SOMETHING
COMING
THROUGH

SOMETHING COMING THROUGH

PAUL McAULEY

GOLLANCZ

LONDON

First published in Great Britain in 2015 by Gollancz
An imprint of the Orion Publishing Group
Orion House, 5 Upper St Martin's Lane, London WC2H 9EA
An Hachette UK Company

A CIP catalogue record for this book is available
from the British Library

ISBN 978 1 473 20393 8 (Cased)
ISBN 978 1 473 20394 5 (Trade Paperback)

1 3 5 7 9 10 8 6 4 2

Typeset by GroupFMG using Book Cloud
Printed in Great Britain by CPI Group (UK) Ltd, Croydon, CR0 4YY

The Orion Publishing Group's policy is to use papers that
are natural, renewable and recyclable products and made from
wood grown in sustainable forests. The logging and manufacturing
processes are expected to conform to the environmental
regulations of the country of origin.

www.unlikelyworlds.blogspot.com
www.orionbooks.co.uk
www.gollancz.co.uk

For Al Reynolds,
and for Georgina.

1. Just Another Snake Cult

London | 2 July

Four days till she was due to appear before the parliamentary select committee, Chloe Millar couldn't take it any more. The rehearsals and group exercises, the pre-exam nerves and pointless speculation, the third degree about the New Galactic Navy . . . No to all that business. She banged out of there and minicabbed it down the A13 to check out a lead in Dagenham. Traffic glittering in hot sunlight, factories, housing estates and big box retail outlets, sewage works and power stations. A glimpse of the Reef's dark blister and the river beyond. A welling feeling of relief with an undercurrent of guilt that she tried to ignore.

The minicab was negotiating the Ripple Road junction when her phone rang. Jen Lovell, Disruption Theory's office manager, wanting to know where she was and what she was up to.

'I'm chasing a lead. A good one.'

'We've all had to give up our Saturdays. Even you, Chloe.'

'There's a cult. Definitely turned, about to break out. They announced it on Facebook, a public meeting supposed to start at one o'clock. I'm late, but these things never run to schedule. I won't have missed anything important.'

'Preparing for the select committee: that's what's important.'

'They haven't shut us down yet,' Chloe said. She wasn't going to feel guilty. She was doing her actual job. 'It's probably just another snake cult, but I can't be certain until I see it in action.'

Her destination was a displaced-persons camp at the eastern edge of Old Dagenham Park. A row of single-storey prefab barracks and half a dozen L-shaped stacks of repurposed shipping containers, built a decade ago for refugees from flooding caused by climate change and rising sea levels, privately rented now.

Chloe found a bench in the shade of a gnarly old chestnut tree, ate chips out of a cardboard clamshell, and watched people gathering around a makeshift stage where a scrawny old geezer in tattered jeans and T-shirt was setting up a microphone stand and a stack of speakers. Young children ran about, transformed by face paint into rabbits and tigers. A pair of policewomen watched indulgently. They were wearing new-issue stab vests, spun from tough self-healing collagen derived from a species of colonial polyp that rafted on Hydrot's world ocean. The Met's logo stamped in dark blue on the pearlescent material. High above, an errant balloon bobbed on an uncertain breeze, a silvery heart blinking random Morse code in the hot sunlight.

It reminded Chloe of the music festival where she'd first been kissed, seriously kissed, by a boy whose name she'd forgotten. She'd been, what, fourteen. A late starter, according to her mates. She remembered a Hindu procession that wound through the streets of Walthamstow to the temple each year: drummers, men with painted faces in fantastic costumes, men animating giant stick-puppets of gods and dragons. She remembered one Hallowe'en, the first after First Contact, when every other kid had dressed up as a Jackaroo avatar.

The geezer bent to the microphone, dreadlocks hanging around his face as he gave it the old one two one two. And a shadow fell across Chloe and someone said, 'Give us a chip.'

She looked up, saw Eddie Ackroyd in his uniform of black jeans, black T-shirt and abraded and creased black leather jacket. His pallid face was shaded by a straw hat; his ghostly blue eyes swam behind slab lenses in heavy black frames.

'The café's over by the tennis courts,' Chloe said. 'You've plenty of time to get there and back before the fun starts.'

Eddie didn't take the hint, settling beside her with a grunt and sigh, taking off his hat and fanning himself with it, fixing it back over greying hair he'd backcombed to hide a bald spot. He smelled of kif smoke and old sweat. The slogan on his T-shirt read *I'm a secret lesbian*.

2

'Lostgirl X, large as life and twice as pretty. You may have taken the corporate shilling, but you still dress like you work the street. Kudos.'

'When did you become the fashion police, Eddie?'

Chloe was wearing her usual weekend gear: baggy knee-length shorts, a market-stall T-shirt with a stencilled peace symbol, New Balance hiking shoes. Her messenger bag, one seam patched with Elephant tape, leaned against her thigh.

Eddie said, 'I bet you still carry that little blade. The one you pulled on Gypsy Nick that time.'

'Keep pushing me and you'll find out.'

The members of this little cult were driven by urges they probably didn't understand, prompted by some kind of alien algorithm or an eidolon, a memory fragment, that had crawled out of an Elder Culture artefact and infected them like bird flu, but they were also having fun. Chloe had been happy, waiting for them to put on their little show in the summer sunshine, but now Eddie Ackroyd's sour little cloud was raining on her parade.

He said, 'It's been a while, hasn't it? I don't see you in the market or the Ten Bells . . .'

His fish-eyed stare reminded her that he was the kind of guy who liked to sneak a glance at your tits when he thought you weren't looking

She said, 'I guess we move in different circles now.'

'And you don't seem to be editing on LFM any more.'

'You said that the last time you saw me, Eddie. Remember what I told you?'

Chloe resented his assumption that they were colleagues. They had both been part of the Last Five Minutes wiki since its early days, they were both in the Elder Culture business, but as far as she was concerned that was it.

When he didn't answer her question, she said, 'I quit. I have other things in my life now.'

'We could use your help. There are still too many crazy people trying to impose their crazy ideas.'

'That's why I quit.'

It wasn't the only reason. It wasn't even the main reason, which was that she'd finally realised that she'd never find out what had happened to her mother, and she wasn't angry about it any more. But yeah, she'd also become tired of dealing with the relentless bat-shit paranoia of the green-ink merchants, and she'd suspected that Eddie and some of the other editors had been actively colluding with them. Most of the people involved with the maintenance and curation of the LFM wiki had lost parents or partners or children; Eddie had become an editor because he loved conspiracy theories, liked to believe that he was one of the chosen few with special insights about the Jackaroo and the Spasm, the lone-gunman plague, the Big Melt, blah blah blah.

He said, 'So how's it going, running errands for those sociologists? Looking for stuff to prop up their theories – is that why you're here? Or are you doing a little work on the side?'

'I'm chasing a lead, Eddie. How about you?'

'Well, right now I'm wondering if you're following me.'

'I might wonder the same thing about you.'

Eddie pointed his chin towards the people bustling around the stage. 'I've been working on them for three weeks. And this is the first time I see you.'

'You've been working on them? What does that mean? Interviewing them? Gaining their confidence? Becoming their best friend?'

'I've been keeping close tabs on them. Recording their stories for a client. And now they're about to reach critical mass, the first time they try to reach out to the world, you just happen to pitch up.'

'It isn't a secret,' Chloe said. 'They put it up on Facebook.'

It wasn't much, a poster designed by someone who thought that rainbow gradients and dropshadowed text were cool. An image of a man with a Santa Claus beard photoshopped against a false-colour alien landscape overprinted with *The Master Is Coming!!!* in a shimmering banner, and a modest line of type stating time, date and place. A typical symptom of a small-scale breakout, but this one had caught her attention, she'd needed a distraction from the nonsense about the select committee, and here she was.

'I found them,' Eddie said, staring at her from beneath the brim of his hat, 'the old-fashioned way. Asking questions, following leads. One of them from LFM, as a matter of fact. Someone who thinks they can predict significant breakouts. You would have seen it too, if you hadn't "quit".'

He actually drew the quote marks in the air.

'I found them because they're trying to reach out to everyone,' Chloe said. She was amused by Eddie's petulance, wondered if he'd already taken a down payment for something he knew he probably couldn't deliver. 'Don't take it personally. Besides, it doesn't look like they're anything special.'

'That's what you think,' Eddie said. 'I'll tell you what we'll do. How we'll sort out this little conflict of interest. I found them first, so I get first dibs on whatever these people are selling. After that, if your pointy-head academics want to interview them, add them to their database or whatever, it's fine by me.'

Chloe smiled. 'We aren't in the playground, Eddie. If these people stumbled on something useful, came into possession of an active artefact or whatever, I'll tell my boss, and he'll make an offer. And you and your client, if you have a client, can do the same.'

Eddie stuck out his lower lip like a disappointed child. 'So it's like that.'

'Same as it's always been,' Chloe said, 'out here on the street.'

Eddie stalked off to a spot in the shade of a stack of shipping-container flatlets and fired up a small drone that wobbled away towards the stage. A tall young man wearing blue jeans and a black windcheater was chatting to the two policewomen. Chloe spotted the Bluetooth headset plugged into his right ear and guessed that he was from the Metropolitan Police's Breakout Assessment Team, a junior officer who'd drawn the short straw and given up his Saturday afternoon kick-about to check out this little gathering.

Girls and boys in grey jumpers and black trousers or black skirts filed onto the stage and, conducted by a motherly woman in a dashiki, began to pipe out 'Amazing Grace' on recorders.

Chloe dumped her half-eaten lunch in a recycling bin, put on her spex and walked towards the stage, and the guy in the black windcheater cut across the grass to intercept her, saying that he was surprised to see someone from Disruption Theory.

'Isn't this pretty vanilla for you guys?'

'Everything's a data point,' Chloe said, quoting her boss, Daniel Rosenblaum.

'Are you planning to interview Mr Archer and his acolytes?'

Chloe supposed that Mr Archer was the white-haired guy on the Facebook page. She said, 'Would that be a problem?'

'Depends on how they do. Probably not. What about Mr Ackroyd?'

'You'll have to ask him.'

'I expect I will. Take care, Ms Millar.'

Just to let her know that he had her number.

The schoolkids ran through a pretty good version of 'Scarborough Fair', bowed to the scattering of applause and were led off the stage by their conductor. Chloe could feel an energy gathering in the little crowd. An MC took to the stage, an amazingly confident young woman dressed in a metallic silver leotard and black tutu who hunched into the microphone and to a backing track of car-crash rhythms began a rap about the great change coming and hard times ending. When she was done and the whoops and applause had died down she asked everybody to raise their hands for the man with the plan, the man who knew.

'Give it up for Mr Archer. Mr Archer going to speak the truth to you right now.'

There was an awkward pause, some kind of hitch. The MC stood at the edge of the stage, talking to people, shaking her head. The sound system started to reprise the clanging smash of her backing music, then cut off abruptly. Several people were helping someone climb onto the stage.

Mr Archer was a slight old man wearing what was probably the suit he planned to be buried in. His white beard was neatly trimmed; his pink scalp showed through his cap of fine white hair. The MC ushered him to the microphone stand and he clung to it and looked around like a grandfather dazed with pleasure at his own birthday party. A hush fell over the small gathering.

Chloe's spex were capturing everything. Eddie's little drone hung in the sunlit air. The moment of silence stretched.

'Uth,' Mr Archer said. 'Uth! Uth!' And, 'Penitent volume casualty force. Action relationship. Flow different. Uth! Uth!'

Most in the audience chanted *Uth! Uth!* too. Those who weren't part of the cult, who hadn't drunk the snake oil, looked at each other. A couple of kids in front of Chloe started to jeer.

Chloe felt a sinking sense of disappointment. She'd seen it all, in her time. Fiery-eyed preaching. A woman who spoke through a pink plush alligator. People standing face to face, staring into each other's eyes, sharing significant gazes. Ritual bloodletting. A young girl walking amongst her followers with a silver wand, touching them at random, causing them to fall into faints and foaming fits. A hundred different attempts to express thoughts for which there were no human equivalents, no words in any known language. Speaking in tongues was commonplace. She'd seen it a dozen times.

Mr Archer spoke for some time, enthusiastically expounding his thesis in his private language, repeating his catchphrase at intervals, smiling as his followers chanted in response. The two kids who'd been jeering walked away; others followed. Chloe wondered how it would end, a procession or a mass hug or a conga line, but instead the old man simply stopped speaking, laboriously stepped down from the stage, and hobbled off at the centre of a cluster of acolytes. His audience gathered up their children and drifted towards the camp. They looked pleased. They had spoken in public. They had marked their territory. They had let out the ideas jostling in their heads, like that ancient rock star who'd shaken out a box of butterflies at an open-air concert in Hyde Park. Most of the butterflies had died, but it was the gesture that counted.

This was something that couldn't be quantified by Disruption Theory's surveys: the happiness of the people possessed by alien impulses and strange memes. The ecstasy of expression. The simple childlike joy of creating a channel or connection. Although the breakout was nothing special, Chloe was glad to be reminded of that. She took a flyer from one of the kids who were handing them out to the few non-believers who remained, slipped it into her messenger bag and got out of there while Eddie Ackroyd was packing up his drone.

It was too late to head back to Disruption Theory, and she was too buzzed to fold herself into her studio flat. She returned to the park's café and sat with a carton of iced coffee and wrote up a short report on her tablet. She studied the flyer: the speaking-in-tongues Santa Claus, Mr Archer, photoshopped against an alien landscape, with a single word, *BELIEVE*, printed above his head. After a minute, she pulled up the copy of the Facebook page that had led her to the park. The same kind of landscape in the background, a cluster of towers or spires in some kind of red desert.

Chloe looked from screen to flyer, flyer to screen, then dropped the Facebook page into an image editor, cropped out a portion of the background and fed it into a search engine. Got a hit for the website, a bunch of old sci-fi flicks, landscape photos from the fifteen worlds gifted to the human race by the Jackaroo . . . And, hey, look at that, a set of images posted on a tumblr by someone calling themselves Mangala Cowboy. Drawings and paintings of red cliffs, dunes of red sand saddling away towards distant hills, a crowd of thorny spires glowing in orange sunlight. A view of the spires from a distance, a view from a high angle, as if from a plane or helicopter. The same spires at night, outlined in dabs of red phosphorescence. A close-up of thorny projections silhouetted against a pink sky. They looked like teeth, or the ends of broken bones. A tangle of grey vegetation with a fleck of incandescent yellow burning in its centre. A pavement of black slabs winding around red rocks. Some kind of room or space outlined in dense black scrawls. A flock of what might be balloons drifting across the freckled face of a fat sun. And over and over again, the same cliffs, the same dunes, the same spires.

One summer, fifteen years old, restless with self-pity and un-examined anger because she felt that the death of her mother, how her mother had died, had denied her any kind of ordinary life, Chloe had taken to cycling long distances. From Walthamstow into the City of London. Down the course of the River Lea, past the Olympic Park to Bow Creek, where she now worked. Across Epping Forest, through the banal suburban landscapes and strip malls of Enfield. She'd taken her bike on trains out to Kew and Richmond; once, one day close to midsummer, she'd ridden all the way to Amersham. And from Amersham she had cycled through a maze of B-roads into the Chilterns, and as the sun had begun to set she'd come out at the top of a ridge and seen a patchworked valley spread beyond: immemorial England parcelled into fields and stands of trees aglow in that magic hour when light is a property of the air. As if she had intruded on a secondary world, a fairyland where everything wore its True Name.

She felt that same vertiginous recognition now. A freezing pleasure, an emotion as deep and poignant as nostalgia for places she'd never before seen. And then she thought of Eddie Ackroyd, slouching like a malignant shadow through the displaced-persons camp, searching for Mangala Cowboy, and a sliding sense of urgency seized her and sent her hurrying through the late afternoon sunlight and the ordinary little park.

The stage and sound system had been cleared away, but a gang of little children were chasing each other across the dry grass and several pre-teen girls clustered around the bench under the chestnut tree, sharing images and clips on their phones. Chloe went up to them and got into a conversation with their leader, Niome, a sharp-faced girl dressed in pink shorts and a blue T-shirt, hair scraped up and exploding in an afroball at the top of her head. Chloe told her about Disruption Theory, asked about Mr Archer. Who'd just been this geezer until a couple of months ago, apparently. No bother to anyone, spent most of his time sitting outside his front door or in the café gossiping with other geezers. He carved stuff, Niome said, birds and shit like that from bits of wood. Sometimes gave them away, sometimes sold them in the local street market.

'Then he started having meetings,' Niome said. She was perched on the back of the bench, leaning forward with her elbows on her knees and her bright red sneakers planted on the seat. 'Him and a few geezers at first. Then other people too. It was like they were in church. Like Mr Archer was giving a sermon, or they were singing hymns. But in this funny language.'

Chloe asked her if she or her friends had ever gone to these meetings.

'*I* didn't,' Niome said. 'Get mixed up with that chump ranking? No way. But Bunny did. Her mum got caught up, and she took Bunny along. She played recorder today, didn't you, Buns?'

Bunny was a shy plump girl who ducked her head and shrugged.

'Tell her what it was like,' Niome said.

Bunny shrugged again, pleased and embarrassed, said she couldn't exactly explain.

Chloe showed the flyer to Niome, said that she was wondering who had made the picture.

'Oh, that,' Niome said. 'That's one of Freddie's.'

Freddie Patel and his little sister, Rana, had come to live in the camp about three months ago. No sign of their parents, according to Niome, who didn't seem to think it was anything unusual. Mr Archer was Freddie's upstairs neighbour, she said, and the old man had taken a shine to him because of his drawings.

Chloe said, 'Is he part of this thing of Mr Archer's?'

'He isn't really part of anything.'

'But he did the flyer for Mr Archer. And a poster they put up on Facebook.'

'Yeah, but Freddie was never into Mr Archer's church stuff. I mean, you never seen him there, did you, Buns?'

Bunny shook her head.

'Freddie mostly keeps himself to himself,' Niome said. 'Man of mystery innit.'

'Niome's in love with Freddie,' one of the other girls said, half-singing it in a teasing lilt, and Niome said, 'I am so not. He's lush, yeah, but he's sort of weird, too.'

'Weird in what way?' Chloe said.

'Like he's lost in his head. You say hi to him, he say hi back. But otherwise it's like he don't see you.'

'What about his sister?'

'Oh, Rana's just a cute little thing.'

'A normal little girl.'

'I guess.'

'She doesn't ever talk about ghosts, or anything similar?'

The stuff that encoded eidolons interacted with people's optic nerves on some deep quantum level, generating weird, blurry images. Shadows and shapes. Ghosts and monsters.

Niome said, 'I don't think so. She's just this little girl.'

Chloe said, 'Have you seen anything weird, you and your friends?'

Niome laughed. 'You mean like spooks and such?'

'Or strange animals, strange noises, strange dreams.'

'What kind of strange dreams?'

'Dreams about the kind of places Freddie draws, for instance.'

Niome asked to see the flyer again. She studied it carefully, shook her head, showed it to her friends. 'This mean anything to you?'

More head-shaking.

'There's this bunch of shiners who sit around the other end of the park,' one of the girls said. 'They see all kinds of stuff that isn't there.'

'She means ordinary people seeing, like, super-strange paranormal shit,' Niome said, and smiled at Chloe. 'If you want, we can ask around. Do some detecting.'

The girl was bright and bold and inquisitive, far more together than Chloe had been at her age. It occurred to her that Niome had never known a time when there hadn't been aliens in the sky and a lottery for easy travel to other planets. It made her feel old.

She gave one of her cards to Niome, and a couple of five-pound coins for her help. Niome asked if that meant she was one of Disruption Theory's informers now.

Chloe said, 'Be sure to let me know if you hear about any super-strange stuff. Meanwhile, how about pointing me at Freddie's home?'

It was in the nearest cluster of container flatlets. The steel boxes had big windows at either end and were stacked side by side in an L shape three storeys high, with steel-mesh walkways on the inner side. People sat on stairs, in open doorways. The mingled murmur of TVs and radios, a domestic hum and clatter.

Freddie Patel's flatlet was in the middle of the second storey of the short arm of the L. Like most of its neighbours, its window and glass-panelled door were blanked with curtains. Freddie Patel twitched the heavy blue material aside when Chloe rapped on the glass, then cracked the door open to ask what she wanted.

He looked much younger than she'd expected, a slender teenager a good head taller than her, dressed in cargo shorts and an oversized T-shirt. When Chloe showed him the flyer and asked if he was the artist, his suspicious look darkened.

'Who wants to know?'

Chloe introduced herself, speaking quickly before he could shut the door in her face. 'The people I work for are interested in happenings, festivals, that kind of thing. Like the one here today? I was wondering if you could help me, answer a few standard questions for a survey. It will only take a couple of minutes, I promise. And there'll be a small payment for your time and trouble.'

'Mr Archer's meeting? I wasn't even there. You want to know about that, you should talk to him,' Freddie Patel said.

He was looking past her, scanning the walkway as if expecting to see someone else. Over his shoulder, Chloe could see a wedge of wall tiled with a mosaic of mostly red drawings.

She said, 'You helped Mr Archer with his flyer. His website, too.'

'So?'

'It caught my attention. It's a sweet piece of work. Would you mind talking about it? Your inspiration, and so on,' Chloe said, putting on her spex.

'You want to record this?'

'It's our standard procedure. I mentioned a small payment, didn't I?'

'No way.'

'That's okay, we can do it without,' Chloe said, and made a big deal of taking off her spex and folding them away. Hoping that she'd got a nice steady shot of the pictures.

A chubby little girl of four or five, cute as a button in dungarees with an appliqué flower on the bib, came up behind Freddie and gave Chloe a bold stare. When Chloe said hi she looked away, looked back. Ringlets tangled over her forehead. A piece of paper was crumpled in one fist.

Chloe said to Freddie, 'Is this your sister?' Said to the little girl, 'How are you, sweetie? Rana, right?'

'I made a drawing,' the little girl said, and held up the multi-coloured scrawl so that Chloe and her brother could inspect it. A red string was tied around her chubby wrist, a single green bead threaded on it.

Freddie told her, 'I'll take a look in a minute. Go on inside now.'

'Ugly Chicken says she's nice,' the little girl said.

Freddie's tone hardened. 'Go on inside. Now.'

The little girl waved bye-bye, hand flapping at her wrist, and toddled away.

Chloe said, 'So your sister's an artist too.'

'Exactly what is it you're trying to sell me?'

Freddie Patel was attempting to project an attitude, but he looked away when Chloe met his gaze. He didn't have the fuck-you stare of a real street kid.

'I work for a little company, Disruption Theory. Here's my card,' she said.

Freddie glanced at it, shrugged.

'You can check out our website, see that we're totally valid. What I'm interested in, *all* I'm interested in, are your pictures. If you have anything else like the flyer, I'd love to see them, talk about them.'

'No way,' Freddie said again, and started to close the door.

Chloe said quickly, 'Maybe I could buy one.'

'You don't go away, I'll call the police,' Freddie said, and the door clicked shut and the curtain fell.

Chloe wrote *call anytime* on the back of the card Freddie hadn't taken from her, and stuck it between the glass door and its frame. A bare-chested man sitting on a canvas stool at the end of the walkway was watching her. She resisted the urge to give him the finger and went down the stairs, feeling that something or someone was tracking her, following her through the stacks of containers and into the park beyond. But when she looked around, half-expecting to see Eddie Ackroyd or his damn drone, there was no one there.

2. Landing Day

Mangala | 24 July

Astronauts and aliens paraded down Petra's main avenue. The astronauts were the surviving members of the Thirty-Eight, the first people to land on Mangala. Dressed in white tracksuits and standing on the backs of two flatbed trucks, waving to crowds that pelted them with confetti and paper streamers. The aliens marched behind the trucks. Lizard aliens, frog aliens, cat aliens, gorilla aliens. The cats brandished ray guns; the gorillas wore space helmets with spiral antennae. There were people dressed in black leotards stuck all over with clusters of black balloons; people in aluminium foil costumes and silver facepaint and blue wigs. A solitary Dalek trundled along, squawking about extermination. There was a troupe of dancers costumed as Jackaroo avatars, black suits and white shirts and gold-tinted plastic masks, high-stepping in jerky stop-go synchrony. There were floats and three school bands, a steelpan orchestra on the back of a truck decorated with artificial turf and fake palm trees and two real parrots. The Mayor and his wife rode in a vintage open-top Mercedes imported by a tomb raider who'd struck it rich, followed by a phalanx of motorcycle cops, four fire engines, the Salvation Army brass band, representatives of two dozen professions and trades, and a group selected from the latest arrivals on Mangala, newbies dressed in white T-shirts and blue jeans and blue denim jackets, the uniform of the orientation camp.

It was the thirteenth anniversary of the first landfall of the shuttle that tirelessly cycled between Earth and Mangala, of the first human footsteps on one of the fifteen worlds gifted by the Jackaroo. The shuttle had returned from its latest trip to Earth

14

just two days before. A ring of fireworks had exploded around the giant spacecraft as it slid out of the sky, and there were more fireworks now, flowering in the chill sky above the city.

The last cannonade was fading and falling as Vic Gayle plunged into the narrow streets of the old quarter, heading towards a Landing Day party with a bunch of comrades from the early days. Back then, this had been all there was to the city. Quonset huts, a couple of big steel-frame sheds, small mud-brick domes built over the entrances to cut-and-cover bunkers. A precarious foothold in the howling alien wilderness. There were almost a million people on the planet now, most of them living in Petra, and the huts and bunkers in the old quarter had been made over into restaurants and tanning parlours, cafés and souvenir shops. Man, look at that: a Starbucks.

Vic's friends had taken over the big round table at the back of the city's oldest Chinese restaurant. They were all veterans of the second shuttle to Mangala, making a lot of noise, helping themselves from little dishes and bamboo baskets as waiters brought more food and fresh bottles of wine, brought Vic a bottle of Tiger beer. Most were much older than Vic, baby boomers who'd won the emigration lottery and decided to shed their old lives and chase after dreams of their Space Age childhoods. Thomas Müller owned two super-markets and a thriving import/export business. Alice and Marek Sienkiewicz dealt in Elder Culture artefacts. Victoria Cheshire had built up a transport company that ran road trains between Petra and Idunn's Valley. There were lawyers, surgeons, teachers. Maria Luis Pereira owned a chicken farm, the biggest on Mangala.

Vic Gayle was an investigator in the city's police, a stocky middle-aged man in a dark brown suit and black shirt and green tie. Close-trimmed hair going grey at the temples, sleepy eyes that didn't miss much. Sitting quietly amongst his friends as they ate crispy duck and pancakes, drank white wine from Idunn's Valley or imported beer, talked about the old days, their children and grandchildren back on Earth, the latest political scandals, the big dust storm blowing up out of the west, the panic buying in shops and supermarkets. Vic finished his beer and switched to jasmine tea. Although he was on call, working on Landing Day

15

so that colleagues with families wouldn't have to, he'd decided at the last minute that he didn't want to miss the annual party with his old friends, had told his new partner to hold the fort for a couple of hours, ignore the phone if it rang, call him if there was a problem. But now that he was here, he was feeling out of place. Everyone was talking about new business opportunities, their new cars and houses, their kids, their plans for the future, and he was back to living in an efficiency apartment, his ex was nagging him about collecting the last of his shit from what had been their home, and he was still working violent crimes, putting down murders. A righteous calling, no doubt, but after seven years it was beginning to feel like the same old same old.

Someone said, 'Next year, we should do this in Red Rock Falls.'

Someone else said, 'Only tourists and newbies go to Red Rock Falls these days.'

'Time we reclaimed it, then.'

'Who ordered these chicken feet?'

'I hear StrangeWare is organising another attempt on the North Pole.'

'Those people have more money than sense.'

'They can afford to bet on long shots. And who knows what's under the ice?'

'A secret Jackaroo base.'

'Atlantis.'

'Every sock ever lost.'

'The mapping satellite didn't find anything.'

'It's a lot of ice.'

'It had sideways radar.'

'It's a *lot* of ice. Forty kilometres deep in places.'

Familiar faces animated in the red light of the sconces on the red and gold walls. Laughing and talking. Hands wielding chopsticks, fluttering in the air over bowls and glasses.

'Did anyone ever find out what happened to that satellite?'

'A secret Elder Culture city shot it down.'

'Two of its gyroscopes failed,' Maria Kawelec said. She was an engineer and an amateur astronomer. 'It couldn't be aimed at anything any more, so it was de-orbited.'

'They should put up another.'

'They should send probes to the other planets. Seriously,' Maria said. 'Anything could be out there.'

'That's where we should go for our fiftieth. The North Pole.'

'And miss the parade?'

'I wouldn't miss it. Every year the same.'

'That's why I love it.'

'The kids love it.'

'My kids don't. Too old. Jaded at eight and ten,' Faith Madeuke said, and looked across the table at Vic. 'Are you okay, honey?'

'Absolutely,' Vic said.

'You're quieter than usual, is all,' Faith said. She wore a gold and red dress and had wrapped her dreadlocks in a matching scarf. She had been the first in their circle to have children here, some of the first children born on Mangala.

'I thought of skipping the bash this year,' Vic confessed.

'I'm glad you didn't. Tell me one of your horrible stories.'

Vic smiled. 'About police work or about my life?'

Mark Brown leaned in. 'There was a shooting in my neighbourhood two weeks ago. In the park. A motorcycle went past some young men hanging out by the café and the pillion passenger popped off a couple of shots. This was Saturday afternoon,' Mark said, his voice rising with indignation. 'People were having picnics. Families were out with their kids.'

Vic had heard about it in the daily briefing, told Mark that the perps were being tracked down.

'Probably gang-related,' Thomas Müller said.

'My question is, where do they get the guns?' Mark Brown said.

'People smuggle them in,' Thomas Müller said. 'People print them. Am I right, Vic?'

'There are definitely too many guns,' Vic said.

'Kids with guns,' Mark Brown said. 'When did that start happening?'

Faith said, 'Did you see the newbies in the parade? Didn't they look weirded out?'

Vic, grateful for the change of subject, said, 'You land on a strange new planet and – wah gwan? You're marching behind

17

the Salvation Army band and the crookedest politician in twenty thousand light years, who's waving at the crowds from a vintage car. Who wouldn't be weirded out?'

'Anyone interesting in the new batch?'

'You mean anyone famous or anyone useful?'

'Famous people are famous on Earth, so why leave?'

'They'd be more famous here.'

'They'd be famous for being famous for about five minutes. And then what? What would Robert Pattinson do here?'

'I have a couple of ideas,' Faith said, and gave her trademark filthy laugh.

'What happened to that guy who came here to make movies? Sci-fi movies on an actual alien planet.'

Vic said, 'We had a nuclear war, we had an alien invasion, and now we're living on alien planets. How could you make up anything to beat that?'

There was a vibration in the pocket of his jacket. His phone. He left the table and found a quiet spot near the restaurant's pass-through.

'We've got one,' Skip Williams said.

Vic automatically checked his watch. Seven twenty-two.

He said, 'You picked up the phone. Didn't I tell you about not picking up the phone?'

'Sorry about your meal and everything, but I was the only one here. Bodin and Espinosa are attending a shooting over at the Flats.'

Vic gave the address of the restaurant. 'You'd better come by and pick me up.'

3. Disruption Theory

London | 4 July

Disruption Theory's office was near Bow Creek, the top floor of a Victorian warehouse protected from the extended reach of the Thames by a construction-coral stopbank. Chloe commuted to work by ferry, across the river from Greenwich. The first to arrive on Monday morning, she disarmed the security system and primed the industrial coffee machine; after a sequence of thumps, rattles and jets of steam the earthy scent of its brew began to permeate the quiet still air of the open-plan workspace. Sunlight fell through the glass wall that fronted the conference room and Daniel Rosenblaum's corner office, glowed on the workstations and tables under the oak beams and dusty skylights of the high ceiling.

When Jen Lovell came in, Chloe was reviewing the cut she'd made from footage of the breakout meeting and the brief interview with Freddie Patel. Jen clattered about her office for a couple of minutes before pouring herself a cup of coffee and carrying it across the room to the table where Chloe sat.

'How did your lead pan out?'

'Better than expected,' Chloe said. 'It definitely wasn't your average snake cult. In fact, I'm hoping to follow up on it.'

Jen didn't rise to that. A calm, chunky woman who favoured business suits and amber jewellery, she took a careful sip from her cup of coffee and said, 'There's a meeting in an hour, to go over today's schedule and raise any snags. After that you have a one-on-one with Helena to fine-tune your preparations. And then there's the group briefing this afternoon.'

'I don't know why we're making such a big deal of the New Galactic Navy thing. Even the tabloids said we had nothing to do with it.'

19

Jen took another sip of coffee. 'I don't blame you for being nervous. We all are.'

Disruption Theory was in the gunsights of Robin Mountjoy, one of the leading lights of the Human Decency League. His party campaigned on a single issue: the removal of all traces of the Jackaroo and their fellow travellers from Great Britain. It had made big advances in the last general election; although the minority Conservative government hadn't entered into a formal alliance with it, there had been several major concessions. Which was why Robin Mountjoy was chairing the Alien Technology Committee. He wasn't about to take on the multinationals, so he was going after small companies like Disruption Theory instead. And Disruption Theory was an especially tempting target because of Daniel Rosenblaum's high-profile promotion of its work, and because it was bankrolled by Ada Morange, the controversial French entrepreneur. Her company, Karyotech Pharma, had been a leading contender in the early days of exploitation of Elder Culture tech and alien biota, with a presence on ten of the fifteen worlds. At one point, after Karyotech Pharma's initial public offering of shares on Euronext, she'd been a paper billionaire, but much of her fortune had dissipated in a long battle against a hostile takeover and a series of lawsuits over patents and prior art. So Disruption Theory was squarely in the sights of the select committee, but lacked the defensive firepower of the big players. Robin Mountjoy was boasting about taking a tough line with what he called fellow travellers of the Jackaroo; Ada Morange was threatening to shut down Disruption Theory or move it to France, absorb it into one of her companies; everything was up in the air.

Chloe was tired of all the fuss, the preparations and anticipation and anxiety, but knew that she shouldn't take it out on Jen, who'd probably spent her Sunday doing all the admin work that she hadn't been able to get done last week, and said meekly, 'What time is my one-on-one?'

'Helena will be here at eleven,' Jen said. 'You're the first on her to-do list. Take her advice seriously, Chloe. She actually knows what she's talking about.'

Chloe promised that she'd behave. She flicked through the images she'd snurched from Mangala Cowboy's tumblr and spent a little time with Ram Varma, then sat around the long table with the rest of Disruption Theory's small crew while Jen Lovell went over the last preparations for the committee and reminded everyone not to talk to the press or the blogging community. When she'd finished, Daniel Rosenblaum gave a brief homily: we're in great shape, one last push and we'll be bombproof, don't believe anything you see on the news feeds, so on, so forth.

Chloe moved quickly when the meeting broke up, sidestepping Jen, asking Daniel if she could have five minutes to discuss something really interesting that had turned up.

'You have a call from France at eleven,' Jen told him.

'I haven't forgotten,' Daniel said.

'Also a month's worth of worksheets to sign off.'

Daniel looked at Chloe. 'Five minutes, you said?'

'It might take ten,' Chloe said, chancing it.

'The artist is Freddie Patel, aka Mangala Cowboy,' Chloe said. 'Seventeen, eighteen years old, whereabouts of his parents unknown, lives with his little sister in a box he rents in a DP camp in Dagenham. He moved in about three months ago. Soon afterwards, some of his neighbours started speaking in tongues. And then they had a little breakout.'

Daniel said, 'This is the thing you ran off to on Saturday.'

'I'm seeing the lawyer after this, and I'll be at the briefing this afternoon,' Chloe said. 'Anyway, the breakout wasn't anything special, but then I found out about Freddie Patel and his pictures.'

They were in Daniel's office, a corner room with big steel-framed windows that looked across the flat top of the stopbank and the flood of the Thames to Greenwich. Ladders of shelves were cluttered with books and mementos of past investigations. Disintegrator-ray projectors powered by AA batteries, components of antigravity machines, teleportation devices and other improbable and completely non-functional devices built by monomaniacs infected with Elder Culture algorithms and eidolons. A row of 3D printed avatar faces, like golden death

21

masks of matinee idols. Jackaroo dolls. A model of a Jackaroo spaceship made from toothpicks. File boxes stuffed with self-published theses about the location of the Jackaroo's home world, conspiracies linking the Jackaroo to nationalist groups and rogue states supposedly behind the nuclear bombings and other terrorist spectaculars of the Spasm, or hidden images of the Jackaroo and other aliens in Palaeolithic cave paintings, Ancient Egyptian wall paintings, Mayan calendars, and Indian temple sculptures. Attempts to unify classic and quantum physics using only algebra. Notebooks written in cyphers or secret languages or 'automatic' writing. All of it evidence of deep changes in the collective human psyche, according to Daniel Rosenblaum. The usual detritus of ordinary craziness and eccentricity skewed by the strange attractor of the Jackaroo, according to his critics.

Daniel sat with his back to the riverlight, a tall, imposing man with a corona of curly grey hair, wearing one of his trademark brightly patterned waistcoats over a black shirt. Images from the tumblr hung in a cube of virtual light over his desk. Watching her boss carelessly flip through them, Chloe realised that they didn't speak to him the way they spoke to her, didn't evoke the kind of recognition she'd felt when she'd first seem them.

'I admit they're very nice. Exemplars of their kind,' Daniel said, ruffling through the pictures again. He stopped at one of the briar-patch scribbles, studied it. 'This is rather intense.'

'Some kind of room, I think,' Chloe said. 'Ram and I tried to match the pictures with Elder Culture sites on Mangala and the other worlds. No luck so far. There are ruins on First Foot that look a bit like those spires, but only a bit. And they're in the middle of a lake.'

'This kid is involved with an outbreak of an Elder Culture meme,' Daniel said. 'All around him, people are trying to express the new ideas that have infiltrated their minds. This is his attempt, pieced together from images of the fifteen worlds, from ads and sci-fi films, from his imagination. It's interesting, but why is it special?'

'It's the same landscape, over and over. The same spires, different views, close-ups of different parts. It's a place that's very real to him. And it seems very real to me. Authentic; Chloe said, disappointed and frustrated that Daniel wasn't seeing what she saw. 'I think that something got inside his head, and then it got inside the heads of his neighbours. It may have infected his little sister, too. She mentioned something she called Ugly Chicken. The question is, what is it? And where did it come from?'

'You're certain this kid was the primary?'

'According to my information, the leader of the cult started behaving strangely soon after Freddie moved into the flat below his. So that's one thing. But there's something else, too. A freelance scout, Eddie Ackroyd, was on the scene. He's been chasing Elder Culture artefacts for longer than I have. He told me that he has a client interested in the cult and its breakout—'

That got Daniel's attention. 'Who, exactly?'

'I don't know yet. The thing is, Eddie told me that someone on the Last Five Minutes wiki had tipped him off about the cult.'

'The bomb thing?'

'The bomb thing.'

The bomb was the nuclear device that had detonated in Trafalgar Square fourteen years ago. 12 September, 12:21 p.m. Just before the Jackaroo had made contact, when every country in the world had been caught up in riots, revolutions and counter-revolutions, civil wars, border wars, water wars, netwars, and plain old-fashioned conflicts, mixed up with climate change and various degrees of financial collapse. All this craziness culminating in a limited nuclear missile exchange and a string of low-yield tactical nukes exploding in capital cities. The Spasm.

The Trafalgar Square bomb had been a tactical weapon stolen from the stockpiles of the former Soviet Union, with an estimated yield of 0.4 megatons. It had obliterated a square kilometre of central London, igniting enormous fires and injuring over ten thousand people and killing four thousand. Including Chloe's mother, who had been working at the archives of the National Portrait Gallery – research for a book on Victorian photography – and had vanished in an instant of light brighter and hotter than the surface of the sun.

Chloe had been twelve when the bomb had exploded her world, had just turned thirteen when the Jackaroo revealed themselves and told everyone in the world that they wanted to help. A few years later, she discovered the Last Five Minutes wiki, a gathering of people dedicated to analysing recently released CCTV footage from that day. There was video footage from traffic and security cameras, too, and photographs and video clips posted to the web or sent by email just before the suitcase nuke detonated.

One sequence was infamous even before the pixel wizards had started to work on it. It had been shot by a CCTV camera on the east side of Trafalgar Square, across the road from St Martin-in-the-Fields, and began forty-eight seconds before detonation.

A beautiful sunny September day. Traffic at a standstill along Charing Cross Road. Sun flashing off the roofs of cars and vans, people walking past, a young woman lighting a cigarette, another young woman gesturing animatedly as she talked into her phone, a living statue painted grey and standing on a plastic crate, a man photographing two women, the twinkle of a child's balloon drifting in the middle air. And someone flings open the door of a white van and jumps out and runs. A man, white, young, blue jeans and a grey hoodie. Threading between two black cabs, elbowing past a knot of Chinese tourists, running across the square at a slant, past the plinth of one of Landseer's bronze lions, startling pigeons into flight. A policeman in a yellow stab jacket chases after him, head dipped as he says something into the radio clipped to his vest, both of them passing out of the camera's field of view, and the footage ends in blocks of frozen pixels at the instant of detonation.

The chase had been caught by other cameras, but this was the best view. Recovered from a hard drive in the CCTV centre in the ruins of Oxford Street, every millisecond and pixel of the sequence had been analysed by a small army of experts and amateurs looking for clues to the identity of the perpetrators, whose names and motives were still unknown after years of investigation by police and MI6 and MI5, government enquiries, and millions of words of speculation in newspapers and on the internet. Chloe had watched it hundreds of times, unsuccessfully searching its fringes and deep background for glimpses of her mother.

Records from her mother's mobile phone put her in the blast zone. She had called a friend at the British Museum; they had arranged to have lunch together. The friend had survived, had told Chloe and her brother that their mother had called her a few minutes before the bomb detonated, saying that she was running a bit late. Chloe knew that her mother was dead, but didn't know how she had died. Whether she had been mercifully close to ground zero and had died instantly, or whether she'd been at the edge of the nuclear fireball. Chloe, who'd seen the horrors of the bomb's aftermath in documentary footage, wished and wished and wished that her mother had vanished in a bright instant, dead before she knew that she was dead.

She had spent a solid year working on the LFM wiki, studying footage, posting theories, chasing leads. LOSTGIRL_X. Up in her childhood bedroom, curtains drawn, eating random meals at random times. It was the only time she and her brother ever had any real stand-up fights. She'd thought then that he'd been conspiring to stop her finding out the truth; she knew now that he'd been worried that he'd lose her to her obsession.

Although she had failed to discover any trace of her mother, she had found a great deal of comfort in the community of like-minded people that had grown around the wiki. Her first real boyfriend had been one of its image-processing experts. Jack Dennis, a seventeen-year-old computer whizz who'd introduced her to another polder of obsessives: the scouts for Elder Culture artefacts and other alien stuff brought back on the great shuttles that travelled between Earth and the fifteen worlds gifted to humanity by the Jackaroo. Her thing with Jack hadn't lasted long, but by the time she left school she already had a part-time job helping a woman who had a stall in the Sunday market in Spitalfields, selling alien fossils and polished slices of rock from half a dozen worlds. From there, she'd worked up a freelance career as a scout in the artefact trade, sourcing lucky stones from Spire Lake on First Foot, raptor teeth from Hydrot and fragments of so-called temple carvings and 'heavenly beads' from Naya Loka. She'd made and sold jewellery incorporating off-world gemstones or fragments of Boxbuilder polymer, had done some work for the University of Middlesex, chasing rumours of escaped alien animals and plants. Which was how she'd met Daniel Rosenblaum, and joined Disruption Theory.

Now, Daniel was giving her a look of tender concern. He knew about her mother, how she had died. He said, 'I thought you'd given up on that.'

'I had. I have.'

Over the years, the LFM wiki had been infiltrated by conspiracy geeks. They filled its bulletin board with their chatter, subverted every discussion thread with their crazy ideas. That humans controlled by the Jackaroo had planted the bombs. That the Jackaroo had been influencing human history for centuries. That they were actual devils, or the distant ancestors of humans, or godlike artificial intelligences playing an elaborate game for their amusement, on and on, an endless tide of stupidity and insanity. Chloe had more or less given up on it around the same time she'd joined Disruption Theory. Her brother had been pleased. He thought that she had grown up at last, was putting the past behind her.

She told Daniel, 'The thing is, Eddie is one of the wiki's editors, and he told me that someone was posting predictions of significant breakouts on it. So I had a look, and I found something interesting.'

Actually, because she was slightly paranoid, because she believed that Eddie Ackroyd might be keeping watch and didn't want to give him the satisfaction of knowing that he'd made her look, she'd asked another editor, her friend Gail Ann Jones, to check it out. Gail Ann had found a folder on the editor's board that Eddie checked regularly. It seemed to be empty, but Gail Ann had been able to retrieve three erased postings.

'None of them has any text,' Chloe told Daniel. 'Only headers. But all of them point towards places where breakouts have occurred. Godyere, the name of a landowner, which mutated into Golders Green. There was a breakout there a year ago, in one of those big gospel churches. Chilly Field, the original name of Chelsfield Village in Bromley, where patients in the hospital were affected by singing sickness. And Decca's Homestead. The original name of Dagenham.'

She watched Daniel think about that. He said, 'So these are hints about the general area. But how would Eddie Ackroyd pin them down to a specific place?'

'The same way I work. Checking out blogs and the local media. Pounding the pavement. I'm wondering,' Chloe said, 'if the person sending these messages is Eddie's client.'

'But why all this cloak-and-dagger nonsense? And why doesn't this client check out the breakouts himself?'

'I don't know, but I'd like to find out. The point is, someone seems to be able to predict breakouts. It would be pretty amazing if we could make use of that.'

'You know what they say about Dagenham? It's two stops past Barking,' Daniel said.

'I know it sounds like crazy shit—'

'It could be a scam. The messages could have been sent after the breakouts, with false dates.'

'That's one thing I need to check out. The veracity of those messages, and who sent them. I'd also like to interview Freddie Patel again,' Chloe said. 'I left my card, but he hasn't called. I thought I could go back and talk to him again. I'm pretty sure that he owns some kind of Elder Culture artefact. Something containing an active eidolon or some kind of bad algorithm. It would be a good idea to make an offer for it before Eddie Ackroyd does. It wouldn't be much. A few hundred pounds—'

She'd gone too far. Daniel held up his hand like a traffic cop. 'I don't doubt your enthusiasm. And maybe there's even something to these mysterious messages. But right now, Chloe, we have to put our work on hold. We have to focus all our energy into justifying ourselves to a committee of unfriendly politicians who have the power to cause us all kinds of trouble. Once we get past that, we can get back to work. Okay?'

He was staring intently at her.

She said, 'Okay.'

Daniel sat back, steepling his long fingers across his waistcoat. He bought them from a little shop in Brixton Market. He said, 'If you don't mind me saying so, you seem a little agitated. Febrile, with a touch of monomania. You might have caught a touch of

27

meme fever from this kid, or from the breakout. Perhaps that's why these pictures seem so important.'

'If I start speaking in tongues you'll be the first to know,' Chloe said, trying to turn it into a joke.

But Daniel wasn't listening to her. 'Ever since first contact, our minds have been altered by alien memes and ideations. Even the simple fact of the Jackaroo's existence has changed our ideas about what we are, and our place in the universe. Before we can understand the Jackaroo and their gifts, we must understand what they are helping us become.'

He was treating her to the full wattage of the sincerity and charm that had served him so well when he'd helmed a popular TV series that had put a contemporary spin on Charles MacKay's *Extraordinary Popular Delusions and the Madness of Crowds*. He'd been a professor of anthropology in Middlesex University then, a consultant on what he called peripheral phenomena for several financial companies, author of a bestseller about what he called human fallibility. After the Spasm, after the Jackaroo's presence had begun to leak out on the internet, after their avatars had appeared at the UN General Assembly, he had immediately offered his services to the British government. And when he'd been rebuffed, he'd persuaded Ada Morange to bankroll his investigations of phenomena that were, according to him, manifestations of the ways in which the Jackaroo were, by design or by accident, altering human collective consciousness.

Chloe laughed. 'Jesus, Daniel, you don't have to make your pitch to me.'

He had the grace and self-knowledge to look embarrassed. 'After the last couple of weeks it's become force of habit. You should hear the lectures I give to the bathroom mirror every morning. Listen: I don't want you to think I'm making light of your passion. I hired you because of your expertise in chasing down apparitions and artefacts. Because of your talent. You're good at it. You see things that others don't. But this isn't the time to explain it to me. Right now, everything has to be put on hold until we get past the select committee. Promise me, no more bunking off. And I promise you that I'll give this my full attention as soon as I can. Okay?'

Chloe promised she wouldn't bunk off again. She sat through the briefing with Helena Nichols, Ada Morange's lawyer. She attended the strategy meeting that stretched out all through the afternoon. She was on the ferry back to Greenwich when her phone rang. It was Niome. She said that she had some news about Freddie Patel.

'He's only gone and done a flit.'

4. The Shadow of the Shuttle

Mangala | 24 July

The murder scene was near the gate of the shuttle terminal's freight yard, at the end of a track that ran past a construction site and petered out in a slope of grey heath. The shuttle's tapering skyscraper reared into the dark blue sky like God's own exclamation mark, its vast shadow falling across the yards and the low white terminal buildings, the construction site and the four-lane highway that ran out towards the city. Beyond the shadow's edge, the playa burned like hot iron in the sunlight.

A cold wind blew across the heath. Clots of vegetation shivering in the dull half-light, ropes of red dust curling down the unpaved track. Vic Gayle had attended wrongful deaths in every kind of location, from luxury 'executive' apartments to Junktown hovels. As far as he was concerned, this one was about as bleak as they came.

The security guard who had found the body was sitting with her Alsatian in a golf buggy, parked behind the cruiser of the uniform who'd responded to her call. He leaned against his vehicle, smoking a cigarette, watching the two investigators work. A veteran who knew to keep away from the body. You can only kill someone once, but you can murder a crime scene a hundred times in a hundred different ways.

It was on its back, the body: a white male, late thirties or early forties, dressed in a thin black jacket over a grey sweater, black trousers, work boots. So freshly dead that a trace of astonishment could still be recognised in his face. Eyes half-open, not yet glazed or sunken. Blood had run from his ears and puddled under his head.

A scooter lay a little way off, a dent in the bodywork under its saddle. Skip Williams pointed out the rental sticker in the lower left-hand corner of the windshield and said it should be easy to trace.

'My guess is our guy isn't a local.'

'Anyone can hire a scooter,' Vic said.

They were wearing plastic bootees over their shoes, blue nitrile gloves.

Skip said, 'For sure. But his clothes and boots look brand new. Could be he's fresh off the shuttle.'

'Let's not jump to conclusions,' Vic said, and winced when Skip walked directly to the body. It was Vic's habit to circle it first, spiralling inward, checking everything around it, but hey, the kid had answered the phone. The case was his, he had to learn by trial and error how to do things the right way.

Skip Williams had been assigned to violent crimes a week ago. Vic, who'd been working alone since his long-time partner had retired, had been saddled with him. 'Try not to break him,' Sergeant Mikkel Madsen had said.

Investigators in the violent-crimes unit usually worked in two-person teams. The person who picked up the phone when a call came in became the principal on the case. Anyone with too many open cases got a Hail Mary pass, but it wasn't a good idea to accumulate unsolved cases because you'd have to explain yourself to Mikkel Madsen and Captain Colombier. You were answerable to the captain, she was answerable to the chief on the sixth floor, and he was answerable to the city's mayor and the UN commissioner. Who were currently unhappy with the homicide rate – 637 last year in a city of less than a million people – and the percentage of unsolved cases.

Skip Williams was young, a big blond handsome guy in his late twenties whose shoulders strained the seams of his suit jacket. Unusually, on a world where most of the population was from Europe, he was Australian. Winners in the UN emigration lottery were free to choose their destination, but most preferred the world where people like them lived, served by a shuttle that took off from their own country or close to it. The shuttle to Mangala took off from France; most of the settlers were from the European

Union. On First Foot it was Americans, Canadians and, because of an odd geopolitical agreement, Taiwanese and a good number of people from Hong Kong. On Hydrot, mostly West Africans. On Yanos, mostly Russians. And so on. But Skip had been working in London when he'd won his ticket, and instead of returning home and taking the Timor shuttle to Syurga, he'd chosen instead to go up and out via the nearest shuttle, to Mangala.

Like all new arrivals who either couldn't afford to buy their way out or lacked a professional qualification that would exempt them, he'd spent his first three months on Mangala in the civic labour programme, earning his right to become a citizen. He'd done his stint on a farm in Idunn's Valley before moving to Petra and joining the city police. He'd been quickly promoted from foot patrolman to investigator, working for just a year in street crime before moving to the Mayor's security detail, which had given him the boost to violent crimes. There was a rumour that one of the colonels had taken a shine to him, was grooming him for the prosecutor's office.

He was cheerful and easy-going, and seemed smart enough, but Vic believed that he was inexperienced and had been promoted too far, too fast. Most murder police were seasoned and cynical. They needed to be, because they had to deal with the worst thing one human being could do to another. Skip was too quick to jump to conclusions, to take things and people at face value.

But he had answered the phone. It was his case. He had to decide where to take it, and Vic had to throttle back his impulse to take charge or give unwanted advice.

Now Skip switched on his torch and ran its light over the body, staring at it as if trying to force it to yield its secrets by sheer willpower. The secret was that it was dead, and didn't care. It was up to Skip to care. It was up to him to speak for his dead.

At last, he clicked off the torch and said that there was no sign of gunshot or stab wounds.

Vic said, 'That you can see. I had a case a few years ago, a guy lying dead in the street, not a mark on him. I couldn't find anything, the crime-scene techs couldn't find anything. It was like he had dropped dead from a heart attack. Then they rolled him, and a bullet fell out of his ear.'

'If this bloke was shot, he managed to put up a struggle first,' Skip said, gesturing at the trampled vegetation around the body. It was a dense tangle of thick wires, knee-high, springy as pubic hair. What they called wiregrass, although it really wasn't much like grass. The cuffs of Vic's trousers already bristled with friable fragments. The area around the body had been crushed and flattened. Broken stems gave off a sharp, not unpleasant smell, a little like mentholated mouthwash.

'You can check any pockets you can reach,' Vic said. 'But don't roll him. Leave that for the techs.'

'I know,' Skip said mildly. He squatted beside the body and felt inside the thin jacket, then reached into the front pockets of the trousers with scissored fingers.

'Watch for needles,' Vic said.

'A guy dressed like this won't be a skin-popper,' Skip said, another assumption he shouldn't have made, and pulled out a wallet, holding it up between ring- and forefinger. He showed Vic the items it contained. A credit card issued by the Petra City Bank in the name of John Redway. A fat fold of plastic notes, UN scrip, in a money clip. Several business cards: John Redway, consultant, Cybermat Technologies Inc, an address and telephone number in London. And a key card from the Hotel California.

'So I was kind of right,' Skip said, as he dropped the wallet into an evidence bag. 'Our Mr Redway is a newbie, all right, but a corporate newbie. A legitimate businessman who fell into bad company. This is just the kind of place for a clandestine meeting. Or a shakedown. No cameras. There was an argument, our guy got himself shot, and the bad guys bailed when they saw the security guard coming.'

Vic didn't say anything.

Skip said, 'So what's wrong with that picture? What did I miss?'

'I don't think you have enough to make a picture,' Vic said.

'We should definitely check where he was staying.'

'We can do that once the techs arrive.'

'I called them again,' Skip said. 'They're still caught up in that bar killing, checking everyone who was in it for blood spatter and whatever. Might be another hour.'

'Our friend isn't going anywhere.'

Vic cast around, found tyre tracks in the vegetation cutting away towards a string of Boxbuilder ruins at the top of the slope. He stared off in that direction, then walked back to the road, where Skip was interviewing the security guard.

She had been walking the perimeter fence when she'd heard what sounded like fireworks, her dog had started to bark, and she'd glimpsed a van bucking away across the heath. She thought it was white; she didn't know its make.

Skip went through this twice, with gentle patience. When he was finished, Vic asked the guard how many scooters she'd seen.

The woman gave him a suspicious look, as if he'd asked her a trick question. 'Just the one. Over there by the poor man.'

Skip and Vic walked a little way off down the road. Skip said, 'What was that thing about how many scooters?'

Vic showed him the tracks. 'There are two sets. These must be the van's. And these are a scooter's. I'd say one was chasing the other.'

'You think our man had a pal?'

'I think we should follow the tracks, see if the people in the van caught up with the guy on the scooter.'

Skip drove slowly over the bumpy ground, wiregrass scraping the underside of the car, while Vic leaned out of the open window and called out directions. The tracks cut past the Boxbuilder ruins, curving back towards the highway to the city, disappeared when the vegetation petered out into a broad stretch of stony sand. They got out of the car and cast around, but if there had been any tracks in the sand the wind had erased them. Several warehouses stood a little way off, strung along the highway. Sunlight burning off the flat land beyond. The shuttle looming over everything.

Back in England, in Birmingham, they'd have had a full squad of police and specialists at the scene, access to a network of traffic cams that watched every centimetre of the road system, and drones imaging everything in HD and infra-red and ultraviolet, sniffing for DNA and trace chemicals, following the spoor of the scooter and van like bloodhounds. Here on Mangala, they had to make do with a couple of investigators using their eyes and instincts, the promise of a cursory examination by overstretched techs, and more questions than answers. Such as: did the guy on the second scooter get away, or was he lying dead somewhere out there?

Vic said, 'We might be able to call in some uniforms tomorrow, have them search the area.'

'I hope he escaped,' Skip said. 'And I hope he has the good sense to come in and tell us what he saw.'

'He was most likely involved in a criminal enterprise. Good sense doesn't come into it.' Vic turned from the cut of the wind, stared up at the shuttle's enormous exclamation mark.

He said, 'This guy gets a ticket to ride an alien spaceship to another world. He's here two days and gets himself whacked. If I were him, I'd ask for a refund.'

5. Midnight Flit

London | 5 July

The Jackaroo avatar stood on a dais made from an upturned plastic milk crate and a circle of silver-painted plywood, confronting a cluster of tourists taking turns to be photographed with it. Black suit, white shirt; black tie, white gloves; a Hallowe'en mask of gold-tinted plastic gleaming under a bowler hat. When one of the tourists dropped a coin in the cardboard box in front of the dais, the avatar gave a stiff robotic parody of a bow.

Other costume artists stood along the path at the edge of St James's Park. Mickey Mouse. Superman. Batman. Super Mario. A generic Disney Princess.

Phone and tablet flashes stuttered as the avatar removed his bowler hat to reveal a shaven head painted gold and a headband with two springy antennae that terminated in gold-painted ping-pong balls.

Chloe walked on through the shade of a row of young gingkos, replacements for plane trees blasted and burned by the Trafalgar Square nuke. A photograph of the trees all aflame was one of the iconic images of the atrocity, like the refrigerated trucks packed with the dead and parked nose to tail along South Carriage Drive in Hyde Park, or the Union Jack fluttering from the jib of a crane elevated above smoking ruins. Chloe hadn't seen any of that at the time. She'd been in school in Walthamstow, had been evacuated with her classmates and everyone else in the long transect of East London threatened by the radiation plume, had ended up in a holding camp outside the ring of the M25. That was where her brother had found her a week later. She remembered that she'd flinched away from him when he had stooped into the tent she shared with five other girls. This strange gaunt unshaven stranger suddenly becoming her brother, gathering her up into his arms and both of them howling. Neil had hitchhiked down from York, where he'd been at university, walking the last ten miles cross-country to avoid army patrols and checkpoints. His first and last big adventure.

Now Chloe wanted to ask him for a favour. They'd arranged to meet after work in a café on top of the construction-coral dyke that held back the Thames, close to the asymmetric apartment block that occupied the site of old New Scotland Yard. The dark red dyke was topped by a broad promenade where gravel paths wound between lush islands of palmettos and bamboos and flowering bushes, and gave spectacular views across the mud-brown flood of the Thames. High above, a sky-whale black with sequestered carbon drifted on the summer breeze, accompanied by a small school of freshly budded juveniles.

Neil was nursing a bottle of beer at a table at the edge of the crowded outdoor café. Her tall handsome brother, rising to hug her. He was dressed in Lycra shorts and a red jersey. A rucksack containing his suit sat at his feet; the bicycle he used to commute from Walthamstow every day, summer and winter, rain or shine, was no doubt chained to one of the racks at the foot of the dyke. Chloe bought an iced coffee and they sat in the sunshine and caught up with each other's lives. Neil said that he was glad she had stopped dyeing her hair blonde, it had never really suited her; Chloe asked about his wife and his daughter, her niece, nine years old now, hard to believe.

'You should come visit,' Neil said.

'Please don't make me feel guilty.'

'The last time was Ellie's birthday.'

'That's what I mean about that guilt thing.'

Neil knew exactly how to push her buttons. After he and Chloe had been allowed to return to the little house in Walthamstow, he'd given up his university course and joined the civil service and put Chloe through school with the help of their aunt and uncle; their grandparents on their mother's side were dead, and their father had abandoned them long before and was raising a new family in St Andrews, where he lectured on medieval history. Neil was stable and stolid and utterly conventional. He'd taken refuge from their mother's death and the arrival of the Jackaroo in a life as ordinary as possible in a world grown wild and strange. Chloe had embraced that strangeness; Neil had turned his back on it. They were, their aunt Beth said, two sides of the same coin.

They talked about their work, his in the Ministry of Transport, hers with Disruption Theory. Neil asked if she was ready for her big day tomorrow, in front of the select committee. 'You look as if you've dressed for it,' he said.

'That's what I thought.'

Chloe was wearing black trousers, a white shirt that an old boyfriend had left behind, and her black denim jacket, little tin badges printed with the faces of dead cosmonauts pinned to one lapel. She'd found them on a stall in the Reef run by a Russian guy who'd assured her that they were genuine antiques. Well, maybe. But even if they were fakes, they were powerful juju, the faces touchingly noble, romantic. Lost boys from a forgotten heroic age.

She said, 'According to the high-powered lawyer who's been preparing us, this isn't quite the thing. She's going to lend me something appropriate. I dread to think.'

'Because it'll be something an actual grown-up would wear?'

'If this is what being a grown-up is like, big brother, you can keep it.'

Chloe had spent most of the afternoon shut in the conference room with the rest of Disruption Theory, being briefed by Helena Nichols and her two startlingly young and capable assistants, taking part in a group discussion that was supposed to analyse their strengths and weaknesses. After the lawyer finally wrapped things up, Daniel Rosenblaum had given another pep talk, telling them that he was immensely proud of their work and was certain that their abilities and enthusiasm would carry the day.

'I can promise you,' he'd said, 'that we'll be getting the best kind of support. So go home, rest up, relax. This is a big challenge, but it's nothing we can't handle.'

Neil told several gossipy stories about the antics of the Human Decency League and their supporters. Like all civil servants, he had a healthy cynicism about politics and politicians.

'Last month one of their swivel-eyed MPs made a speech in the Commons about how the UN lottery was blatantly rigged,' he said. 'How it favoured people from the Third World, how they were flitting off to enjoy and exploit the riches of the new worlds and leaving behind the mess they'd made, because everyone knew the Spasm had started in Pakistan and India. When Robin Mountjoy was asked about it, he claimed that it was an example of the kind of robust discussion that made his party so strong. The fact is, they're an unstable amalgamation of every far-right prejudice and crackpot theory. The only thing they have in common is a visceral hatred of the Jackaroo.'

Helena Nichols had told the same story during a background briefing. 'I know I should care about the select committee, but I really don't,' Chloe said, and diverted the conversation to the little cult and its breakout.

She pulled up some of Mangala Cowboy's pictures on her tablet. Neil, flicking through them, said, 'They look like covers for old sci-fi paperbacks.'

He couldn't see what she saw, either.

Chloe said, 'I think they're authentic. Pictures of a real place. Some undiscovered ruin on one of the fifteen worlds, or maybe on a world we haven't been given access to. I think the guy who made these was exposed to an active artefact. Something that got inside him and compelled him to draw these pictures. And it affected his neighbours, too. They had a breakout on Saturday. And on Sunday, our artist did a midnight flit.'

She had returned to the displaced-persons camp yesterday evening, after Niome's phone call. The girl had been waiting for her on the bench by the chestnut tree, told her that Freddie and his sister had moved out. 'Here yesterday, gone today. Happens a lot in this place.'

She hadn't seen them leave, shrugged when Chloe had described Eddie Ackroyd. 'I only found out about it when I come back from school. But this boy I know, he said he saw Freddie and a couple of heads stuffing cardboard boxes and clothes and shit in the boot of a car parked over by the gates. This was about eleven, twelve last night.'

'I don't suppose your friend would remember the number of the car?'

'He was so blasted I'm amazed he recognised Freddie. So, what's this hot news worth?'

Chloe gave Niome another five-pound coin, told her to keep watching the skies. No one answered when Chloe rapped on the door of Freddie Patel's flatlet. She went upstairs, hoping to talk to Mr Archer, but the old man's wife answered the door and said that her husband was resting and didn't want to be disturbed.

'I saw his performance yesterday,' Chloe said. 'It was impressive. In fact, that's sort of why I'm here.'

'Do you know your Bible?' Mrs Archer said.

She had sharp blue eyes, this thin old woman with a cap of white hair, clutching a cardigan draped over her bony shoulders.

'A little,' Chloe said.

For two years after the Spasm, she had gone to church with Neil and their aunt and uncle every Sunday, but at age fourteen she'd rebelled. Apart from weddings and christenings that had been that, for her and religion.

Mrs Archer said, 'Perhaps you remember the passage that describes how the holy dove descended on the apostles, and they could understand every language.'

'Your downstairs neighbour, Freddie Patel. Does he have that gift?'

Mrs Archer's smile went away. 'Someone else came here yesterday, asking the same questions. As I told him, I really don't know anything about the boy.'

Chloe had a falling sensation. She was losing her edge. She'd let Eddie Ackroyd beat her to the prize. She said, 'Was that a man wearing a hat and an old leather jacket, smells funny and won't look you in the eye? He isn't any friend of mine. Was he causing trouble? Did he have something to do with Freddie leaving?'

'I wouldn't know,' Mrs Archer said, and started to close the door.

Chloe said quickly, 'Do you have a relative or a friend who won the emigration lottery?'

'Not today, thank you,' Mrs Archer said, and the door snicked shut.

Her neighbours didn't know anything about Freddie Patel or weren't prepared to tell Chloe. Several had the shiny-eyed look of the meme-struck.

'Either he did a deal with one of my rivals,' Chloe told Neil, 'or he got spooked by the breakout, or by my interest in his pictures . . . He was definitely nervous when I talked to him. And when I called the letting agents, I found out that his real name is Fahad Chauhan. They had a photocopy of his ID card in the lease documents. Fahad Chauhan, eighteen years old.'

She'd pretended to be from the immigration services, but there was no need to tell her brother that, he'd only get upset.

'I'm pretty sure he's hiding from someone,' she said. 'On the run from some kind of trouble.'

'Perhaps you should talk with this rival of yours, ask him what he knows,' Neil said.

'Even if he knew anything about it, he'd probably lie.' Chloe didn't want to say Eddie Ackroyd's name. If she did, he might appear in a puff of stale kif smoke. 'There's something else, too. Apart from his tumblr, Fahad seems to be totally off grid. I did the usual Googling and found plenty of Fahad Chauhans, but none of them seem to be the one I'm looking for. There's a pop star in Pakistan called Fahad Chauhan. A film director in India . . . They're either too old or too young, or living in the wrong place. My guy doesn't do Facebook or Friendster or Snapchat. He isn't listed on TownSquare or AsianCafé. Maybe he's on one of the walled networks, or maybe he lurks in the darknets, but as far as his public profile goes he doesn't have one. It's as if he's purged every reference to him. There are worms that do that. Erase your profile, or improve it by hunting down and deleting those embarrassing selfies you took when you were a teenager.'

'Isn't that illegal?'

'Only if you try to use it on a government site, attack your police records. The kid's a ghost. But I did find something about his family, and his history. To begin with, his father is some kind of biochemist, moved here from Pakistan seven years ago.'

Gail Ann Jones had pointed her towards a news snippet buried in an industry newsletter. A brief paragraph about Professor S. A. Chauhan, formerly of the University of the Punjab, taking up a new job at the GlaxoSmithKline R&D site in Uxbridge.

'And you know this Professor Chauhan is your man's father because?' Neil was smiling: he liked to read thrillers, derived vicarious pleasure from Chloe's stories about tracking down alien artefacts.

Chloe said, 'Because about a year after Professor Chauhan moved here, there was an article in the *Hillingdon Times* about a tropical garden that his wife created. And one of the article's photos showed Professor and Mrs Chauhan and their son Fahad. It's one of those sad stories with a sweet ending. In their home country, the father was caught up in a government campaign against universities. Labs and libraries burned down, denunciations, student strikes . . . A bit like the anti-intellectual riots we had here, but with assassinations and mass arrests. Anyway, Professor Chauhan was arrested, Mrs Chauhan and Fahad came here, and the family was reunited some years later, after the new government released the Professor from prison. So one of my questions is, if Fahad and his sister are on the run, where are their parents?'

'Oh dear. I think I can see where this is going.'

'You've done it before.'

'And the last time I did it we agreed it would be the last time.'

'Fahad and his little sister are in bad, serious trouble. They're on the run because something has got hold of them. Some Elder Culture thing. An active artefact, an eidolon . . . It's already caused a breakout. Next time it could be something that puts them in real danger. All you have to do,' Chloe said, 'is search the DVLA database for their father and mother. A quick peek. In and out.'

'Suppose they don't have driving licences?'

'There was a photo of the front of the house, with two cars in the drive.'

'Just one quick look.'

'You're a star. Just one other thing—'

'Just the one thing, Chloe. Otherwise I might find myself having to answer some hard questions.'

'This isn't about the DVLA. I'm wondering how Fahad got hold of an artefact. I've already checked the emigration lottery winner lists, no luck there. So I thought,' Chloe said, 'you could ask your old university pal David, over in the Foreign Office, if he could check the lists of shuttle passengers whose tickets were bought by companies and governments. See if Professor Chauhan was sent up and out by his employers.'

6. The Hotel California

Petra | 24 July

Back in the day, the Hotel California had been a camp for scientists employed by the UN. The original building, a chain of modules perched on A-frame stilts, now housed the hotel's reception and administration offices; guests were accommodated in cabins scattered across a landscaped park of terrestrial trees and plants cupped beneath a geodesic dome.

It was dusk inside the dome – a scattering of window lights amongst clumps of trees and bushes, fairy lights twinkling along the paths – as the manager led Vic Gayle and Skip Williams to the cabin rented by the late John Redway and his colleague, David Parsons. A clapboard cabin with a corrugated-iron roof, perched above a mossy pool fed by a little waterfall and approached by a humpback wooden bridge. No lights showing at the windows.

The manager had printed out scans of the passports of the two men, and made a copy of CCTV footage of them leaving the hotel at around four p.m. Parsons was older than Redway: a forty-two-year-old white male according to his passport, brown eyes, cropped black hair, one metre ninety. Clearly the boss, the manager said.

Both men were British. Parsons had paid for their cabin with a card drawing on credit deposited with the Petra City Bank in an account apparently opened by Cybermat Technologies.

The manager, a brisk young Spanish woman, stood back as Skip took out his gun and gave a good police knock, three hard raps with the side of his fist, and announced that the police were outside. No reply. Frogs peeped everywhere. They'd been introduced to control an infestation of flies, and had multiplied enormously. Vic sweated inside his suit. The warm air was heavy with the scent of the honeysuckle that curtained one end of the porch. A line from the old song which had given the hotel its name ran through his head. The one about checking out but never leaving.

Skip knocked again, exchanged a look with Vic, and ran the key card through the slot. The pinlight changed from red to green and Skip turned the handle and shouldered through the door, leading with his gun. Vic followed, into a living space under a slanting ceiling, lights coming on when Skip found a switch by the door. A leather sofa and leather armchairs, a big stone fireplace, a flat-screen TV on a sideboard. One wall was covered by a blow-up of the famous photograph taken by Marianne Hækkerup as the first shuttle flight had approached Mangala. A half-globe banded like an Easter egg: ice cap, desert, the bitter equatorial sea, desert, ice cap.

The manager stood in the doorway while Vic and Skip pulled on gloves and checked the two bedrooms and the bathroom. There was nothing to identify the men or the nature of their work. No papers or tablets, no data sticks. Anonymous clothing from Matalan and Marks and Spencer. White shirts, grey and black slacks, grey jackets, black sweaters, black socks. New toiletries. One of them had used an electric razor, the other disposable Bics.

Vic and Skip stripped the beds, moved furniture, checked under drawers, lifted rugs. Nothing.

'I'll call in the CI techs, get them to take DNA from the razors and toothbrushes,' Skip said. 'I guess I should post uniforms, too. Although I reckon Mr Parsons won't be coming back.'

'No doubt. But the people who killed his friend might stop by,' Vic said.

They came out of the dome's soft warm dusk into harsh sunlight and a cold wind. The fat orange sun hung above the roofs of the city. It was a hair past eleven in the evening, and it was the long afternoon of the day-year. Thirty-one days of light; then thirty-one days of night. After thirteen years Vic still hadn't accommodated to it. Most people hadn't. Across the street, a strip of bars and restaurants was buzzing with Landing Day revellers.

45

Skip said, 'I should check with the British consulate, see if they know anything about these two. Maybe this is some kind of corporate espionage caper.'

'I'll tell you exactly what it is,' Vic said. 'It's the worst kind of case. The kind of case that'll keep you awake at night, keep Sergeant Madsen breathing down your neck. I pity you, man, I really do. First time you answer the phone, you get a full-blown twenty-four-carat whodunnit.'

7. Bob Smith

London | 6 July

'We came in peace,' the alien said, 'for all humankind. And I've come here today, Mr Chairman – and please forgive me if I'm being presumptuous – to remind you of that.'

Eleven o'clock on a drowsy summer morning in Committee Room No. 3, the fifteenth floor of Kingdom Tower. A chill edge in the air-conditioned space, tall windows polarised against blinding sunlight, dimming the view of the huge construction site where the half-completed reconstruction of the Palace of Westminster stood inside a cofferdam. The Jackaroo avatar had walked into the committee room during the chairman's opening remarks, causing a major stir and forcing the chairman to wait a full five minutes, grim-faced, before the fuss had died down and he could resume his speech. Dressed like an old-school rap star in a brand-new black Adidas tracksuit and box-fresh sneakers, vintage Ray-Ban Aviators masking its blank eyes, the avatar sat behind a table cluttered with microphones and plastic-wrapped glasses and sweating jugs of ice-water, an unscheduled special witness facing the four members of the Alien Technology Committee.

In the early days of First Contact, the Jackaroo – or rather, their avatars – had been everywhere, from Antarctica to Zimbabwe, but in the years since they had pulled back, become more like ambassadors than tourists, appearing at government functions and ceremonies, occasionally interviewed on news or talk shows, but rarely seen at large, out in the world. Years ago Chloe had glimpsed, from the top deck of a bus, an avatar ambling up Walthamstow High Street in the middle of a scrum of officials and police. Bus passengers crowding to the windows, passers-by

47

gawping, traffic slowing in a blare of horns as the avatar and its followers crossed the car park towards the town hall. That was the closest she'd been to one, before today. Now, sitting with the rest of Disruption Theory's crew in the first row of chairs and waiting her turn to be questioned, she could almost reach out and touch it.

She supposed that its appearance was what Daniel had meant by 'the best kind of support', wondered if it had something to do with Ada Morange, who was being shadowed by a !Cha that was collecting her life story. The !Cha had arrived with the Jackaroo, although it still wasn't clear if they were servants or hitchhikers, clients or secret masters, or something else. Insatiably curious, they travelled inside tough mobile aquaria that could, as several gangs of would-be kidnappers had discovered, shoot skywards at high velocities. There weren't many of them: a hundred or so. Beautiful Sorrow. Brilliant Mistake. Strange Attraction. Useless Beauty. Actual aliens wandering the world, searching for wonders.

Yes, it was possible that Ada Morange's !Cha — it called itself Unlikely Worlds, Chloe remembered — had reached out to the Jackaroo, had asked them to give its friend's employees a little help. Or maybe Unlikely Worlds had heard a rumour on some kind of alien gossip node that the Jackaroo were planning to make an appearance before the select committee, and had given the entrepreneur a heads-up.

Daniel was at the far end of the row, tall and rumpled in an ancient Savile Row pinstripe suit and a silvery waistcoat decorated with bright green banana leaves. During the preliminary announcements and the beginning of the chairman's opening remarks he had slouched in his seat, studying something on his phone, but like everyone else he'd turned his full attention to the Jackaroo avatar when it had arrived, watching now as it placed its hand on the copy of the Bible held by the clerk of the committee. It was rare to make witnesses to select committees swear to tell the truth, but the chair, Robin Mountjoy, had insisted on it.

The avatar recited the oath with apparent sincerity, but added, to general laughter, 'You will note that neither I nor your sacred book have burst into flame.'

No one had ever seen one of the Jackaroo in the flesh. They could be devils with bright red skin and horns and hooves and barbed tails, or angels, or anything in between. Gas bags evolved to ride the frigid winds of an exoJupiter. Machine intelligences. Self-organising magnetic fields. No one knew. And no one knew whether or not the Jackaroo actually inhabited their floppy space-ships – the tangles of restless vanes that had somehow towed the mouths of fifteen wormholes, each mounted on the polished face of an asteroid fragment, into L5 orbit between the Earth and Moon. Soon after the Jackaroo had revealed themselves, one of their ships had been vaporised by a thirty-kiloton nuclear bomb delivered by a Chinese Long March rocket. The Chinese had immediately claimed that it had been the act of a rogue element in their army, and the whole world had held its breath, waiting for the Jackaroo's response, but the other ships had simply absorbed the debris and the Jackaroo had never mentioned the incident, had deflected all questions about it. It was possible that the ships were no more than relays transmitting signals from elsewhere, although no such signals had been detected. Or that the Jackaroo were clones or machines who had no concept of individual death. Or that the ships weren't really ships at all, but decoys to divert attention from the Jackaroo's actual presence (whatever that was). Props to satisfy human tropes of alien inva-sion. In the end, the destruction of the ship and the lack of any acknowledgement or response proved only that nothing, really, was known about the Jackaroo.

This one called itself Bob Smith. Like all of its kind, it appeared to be male ('We prefer not to challenge certain social norms,' the Jackaroo said, when asked about this), had translucent golden skin and was blandly handsome, its features a composite of an international selection of film stars with just enough artful asym-metry to avoid the uncanny valley effect. A machine passing for human: an animated, remotely controlled showroom dummy as hollow as a balloon. X-ray spectrometry, multispectrum imaging and other forms of remote probing suggested that the musculature and circuitry of Jackaroo avatars were entirely contained within their skins, but no one had ever managed to analyse one directly.

They evaporated if trapped or damaged, fizzing away into water, gases, and trace elements. The ultimate golden vapourware.

Bob Smith gestured languidly, its body language a precise simulation of a person in command of their facts, relaxed and happy to cooperate. Answering, in a mellow, agreeable baritone, questions from the four MPs about the latest discoveries of ancient alien technology on the various new worlds. Stuff excavated from ruins and tomb cities, found in forests and deserts, fished from alien seas. Agreeing that these things could be dangerous, 'But only if used in the right way.' Claiming to know very little about Elder Culture artefacts. Saying, after being challenged about this, 'We do not spy on our clients. We try to minimise contact. We try not to influence them. We let them find their own way. So we do not know what our previous clients left behind. By now, in fact, you probably know more about that than we do. You are a clever and versatile species. Very adaptable. Very plastic. We are sure that you will discover interesting new uses for everything you find.'

The Jackaroo were masters of flattery and misdirection, deflecting hard questions with humour, salting their sweet talk with a smattering of obscure cultural references to flatter the cognoscenti. With their outsider's perspective and millions of years of experience in dealing with no one knew how many intelligent species, they understood people better than they understood themselves. Bob Smith's imitation of a human was somehow more than human: a behavioural superstimulus like the red ball a male robin, believing it to be a rival, would exhaust itself attacking.

Chloe definitely felt the avatar's film-star allure, its fairyland glamour. Glancing around, she saw that almost everyone else in the room – witnesses, advisers, journalists and members of the public packing the rows of seats, even the security guards standing at the door – had a kind of avid shine to their gaze. They felt it too.

She was dressed in a black Jaeger trouser suit which Helena Nichols had lent her. It wasn't a bad fit, but it felt like a costume for a play. Her palms were sweating. Stray lines from yesterday's rehearsals kept running through her head. She hoped that the avatar's appearance would deflect attention from Disruption

Theory, from herself, but she also knew that people all over the world would be watching it, that specialists would be analysing every word, every gesture, and pretty soon they would be watching her, too. Trying not to think about that invisible audience, as per Helena Nichols's advice, was kind of like not thinking about a white rhinoceros while you tried to turn boiling water into gold.

Robin Mountjoy was making a decent attempt to appear to be unaffected by the avatar's charm. He was in his mid-fifties, a burly man with thinning blond hair and a florid complexion, dressed in an off-the-peg suit. Although he was a multimillionaire, having made his fortune constructing and servicing displaced-persons camps, his PR painted him as a bluff, no-nonsense man of the people whose common sense cut through the incestuous old boys' networks of the Westminster village.

He put on his gold-rimmed glasses to read something on his tablet, took them off again and leaned forward, blunt fingers laced together. 'It seems to me that after thirteen years you have nothing new to say to us, sir. You offer only the same platitudes, the same empty reassurances.'

'You ask why we do not change,' Bob Smith said. 'We are as we always have been because that is how we are. The question should be: have *you* changed?'

'Voters elected thirty-six MPs in my party,' Robin Mountjoy said. '*We* represent change. A change in attitude to your kind. We are challenging you. We intend to see through you.'

'Everyone can see through us,' Bob Smith said, with that very human shrug.

Robin Mountjoy waited out the laughter. 'We see your avatars, but we do not see you. If you truly have nothing to hide, why don't you show yourselves?'

'When you have a telephone conversation with someone, do you treat them differently? Do you trust them less?'

'You answer my questions with more questions. But our business is to get some answers.'

'Perhaps you are not asking the right questions.'

More laughter.

'There's only one question,' Robin Mountjoy said. 'Why are you really here? You say you want to help. What do you expect in return?'

'We hope that you will discover your better natures.'

It was a statement that the Jackaroo had made a million times. Chloe realised that Robin Mountjoy wasn't interested in digging out anything new. He was not vain enough, not foolish enough, to think that he could succeed where thousands of politicians, scientists, philosophers and journalists had failed. Even the infamous Reddit AMA had failed to get inside the Jackaroo's mischievous sophistry. No, he was grandstanding, playing the role of a fearless interrogator armed with what he would no doubt call good old-fashioned English common sense. The appearance of the avatar had put him in the spotlight, and he was milking the opportunity for all it was worth.

He said, 'The business of the committee, sir, is not airy-fairy speculation about human nature. It's the important and immediate question of dangerous and out-of-control technology.'

'Ah! The best kind of technology.'

And so it went, back and forth. Despite the presence of an actual fucking alien right in front of her, Chloe's attention drifted. The seats facing the committee were set out in a horseshoe; although she was seated in the front row, she could watch part of the audience. Some were taking notes, some looked as bored as she was beginning to feel, a few watched with the avid rapture of true fans. A woman clutching a copy of the order papers to her chest. A man with a stony intent expression, sitting as still as a statue. Another man sketching on a pad, shooting quick sharp glances at the avatar.

At last, the committee ran out of questions and Robin Mountjoy thanked the avatar for taking the trouble to attend. Bob Smith smiled and said that it was always a pleasure to serve. 'And let me reassure you that I do not allude to the culinary sense of the verb.'

Two security guards moved forward as the avatar stood, and someone else was moving too. A man rushing forward, a pen flashing in his hand.

No. It was a knife.

Chloe saw everything clearly. The man's blank expression as he sidestepped one of the guards, the avatar turning towards him. It was still smiling. Its hands spread as if greeting an old acquaintance. She saw the man raise the knife. Saw that its fat handle was wrapped in black tape. Saw that it had a double blade, two finger-length spikes. Saw fat blue sparks snapping in the narrow gap between them as the man stabbed the avatar in the chest. There was a pungent smell of burning plastic, the avatar shuddered and collapsed against the man, and Chloe shot to her feet and grabbed one of the jugs of water from the table and swept it up and around, intending to hit the man. He ducked away, but water cascaded over his chest and arms. The knife exploded in his hands, and then both he and the avatar were down on the floor, jerking and flailing like landed fish, and a security guard caught Chloe around the waist and hauled her backwards. She was breathing as hard as if she'd just run a ten-kilometre race. Her heart jackhammering. She was shocked and amazed by what she'd done, wondered if the guard thought that she was an accomplice of the assassin, wondered if she was going to be arrested.

Robin Mountjoy was shouting something, but no one in the room was paying any attention to him. The security guards roughly lifted the man, the assassin, to his feet. The avatar was face down on the navy-blue carpet, twitching and shuddering, a crown of white smoke burning off its head, white threads rising from the wrist and ankle cuffs of its tracksuit, its golden skin turning black, splitting, flaking, disintegrating.

People were jabbering into phones, taking photos, putting on spex. Someone was stupidly calling for a doctor. Someone else was shouting about death to aliens, long live the Human Resistance. It was the assassin, raving at the cameras aimed towards him as the security guards dragged him away. Chloe saw Daniel Rosenblaum hunched over in his seat, one finger in his ear as he talked urgently into his phone, saw Ram Varma snapping on a pair of vinyl gloves, saw him kneel by the collapsed tracksuit and unscrew the cap from a bottle of mineral water and scoop something from the floor.

8. Actual Ray Gun

Mangala | 25 July

The next morning, the start of their shift, Vic met Skip Williams at the city morgue in the main hospital. Skip had already put David Parsons on the watch list and distributed his description and photo to the day briefings, applied for a trace on transactions involving his company account credit card, and phoned around the city's hotels. No luck so far: either Parsons had gone to ground or he was in a shallow grave somewhere out in the playa. And now they had to wait for John Redway's body to take its turn on the table. Three mutilated bodies had been found in an empty house at the edge of Junktown, a slaughter related to an ongoing turf war between rival gangs over control of marijuana growups. And because the Mayor had made control of drugs a major plank in his re-election campaign, the case took precedence over everything else.

In the opinion of Alain Bodin, the investigator who'd caught the triple, things were going to hell.

'I can't work out if it's because we have let the bad guys get away with it, or if there is something in the magnetic field of this goddamned planet.'

'If there was, you and me would have gone crazy long ago,' Vic said.

They were standing on the morgue's loading dock, drinking coffee out of cardboard cups while Alain and his partner, Maria Espinosa, waited for the three bodies to be prepped.

'Maybe we did.' Alain, a stocky man with close-cropped iron-grey hair and a blunt, belligerent manner, was a veteran like Vic, come up on the fourth shuttle flight. 'But immigrants these days, they're definitely crazier. Mad and bad in a way they weren't, back in the beginning.'

'When did we start calling them immigrants?' Maria said.

Alain ignored her, telling Vic, 'That case last year, the guy who killed women and kept them in his basement. He'd been here, what, a year? You come out to a new world, you have a chance at a new life, to make yourself over, and you do that. Tell me it isn't the definition of a new kind of crazy.'

'Well, we didn't have basements back then,' Vic said.

'That's right,' Alain said, very serious. 'We had to make everything we needed. Now you can just buy it. Or steal it. Kids come up with just the clothes on their backs, tattoos, rings in their ears and noses and who knows where else. What are they going to do here? Strike out for the territories? No, they do what they were doing back on Earth. They do drugs and steal to maintain their habit, or they sell drugs and kill each other over territory.'

'They're different, no doubt,' Vic said, beginning to tire of the conversation, aware that Skip was watching the to-and-fro as if it was a tennis match.

But Alain wouldn't let it go. 'Back then, we were too busy growing the city. Now things are pretty much like they are on Earth, so we get the same kind of problems as any city back home. You ask me, they should think about restricting the lottery. Screening out people with a criminal record – there's something that would ease our troubles.'

'But if you start doing that,' Skip said, 'where would you stop? Next thing you know, governments would only let people who voted for them come up.'

Alain said to Vic, 'You see what I mean about the quality of immigrants these days?'

Skip stood his ground. 'Or let's turn your idea around. Suppose they decided to send only criminals?'

Alain spat over the rail of the dock. 'As far as I'm concerned it wouldn't make much difference.'

'Alain misses the frontier life,' Maria said. 'When men were men, women knew their place, and the bad guys wore black hats for ease of identification.'

'Just thirteen years ago,' Alain Bodin said. 'How did we go so wrong so fast?'

Maria turned the conversation to the dust storm, saying to Vic, 'You were here for the Big Blow. They say this one could be bigger.'

'I don't know about that,' Vic said. 'But I guess it has room to grow.'

The storm was rolling eastward around the northern hemisphere. Forecasters reckoned that it would sweep across Idunn's Valley in five or six days; a few days later, it would reach Petra. The news channels were showing video clips shot by a survey plane. A tawny cliff rearing kilometres into the sky, with tawny clouds rolling at its feet. Dust devils whirling across stony plains like crazed ballroom dancers, leaving black tracks scribbled on red ground, red dunes. Flickers of dry lightning. Portents.

'They cleared out the courtroom jail yesterday,' Alain said. 'Put bunk beds in the cells for when we go to emergency duty. Man, if I can't get home, I sleep at my desk.'

'I have an air mattress,' Maria said.

'We should get in food,' Alain said. 'Wine too. Get it before the supermarkets are stripped.'

Skip said, 'There are already big queues everywhere.'

Alain nodded. 'We go straight from Landing Day into crisis mode. One thing, we will make good money on the overtime.'

'We tried to buy some plastic sheeting,' Skip said. 'All gone. Hardboard too.'

'I suppose you've never seen a storm before,' Maria said.

'A little one, in the Valley,' Skip said. 'Everyone has been saying we're overdue a monster. I guess this is it.'

'Seal the edges of every window that opens with mastic. Every door too, but one. You have a chimney? If you cannot cap it,' Alain said, 'put a balloon up it.'

'There was a fist fight in the supermarket yesterday,' Skip said. 'I had to wade into the middle of it. Two guys duking it out over the last bags of rice.'

'Get canned food,' Alain said. 'Dry food needs too much water. And if the power goes, you can heat cans over a camping stove. Or eat it cold.'

Vic listened to them talk, remembering the Big Blow. Two years after the first shuttle flight had arrived on Mangala. He remembered having to wear a respirator and hooded coveralls to go outside, remembered the dim light, the fog of dust thickening in every direction. Remembered navigating the rudimentary streets of the city by using lines strung between buildings. More than a hundred people had managed to get lost and die before they could find their way back to shelter. There had been a rash of suicides. He remembered the devil's itch of dust in every crevice of his body, the iron taste of it, the grit between his teeth in every mouthful of food. None of the buildings had been completely sealed. If you left a glass of water out for ten minutes a faint scum would bloom on its meniscus. Every surface coated in red powder.

The Big Blow hadn't been a local dust storm, like the one coming in: it had blanketed the entire planet for two sidereal years, a shade over sixty-two days. One day-year, one night-year. Polytunnels and greenhouses had collapsed under the weight of settled dust; eighty per cent of the crops had been lost. There'd been rationing, several murders over hoarding, a rumour about cannibalism in a stranded road crew. Everyone in the new colony had relied on food supplied by the shuttle, which had not been affected by the storm, arriving and leaving on schedule, as indifferent as God to the works of nature and man.

This storm was nothing compared with that monster. According to the weather people it would envelop Petra for no more than two or three weeks before it blew past. But the Mayor had already made an appeal for calm, and the news channels were showing queues for food and dry goods, interviewing people who'd fled from outlying settlements in Idunn's Valley, and fielding pundits who questioned the city's resilience.

'The only good thing,' Marie said, 'it will lock down everyone. Civilians and bad guys. And afterwards people will be too busy digging themselves out to get into any serious mischief.'

'Let's hope so,' Alain said.

'The last big storm we had, crime went down more than twenty per cent,' Maria said.

'And before it hits?' Alain said. 'We get an uptick in killings because gangs are out in force, supplying addicts and fighting each other over territory. Also in low-level crime, as addicts scramble for quick cash. Because while civilians are stocking up on canned goods and bottled water, shiners and meqheads are stocking up too. I tell you this, my friends: when the storm comes, we'll be glad of the holiday.'

After Alain Bodin and Maria Espinosa were called into the autopsy suite, Vic and Skip waited in the hospital canteen for their turn, and caught up on paperwork. Vic had a court appearance in a couple of days, and went over his contemporaneous notes because the damn defence always liked to compare your version of the story with the perp's. Skip took a phone call from one of the crime-scene techs: no useful traces on the victim's clothes or skin; nylon and polyester-cotton fibres from two common brands of outdoor clothing caught in the wiregrass; a cast of tyre tracks that would be useful in identifying the van if it was ever found. He had also received a reply to the request he'd sent by q-phone to Interpol headquarters in Lyon, France. They were little miracles that fused human and Elder Culture technology, q-phones: paired handsets that shared entangled electrons whose quantum superposition enabled instantaneous transmission of information anywhere in the universe. The first q-phones had been as expensive as communication satellites, and using them to send an image had been like emptying a swimming pool through a straw; the second generation were no more costly than a villa in Bel Air and worked pretty much like regular phones. Skip had sent the images and passport details of John Redway and David Parsons, asking for further information. Now he told Vic that their passports appeared to be bogus, and there weren't any records for Cybermat Technologies Inc at Companies House in London, or in the European Business Register.

'Do you think these guys could be spooks? From MI5 or whatever?'

'If they are, it would be MI6, the extraterrestrial section,' Vic said. 'And I hope to God they aren't, because it would drop us in a world of shit.'

At last Skip was bleeped and they rode the freight elevator down to the basement. Outside the cutting room, the pathologist, Heather Ngu, told them that the deceased was a white European male who had been in good health when he died, with no tattoos, mods, or other identifying marks.

'He broke his left wrist some years ago. There's also an old healed fracture of his left tibia. Bloodwork showed no alcohol, no drugs. He wasn't any kind of smoker. And the ratio of stable isotopes indicates that he had been eating food from Earth, rather than local stuff.'

'We already know he and his mate just arrived on the shuttle,' Skip said. 'I checked with immigration.'

Vic said to Heather, 'Was he circumcised?'

'After we sewed him up we put him back in the freezer. But if you want to look, investigator, we can wheel him out for you.'

Heather Ngu was a brisk capable woman dressed in a blue smock, black hair pinned up under a blue cap. She and Vic had had a brief thing ten years back. Vic remembered that she'd liked to shower together before and drink brandy afterwards, lazy as a cat in what she called the afterglow. Oh man. Good times. Now she was married with two kids, and Vic was freshly divorced and living in an efficiency in one of the municipal apartment buildings.

She said, 'I can reveal that his last meal was a hamburger.'

Skip asked what kind.

'A cheeseburger, with fries.'

'I mean was it a Big Mac or what?'

'We're good, but we can't yet tell the difference between a half-digested Big Mac and a Whopper,' Heather said.

'What about the cause of death?' Skip said.

'There was some superficial bruising to the face and trunk, but no significant tissue damage. No fractures to the skull, no broken bones, no sign of blunt force trauma to the liver or other internal organs. No gunshot or knife wounds. But I did find something significant,' Heather said, and paused.

She liked to build up to the big reveal. When she and Vic had had their thing, she'd been writing a novel, said that it would be the first novel about the early days of settling and exploring Mangala. Last he'd heard, she was still working on it.

Skip took the bait. 'What kind of significant something?'

'A burn at the base of the skull, just here,' Heather said, touching the back of her neck. 'A charred spot three millimetres in diameter. Small enough to miss, if you don't know what you're looking for.'

'Like a cigarette burn?'

'Not exactly. There was no entry wound, but there was a line of cauterisation extending through the brain. As if someone had rammed a thin and very hot wire through it. It pierced the hypothalamus and the right cerebral lobe. Death would have been instantaneous.'

She was looking at Vic, as if expecting him to respond.

It took him a few moments to make the connection. 'The ray gun.'

Skip said, 'You mean like an actual ray gun, or some kind of laser?'

Vic said, 'We're on a planet littered with Elder Culture shit. Why should you be surprised that someone found themselves a ray gun?'

Heather said, 'There have been other victims with similar injuries. The weapon has not yet been identified. Something that fires a tightly focused high-energy beam. Like a very powerful laser, or a plasma or particle-beam weapon.'

Skip had a blank look, not understanding that he'd lucked out.

'Four other victims,' Vic said. 'Redway is the fifth.'

Skip still didn't see it.

Vic said, 'What we should do now is find Alain Bodin, tell him the news.'

Skip said, 'And why should we do that?'

'Because he took the call on the first ray-gun murder,' Vic said. 'Which means all the others are his. Including Redway's.'

9. Carbon-Based Life Form

London | 6 July

The police released Chloe after three hours, told her that they would escort her home. It was the kind of offer she couldn't refuse, but after a brief argument she persuaded them to take her to Disruption Theory's office instead of to her flat.

They gave her a ride in a police launch, banging up the centre of the river past embankments of construction coral and rakes of pontoon apartments and clusters of houseboats. She called Daniel and told him she was okay.

'How were the police? Did they treat you all right?'

'They interviewed me and let me go. Right now they're bringing me back to the office. In, guess what, a police launch.'

She was hunched over her phone on the bench seat behind the helmsman and a policewoman, earbuds plugged in, speaking close to the screen. Her hands trembling ever so slightly. Spray gusting over her as the launch passed under Blackfriars Bridge.

Daniel said, 'I wondered why all the noise.'

'I've decided it's the only way to commute. I asked them to turn on the siren and lights, but the guy driving this thing— Wow.'

'Are you okay?'

'We went over a bump or a wave or something. The guy said I'd already attracted enough attention.'

She was trying to make light of it, to assure Daniel that she was okay. To assure herself.

Daniel said, 'Helena tried to get access to you. So did I. They invoked the usual terrorism bullshit. Jen and I are with Helena in her chambers right now, in fact. Did they make you sign anything?'

'They took a statement.'

'But did you sign it?'

'They didn't ask me to sign anything,' Chloe said. 'And I only told them the truth. If you want to check it, I have a copy.'

'I'll take a look. So will Helena.'

'I didn't do anything wrong.'

'I know. Did you say they were taking you to the office?'

'I didn't want to go home.'

'I'll get there as soon as possible,' Daniel said. 'Hang in there. Don't talk to anyone.'

She wanted to ask him about Ram scooping up fragments of the disintegrating avatar, but he'd rung off.

There were no journalists waiting for her at the little dock that stuck out from the low wall of the stopbank, no journalists waiting outside the entrance to the warehouse. She stood in the shadowy street under the plaque on the wall that indicated the new level of the river and called Neil. Because she wanted him to know that she was okay; because she needed to ask him something.

He'd seen a clip of the attack on the BBC news, wanted to know if she was all right.

She told him she was fine. 'Did you know there are police cells in Kingdom Tower? I was locked up in one for more than an hour before they realised that I didn't have anything to do with the so-called assassin.'

'Apart from knocking him to the ground,' Neil said.

'By total accident. I was trying to brain him, and splashed that stupid knife thing of his instead. I had no idea it would blow up like that. Anyway, the police took a statement, released me without charge, and gave me a ride back to work.'

'You did the right thing,' Neil said.

'I'm not so sure. The one thing you're never supposed to do when something kicks off is get in the middle of it. And by the time I reacted, it was too late.'

'You did the right thing,' Neil said again. 'My sister, the hero. A reporter from the *Daily Mail* called me. She got hold of my mobile number, offered cash for photos of you.'

'I hope you accepted. She'd be paying for what everyone can get for free on the web.'

'She wanted childhood photos,' Neil said. 'You know, with Mum.'

'Oh.'

'Don't worry. I told her exactly where to go.'

'I bet you did.' Chloe smiled, imagining Neil's freezing politeness.

He said, 'If you need a place to hide out until this blows over, Sue and I can put you up. We'll put up the barricades, send out for some Indian from Raja.'

'I don't want to put you guys in the middle of this. And I think my boss is going to come up with some kind of plan.'

'As long as you're okay.'

'I'll tough it out.' Chloe paused, then said as casually as she could, 'By the way, did you get around to checking that database, and asking your friend if he could help out?'

Only Ram Varma was in the office. He wasn't surprised to see Chloe: Daniel had told him she was on her way.

'You're famous,' he said. 'All over the media.'

The big monitor on his workbench was patched with half a dozen windows playing loops of the assassination. From the committee room's cameras, from the TV crew's camera, from Jen Lovell's phone. There were feeds from BBC 24 and Sky News, too. The avatar smiling at the assassin as the knife came down, a blur of motion off to one side resolving into Chloe swinging at the man with the water jug, a white flash, the man and the avatar collapsing. Different angles. Slow-motion recaps. Stills.

According to the BBC, the assassin was Richard Lyonds, an unemployed accountant. He'd been fired from his accountancy firm for stealing from a client's account, had just been released after spending two months in prison for shoplifting, did not appear to have been associated with any of the anti-Jackaroo groups.

'He used a taser knife,' Ram Varma said. 'They aren't commer-cially available, but there are build instructions on the net. Take two thin blades, glue them together with an insulating spacer, wire them up to a battery and capacitor stack in the handle, and you're good to go. You shorted out the capacitors when you threw water over the guy. He got the full benefit of their stored charge.'

'How did he get it past security?'

'He hid in a cleaning cupboard, sneaked out when the session began. Someone in security is going to catch it,' Ram said. 'Bad luck for the avatar that it was so lax, but good luck for me.'

He told Chloe that he'd just received the preliminary results of the analysis of the avatar fragments that he'd dropped into ice-cold mineral water and managed to smuggle out in the confusion after the attack.

'I rode down in a lift full of policemen, sweating like a pig. And once I was outside I realised that I couldn't do my prize justice. So I called one of Ada Morange's people, an exobiologist I met at that conference in Lyons last year. Ten minutes later a courier on a motorcycle appeared, and rushed it over to a lab in Imperial College. They did a quick combustion analysis, and ran a sample through an atomic-absorption spectrometer,' Ram said, and pulled up graphs of spiky lines on the big monitor.

'I see it, but I'm not sure I understand it,' Chloe said.

'It's mostly carbon, hydrogen, oxygen, and nitrogen. A carbon-based life form. Also calcium and phosphorus,' Ram said, pointing to different spikes. 'Potassium and sulphur, sodium, small amounts of iron and copper . . . Pretty similar to the composition of the human body. The stable isotope ratio suggests that either it was made here, or it was doped to make it look as if it was. The Americans probably know this stuff already, and much more. The Chinese and the Russians and Indians too. The Brazilians . . . Anyone who has managed to get hold of a fragment. But no one shares information, and there's a ridiculously high signal-to-noise ratio in the rumour mill. So all of this is new to us. I'm told that Dr Morange herself is very interested.'

Ram was smiling like a kid whose every Christmas had come at once. He was about Chloe's age, soft-spoken and capable, one of the smartest people she knew.

'It was a cool move,' Chloe told him. 'Actually pulling something useful from this mess.'

'Most of the sample had dissolved by the time it reached the lab, but the people at Imperial managed to filter out and stabilise what appear to be fragments of a giant macromolecule. Like DNA, but much, much bigger. Maybe the avatars are woven from a single such molecule. Different sections could have different properties, different functions. Memory storage, information processing, musculature and so on. Amazing, right? Way ahead of anything we can make. As you might expect. Right now, I'm waiting for the results of electron and atomic force microscopy. Hopefully before the police and security services work out what I did. Because while we're analysing the fragments, they'll be analysing every microsecond of footage of what went down. It's like a race where you know you won't reach the finish line, but try to get as close as possible.'

Ram switched the monitor back to the tiled news feeds. One of them showed a woman scurrying from the front door of her house to a taxi, barging through a scrum of reporters and cameramen and photographers. Richard Lyonds's ex-wife, according to the chyron. Chloe felt a pang of sympathy.

'There you are,' someone said.

Chloe turned, saw Daniel Rosenblaum and Jen Lovell in the doorway.

'Let's go into my office,' Daniel said. 'We need to talk.'

He asked if she wanted coffee or tea or maybe something stronger. She said that she'd drunk about a gallon of bad coffee when she'd talked to the police, and handed over the envelope containing a copy of her statement. Two pages, single-spaced. Daniel gave it to Jen, asked her to copy it to Helena.

'I only told them the truth,' Chloe said.

It still sounded weak.

'If there's a problem, Helena will deal with it,' Daniel said. 'She's on your side. We all are. Ada Morange is very pleased.'

'Ram told me. I have some other news. About Fahad Chauhan—'

But Daniel wasn't listening.

'Ada suggested a press conference, but I have a better idea,' he said. He was drinking tea from a big white mug with WORLD'S BEST DAD printed on it.

'I really don't want to have anything to do with the press,' Chloe said.

'This would be a one-on-one interview. One of my friends from the production company that did my series? He works for

Channel Four now. He'll give you the questions before it starts, and you can choose which ones to answer, let me handle the rest. It will be very friendly, very relaxed. It will be great PR,' Daniel said enthusiastically, 'and it will give us control of the story.'

Chloe thought of Neil. She thought of Richard Lyonds's ex battling past cameras and shouting reporters. She said, 'Will it get the press off my back?'

'No doubt the bottom-feeders will try to dig up some dirt, but the rest will be happy to rerun footage of the Q&A. You aren't the main story, Chloe. The crazy accountant is. But we can definitely make good use of this. Put out our side of the story. I've already talked to the press, of course. When you were arrested, and a brief statement after you told me you'd been released. But they need to hear you tell your story. You need to put it out there.'

'Just a few questions.'

'They'll be gentle lobs over the net, I promise. All you have to do is pat them back.' Daniel took a noisy slurp of tea, twinkled at Chloe over the top of his mug. 'How are you holding up?'

'I didn't know what I was thinking when I did it,' she admitted. 'I'm trying to work out what I think about it now.'

'And?'

'I feel like a fraud.'

'Far from it. You're a hero. And that's another thing we need to talk about. Richard Lyonds is probably a lone nut who blames the Jackaroo for everything that went wrong in his life. But there are plenty of people who agree with him, inside and outside the Human Decency League. So I think that we should find a place where you can lie low for a few days. Just in case.'

'You're saying what? That I might be a target because I tried to save the avatar?'

Daniel nodded, suddenly very serious.

'Have there been actual threats?'

'So far, no more than the usual garbage from people who think we are interfering in things man was not meant to know. But it'll get worse before it gets better. You're still required to appear before that committee, but after that I think we should find you a nice quiet place where you can wait out the fuss. Ada Morange has offered to fly you out of the country. Or there's the bothy my family owns in Orkney—'

'You're kidding.'

'It's very cosy, very quiet.'

'And if any crazies find out where I am, it'll feature a re-enactment of *Straw Dogs*. I have a better idea,' Chloe said. 'You remember Fahad Chauhan, the kid who drew all those pictures? He and his little sister were hiding out in the DP camp where that breakout occurred. Before that, it turns out, they were living in Norfolk. Martham, this little town in the middle of the Flood.'

'I don't think this is the time to get into that again,' Daniel said.

'Hear me out and you'll see how we can kill two birds with one stone. Three years ago, Fahad's father went up and out, to Mangala. His ticket was paid for by a construction company, Sky Edge Holdings. He was acting as a consultant on a project to build a pharmaceutical plant. Still is, I guess, because he hasn't come back.'

Neil had passed on that information from his friend in the Foreign Office, telling her that she should keep it to herself. It wasn't exactly against the law, he'd said, but it was against procedure. Chloe had promised that she wouldn't tell a soul, but this was kind of an emergency . . .

Daniel studied her for a moment, then smiled, showing most of his big white teeth. His smile always reminded her of a picture of Red Riding Hood's wolf in the fairy-tale collection she'd been given one Christmas.

He said, 'You think the father sent his kids a souvenir. Some kind of artefact. And you want to go look for it.'

'I want to check out where they used to live,' Chloe said. 'It'll get me out of London, away from all the fuss. And it's in Norfolk, way out in the Flood. Who would expect to find me there?'

'Did you think of this just now?'

'I was going to ask you anyway. But you can see how the two things fit together. You want me to get out of London; I want to follow up on that breakout. Fahad's father went up and out, but his mother might still be living in Martham. She might know where Fahad and his sister are. They might even have returned home. And there might be other artefacts. The father has been gone for three years. He might have sent more than one.'

'Or this might just be a wild-goose chase.'

'Eddie Ackroyd's client thinks otherwise. And even if there is nothing to it, it'll still get me away from media attention.'

Daniel studied her. 'It really has hooked you, hasn't it?'

'I think it's something real. And didn't you hire me because I can tell real artefacts from fakes?'

She felt her heart beat while Daniel thought about that. She told herself that if he said no, fuck it, she'd go anyway.

At last, he said, 'I'll have to talk with Ada Morange's people. And if I do let you go, it will have to be after the committee reconvenes. None of us are going anywhere until then.'

'Okay.'

'Also, I wouldn't feel right if you went alone—'

Jen Lovell knocked on the frame of the open door. 'There's a problem,' she said, and before she could explain more two men appeared behind her. One was flourishing a piece of paper as he shouldered past, telling Daniel that he was being served with a warrant that ordered him to surrender all fragments of the avatar at once.

The man with the warrant identified himself as Chief Inspector Adam Nevers, of the Met's Alien Technology Investigation Squad, otherwise known as the Hazard Police. Like the Breakout Assessment Team, they dealt with possible and actual threats created by contact with the Jackaroo and Elder Culture artefacts. Disruption Theory had a fairly good working relationship with BAT, which monitored cults, sects, self-styled prophets, and crazes, manias and other behavioural changes that could be traced back to contact with artefacts, algorithms and eidolons, but the Hazard Police, which tracked down illicit imports and hazardous artefacts, was more belligerent and had sweeping search-and-seizure powers.

Daniel scanned the papers and said that he had never been in possession of the items in question. Adam Nevers said, 'If you don't hand them over or tell me where they are, Dr Rosenblaum, we will have to search the premises.'

'I'm afraid I must plead commercial confidentiality.'

Chloe watched the two men standing up to each other, Daniel beginning to realise that he was outgunned but refusing to back down.

Nevers said, 'Perhaps I should give you a moment to consult with your employers, sir. I'm sure they'll advise you to do the right thing.'

'I'm in charge here.'

'But you answer to Dr Morange.' Nevers pronounced it the right way, with a hard *g*. 'Tell her people why I'm here, and what I'm looking for. We'll wait outside.'

Inside the office, Jen and Daniel had a brief intense exchange, Daniel spreading his hands in a gesture of surrender, pulling out his phone. Outside, Chief Inspector Adam Nevers said to Chloe, 'I saw what you did. Pretty cool, stepping up like that.'

He was an imposing guy in his early forties, dressed in a light brown summer-weight suit and a crisp white shirt and a gold tie with an impeccable Windsor knot. He nodded to his partner, a younger man with a mop of blond hair, who started to amble slowly around the big room. No doubt scanning everything in it with his spex and, Chloe was pretty sure, giving Nevers time to try to dig something useful from her.

She said, thinking of the best form of defence and all that, 'Is it true that you lot report directly to the Human Decency League?'

'As a matter of fact we came here to retrieve property that belongs to the Jackaroo. It isn't a good idea to piss them off. They aren't always as friendly as they like to make out. As I'm sure you know.'

The other policeman was standing in a corner of the workroom, spex glinting as he looked around.

Chloe said, 'I thought the HDL set up the Hazard Police because they're against all things alien. But you're here to help the Jackaroo?'

'We're helping to protect people from meddling in things they're not meant to know,' Nevers said, with a nice little smile.

'Like q-phones, construction coral, biomachines that clean up the sea and the air, easy travel to other planets . . .'

The two of them were sparring, having fun.

He said, 'Do you enjoy your work, Ms Millar?'

'If I didn't, I'd be doing something else.'

'And you get on with your colleagues.'

'Why shouldn't I?'

'What about Dr Morange? Have you ever met her?'

'Just once, for about thirty seconds.'

It had been a couple of years ago, soon after Chloe had joined Disruption Theory. They'd all been Eurostarred to Paris, a party held in a section of the catacombs. Vaults and passages done up with swags of blue material, video screens, big tropical plants, three different bars, a seafood buffet, fairground rides. It was impressive, but not a patch, apparently, on the Wagnerian debauches of the company's heyday. Disruption Theory's crew had huddled together, outnumbered by Karyotech Pharma's teams of scientists and philosophers, lawyers and administrators, but Daniel had seemed completely at ease, glad-handing a group of investment managers, taking the arm of one of the chief scientists and walking away through a stand of tree ferns, deep in conversation. Later, he'd taken Chloe to meet their host. Ada Morange, who had suffered from an exotic variant of lymphoma for twenty years and required a hospital's worth of advanced medical technology to keep her alive, sat in a carbon-fibre wheelchair within a bower of ferns and orchids. Chloe, slightly tipsy from three glasses of vintage champagne, wondered if she should curtsy when Daniel introduced her. The thin ravaged old woman, with her fierce gaze and cap of synthetic hair white as snow, had a queenly presence.

One of her assistants bent to explain who Chloe was; the entrepreneur fixed Chloe with her dark gaze, saying, 'Daniel tells me that you have a talent for finding the strange and new.'

'I spend a lot of time on the streets.'

'One day something will come through that will amaze us all. Perhaps you will be the first to see it.'

'Please enjoy our party,' one of the assistants had said, before Chloe could think of a reply, and that was that, for the interview.

Nevers said, 'She's one of those people who think they can change history. I'd like to ask her what makes her think she has the right. By the way, how did you enjoy that little display in Dagenham?'

There it was.

Chloe thought of the two policewomen and the BAT officer, of Eddie Ackroyd. It wouldn't surprise her in the least to discover that Eddie was feeding information to the feds.

She said, 'I thought that the Hazard Police are trying to close down people who deal in illegal imports. Why would you be interested in a silly little breakout?'

'Was that what it was?'

Chloe, with a sharp uptick of unease, saw the other policeman go into Ram's tech suite. She said, 'Sure. Just another snake cult.'

'*Conan the Barbarian*,' Adam Nevers said. 'Great little film. Arnold Schwarzenegger and James Earl Jones. Arnie is searching for the man who killed his mother, finds what he thinks is a harmless cult. Except, as it turns out, it's a lot more than that. You never know what a silly little cult might grow into, never know when one of their so-called breakouts might become a problem. Start infecting innocent people, spreading . . . The trouble with this Elder Culture stuff is that we don't know what any of it really does. It's completely outside our experience. We're like a bunch of toddlers hitting an atom bomb with hammers.

'I used to work in the drug squad. I saw some sights then I can't forget. Shine isn't too bad at first. Users become comatose, have vivid dreams. But those heavenly visions turn into terrible nightmares, real heart-stoppers, unless users up the dose. Soon, they have to take massive amounts just to maintain, and the residue destroys their circulatory systems. People lose arms, legs, they have strokes . . . And meq is much worse. Repetitive behaviour, full-blown psychotic attacks, self-harm, what users call wilding.

'The first dead meqhead I saw had killed herself by banging her head against the floor until she fractured her skull, turned her brain to jelly. Her kid was in the next room. A four-year-old girl, watching TV. Too frightened to talk for more than six months afterwards. Some people say, well, that's what happens if you use illegal drugs. But meq and shine are far worse than anything we had before the Jackaroo came. We can't handle them.

And what does it say about us,' Nevers said, in a level, serious voice, holding Chloe's gaze, 'when just about the first thing we do when we reach other worlds is look for stuff to get us high? That when we find things that are a cross between animals and machines, all we can think to do with them is squirt extracts of their blood into our veins. That's some sorry shit, right there.'

'And that's an impressive speech.'

Chloe was wondering if she was supposed to agree with him, to renounce her work right there and then.

'You and I know it isn't all shiny new toys, don't we?' Nevers said.

'But the difference is, maybe, you see the worst in people, and I hope for something better.'

'That we'll find enlightenment, make the Jackaroo worlds into utopias, that kind of thing?'

'Why not? Why measure us by the worst we do?'

'Like the New Galactic Navy, for instance?'

'That didn't have anything to do with Elder Culture tech,' Chloe said.

'They killed themselves right after you talked to them. Can't have been a nice feeling.'

'It was six weeks later.' She knew that it sounded defensive, knew that he knew it too, and felt a hot twist of anger. She'd been through talking therapy, afterwards, she'd put it behind her, and now Nevers and the select committee wanted to dig up the bodies and use them against her.

Nevers said, 'You get involved with people who do something stupid, it isn't your fault, but it stays with you. I've been there myself.'

'I can't really discuss it,' Chloe said. 'Not until after I'm called back to the select committee, anyway.'

'And I'm not going to pry,' Nevers said. 'We're just having a friendly chat. Sharing notes about our common interests.'

He asked her how she liked interviewing people, said that it must be different from chasing down Elder Culture artefacts and alien beasties. She said no, not really. In the artefact biz you have to know how to find leads, and that means talking to people, getting them to give up what they know.

She'd shadowed Frances Colley at first, watching her talk to all kinds of people about their crazy theories. Although most of them didn't seem crazy. Serious and intense, but not bug-eyed gaga. They were functional. They held down jobs. They were mostly of above-average intelligence, many of them professionals. Teachers, IT technicians, even a policeman, trying to make sense of the changing world by what Frances called dangerous simplifications. Chloe had learned from Frances how to maintain a non-judgemental attitude, how to let people explain their ideas in their own words, without leading them.

She was telling Adam Nevers about her first solo interview when Jen asked him if he and his colleague would like to join a phone conference with someone from Ada Morange's research lab. Chloe drifted across the workspace, ducked into the tech suite. Ram said it was all good, that the policeman had just looked around, hadn't touched anything or asked him about the breakout or the kid's pictures.

'He was scanning the shit on my workbench. The so-called eidolon detector Frances brought in the other day. I told him if he could make sense of it he could get a job here any time.'

Chloe felt a little better, but then saw, lying on the tray of the big archival scanner, Mr Archer's flyer.

10. Do The Right Thing

Mangala | 25 July

As they drove back to the UN building, Skip at the wheel, Vic explained why they'd caught a break, how the whodunnit could be rolled up into Alain Boudin's ongoing investigation of the ray-gun murders.

'They were all drug-related. And Alain knows who did them. Cal McBride. He calls himself a businessman, but deals in meq. Runs a little gang of hooligans who trap biochines, extract the precursor from their blood, cook it, and sell the resulting product. We'll show Dr Ngu's report to Alain and point out that she concludes the cause of death is identical to his cases. And he'll have to eat it. How about that? I'm beginning to think you aren't such bad luck to have around after all.'

Skip didn't look particularly grateful, saying, 'So why isn't this guy in prison? I mean, I guess he can't be, if you think he did Redway.'

'He was in prison, as a matter of fact, but not for the murders. Alain was putting the case together when McBride went down for something else. Some kind of sting run by drug enforcement. Alain and the prosecutor tried to get him to agree to add the murders to the other charges, time to be served concurrently, but McBride's lawyer wouldn't have any of it. McBride went to jail and the murder cases went cold. But if he can be put in the frame for this one, he'll fall for all the rest, too.'

Skip drove, thinking about that. As if it needed thinking about. But he had a hard-on for this, his first murder, and Vic thought that he might have to lean on the kid to make him see sense. He remembered his own first time. A domestic, a woman stabbing her boyfriend to death in his sleep because he'd pimped her out

74

for drug money and beaten her once too often. She'd confessed to it right away, explained that she had bought a bottle of vodka to make sure he would pass out before she killed him. Vic had written it up and she'd signed it, and that was that, she'd gone down hard, thirty years building roads or working in one of the factories that the multinationals were beginning to build in what had then been the outskirts of the city. After she'd been sentenced, Vic's partner had taken him to a bar and said that if she'd gotten her story straight she could have claimed that she'd stabbed the boyfriend while he was attacking her, got off with a couple of years for manslaughter at the most. Vic had asked if he should have given her that option, wondering if he'd done something wrong, and his partner had said, hell no, the dumb bitch had made her own bed, let her lie in it. 'We let them talk if they want to talk; get them to talk if they don't. We put the case down, and we move on.'

Chris Okupe. His partner for ten years, until Chris had to have heart surgery and quit the force because he didn't want to spend the next ten years pushing paper in some bullshit medical-exemption job. A week after he left, on holiday in Idunn's Valley with his wife before he started his new job, running security at the French consulate, he'd dropped dead of a heart attack in the foyer of a hunting lodge.

Now Skip stopped at a red light behind a swarm of bicycles and mopeds, looking at Vic and saying, 'It could be that Redway and Parsons came out to do business with Cal McBride. They had a meeting, it went wrong . . .'

'No point speculating on the why,' Vic said. 'Especially as we can hand this one off to Alain. Poor guy, he starts the day with three fresh bodies, and now he has four. And it isn't even lunchtime.'

But that wasn't how it worked.

When Vic started to lay it out, Alain shook his head and said, 'There is no way I am taking this.'

'The man was done like all the others,' Vic said. 'Some kind of ray gun zapping his brain. You have four just like it. What's one more?'

75

'I have four people killed with what appears to be the same weapon,' Alain said. 'But apart from some street talk that is all that connects them.'

'But you know who did it, don't you?' Vic said.

'I am certain McBride was involved in at least two of the killings, yes. He had motive and opportunity, and I sweated an admission out of one of his corner boys that he had been boasting about them. Letting people know what would happen if they stepped out of line. I brought McBride in and told him this, but he did not even blink, and soon afterwards the corner boy disappeared. And then drug enforcement fucked me in the arse with that sting. They promised they would make him an offer, ask him to confess to the murders in exchange for a break in sentencing. Assuming, you know, that McBride was as stupid as they were. Which he was not. So he went down for their thing, my cases went cold, and fuck it,' Alain said, 'I moved on.'

They were talking in the violent-crimes squad room, on the fifth floor of the UN building. All of them in shirtsleeves, ID cards dangling from lanyards around their necks. The squad room was a square space divided by chest-high partitions into a dozen cubicles, each containing two desks. There were glass-fronted offices for Captain Colombier, Sergeant Madsen, and the captain's secretary and the information clerk down one side, two small interrogation rooms and the locker room on another. A poster by the door to the locker room showed a Jackaroo avatar dressed as Uncle Sam, pointing a white-gloved finger under the caption *I Want You for Anal Probing*.

'And now McBride is out of jail, and he's back to doing what he does,' Vic said.

'And you want me to eat your body, and bring those cold cases back into play?' Alain said. 'It is not going to happen.'

'We aren't handing you another cold case, Alain. We're handing you a red-hot lead. The opportunity to crack all those murders and make the captain happy.'

'They're cold cases, my friend. No longer my problem. And think about this: you say that this guy was killed by a ray gun. Fine. But was it the same weapon as those cold cases? Maybe there are two ray guns. Maybe more.'

'Maybe. But I don't believe anyone was zapped in the head while McBride was in jail.'

'I put that to the prosecutor one time. She said forget it, it is pure speculation. And even if it was the same weapon, it does not mean that the same person used it. Perhaps McBride sold it on or gave it to someone as a Christmas present. Also, you have no evidence that this is in any way drug-related.'

'My young friend has a theory that Redway and Parsons came here because they're representing the other end of McBride's supply chain, back home,' Vic said. 'They met with McBride, things went bad, McBride zapped Redway in the head.'

'Nice story. Here's another. It could be this guy really is some kind of businessman. He got lost, he was mugged, put up a struggle, and zzzt . . .' Alain touched his forefinger to the back of his neck.

Vic said, 'A mugger with a ray gun?'

Alain shrugged. He had that stubborn, smouldering look. 'On this world, why not? No, my friend, this one belongs to your partner. I am not eating it for him.'

Skip said, surprising Vic, 'You don't have to. I want to follow it through.'

It surprised Alain too. After a moment he smiled and told Vic, 'How is it that only this kid knows the right thing to do?'

11. Sleuthing

London | 7 July

'I have a free day,' Chloe said. 'I could sit around here, or in my flat with the curtains drawn, hiding from reporters. Or I could do something useful.'

'If you want to do something useful, you should rest up for the rerun of the committee hearing,' Jen said. 'But I know you won't.'

'This can't wait,' Chloe said. 'Not with Chief Inspector Nevers on the case.'

'We've already been over that,' Jen said. 'All he wanted was those fragments that Ram took. Now he has them, that should be the end of it.'

'I don't think so. He wanted me to know that he was interested in the breakout in Dagenham. Plus his friend saw the flyer, so they know we're interested in it too. In Fahad Chauhan.'

'Do you really think this boy is in trouble?'

'I think he's hiding from someone. Hence the midnight flit. And then there's the number the artefact is doing on his head.'

'Because if he is in trouble,' Jen said, with relentless patience, 'wouldn't it be best to let the police help him?'

'Not if he's hiding from the police. And suppose Eddie Ackroyd finds him first?'

They were talking in the sunny kitchen of Jen's roomy semi-detached house in Finchley, after Jen's husband had left for his job in the City and Jen's daughters had been dispatched to school, joining a walking train of children escorted by four parent volunteers. Chloe had spent the night on the sofa. Her flat was being staked out by a small gang of journalists; there'd been a clip on Sky News showing them outside the entrance of the tower block,

78

followed by a twenty-second interview with a bewildered neighbour. Apparently Chloe had always been 'quiet'. She couldn't go
home, she'd had to switch off her phone because some hacker
had outed its number, and her Facebook wall was plastered with
messages from journalists offering to treat her side of the story
sympathetically and a spew of anonymous threats and insults.
She was going to have to ride out this moment of notoriety and
hope it passed quickly.

At least she'd been able to put across her side of things in the
TV interview. It had been set up in neutral territory, a room in
a hotel in Bloomsbury. Daniel's friend Jim Ford, a man in his
sixties Chloe had seen on TV now and then, with snow-white
hair and dressed in a vintage Paul Smith suit and a brightly
patterned tie, had quickly and charmingly probed her background
and established what she wanted to talk about, and then they'd
got down to business. Two armchairs facing each other under
bright lights, a woman behind a video camera, another woman
who'd dusted Chloe's cheeks and forehead with powder and
fastened the microphone beneath the top button of her blouse,
Jim Ford with a prop clipboard. It had taken just twenty minutes.
Jim Ford and his crew had zoomed off because they needed to
edit the footage for the seven o'clock news; Daniel had treated
Chloe and Jen to dinner in the hotel's restaurant, and Jen had
taken Chloe back to her house.

Now, in Jen's kitchen, in the borrowed trouser suit she'd worn to
face the committee, her hair wet from Jen's shower and smelling
of Jen's apple shampoo, Chloe promised that she wouldn't get
into any trouble, or talk to any strange reporters.

'At least tell me where you're going,' Jen said.

'Spitalfields, to begin with. I thought I'd do a little sleuthing,
and ask some old friends for a little help.'

Chloe rode the Tube to Liverpool Street station, where she bought
two pay-as-you-go phones from a booth that printed them for
her right there. She used one, still warm in her hand, to call Jen
and give her the number.

'Just in case anything comes up at your end. How's Daniel?'

'He's doing interviews. Helena isn't too happy about it, but you know Daniel.'

'Has he mentioned anything about my field trip to Norfolk? I know he was going to talk to Ada Morange's people. Maybe you could ask him if he remembered to mention that the Hazard Police are interested in this thing.'

'As a matter of fact,' Jen said, 'Dr Morange's security people have reached out to us.'

'What do they want to know? If you give me their number, I could talk to them directly.'

'I don't think you should discuss it over the phone,' Jen said. 'You need to come in for a briefing.'

'I have my own thing to do first,' Chloe said, adding, when Jen started to object, 'I'll call when I'm finished.'

She felt a mixture of excitement and dismay, a sense of things moving out of her control. More than ever, she needed to find out everything she could about Fahad Chauhan, and Eddie Ackroyd and his client. She needed something she could use to prove her worth, to keep herself in the game.

She headed out of the station in the river of rush-hour commuters, trying not to look at the big screen where BBC 24 was replaying a clip of the assassination, dodged through the traffic juddering and honking down Bishopsgate, and cut across Spitalfields Market. She walked fast, head down, trying to blend in, tingling with anxiety and exhilaration. A spy in her own city, a fugitive on an urgent clandestine mission. The game was on, and she had only a small window of independence before Ada Morange's people started to interfere.

Tonani's, the café frequented by runners and scouts before most of them had decamped to the Reef, was dismayingly empty. The orange plastic chairs and white tables, and the poster-sized photographs of alien land- and seascapes, were still there, and the owner, Rosa Jenners, still presided over her hissing Gaggia, but where there'd once been a buzzing crowd of people looking for deals, making deals or boasting about deals, there were only a couple of bemused Chinese tourists and a guy Chloe didn't recognise poking at a tablet. After she had answered the inevitable questions about Richard Lyonds and the Jackaroo avatar, saying that, no, she didn't think she'd be getting any kind of reward or medal, Chloe asked Rosa if she'd seen Eddie Ackroyd recently.

Rosa, a short, thick-waisted woman, grey hair done up into a bun skewered with a pink and purple robber-worm quill, wanted to know what kind of trouble Eddie had got himself into now.

'I just need to ask him about something.'

'Because we had the police in earlier, asking after him.'

'A tall white guy, Adam Nevers?'

'No, it was two young men from the Hazard Police. Are you all right, dear?'

Rosa sat Chloe at a table and gave her a mug of builder's tea fortified with a heaping spoonful of sugar, and Chloe told Rosa that things were moving faster than she'd expected, and explained about her encounter with Eddie at the Dagenham breakout, his boasts about his mysterious client, the clues sent to the LFM wiki board.

'I was wondering if Eddie knows anything about the where-abouts of this kid who was involved in the breakout,' she said. 'And who his client might be. If he has a client. If the story isn't a weird practical joke.'

'Eddie lacks the imagination for that kind of thing,' Rosa said. 'Fast Eddie, we used to call him. Always on the make, always on the take. This was before you came on the scene, dear. While the UN quarantine was still in force. Everyone in the arte-fact business was chasing specimens that leaked back to Earth via diplomatic pouches, clandestine loads smuggled amongst licensed material by companies and criminals, souvenirs brought back by UN personnel . . . Eddie knew how to make the most of his contacts, but he lacked common sense and got himself into trouble with the police several times. He thought he was cleverer than he was and cut too many corners. Went down for it, eventually.'

'I know he did six months in Wandsworth,' Chloe said. 'He used to boast about it, like it was a badge of honour. He still comes in here, doesn't he?'

'He has a stall in the Sunday market,' Rosa said. 'But I haven't seen him for a month or more. Maybe he's moved out to the Reef, like most of the other traders. The market isn't what it was. Mostly replicas and fakes, or the cheap stuff the Chinese and Indians are importing by the ton from Tian and Naya Loka. And then there's all the nonsense from the Human Decency League. They set up a stall by the entrance of the market every Sunday and hand out leaflets with pictures of dead meq addicts. They're petitioning the council to close the market down, although why they bother I don't know. It'll die a natural death soon enough.'

Rosa didn't have Eddie Ackroyd's phone number or address, and didn't know anyone who did – he wasn't exactly blessed with an abundance of friends – but said that if she saw Eddie she'd tell him that Chloe was looking for him, and would ask around about Eddie's mysterious client, too.

Chloe's anxiety had been ratcheted up by Rosa's mention of the police. She was stupidly aware of every CCTV camera as she headed towards her rendezvous with her friend Gail Ann Jones. They met in a tapas place in King's Cross. Gail Ann was late, as usual, telling Chloe, 'I called to say I was held up, but you didn't answer.'

'I had to buy a new phone,' Chloe said.

'My filthy colleagues have been giving you trouble, I bet. A glass of house white,' Gail Ann added, as the waiter handed her the menu. 'You aren't blonde any more. Good move. That trouser suit really isn't you, though. Not even you in twenty years.'

'I borrowed it for the nonsense yesterday. Haven't had the chance to change.'

'Your wicked ninja episode. Tell me everything you didn't tell the TV news. Give me something exclusive, and I promise I'll have your babies.'

Gail Ann was almost exactly Chloe's age, pale skin emphasised by her trademark red lipstick, dressed in a boiler suit with a swirling brown paisley pattern, a black denim jacket, cherry-red Doc Martens boots, and a red leather satchel – the exact shade of her lipstick – slung over her shoulder. They'd met when Chloe had joined the LFM wiki's editorial board;

Gail Ann, who'd lost her older brother to the bomb, had been one of the founder members. She was a freelance journalist now, selling articles to the glossies and news sites, running a feed about street fashion.

Chloe said that there hadn't been any new developments about the thing with the avatar, told Gail Ann about Chief Inspector Nevers's visit to Disruption Theory and his hint that he had an interest in Fahad Chauhan.

'So this is a real thing,' Gail Ann said.

'It always was.'

'I mean it's a real story. A kid on the run, his mind altered by some kind of weird alien artefact. You want to save him from the clutches of Eddie Ackroyd and his mysterious client. And now from the police.'

'You said that you'd dug up more stuff about Fahad.'

'About his family. Rather a sad story, actually.'

They ordered half a dozen small plates of food. Gail Ann said that she had a friend who was in the genealogy business. Actually a friend of Noah, her on-again off-again boyfriend.

'He practically lives in the National Archives, knows how to find his way around old newspaper records and so on. And also has serious google-fu. He found that squib in the trade journal.'

'Then I owe him one.'

'*I* owe him one,' Gail Ann said. 'And you owe me.'

'After I catch up with Fahad, I'll tell you all about it. Cross my heart. What's this sad story?'

'To begin with, Fahad's mother is dead. It happened about five years ago.'

Chloe thought of the little girl, Rana. She said, 'Did she die in childbirth?'

'She died in Uxbridge. A traffic accident, apparently. I expect my friend could find out if you need to know,' Gail Ann said. 'About a year later, Fahad's father was declared bankrupt. And either he lost his job with GlaxoSmithKline or he quit, because he moved to Norfolk.'

'To a little town, Martham,' Chloe said.

'You've been doing some digging, too.'

'I didn't know about the mother, or the bankruptcy. But I did find out something else. The father, Sahar, went up and out to Mangala.'

'And you think he came back with some kind of alien artefact.'

'He didn't come back. It was a one-way ticket sponsored by a property-development company, and he isn't on any of the passenger lists of flights back to Earth. I was going to look for Fahad's mother in Martham. Now I guess I'll be looking for the people who were taking care of him and his kid sister after his father left. As well as trying to find out what his father was doing there, and his connection with this company. I want you to have this,' Chloe said, and laid the second new phone on the table. 'In case I need to call you for backup, or some more of Noah's friend's google-fu. My new number's in it.'

'Ooh, super-secret spy shit.'

'The press got into my phone,' Chloe said. 'This is just in case they get into yours.'

Gail Ann studied her. 'This has really got under your skin, hasn't it?'

'It did cross my mind that the thing that got into Fahad's head has also got inside mine,' Chloe confessed. 'But how could I tell?'

'Knowing how you get when you decide to chase after something,' Gail Ann said, 'I don't think that it would make much difference.'

12. Take Me To Your Leader

Mangala | 25 July

Skip said, 'This guy is something else. Came up eight years ago, but before that spent two years fighting for his right to emigrate. The British authorities claimed that the company that bought his ticket was a front for, quote, "an extensive and ruthlessly violent criminal enterprise run by his family". McBride took them all the way to the House of Lords and won.'

They were driving to Cal McBride's house, Vic at the wheel, Skip in the passenger seat, reading the file that Alain had ported to his phone.

Saying, 'He muscled into the local meq trade, was implicated in exporting the stuff back to the UK. Also murder, kidnapping, extortion, bribery of elected officials . . . He went down when an investigator posing as a visiting businesswoman got him to agree to smuggle Elder Culture artefacts back to Earth inside finished electronic goods.'

'What Alain was bitching about,' Vic said.

'Yeah. It says here that the prosecutor used the arrest to go through his books, found evidence of money laundering, asked for thirty years concurrent. McBride's lawyers argued entrapment, bargained the sentence down to five. He served less than two, got out six months ago.'

Vic said, 'And you can bet he's back to doing what he does.'

He was gripping the steering wheel with both hands, overtaking everything on the ring road. Swarms of mopeds, cars, trucks, a road train of five container units hauled by a big diesel rig with chromed exhausts, headlights and the spots above its high cab blazing. There was a faint pinkish tinge in the lower part of the sky. A thousand kilometres to the west, the dust storm was getting close to Idunn's Valley. Farmers were rounding up livestock and shutting them in barns, harvesting crops and unripe fruit, wrapping trees in orchards and vines in vineyards in shrouds of bubblewrap, sheeting over greenhouses. There had been a piece about it on the TV news that morning.

Vic said, 'You know the reason for the sting that wrecked Alain's case? The Mayor was up for re-election and one of the supporters of his chief opponent was in McBride's pocket. So the Mayor put pressure on the police commissioner to arrest McBride, hoping to smear his opponent. But McBride wouldn't give up his friends, ate the prison sentence to keep his political influence. Remember that when you talk to him. He's smart, and he has influence in high places.'

Skip said, 'You know, I met him at a reception a few months back. I'd forgotten all about it until I saw his mug shot.'

'This was when you were driving for the Mayor.'

'It wasn't just driving. I was part of the close-protection team, I had to stand with him at parties, official receptions. Any place public.'

'The Mayor being such a popular, fun-loving guy.'

'He was always straight with me. A regular bloke.'

'Who needs a bunch of bodyguards in case one of his many enemies tries to take a pop at him.'

'He knows he isn't going to win the next election. He's okay with it. Anyway, McBride was at this reception. One held by the British consul.'

'McBride being a fine upstanding representative of everything that puts the great into Great Britain.'

'There were all kinds of people there. Everyone in black tie or cocktail dresses. McBride shook hands with the Mayor. They exchanged a few words. He seemed to know a lot of people.'

'We should keep this meeting nice and informal,' Vic said. 'A routine enquiry about where McBride was last night. He'll want to know why. Tell him it's about a suspected murder, but don't give away any details. Don't even mention Redway's name. Save all that for the actual interrogation.'

86

'I know how to handle a suspect,' Skip said.

'This is a murder investigation. A horse of another colour.'

'Look, can I ask you a question?'

'That's why I'm here. To give you the benefit of my years of experience.'

'Were you trying to hand off the case because you think I'm not up to it?'

'Of course not. I was trying to do Alain a favour. You too, for that matter.'

Skip seemed to buy that. Or at least, he didn't push it. He said, 'Just to be clear, I should be the one asking the questions when we get into it with McBride.'

'It's your case, Investigator Gayle. Go to it.'

Cal McBride's house was set in a green garden behind a perimeter wall, a low rambling building with a red-tile roof. A square tower at one corner rose three storeys to a crenellated top. A big flag divided diagonally between red and black flapped in the brisk wind up there.

'I believe that's the anarchist flag,' Vic said. 'Looks like your man likes to think of himself as a libertarian. The kind that doesn't believe in the law until someone steals their shit, and then they can't get enough of the police.'

He and Skip were waiting beside their car, at the arched gateway. No one had answered when Skip had buzzed the intercom at the locked gate; if anyone was inside they weren't in a hurry to check them out.

'It doesn't look like anyone's in,' Skip said, after a couple of minutes.

'A place like this, someone is always in, keeping watch. Why do you think he built that tower? Lean on the horn again. Or wait, let me try something else.'

Vic reached through the open window of the car and hit the switch that activated the siren and the lights. The noise echoing down the broad curved street where other big houses stood behind high walls or hedges. Bel Air, the residential quarter of Petra favoured by top UN officials, diplomats and business people. The Mayor had a house two streets over.

Someone came out of the house and walked along the drive. A short tubby man in jeans and a roll-neck sweater, squinting against the blue stutter of the car's LEDs, asking – shouting – to please turn that fucking thing off, you've made your point.

Vic flicked the switch, walked up to the gate in the sudden silence. The man staring at him through the bars, saying, 'You got a warrant?'

'Why would we need a warrant? This is just a social call.'

'I don't let in any police without a warrant.'

'David Carson,' Skip said. He had put on his spex. 'Aka Little Dave. Came up here five years ago, served six months for failing to do mandatory civil work on arrival, with an additional two months for three counts of burglary.'

The man spat between his feet. He had the truculent look of someone always ready to be disappointed by life. 'You can't walk down the fucking street without some cop glassing you and getting in your face.'

'We aren't here to talk about your misdemeanours,' Skip said. 'We want to talk to Cal McBride.'

'He isn't here.'

'I'd like to check that for myself.'

'I tell you he isn't here, then he isn't here.'

'And when someone like you tells me that the sun is shining,' Vic said, beginning to lose his patience, 'I immediately phone the weather bureau, ask the chief meteorologist if that's the case. So why don't you open the gate.'

'He isn't here,' the man, Little Dave, said. 'Phone who you like, it won't change things. And if you want to come in you need a warrant.'

They stood there with the bars of the gate between them, in the shadow of the tall archway.

Vic said, 'Investigator Williams, would you mind giving me the warrant so I can show it to this man?'

They'd talked about how to do this on the way over.

'Sure thing,' Skip said, and handed over a sheet of blue paper folded three times.

Vic took a step closer to the gate, held up the folded paper, its edge just touching the bars, twitched it back when Little Dave snatched at it. The man lunged without thinking, and Vic dropped the folded sheet of paper – a crime-scene form – and grabbed his forefinger and bent it up.

Little Dave gasped, his face turned sideways and pressed against the bars.

'Careful,' Vic said, bending the finger a little more. 'If you move the wrong way it might break. Now, how about opening the gate?'

'Let me go, you fucker.'

'After you open the gate.'

'I can't do it when you've got my fucking finger!'

Vic said, 'You have a phone, don't you? Call the man watching us through the security camera up there. Tell him to do it. Then you can take me to your leader.'

They walked up the drive, lawns and beds of heather and conifers on either side. Plants from Earth. Ferns growing in a wrinkled hump of native rock.

'Must be a lot of work, keeping these alive,' Vic said.

Little Dave didn't answer. He was flexing his right hand, scowling.

'Those floodlights, I suppose they keep things growing during the night-year,' Vic said. 'Places like this, they shine as bright as day then. But I'm wondering, what will happen to all this when the dust storm hits?'

Little Dave didn't have an answer for that, either. They went up a broad fan of steps to the house and he pulled open the door, oak planks studded with iron bolts, and walked through without looking to see if the two policemen were following.

The hall was as big as a hotel foyer. Wooden crates lined along one wall. Canvas equipment bags and backpacks. Toolboxes and plastic cases. A thin snow of styrofoam packing chips on the red floor tiles.

'Wait here,' Little Dave said, and walked off towards an archway at the far end of the hall.

Vic surveyed the supplies. Sleeping bags, tents, boxes of freeze-dried ready meals. He pointed to the stencilling on a small plastic case, said, 'Know what a pulsed field magnetometer does?'

Skip was looking at a rock spotlit on a pedestal in a recess. A skull-shaped lump of what looked like sandstone finely layered in muted yellows and oranges and greys, like a section through a book.

He said, 'You reckon this is some kind of artefact?'

'It's from a Riverine B site,' someone else said. A man about Skip's age, dressed in a blue linen suit, standing in a doorway. 'Not much left of it after a million years, of course. Mostly rust and carbon strands and what they call differentiated spherules. Perhaps it was once some kind of machine, but who really knows?'

He stepped forward. Tall and tanned, thinning black hair brushed back from a high forehead and caught in a ponytail. His glance sliding off Vic, fixing on Skip.

'Do forgive the mess. We're getting ready for a little expedition.'

Skip showed his badge to the man, and introduced Vic. 'We want to speak to Cal McBride.'

'I understand you have a warrant. Perhaps I could see it.'

Skip said, 'And you are?'

'Danny Drury.'

'You work for Mr McBride?'

'Mr McBride doesn't live here any more.'

Skip glanced at Vic. They'd worked up a rough plan to deal with Cal McBride, but now he wasn't sure what to do.

Vic said, 'This is his house, isn't it?'

'I fear you've been misinformed.'

Drury's smile projected the kind of arrogant superiority that irritated the fuck out of Vic. He wondered if Skip understood it – that there was a class of English people who never questioned their unearned privilege, believed that it was their God-given right to take the best jobs and all the rest of the good stuff. There had been several of them in the force, back in Birmingham. Straight out of Oxbridge into the promotional fast track.

It didn't help that Drury was directing most of his attention to the only other white guy in the room.

Skip tried to recover the initiative. 'You bought this house from Mr McBride?'

'Not exactly. I suppose you could say I inherited it. A perk of the job.'

'And your job is what, exactly?'

'I'm the managing director of Sky Edge Holdings.'

Vic realised what had happened. What Alain fucking Boudin had done to them. He'd given his case file to Skip all right, but hadn't bothered to tell them that it hadn't been updated. A little fuck-you for trying to dump the whodunnit on him. Skip hadn't checked because he didn't know any better, and Vic hadn't bothered to check either. Damn.

He said to Drury, 'You took over McBride's house and his business. What did he have to say about that?'

'It is his family's business. I run it on their behalf.'

'And how is the meq trade, these days?'

'Do you really expect me to answer that, investigator?'

'I'm wondering if this "little expedition" of yours is all about hunting biochines.'

Drury inclined his head. 'Is this an interrogation? Because if it is, perhaps I should call my lawyer.'

'Routine questioning,' Vic said. No point in telling this guy more than he needed to know. 'When Mr McBride moved out, did he leave a forwarding address?'

'You'll probably find him at the folly he's building near the old Westside fighting pit. Are we finished? Because I really am very busy.'

At the front door, Skip turned to Drury and said, 'By the way, where were you last night?'

Drury didn't even blink. 'The Mayor's Landing Day Ball at the Hilton. Quite an event. Everyone who is anyone was there. Good day, investigators.'

As they walked up the drive, Skip said, 'He was ready for me to ask that, wasn't he? I mean, he didn't even ask me why I wanted to know.'

'We'll make a murder police of you yet, Investigator Williams.'

'I guess I should have done my homework a little better.'

'We both fucked up,' Vic said, and meant it. 'But it isn't anything we can't fix. Drury is an interesting character, isn't he? That pony-tail is straight out of central casting for film villains circa 1990.'

'I can't help wondering if he inherited the ray gun along with the house and the meq business.'

'Something else to ask Cal McBride. I assume you still want to talk to him.'

13. Devil Squid

London | 8 July

The select committee reconvened in the same room, 10:00 a.m. Thursday. It was closed to journalists and members of the public because security was jittery after the assassination of the Jackaroo avatar, but Chloe and the rest of the Disruption Theory crew had to push through a gauntlet of reporters and cameras at the entrance of Freedom Tower. Chloe put her head down and stayed close to Daniel Rosenblaum's broad back.

The committee chair, Robin Mountjoy, began by reading out a short formal statement thanking Chloe for her intervention two days ago. After that everything went quickly downhill.

Daniel was called to give evidence. Mountjoy peppered his interrogation with secondary questions and snappish asides, asking him to clarify what he meant by algorithms, eidolons, breakouts. When Daniel started to explain about memes, how ideas became infectious and spread from person to person like a catchy tune, Mountjoy looked at him over the top of his gold-rimmed bifocals and said, 'And these so-called memes originate with the Jackaroo.'

'Actually, we don't have any evidence that they do. We know that some of the cults are inspired or driven by algorithms or fragments of intelligences, eidolons, embedded in certain Elder Culture artefacts. That's a major facet of our work. But we are also interested in the ways in which the presence of the Jackaroo has affected every aspect of our society and culture. Thirteen years after first contact, we still know very little about them. In the absence of hard facts, all kinds of speculations flourish. Theories, rumours, ideas. And some ideas are more attractive than others.

They spread quickly and they spread widely. That is what we are trying to map. Ideas which have cultural significance, cultural currency. If they don't tell us anything about the Jackaroo, they certainly tell us something about ourselves.'

'So if it wasn't for the Jackaroo,' Mountjoy said, 'these memes wouldn't exist.'

'They are our ideas about the Jackaroo,' Daniel said, with visible impatience. 'Not their ideas implanted in us. It's an important distinction. And not exactly hard to grasp, I think.'

'By withholding information about themselves, the Jackaroo are manipulating us. So in a sense they are generating those ideas, are they not?'

Robin Mountjoy was making a point, trying to show that Daniel and the Disruption Theory crew were wilfully or carelessly ignoring the danger posed by the Jackaroo. Chloe was reminded of the way certain girls at school enjoyed maliciously twisting your words, tried to redefine their meaning, tried to use them against you. One of the other MPs, a slender white-haired woman in a navy-blue trouser suit, took up the theme. Daniel answered with a freezing politeness, insisting that there was no evidence that the Jackaroo were directly intervening in any way. Another MP asked about the value of tracking the popularity of different ideas.

'Our work is far from theoretical,' Daniel said. 'If you care to examine the appendices of our formal report, there are detailed statistical analyses of the spread of selected memes. We have evidence—'

'I'm sure it's of interest to a few specialists,' Mountjoy said. 'But does it have any actual value in the real world?'

He was speaking for the cameras that were broadcasting the session on one of the parliamentary channels, turning the inquiry into an arena in which he, the plucky English terrier, was nipping at the ankles of the scientific status quo. Standing up for common sense and ordinary hard-working people, accusing Disruption Theory and Ada Morange of meddling in dangerous matters, *things mankind was not meant to know* kind of thing, of encouraging the delusion that the alien invaders had nothing but good intentions, of colluding with the UN and the EC and other bodies which imposed their laws and regulations on Parliament and the English people. Asking Daniel if he had ever carried out illegal experiments with alien artefacts, reading extracts from interviews that Daniel had given immediately after the appearance of the Jackaroo, questioning him about them, asking him if he still believed that they came in peace, and so on and so forth.

Daniel replied with pained dignity, keeping his answers short, trying his best to counter Mountjoy's insinuations. But Mountjoy kept at him and at last wore down his patience.

'Only a fool would try to ignore the Jackaroo,' he said. 'They aren't going away, and people on the fifteen worlds aren't going to stop discovering Elder Culture technology.'

'But we can and will protect the British way of life,' Mountjoy said. 'Instead of trying to undermine it with airy-fairy nonsense.'

'The world has changed, is changing, will continue to change. You can't stop it.'

'Is that a scientific assessment, Dr Rosenblaum? Or simply your opinion?'

'It is a plain fact.'

'It sounds to me like a council of despair,' Mountjoy said, with a jovial smile, and cut off Daniel's reply, thanking him for his time, saying they had to move on.

The clerk called out Chloe's name. As she took her place behind the table, next to Daniel and Helena, she saw that there was a rectangle of slightly brighter blue in the carpet nearby, about the shape and size of a grave. She supposed that the portion where the avatar had fallen and disintegrated had been taken away for trace analysis.

She was sworn in, and the woman MP prompted her to give a brief description of her work. She told the committee that she had been working for Disruption Theory for three years, gave anodyne examples of her work, answered several harmless-seeming questions.

Then Robin Mountjoy said, 'Perhaps you could tell us about the New Galactic Navy.'

She met his watery blue gaze. 'It was an unusual case. Quite outside the ordinary work we do.'

Mountjoy led her through it. How the cult had contacted Disruption Theory and Chloe had been sent to give a preliminary interview with its leader, a former accountant and self-styled Grand Admiral who shared a shabby terraced house in Tooting with fifteen followers. The longer interview that Chloe and Frances Colley had conducted, unpicking the cult's belief that its members had been selected to join a space navy opposed to the Jackaroo, who were suppressing the true ascension of humankind to its rightful place amongst the stars: a blend of sci-fi and occult beliefs involving cosmic minds and a revolutionary leap upwards in the evolution of human consciousness. Their costumes of robes and sashes laden with 3D-printed medals. Their psychic maps of the universe. The rooms painted black, with constellations of glow-in-the-dark stars glued to the ceilings. Glossy printouts from astronomy sites. The bunk beds crowding the bedrooms of the little house, where six weeks later the members of the New Galactic Navy had been found dead, all of them having ingested fatal doses of cyanide-laced orange juice. The message that they had left behind their flesh envelopes to go voyaging as spirits amongst the stars.

Robin Mountjoy said, 'Is it not true that you were the trigger for these unfortunate deaths?'

Helena objected, pointing out that the cult's leader had also contacted national newspapers, the BBC, Sky News, and other prominent news outlets, and the police investigation had concluded that Chloe, Frances Colley and Disruption Theory hadn't had anything to do with the mass suicide, which had been planned long before their interviews. Robin Mountjoy politely accepted that fact. He had made his point, associating the work of Disruption Theory with the deaths of a dozen disturbed and deluded individuals. One of the other MPs, a balding pink-faced man, delivered the *coup de grâce*. He asked Chloe several questions about her sources of information. She mentioned freelance scouts. She mentioned people who trawled the internet and sent in tips. She mentioned visiting schools to check out the artwork of school children.

He said, 'I believe you also visit mental institutions.'

Chloe felt a freezing caution. Beside her, Helena wrote two words on her yellow legal pad. *Be polite.*

'Very rarely,' Chloe said.

'Five times since you began employment with Disruption Theory. Several times before that, when you were working as a freelance scout.'

'I followed leads to wherever they led. That's my job.'

The pink-faced MP tilted his head, as if accepting that. Chloe wanted to say more, wanted to qualify her answers, but Robin Mountjoy banged his gavel and called for a two-hour recess, said that he would complete questioning of the rest of Disruption Theory's staff after lunch.

Outside, in the corridor, the others congratulated Chloe on her performance. Daniel said, 'That wasn't so bad.'

'I'm trying to think how it could have been worse,' Chloe said. She had sweated through the silk blouse Helena had lent her, was shaking slightly from adrenalin.

'You did good. And there'll be a chance for rebuttal later. I'm on the BBC evening news. We'll line up some longer pieces too. We'll get through this, Chloe. Mountjoy is a gadfly. Tomorrow he'll be attacking someone else, and we'll be forgotten . . .'

He was still talking, but Chloe wasn't listening. Chief Inspector Adam Nevers was coming towards them, patting his hands together in mock applause, saying, 'I'm impressed. Coolness under fire and all that.'

'I didn't see you in the committee room,' Chloe said.

'I watched it on the CCTV feed.' Nevers was wearing a shark-grey suit today, a blue tie. He was a head taller than Daniel. He said, 'We need to talk.'

Daniel said, 'If you want to interview my employee, Chief Inspector, you should talk to our lawyer first.'

'Interview her? No, it isn't anything like that. More in the nature of a friendly chat. Let me show you something,' Nevers said, and took Chloe's arm and guided her to the bank of lifts at the end of the corridor.

As they rode down, Chloe said, 'Are you trying to intimidate me, Chief Inspector?'

Because she definitely felt intimidated, wondering where he was taking her, wondering if he knew about her plans.

'I really liked how you handled the questions about the New Galactic Navy,' Nevers said. 'You stood up for yourself, but you didn't blame them. Even though they had obviously been driven crazy by alien ghosts.'

'It was the ordinary kind of crazy, nothing to do with algorithms or eidolons. There were plenty of cults like theirs before the Jackaroo came.'

'But there are a lot more now, aren't there? And many new kinds of craziness. Some of it harmless, some of it dangerous. People meddle with alien technology, and it fucks them up. It's like giving plutonium to a bunch of savages. Shiny stuff that's warm to the touch, glows in the dark. Magic. But then your hair and teeth start falling out, your women give birth to monsters, and if you put too much of it together . . . This way.'

Chloe followed him out of the lift, along service corridors painted institutional green, through a fire door. Warm air, the slap of waves beneath a mesh platform elevated over a cluster of fat pipes, a workman in a high-vis jacket at the far end lowering something, a square mesh cage, over the rail.

Nevers introduced Chloe and said that she wanted to look at the day's catch, and the workman lifted the lid off an ordinary black plastic dustbin. There were monsters inside. Fist-sized knots of pale threads, dozens of them, writhing around each other in a caul of slimy foam. A strong odour like stagnant water in a vase of long-dead flowers, with overtones of burnt plastic. Chloe felt an instant, atavistic revulsion. It was like some parasite found in the bowels of an animal. A nest of corpse worms. A horror-movie special effect.

The workman explained that they were devil squid. Native to Hydrot, brought here as sporelings in bubbleweed, now securely established in the ecosystem of the Thames. The building used river water to cool the heat exchangers of its air-conditioning system, and the devil squid crawled into the pipes, causing blockages and fouling the pumps.

'We put up mesh, but they can squeeze through it,' the man said. 'So now we use traps baited with a pheromone.'

'And you have to clean the traps every day,' Nevers said.

'They keep coming,' the man said. 'Reckon they like it here.'

'If that's some sort of lesson,' Chloe said as she followed Nevers to the other end of the platform, 'I don't quite get the point.'

Nevers leaned against the rail, presenting her with his keen profile as he gazed out across the river. 'People like your boss think they can quantify the influence of the Jackaroo and all the rest, but they really don't have clue one about it. None of us do. That old line about not meddling in things we don't understand – a funny old cliché, right? An awful warning about mad scientists and such. But some of us have realised that it has an urgent truth. We brought back bubbleweed from Hydrot, fast-growing stuff that was supposed to help with the carbon-sequestration effort. And devil squids hitched a ride in it, and they grew and multiplied, and now we can't get rid of them. Just one example of many problems large and small, caused by misplaced arrogance. By people thinking that they can use alien stuff without any blowback. Can I give you a little advice, Chloe?'

'Why not?' Because like she had a choice.

'When Disruption Theory stuck to documenting cults and crazies, all well and good. We didn't have a problem with that. But now it's started to deal in actual alien artefacts, and that's another game entirely. That's *our* game. Do you follow me?'

'This sounds more like a threat than advice.'

'The advice part's coming up. Don't put your trust in Dr Morange or any of her people. She's brilliant, true. But she's also ruthless. If she thinks you're causing her a problem, she will drop you like *this*.'

Chloe managed not to flinch when Nevers snapped his fingers in her face.

He said, 'Fahad Chauhan's pictures have been thoroughly examined by our techs. Who have high-powered pattern-recognition systems, AI risk-assessment programmes . . . They say the pictures are topologically consistent, and contain signatures that suggest they could be the product of a powerful and single-minded eidolon. A type that hasn't been encountered before. But you already knew that, didn't you? I mean, that's your thing. It's what you do.'

'I can tell real artefacts from fakes. Most of the time.'

'And those pictures looked real to you.'

Chloe shrugged. She didn't want to give anything away.

'And you've had plenty of experience with Elder Culture shit,' Adam Nevers said. 'Algorithms and eidolons and all the rest. You know what they can do to people. How they can get inside their heads and mess up their minds. Our chief tech says that the maths packed into some of the algorithms can be very elegant. Simple and profound; beautiful, even. He's used that very word more than once: beautiful. Is that how you see it?'

'I'm not a mathematician.'

'I like motorbikes. My idea of beauty is a Harley-Davidson Duo-Glide. That big, air-cooled V-twin engine, the curve of the fairings and the teardrop tank . . . Or if you're into classics, the Vincent Black Shadow. But jet fighter planes are beautiful too. So are Great White sharks.'

'Aren't they extinct? Great Whites.'

But Nevers refused to be derailed. 'The techs reckon your friend Fahad has been exposed to a seriously dangerous alien mind virus, and I have it on good authority that the kid's father was into some seriously dangerous stuff too, working for some seriously dangerous people. I suggest you look back at the path you've taken so far, Chloe. Think very carefully about which direction you should go next. And any time you want to get in touch, here's my card,' he said, holding it out between two fingers. 'Don't take too long to think about it. Don't leave it until you and your friends are deep in the shit before you call for help.'

Upstairs, outside the committee room, Chloe told Daniel it was nothing. 'I'm not sure if it was a threat or a job offer,' she said. 'But screw it, I'm going to do this thing anyway. And then, maybe, we'll know what happened to Fahad.'

Daniel moved forward unexpectedly and folded her into a bear hug. 'Do good work,' he said. It felt like a farewell.

She redeemed her message bag from the cloakroom. Jen had driven her to her flat early that morning so that she could pick up fresh clothes, a change of underwear, her washbag. It was a postage stamp of a studio flat and she was paying a stupid amount of rent for it, but it was the first time she'd had her own space, her own front door, her own mail box. Before that, she'd sofa-surfed, shared rooms with friends, even squatted one summer in a big decrepit house in Hackney. But as she'd packed, with Jen perched on the corner of her swing-down bed, Chloe had realised that after two years she was still living as if she expected to have to move out at a moment's notice. The furniture was the landlord's; she'd bought the cookware, crockery and bed linen in a mad dash through Ikea; her books, music and movies were in her tablet or the Cloud.

There had been no reporters waiting in ambush outside the block of flats: the news had rolled on past her. And although the little huddle outside the entrance to Kingdom Tower stirred when she appeared, calling to her as she climbed into the taxi that Jen had ordered, aiming phones and cameras at her through the windows as it moved off, none of them bothered to follow.

She asked the taxi to drop her off near Shepherd Market and threaded the back streets to Green Park Tube station, resisting the impulse to look over her shoulder, to look at CCTV cameras on high posts, the corners of buildings. She descended to the Piccadilly line and rode a westbound train one stop to Hyde Park Corner, crossed to the eastbound line and rode back through Green Park. Feeling less like a spy and more like a kid playing hide-and-seek. Because how would she know if anyone was following her, or watching her on security cameras? But it made her feel a little better, made her feel like she was doing something about Nevers's scare tactics.

She stayed on the train to the end of the line. Cockfosters. A low brick-built station, an old-fashioned parade of dilapidated shops on the other side of the road, a battered black Range Rover parked outside a betting shop. The driver, Ada Morange's man, started the motor when she climbed in.

14. Nothing Like Australia

Mangala | 25 July

As he and Skip drove out of the city, Vic called his friend Dario Zanonato in drug enforcement, put him on speakerphone, and asked him for the low-down on Cal McBride. 'I heard he was pushed out of his little operation.'

'Why are you fifth-floor guys interested in him?'

'Short answer, we have a body zapped by a ray gun.'

Dario laughed. 'Are you still sore about that sting?'

'No, man, not at all. It wasn't my case that got fucked up.'

'But now you are thinking of going at McBride again.'

'I'm wondering what happened to him, what he's doing now.'

'What happened, his meq business fell apart after he was jailed,' Dario said. 'His second-in-command was killed in a traffic accident, and everything went to hell. The trappers who catch biochines and bleed them, most of the street-level lieutenants who run the street crews, they went to work for other gangs. And it seems the guy who supervised the lab that cooked the shit tried to defect too. He was found dead a few months ago. Nailed to a wall in a half-built apartment building.'

'I remember that,' Vic had said. 'The crucifixion bit, anyhow.'

'The guy had been shot in the head, but not by a ray gun,' Dario said.

'Yeah. Jerzy Buzek had the case.' Vic believed that it was still open. He needed to talk to Jerzy, see where he was with it.

Skip said, 'How does Danny Drury fit into this story?'

He was at the wheel, driving with a light, two-fingered touch, blond hair ruffling in the breeze from the open window.

Dario said, 'He was sent here by the family to sort things out. When McBride was released, he found himself frozen out. The family decided Drury was doing a better job. Have you guys met Drury?'

'Briefly,' Vic said.

'He's, what do you say, a piece of work. The son of the family's accountant back home, good education, several years in the army . . . Anyway, as I understand it, the family wants to get out of the meq trade here. Go legit. The city's growing. More money in building work and trading Elder Culture shit than drugs. And Drury is their man for the job.'

Vic said, 'So they retired McBride rather than kill him?'

'They wouldn't kill him. He's family. But he's also old school. You know, from the street.'

Skip said, 'What's McBride doing now?'

'Property development,' Dario said. 'According, at least, to him.'

'But guys like McBride never leave the street behind,' Vic said. 'You have anything on him?'

'Not really. The Mayor is breathing down our necks. He wants us to clean up small-time low-hanging fruit to make him look good. You like to go after Cal McBride,' Dario said, 'I'm pretty sure we don't mind.'

Vic thanked Dario, and told Skip, 'We definitely need to find out what McBride thinks of Mr Danny Drury.'

'You think, if Drury has something to do with this, McBride might rat him out?'

'I think we should mention Drury to get under McBride's skin, then ask him where he was last night. See how he handles himself.'

They drove past the dusty edges of the suburbs, past rows of poured foundations, stacks of construction materials and sections of cast-concrete sewer pipes, a yellow bulldozer scraping at a stretch of ground in a cloud of red dust. Past new factories constructed from prefabricated sections shipped from Earth, a half-built shopping mall, hectares of scrapped cars glinting in the level sunlight. Past all that, turning onto an unpaved road that ran across a stretch of playa staked out for further development. The ghostly outlines of streets and lots laid across red dirt. Whipgrass, low stands of greythorn. Yellow surveyor flags snapping in the wind. Gang signs on the flanks of shiprocks.

A red Mitsubishi Shogun sped past in the opposite direction, peppering their car with small stones, trailing a long banner of dust.

Skip buzzed up the window, said, 'Know what this looks like?'

Vic said, 'You mean which part of Australia?'

'It *is* a bit like the Outback, but I was thinking it looks like the deserts outside Los Angeles. That's where the film and TV people went when they wanted to shoot exteriors for sci-fi films. So we think all alien planets should look like Californian desert. Or Death Valley. They shot *Robinson Crusoe on Mars* in Death Valley. You ever see that one?'

'I'm not what you'd call a film buff.'

'It's an old one, but pretty good. The hero has a gun, but never uses it. Even when the slaver aliens are trying to kill him.'

'You're babbling, Investigator Williams.'

'I mean this looks like the old ideas of what Mars looked like, before they discovered what it really looks like. In the city, it's easy to forget you're on an alien planet. But here it is.'

'Enjoy it while you can. The suburbs keep growing.'

There was a short silence. The car sped along the level dirt road. Red dust powdered the windscreen. Red dirt studded with grey and black vegetation stretched away towards the horizon. They turned along a track that crossed the road at right angles. A cluster of sheds and construction machinery, a hoarding showing some kind of green oasis: *Shangri-La: Another Development by CalMac Enterprises.*

'I know you'll remember this place,' Cal McBride said to Vic. 'An old-timer like you.'

They were standing at the edge of a square pit dug into the red earth. It was about half the size of a football pitch, fenced with steel stakes and orange netting. On the far side was a shabby rake of bleacher seats. In the middle distance, a hydraulic drill rig was pounding a foundation spike into a trench, its percussive clang unravelling into the empty playa.

Vic said, 'I remember a murder investigation here, ten, eleven years ago. There was a strandloper in the pit, somehow the man

103

who owned the place fell in, and the thing ripped him from neck to navel.'

'Long before I bought the place,' McBride said. 'Long before I came up, even. Did you ever find out who did it?'

He was a burly man in his fifties, with a stiff shock of white hair. Dressed in some kind of safari suit – a bright yellow hip-length jacket with patch pockets and wide lapels, a cloth belt buckled over the bulge of his belly. Matching trousers tucked into knee-high brown leather boots. An ivory-coloured claw hung on a silver chain around his neck.

Vic said, 'Who pushed him in, you mean? Oh, we were pretty sure that it was his business partner, but we didn't have enough evidence. In the end it was ruled death by misadventure. But it closed this place down, put an end to biochine death matches.'

He remembered the strange pairing that the bodies of the man and the strandloper had made. The man's clothes soaked in blood and tattered with parallel rips. The biochine's segments collapsed between a dozen pairs of slender multi-jointed legs, its brittle carapace shattered by gunfire. Strandlopers were mostly harmless, but two individuals from different packs would fight to the death when they were put into the pit. A territorial thing. The main attraction had been fights between matched pairs of jacka-napes, the quick, vicious biochines that preyed on strandlopers and other grazers. There weren't any around Petra any more. The city council had culled the local population after they'd started straying into the new suburbs.

He said to McBride, 'So now you own the place. Not the first time you've benefited from a death, is it?'

'I bought it from the city, fair and square,' McBride said.

He was building a resort, a cross between a country club and a casino, had insisted on giving Vic and Skip a tour of the construction site. He'd made expansive gestures as he'd strutted along, pointing to the stony stretch of ground where the eighteen-hole golf course was going to be, pointing to the stakes that outlined the extent of the dome under which the main building and guest cabins would shelter amongst a land-scaped arboretum.

'Know the Hotel California?' he'd said. 'Of course you do. This will be six times the area, semi-tropical. Palms, banana plants, that kind of thing. Imagine staying in a place where you can pick oranges or bananas right off the tree. I'm going to bring in animals too. Once my lawyers have cut through the red tape. Monkeys, parrots. Tigers. White tigers in their own enclosure. Paradise.'

Saying now, 'Wouldn't it be something if I could get around that stupid law, get the old pit working again? Revive some of that rough, tough pioneer spirit. I always wish that I'd been here at the beginning, before the UN started imposing its rules and regulations. Before the fucking corporations started coming in. There's a McDonald's drive-through now, you believe that? I couldn't, when I saw it. Shopping malls, for Christ's sake.'

'And golf courses,' Vic said.

'If you want to survive, you have to go with the flow. See where things are going and try to get ahead.'

'Is that something you thought up in prison?' Vic was trying to needle the man, make him annoyed and careless.

But McBride was smiling. 'Fuck, no. I've been diversifying my portfolio for some time now. Set up my own company, everything legit and above board. This project stalled while I was away, but I'm getting it back on track. And I have some serious interests in the Elder Culture artefact business. We haven't explored five per cent of the planet yet, not properly. We don't even know everything about the territory around Petra.'

'So you're starting a new life,' Vic said. 'Trying to go legit.'

'Trying? No, that's what I am now. A businessman. Plain and simple. I was trying to remember where I saw you,' McBride said to Skip. 'And now I remember. You were with the Mayor at some do. I have a memory for faces.'

Skip said, 'We met the new boss of your old business. Danny Drury. Interesting bloke.'

Vic detected the slightest hesitation before McBride said, 'He's a smart boy. Should do well for himself. With my blessing, of course.'

'So no hard feelings between you and Mr Drury,' Skip said.

'He has his business, I have mine. There's plenty of room out here for all kinds, after all.'

'You just gave up on the drug business,' Skip said. 'Walked away from it.'

'You want to see what prison can do, how it can put a man on the straight and narrow, here I am,' McBride said.

Vic said, 'You're talking about the good old days you know nothing about, talking about starting up the pit again . . .'

'Which will probably never happen. Thanks to the fucking conservation regulations.'

'So I have to wonder,' Vic said, 'if you haven't entirely let the past go.'

'Oh, now we're getting into it, huh?'

'You thought it was a courtesy visit?'

'As soon as I saw you, I knew you were trouble.'

Skip said, 'And what kind of trouble might that be, Mr McBride?'

'If this is about those three dealers killed last night, I told you, I'm out of that game. Well rid. Leave it to the Serbs and the French and the fucking Turks, I say,' McBride said, his face perfectly blank. Impossible to tell if he was playing them, or if he really didn't know why they were there.

Vic touched his ear, the signal to change up the game. Skip said, 'Where were you two days ago, around nine in the evening?'

That was the time the security guard had spotted the van speeding away from the murder scene.

'You mean Landing Day?' McBride smiled. 'I was at a restaurant. Area 51. It had a special tasting menu.'

Skip said, 'Would you mind telling me who your dinner companions were?'

'You mean who could give me an alibi? Jesus fucking Christ. You think, just out of jail, getting back on my feet, I'm going to do something stupid?'

'If you didn't do anything,' Skip said, 'there's no harm telling us who you were doing it with.'

McBride stared at him; Skip stared back.

'All right,' McBride said impatiently. 'Just to get you off my back. I was with my good friend Eva Winkler. And I said hello to a couple of dozen acquaintances, too. Ask anyone who was there, they'll remember me.'

Vic said, 'We will. By the way, talking of Elder Culture artefacts, I hear you know something about ray guns.'

'That old shit? All kinds of accusations were made, but none of them were ever proved.'

'Because you went to jail. And while you were there, Danny Drury moved in. Took your house and your business. I was wondering if he also took your ray gun.'

'I wouldn't know anything about it.'

'But I bet you'd like to see Danny Drury go down, maybe get your old business back.'

'If you think I'd grass him up, you got the wrong idea about me,' McBride said. 'Now if you don't mind, I have to get back to work. Paradise doesn't build itself.'

Vic eased into the passenger seat. He felt old and cranky. The car smelled of stale sweat and the disinfectant someone had used recently to rinse off the back seat.

Skip said, 'They both had their alibis ready.'

'I hate to say it, but I think McBride might be telling the truth. Hard to sneak out of a restaurant, kill someone, and come back as if you just went for a piss.'

'But easier, maybe, to sneak out of a big party.'

Vic smiled. 'We both like Mr Drury for this, don't we? But we can't put him at the scene, and we have no reason for him being there.'

'I guess we should check their alibis.'

'Why not?'

As they drove back to the city, Vic thought the playa looked nothing like Australia, and nothing like Mars, either. No, it looked like the world had looked before people had started in on it.

15. Red Weed Country

Henry Harris, the driver of the Range Rover, was a security consultant who worked for Ada Morange's people. A wiry man in his late fifties or early sixties, with a bony boyish face, a deep outdoor tan, and a bright gaze that didn't miss much. Chloe had seen him visiting Daniel a couple of times, knew that he had once been in the army, allegedly in the SAS or some other crack unit.

His presence was a condition of Chloe being allowed 'off the leash', as Daniel had put it. To make sure that she was protected from journalists, to keep her out of any trouble that might attract the attention of Chief Inspector Nevers and the Hazard Police, and to represent Ada Morange's interests.

'Which are also our interests, of course,' Daniel had said.

But not necessarily Chloe's, or Fahad Chauhan's. But there wasn't much she could do about it. If she had headed off to Norfolk on her own it would have been as good as writing a resignation letter. And besides, she'd already told Daniel where she needed to go; Henry Harris would have soon caught up with her.

As they drove towards the M25, he asked her to switch off her phone. Chloe told him that she was using a throwaway. 'I paid for it with cash a couple of days ago. It isn't traceable.'

'Have you used it at work or at home? Yes? Then it's probably compromised. Let me take a look,' Henry Harris said, and held out his hand.

She took it out and gave it to him; he immediately tossed it out of the open window.

'Hey—'

'I'll buy you another. What else are you carrying? A tablet, spex?'

'I need them for my work.'

She had her old phone, too. No way she was giving him that, it had all her shit on it.

'Don't use them. Not even in airplane mode.'

'Are you trying to make me paranoid, Mr Harris?'

She said it with a smile. They were stuck with each other, so there was no point in starting an argument.

'I don't mind if you use my first name, Chloe. Mr Harris, it makes me think I'm your geography teacher. As for what I'm trying to do, it's to keep you out of trouble. The Hazard Police's interest in this thing of yours means that there might be something to it. But it also means we have to make sure we're flying under their radar at all times.'

Chloe said, 'Would you still be interested in this if the Hazard Police weren't interested? I mean, if it was just my opinion that Fahad's pictures were important.'

'You'd have to ask the brass about that,' Henry said. 'Me, I'm just a foot soldier, doing what I'm told.'

He was dressed in a white short-sleeved shirt and tan chinos and battered trainers. He wasn't wearing his seat belt, steered with casual expertise through the thickening traffic, the Range Rover looming like a tank in the buzzing swarm of candy-coloured runabouts and flitters. Its clattering motor was louder than the wind at the window that Chloe had rolled down, and there was a strong odour of frying oil. Her seat was patched with duct tape; the carpet was torn and stained; the back seat was a litter of old pizza boxes, crushed soft-drink cans, newspapers, Kentucky Fried Chicken boxes. There was a stack of box files. An old MacBook Air, its silver clamshell patched with stickers. Whenever the Range Rover went over a bump in the road or turned a corner there was a restless shifting, a clink of rolling bottles.

'Tell me about these missing kids,' Henry said.

He wore a big gold watch on his wrist, the second watch Chloe had seen in three days. Its dial was decorated with the face of someone she knew but couldn't quite place. Dark scowling eyes, a bushy moustache. One of those old film stars who always played villains, maybe. The strap was a cheap strip of grey fabric, fastened with Velcro.

She said, 'Daniel didn't brief you?'

'I want to hear your version.'

She gave him a quick account of the cult's breakout, the flyer she'd picked up, Fahad Chauhan's drawings and her brief conversation with him. She told him about Eddie Ackroyd and his mysterious client, her discovery that Fahad's father had gone up and out to Mangala, his mother's death.

'About the father,' Henry said. 'It seems that Dr Chauhan lost his job soon after his wife died. He was padding inventory expenses, used the money to feed a gambling habit.'

'How do you know this?'

'The Prof has a stake in the company – her person on the board reached out to the head of Human Resources. Anyway, after he was fired, the father ends up in this little town in the back end of nowhere, doing we don't yet know what. And a year later he lands a contract with that property-development company and is sent up and out to Mangala. There's definitely something that doesn't add up.'

'However he got there, I think he sent back something,' Chloe said.

'I bet you've met a few aliens, in your line of work.'

'That depends what you mean by met.'

'You don't count the Jackaroo avatar?'

'We didn't talk.'

Henry was amused by that. He said, 'What about alien ghosts?'

'If you mean eidolons, I've seen a few.'

'Daniel told me you'd been to a lot of seances. Alien ghosts are more popular than dead Indians, he said.'

'We did a survey last year,' Chloe said. 'I saw a woman pretend to drag ten metres of wet muslin from her mouth. I saw a man in black robes and a fez levitate a table.'

'For real?'

'With his knees. They both claimed to be in contact with spirit guides from Elder Cultures, but I didn't see anything that would have surprised Houdini. If you want to see an eidolon, go to the British Museum. They have a tessera from a tomb in the City of the Dead on First Foot that generates one if anyone gets close. It looks a little like a squirrel made of smoke.'

'What about this kid? Is he possessed by one of these eidolons?'

'That's what I want to find out.'

'And that's why we're heading into M.R. James territory.'

'I'm sorry?'

'The writer. Ghost stories. There was one that scared the crap out of me when I was a kid. Saw it on TV one Christmas. That was set in Norfolk. By the sea.'

'I thought I explained that this isn't about that kind of ghost.'

'I never looked at bed-sheets the same, after that,' Henry said.

He was one of those men who like to test the limits of other people's patience because they are impatient with themselves, easily bored. Chloe's last boyfriend had been like that. Had liked to get in people's faces, as he put it, to see what they were really made of. Simon, an ex-soldier she'd met at the gym. They'd had a sort of semi-serious thing for more than a year, and then one day, out of the blue, he'd told her he had taken a security job with BP and was shipping out to Greenland. And after he'd left he'd immediately broken his promise to stay in touch. He'd been gone almost six months now, and she was still a little raw about it.

They drove around the M25 and joined the M11, and just before Cambridge turned onto an A road, passed through a village, and stopped at a small service station on the far side.

'You never know when you're going to find one selling biodiesel these days,' Henry said.

Chloe watched as he pumped fuel into the Range Rover's tank. He popped the bonnet and carefully poured a litre of pinkish fluid into the coolant overflow tank. Looking sideways at her, saying, 'I expect you're wondering why I hang on to an antique like this.'

'I was wondering why you weren't driving something a little less conspicuous.'

'I used to have a BMW. An E39 M5. Nothing to look at, but it was a real road monster. Six-speed manual, 4.9 litre V8. Totalled it in Wales, in a rainstorm near Cader Idris. Banged through a stone wall and flew halfway across a field, walked away without a scratch. This is a classic too,' Henry said, lowering the bonnet.

'Thirty years old, more than a hundred thousand on the clock. They make them with LEAF batteries now, and those tiny little motors that sound like sewing machines. But sometimes you get into a situation where you need a bit of welly.'

They bought sandwiches and coffee from the garage shop, leaned against the Range Rover while they ate. On the other side of the road, a work party of prisoners in orange coveralls printed with the logo of a security company were clearing dense mats of red weed from a stand of pine trees. They used billhooks to haul down scarlet ropes that twined through branches and sagged from tree to tree, chopping them into sections and tossing them into a roaring shredder that spat scarlet pulp into the hopper of a truck. Four guards in blue shirts and black shorts watched them work, tasers on their hips, faces shaded by ball caps, eyes masked by sunglasses.

'Most of East Anglia is red weed country these days,' Henry said. 'They say you can hear it growing, at night. It grows on beaches, salt marshes . . . I saw a housing estate covered in it, out by Ebbsfleet.'

Chloe decided that she wouldn't ask him what he'd been doing in Ebbsfleet.

He ate quickly and neatly, pausing now and then to dab at his lips with a paper napkin. Asked her if she wanted a bite. 'Horse. Very tasty. And much healthier than beef.'

Chloe had abandoned her sandwich: a processed-cheese slice, pallid slices of tomato, bread the texture of packing-foam pellets. She said, 'I don't eat meat.'

Henry took a big bite of what was left of his sandwich, chewed and swallowed, and said, 'Sometimes I could murder for a bacon sarnie. Bacon and fried egg and brown sauce. I hear the Chinese are trying to engineer a new flu-resistant strain of pigs. None too soon if you ask me, and I bet you agree. Every vegetarian I've ever met has lust in their heart for a nice bit of bacon.'

He unfolded a paper map on the Range Rover's bonnet. He didn't use satnav, he told Chloe, for the same reason he didn't use a mobile phone or a tablet if he could help it.

'I like to operate off the grid. Keep things simple.'

'How do you report to your bosses?'

'On a job? I don't. I do what needs to be done, and if it goes wrong it's on me. Not that anything will go wrong.' He traced a route with a blunt forefinger, read out the names of towns and villages, road numbers, then folded the map up. 'Don't worry, I won't ask you to navigate. Let's get going.'

'You need to lose a few prejudices, Mr Harris. Henry. I'm a mean map-reader.'

'And I've memorised the route.'

He started the motor, shoved an actual CD into the antique deck, a compilation of Geezer Rock tracks. Thrashing drums, chugging guitars, male vocals. He told Chloe the name of the band as each track started. Primal Scream. The Wedding Present. New Order. She said that she thought she'd heard of New Order.

'I saw them when I was fifteen,' Henry said. 'In Finsbury Park. What are you into, Chloe? A-pop? Interstellar electronica? Or are you more of a classic-music buff?'

Her mother had liked to play opera very loudly on Sunday morning. It still reminded Chloe of her, instantly, whenever she heard it.

'That's Paul Weller,' Henry said, when another track started up. 'I don't suppose you've heard of him, either.'

They drove past an airbase with a jet fighter angled on a fat pedestal at the front gate, followed a badly maintained dual carriageway for a while, then turned off into a maze of little roads that followed old field boundaries as they wound across a flat agricultural landscape. The sky was enormous. Heat shimmering across yellow hectares of oilseed rape. Froths of cow parsley along verdant verges. Pretty little villages of houses of brick and knapped flint, bungalows with fanatically neat front gardens. Pebble-dashed council houses. Thatched pubs. Once a red telephone kiosk, the first Chloe had seen in the wild for several years. Larger houses beyond high walls and shelter belts of poplars. Immemorial England.

Henry Harris seemed relaxed out here, driving with his elbow cocked at the open window. As they followed the ring road around Acle towards the harbour, he glanced over for the first time in more than an hour and asked Chloe to check the glove compartment.

'It's all the way in the back. You'll see.'

It was a small snub-nosed pistol nestled in a litter of chocolate-bar wrappers and spent biros, its chequered plastic grip protruding from a snug holster of soft black neoprene. Chloe felt an electric shock, as if she'd found a coiled snake.

She said, 'If that's supposed to make me feel safer, it doesn't.'

'It's supposed to make *me* feel safer,' Henry said. 'Especially in a confined space like a ferry. Not to mention funny little towns full of web-footed locals. Hand it over.'

She tried to use only her fingertips. He wriggled in his seat, clipping the holster to his belt, under the tail of his white shirt.

She said, 'Is that legal?'

'I was trained to use bigger guns than this.'

Which didn't exactly answer her question.

'It was a long time ago. The Iraq War, the second one. But I still know which end the bullet comes out of,' Henry said.

Chloe realised who the face on his watch was. The old dead dictator. The ultimate pantomime villain.

Henry told her that he'd once had a spot of trouble with bootleggers out on the Flood. 'They let you lead them to some-thing good, and then they come in and take it. Happened to me once. When I got out of hospital, I swore it wouldn't happen to me again.'

His gaze was neutral, daring her to challenge his story.

She said, 'I shouldn't think bootleggers would be interested in Fahad's paintings.'

'They might be interested in what makes him paint them, mightn't they?'

It was a good point.

They left the Range Rover in a long-term car park and walked along the edge of the new harbour, a raw excavation faced with steel plating. Windrows of trash rose and fell amongst rainbow oil stains on sluggish waves. Gulls wheeled overhead like revenants of a prehistoric age.

The little ferry, its hold just big enough for half a dozen vehicles, churned out of the harbour more than an hour late. It chugged through channels between islands, hugging the shore, calling in at several villages and small towns. At one stop, there was a delay because a pickup truck had trouble backing down the narrow ramp. Men shouted instructions to the driver, who kept sounding his horn, as if for punctuation.

'Left a bit, just a bit more. Now straighten up.'

Beep!

'Straight on, straight on, stop!'

Beep!

'You're over to the right. Ease forward, come on back.'

Beep!

Henry sat on his army-surplus kitbag, watching this. Eating cheese-and-onion crisps, turning the empty packet inside out and carefully blotting crumbs from the corners with a wetted fingertip, somehow reminding Chloe of a squirrel. The ferry chugged on, ploughing through floating reefs of bubbleweed that glinted like frothy spills of blood in the late afternoon sunlight, past a line of pylons standing knee-high in the Flood, past a stretch of railway line on an embankment now colonised by the neat multicoloured shacks, vegetable gardens and wind turbines of fishermen. Most of them Dutch refugees, according to Henry. He'd been out this way a few times, he said, chasing down rumours that hadn't panned out.

'Like I said, there are plenty of ghosts out here. They outnumber the living.'

Past a shoal of small islands. One was completely covered in red weed, like a boil in the blue water. The sun was setting over the long treeline of the shore as the ferry turned due east, running through a channel cut in a wide beds of reeds, coming at last to the little town beyond a long reach of sand dunes, its lights twinkling in the soft summer evening.

16. Just Another Alien

Mangala | 25 July

The parking garage at the Hilton Hotel, where the Landing Day Ball had been held, had a valet service. The supervisor checked the registration numbers of vehicles owned by Danny Drury and his company against her spreadsheet for that evening, told Vic Gayle and Skip Williams that his car had been dropped off at seven-thirty and picked up around midnight, and pulled up footage from a camera that watched the entrance. Drury wasn't driving the car, a shiny black Mercedes M Class, but there he was, getting out of it with a spectacular blonde woman at 7:34 p.m., and there he was again, his stupid ponytail brushing the collar of a white dinner jacket, stooping into the back of the Mercedes at a quarter past midnight.

'There are plenty of ways of getting out of this place,' Skip said. 'He could have sneaked out at any time in between.'

Vic agreed. 'You might want to check if his company owns any white vans.'

'We should have asked him. McBride too.'

'It shouldn't be hard to find out. If they do, you can come back at them, see if they lie. Let's see if McBride's alibi holds water.'

The restaurant where McBride claimed to have been eating that night was at the other end of the Strip, a glitzy cave off the lobby of the Petra Carlton, a six-star hotel used by business people, diplomats and UN top brass when they were visiting from Earth. James Cameron had stayed there just after it had opened, when he'd been scouting locations for a film that had never been made.

According to the restaurant's maitre d', McBride had booked the table for eight p.m., square in the middle of the estimated time of death for Redway, but the maitre d' couldn't confirm if McBride had been late or if he had been at his table all evening. All he knew was that the bill had been signed at around one a.m.

'I believe I spoke to Mr McBride, but we were very busy. We served a special Landing Day tasting menu, more than three hundred covers. And many of our customers socialised in the cocktail bar before and afterwards.'

Skip asked who had been at the table with McBride. The maitre d' said reluctantly, as if revealing a family secret, 'I believe he was accompanied by Ms Winkler. They eat here regularly.'

It turned out that Cal McBride had moved into a suite in the hotel just after he had been released from jail. The maitre d' found one of the waiters who'd worked McBride's table on Landing Day; the woman thought that Mr McBride was at the table most of the time, but said it was hard to be sure.

'A lot of the guests were table-hopping. It was like one big party.'

None of the staff on the front desk remembered seeing McBride leave, and there weren't any security cameras in the lobby. 'We respect the privacy of our guests,' the manager said.

Skip said to Vic, 'I guess we could talk to this girlfriend, see what she has to say . . .'

'If we do it now she'll probably say she was with McBride all night.'

'Yeah,' Skip said, as if he'd already thought of that.

'Better to wait, see if we have anything on McBride first. Then we can use that as leverage, threaten her with a perjury charge if she doesn't tell the truth.'

They were sitting in the car, reviewing what they'd learned.

Skip said, 'What it comes down to, it could be either of them. They were both in crowded places, lots of people coming and going, plenty of opportunities to slip out for an hour or so without being missed.'

'Or it could be someone else. Someone who stole the ray gun after McBride went to jail.'

'Can we get warrants to search McBride's hotel suite and Drury's house?'

'Not with what we have so far. Even if we did, we don't know what the thing looks like, and it might be anywhere. At home, at a place of business, in a safety-deposit box . . . But we do know it was at the murder scene,' Vic said. 'So our best bet is to find someone who was there. Someone who saw McBride or Drury or whoever else with the ray gun in their hand.'

'We're back to looking for David Parsons.'

'There you go. You've put him on the watch list, but you should get out there and do the rounds yourself. Motels, rooming houses, hot-sheet crash pads. Maybe he rented or bought an RV from some Junktown dealer. We can work up a list of likely places and make a start tomorrow. As my grandma used to say, morning makes the world new, every time.'

'Actually,' Skip said, 'I already have a list of motels. I pulled them out of the directory while I was phoning around hotels.'

'And I suppose you want to check them out now.'

'Strike while the iron's hot and all that,' Skip said.

They drove back to the UN building so that Vic could pick up a pool car and they split the list between them, Vic taking places on the west side of the city, Skip taking the east. Vic wasn't keen on the footwork, but what the hell. Drury's arrogance had got under his skin; he'd like nothing better, right now, than to find something that would put the son-of-a-bitch down. And it was kind of enjoyable to be doing some actual good old-fashioned police work. Driving from place to place, showing the photo of David Parsons to receptionists and desk clerks.

A clerk in a motel near the ring road, a young white guy with long hair, bad acne and a strong Newcastle accent, asked Vic if he remembered him; apparently Vic had arrested him six years ago for dealing shine.

'But I'm straight now, Mr Gayle. Working hard.'

The guy had tremors and a pinned-back gaze. If he wasn't doing shine, he was on something else. First rule of the murder police: everyone lies, all the time . . .

Vic checked out the big truck stop on the Idunn's Valley road – no luck there, either – then drove a little way further out to one of his favourite restaurants. It was up on a ridge overlooking the playa and the road arrowing westward towards a distant prospect of hills. A Quonset hut housed the kitchen; there were tables under a canvas awning, a terraced vegetable garden stepping down the slope. A string of Boxbuilder ruins ran off along the top of the ridge, glowing in the soft sunlight.

There were Boxbuilder ruins on every one of the fifteen worlds, but no one knew anything about the species that had built them. Their appearance, their culture, where they had come from, where they had gone. It wasn't even clear how old the ruins were: the cells were constructed from thin sheets of a grainy self-repairing polymer salted with nanotech. Best estimates suggested that the Boxbuilders had occupied the fifteen worlds between eighteen and twenty-two thousand years ago. And twenty thousand years before the Boxbuilders, another Elder Culture had left vast stretches of tombs. Cities of the dead. Some were occupied by eidolons coded in little stones embedded in the walls; some contained artefacts that had kick-started new technologies, including q-phones and computers as small as pinheads. Other Elder Cultures had constructed the so-called factories that sprawled across the forests and coastal waters of Yanos, reshaped mountains and seas, built huge edifices and labyrinths of tunnels, or left nothing more than traces of complex organics and polymers in geological layers.

All had been contacted by the Jackaroo, had accepted their gift of habitable worlds orbiting red dwarf stars scattered across the Milky Way, and had lived on those worlds for varying amounts of time and altered them in various ways before disappearing. No one knew what had happened to them. There were dozens of theories, and each was as valid as any other because none were supported by actual evidence and the Jackaroo refused to answer direct questions about their previous clients.

'We are here to help,' they liked to say.

And, 'Each client finds its own path.'

They sometimes hinted that the Elder Cultures had transcended. That they had discovered something that had enabled them to evolve beyond the understanding of the Jackaroo. That the fifteen worlds were arenas that tested the suitability of intelligent species for inclusion in a Galactic Club so advanced that its activities weren't detectable by those who were not yet fit for membership. Ideas that might have been lifted, like so many of the Jackaroo's hints and teases, from science fiction and pre-First Contact speculations about extraterrestrial civilisations. It was just as likely, according to so-called experts, that previous occupants of the fifteen worlds had suffered culture shock and dwindled away, or had destroyed themselves by misusing technologies left by previous tenants, or had been assimilated by the Jackaroo, as the !Cha might have been. The !Cha said that they had never been clients of the Jackaroo, but as someone once said, quoting a line from a famous old scandal, they would say that, wouldn't they? Perhaps that was the best humanity could hope for: to devolve into pets or hitchhiking commensals.

In Vic's opinion, there was as yet no sign that humanity was going to change any time soon. People had come up and out, built cities, and begun to spread across the empty lands and explore the ruins, and they'd also brought all their old shit with them. A few had managed to reinvent themselves, but most hadn't been able to escape what they already were. Accountants were accountants; estate agents were estate agents; drug dealers were drug dealers. Vic had been a raw constable in Birmingham when he'd won the emigration lottery, and here he was thirteen years later, a murder police unable to maintain any kind of long-term relationship. ('Let's face it,' his ex had said when they'd met for a drink on the day their divorce papers went through, 'neither of us are cut out for marriage.' She had been trying to be kind, but it had still stung.) But even though he had long ago learned that reality fell far short of the ideal of justice, at least he still loved the job. On his good days, anyway. He wasn't yet burned out. He still wanted to make things right by his dead, was still curious about people and this strange, old, vast and mostly empty planet.

The owner of the restaurant, Aarav Sreesanth, a fellow Brummie, hadn't seen David Parsons, either. Aarav had come up on the eighth shuttle, was married with six kids, ran a small fleet of carts that sold partha and curry in the city, and in this little restaurant served the best damn food on the planet. He and his family had roofed over most of the cells of the adjacent Boxbuilder ruins, lived in one half and rented rooms in the other.

Vic worked his way through a plate of thalassery biriyani, chappatis, sambar, and deep-fried banana chips, watched a plainswalker stump past the long tumble of rocks where the ridge ran out. It was a big one, car-sized, the sail turbines that crested its shell flashing in the level sunlight as it headed into the playa. Just another alien in a dry red world like Mars of the old sci-fi imaginings – which was why it had been given one of Mars's old names.

Mangala huddled so close to its small cool star that it should have become tidally locked, like Earth's moon. One half facing the star, permanently lit and scorching hot; the other permanently dark and frozen solid. But an age ago, five million years according to magnetic traces frozen in rocks, back in the Pliocene on Earth, before *Homo sapiens* had turned up on the scene, someone or something had spun up the world. An unimaginable and vast engineering project. Now it rotated in 3:2 resonance, so that a theoretical observer on the surface of its star would see it turn once every two orbital revolutions. One 31-day year in light; the next in darkness. And in the five million years since it had been spun up, dozens of Elder Cultures had lived here and died out or transcended or whatever. Layer upon layer of habitation. Mystery upon mystery.

Vic flicked through his notes about the murder on his phone. The case was exactly twenty-four hours old. They knew who the victim was, who he'd come here with and where they'd been staying. But the dead guy's friend was in the wind, and why they'd come to Mangala, who had sent them, who they'd gone to meet near the shuttle terminal, all of that was still unknown. He was pretty sure that both Danny Drury and Cal McBride were trying to hide something, but he couldn't put either of them at the scene with the ray gun in their hands, he couldn't figure out why they would be there, why they'd killed Redway and tried to kill, or maybe had killed, Parsons.

Most cases were either cracked quickly or went cold, their files growing fatter without yielding fresh revelations until at last they were copied into the vault, and the boxes of bloody clothing and DNA samples and all the rest were removed to the central store. Sometimes an old case was revived when new evidence turned up, or when a suspect in another case said something pertinent. Once, a woman had come into the squad room and asked to speak to a detective and confessed to the murder of a man who'd raped her five years before. But that was rare. Vic knew that if he and Skip didn't turn up something soon, John Redway would die all over again, become no more than a number and name in the cold-case index.

He called the boy detective. Skip hadn't had any luck either. 'You know what really bugs me about this thing?' he said. 'We have two suspects, but we don't have the first idea why Redway was killed.'

'You probably heard that there are all kinds of questions you need to ask about a murder,' Vic said. 'Who did it? How did they do it? Why? What was the victim's background and who did he know? Because most victims are killed by people they know. Man, there's no end to it when you get started. But the most important question, the one you need to focus on, is the first. Who did it? Everything else can be used by the prosecutor to make the case, but the first thing you have to do is find the doer. And then get them in the interrogation room, and break them down.'

'I do have a feeling about Drury,' Skip said.

'Arrogant son of a bitch, isn't he? But not as tough as he likes to think he is. McBride, on the other hand, is old school all the way. You bring guys like him in, you hand them a photo of them standing over the corpse with a smoking gun in their hand, you ask them if they did it—'

'And they deny it,' Skip said.

'And they say, "Get me my lawyer." Drury, though, isn't a street guy. And he definitely thinks he's smarter than us. You can usually get guys like him to talk. They love to hear the sound of their own voice.'

'He was happy to aim us at McBride, wasn't he?'

'There's definitely no love lost between those two,' Vic said.

'It could be,' Skip said, 'that Drury killed Redway with a weapon McBride is known to have used because he wants to put the murder on McBride. He wants McBride out of the way, he can't kill him because he works for McBride's family, so he frames him. Then again, McBride has a beef against Drury, because of losing his business and house and all that.'

'Like I said, there's no end to speculation about the why and the wherefore. Best to stick to what you know, Investigator Williams.'

But Vic thought that Skip might be on to something. Both Drury and McBride were in the frame, but only one of them had that ray gun . . .

Skip said that he was going to check out the last few places on his list, then head back to the UN building and write up the interviews with Drury and McBride. 'Will I see you there?'

'Don't wait up,' Vic said. 'I have one more call to make myself.'

17. Sea Devils

Jean Simmons, the owner of the bleak little caravan park at the edge of Martham, was a stick-thin woman with iron-grey hair and a face pinched by suspicion. The kind of person who was never disappointed when the world failed her, because it confirmed her expectations. She'd lost her farm when the sea level had risen, she told Henry Harris and Chloe, had bought the caravan park with the compensation money. 'More trouble than it's worth, most of the time. You see how I live.'

She perched on the edge of the sofa in the living room of her spartan bungalow, dressed in jeans and a wool check shirt, sipping at a hand-rolled cigarette. She couldn't remember much about her former tenants, she said. Sahar's wife had died before he and his children had come to Martham. Some sudden illness, very sad. Sahar had worked on the local shrimp farm.

'That's what we do here. Fish and farm shrimp. And there are the visitors, of course.'

Jean Simmons meant tourists, and the gangs of volunteers who were attempting to remove invasive species and rewild the flooded coast with native plants and animals. According to her, the Chauhans had lived at the caravan site for about a year, and then Sahar Chauhan had gone away. Jean Simmons said that she thought he had taken up a new job.

'That was three years ago,' Chloe said.

'I suppose.'

'I heard that he went up and out to Mangala.'

'I wouldn't know anything about that. Mr Chauhan mostly kept himself to himself.'

Chloe asked about the children. She had changed out of the borrowed trouser suit, was wearing what she thought of as her Official Interviewing Outfit: black jeans, a thin charcoal turtleneck sweater from Muji, flat-heeled shoes. She hadn't put on her spex: Jean Simmons was spooked enough as it was.

'They stayed on,' the woman said.

'In Martham?'

'Not here. With friends.'

Henry said, 'Could we have the names of the friends? Their address?'

Jean Simmons shrugged again. 'I wouldn't know. None of my business.'

Chloe didn't challenge the obvious lie. If she backed the woman into a corner she'd most likely clam up completely. 'When I met Fahad, he was living in London. Do you know when he and his sister left? And why they left?'

'Well, I know they left. But I'm not sure when. I suppose I last saw them around Easter.'

Chloe asked if Fahad had shown any sign of artistic ability while he was living in the caravan park. 'Did he like to draw or paint? When he moved out did he leave any pictures behind?'

'Pictures? No, nothing like that. He did odd jobs for me. Cleaned the toilet block, the caravans after people moved out. You should see the mess some of them leave. Worse than animals. He did a stint on the shrimp farm too, in the school holidays. There's not much money around here, and you have to work hard for it. Now I think I've told you all I know,' Jean Simmons said. 'And I need to get on. My sister's faring badly. I have to organise a bite of supper for her.'

Outside, in the warm windy sunlight, Henry said, 'She didn't know why the father left? She didn't know who was taking care of his children? Bullshit. She's exactly the kind of landlady who pokes around her tenants' belongings when they're out. I had one like her when I was a student.'

'I think she was spooked because you let her think you were a policeman.'

'It got us through the door. I'm wondering about that shrimp farm where the father was supposed to be working.'

'You think the owners took in his children?'

'There's that. But I'm also wondering what it might be growing besides shrimp.'

'Drugs,' Chloe said, and thought of Chief Inspector Nevers.

'Shine, or something else. Drugs are the only way to make real money out here. Drugs and smuggling. Sahar lost his job in the pharmaceutical industry, he had gambling debts . . . '

Chloe saw a movement at one of the blinds that shuttered the windows of the bungalow. 'She's watching us.'

'Probably while phoning whoever it is she doesn't want us to know about. We should definitely pay a visit to this shrimp farm.'

'I'd like to check the school. I can do that while you go off on your Scooby-Doo quest for evil drug farmers.'

'Where you go, I go.'

'We're on an island, Henry. I'm not going anywhere you can't find me. And I really think I should visit the school on my own.'

'Why? Are you worried I might scare the kids?'

'I'm worried you might scare the teachers.'

The headmistress of the town's little primary school confirmed that Rana Chauhan had been a pupil there until early in May, but refused to tell Chloe who had been taking care of her and her brother. 'I have a duty of confidentiality towards my children.'

Chloe said that she understood, asked if Rana had shown any unusual artistic ability.

'No more than any of the others,' the headmistress said.

Chloe fired up her tablet and paged through Fahad Chauhan's pictures, asked the woman if any of her pupils had produced something similar.

The headmistress's gaze shuttered. 'I'm sure I would remember if they had,' she said, and that was that.

There were examples of children's art posted on the walls of the reception area of the school. Amongst the naive depictions of nuclear families in front of two-dimensional houses, lopsided cows and horses, ships perched on the sea's horizon and superheroes riding blue skies, were drawings of Jackaroo avatars and scenes of other worlds. None of them resembled Fahad's red desert and latticework spires.

126

The village pub where Chloe and Henry Harris had rented rooms was a functional brick building built sometime around the middle of the last century. Henry had paid in advance, with notes peeled off a small tight roll. 'I like to pay cash for everything on a job,' he'd said. 'As far as I know, it's still untraceable.'

There was no sign of him when Chloe returned. She told herself that it didn't matter, but had an edgy feeling that she was losing control, that he wanted to push the investigation in the wrong direction. Away from Fahad Chauhan's pictures, into some mundane conspiracy involving the drug trade.

Her room had a view of the town's little harbour: a clutter of boats and yachts, the open sea stretching beyond the sea wall. A glimmering of stars in the darkening summer sky. A warm breeze fluttering the net curtains. She was leaning at the open window, breathing the fresh salt air and trying to convince herself that even if this didn't pan out she'd made the right decision to escape London and the fallout from the select committee and the assassination, when someone rapped on the door.

It was Henry Harris. Chloe told him that she hadn't had any luck at the school, asked him about the shrimp farm.

'As far as I could tell, it was just a shrimp farm. No locked sheds, no goons with bad attitudes. And the owner was very eager to tell me that he didn't know who had taken in the Chauhan kids after their father left.'

'Reading from the same script as Jean Simmons.'

'Classic small-town mindset,' Henry said. 'Everyone knows everyone else's business, but no one will talk about it with outsiders. Except, lucky old me, I come back here and just happen to meet someone who's more than happy to talk.'

'"Just happened" as in it was no kind of accident?'

'I'm pleased to see that Daniel doesn't employ stupid people. Want to meet my new friend? He's waiting downstairs.'

He was standing at the bar: Jack Baines, a burly middle-aged man with a wind-burned complexion and thinning blond hair.

Saying, after Chloe had been introduced to him, 'I was telling Henry about the sea devils.'

'It's a nice little story,' Henry Harris said. 'Let me buy you a drink, Jack, and you can tell Chloe all about it.'

The pub was the kind of place where a cluster of locals clung to the bar like barnacles while tides of visitors washed in and out. At the long table by the big bay window that overlooked the harbour a group of people in expensive casual clothes were making more noise than anyone else in the place. One of them, a man in a candy-striped shirt, was smoking a fat cigar. Several of the people at the bar were smoking too.

'Visitors like to cruise the Flood,' Baines said, when he noticed Chloe staring at the noisy group. 'It's a thing. Ruin porn and suchlike.'

'There are a couple of tasty yachts in the harbour,' Henry said. 'And a motor cruiser as big as a house.'

'They come and go,' Baines said, 'but they don't see what's really going on.'

'Sea devils, for instance,' Henry said.

'Visitors from foreign parts think this is a backwater,' Baines said. 'Ruins, a few fishermen. But you'd be surprised at what goes on out here. Lights in the marshes, UFO sightings, tracks of strange animals . . . Three porpoises beached themselves last week, and several of my fishermen pals have glimpsed something out at sea. A very big sea serpent by all accounts. Maybe an alien beasty, maybe a new kind of machine. We're a regular Area 51, we are. And because my work takes me all over the marshes, I see more than most.'

Chloe had met a lot of people like Jack Baines. They had all kinds of stories, plenty of inside information they'd disclose if the price was right. She saw him spinning tall tales to wide-eyed tourists, and was pretty sure why he'd glommed onto Henry Harris. She wondered why Henry thought him worth even two minutes of their time.

'Jack knows of a couple of women who were visited by devils,' Henry said.

'Sea devils,' Jack Baines said. 'Thing is, like I told Henry, the women who saw them are friends of Sahar Chauhan. Took in his kids after he left, as a matter of fact.'

Chloe looked at Henry, who gave a little shrug. She said, 'Do you know why the kids ran off?'

'From what I heard, Fahad got it into his head to follow his father,' Baines said. According to him, Fahad and Rana had stayed in Martham, living with two unmarried sisters, after their father had gone off to work on one of the Jackaroo worlds. 'Fahad always was a bit of a loner. Given to bunking off school and such. And then one day he took his little sister out of school and stole a boat that later turned up at Acle. No sign of the two kids then or since, until you come here, saying they're in trouble in London.'

'They're not exactly in trouble,' Chloe said, and gave her explanation, well-honed by now, about Disruption Theory and its work, and why it was interested in Fahad's pictures. 'I'm here to do some background research. I'd very much like to talk to the women who took in Fahad and Rana after their father left.'

'It's interesting, you mentioning the boy's pictures,' Baines said. 'One of them was young Fahad's art teacher, in the Catholic school over in Acle.'

Chloe said, 'And she sees ghosts.'

'Her and her sister. I'll be happy to take you over to talk to them.'

'It's a good lead,' Henry said, smiling at Chloe, daring her to contradict him.

Chloe said, going along with it, 'Do they live here, these two women?'

'Not in town as such,' Baines said. 'Not far away, though.'

'Jack has an airboat,' Henry said. 'He'll take us tomorrow, for a small fee.'

'Just my usual guiding rates,' Baines said. 'I take visitors out into the marsh. We get a lot of birders.'

After the man had left, Chloe said, 'You realise he's a total fraud.'

'But it's a good story, isn't it?' Henry was studying the menu chalked on the blackboard over the open fireplace. 'I reckon the fish must be fresh.'

'I'll have a salad. And you can tell me what this is really about.'

'They don't grow much in the way of vegetables out here. The rise in sea level has poisoned the water table. Everything has to be brought over from the mainland. But fish, that has to be fresh caught. Although fish have faces, and you can't eat anything with a face, can you? How about shrimp? Do they have faces? I don't think so. Not what we'd call faces, anyway. Or scallops, or mussels. Is it true that the Jackaroo are like giant walking shrimp?'

Chloe said, 'You're thinking of the !Cha. Although whatever's in their tanks probably isn't especially shrimp-like. We're being set up for something, aren't we?'

'The art teacher – that was a nice touch. We've definitely attracted someone's attention. They know we're interested in Sahar Chauhan's kids. They know we're not police, and they want to find out exactly who we are, and what we want. Hence Mr Baines.'

'Who is going to take us out of town tomorrow, but not to a couple of women troubled by sea devils.'

'There you go.' Henry raised his hand to get the barmaid's attention.

Chloe said, 'What have you got us into?'

'I intend to find out.'

18. Blue Fairy

Mangala | 25 July

Vic cruised the irregular blocks and alleys of Junktown, eventually spotting the guy he was looking for and pulling over and honking the horn. Rolling down his window as the man ambled up, saying, 'Hey, Dodger. What do you know, what do you say?'

'Let me sit in the back, Mr Gayle. I can't be seen talking to you here.'

Roger 'Dodger' Day was one of Vic's confidential informants, a long-term meq addict with a shock of grey dreadlocks and the gentle shambling manner of an absent-minded academic. He sprawled low in the back seat while Vic drove to a nearby industrial estate. Although Vic kept the window rolled down, Dodger's funky odour of sweat and woodsmoke and the tang of burnt metal filled the car.

Vic bought him a cup of coffee and two doughnuts at a cart, and they sat in the car and talked about Cal McBride and Danny Drury and the ray-gun murders. Roger said that the McBride crew were up and working again, although they were buying their shit from another crew.

'They cut it down to almost nothing,' Dodger said. 'But they work late at night, when most other crews are off the streets. If someone needs a hit, and that's all there is . . .'

'So they still don't have a cook.'

Dodger shrugged. He had eaten the first doughnut in two big bites and was licking powdered sugar from his fingers. His nails were crested with black; his palms were like tanned leather.

'After what happened to the last one I suppose it's been tough, finding a willing replacement,' Vic said. 'You heard how he was killed?'

Dodger shrugged again, took a bite from his second doughnut.

'He was nailed to a wall, and then he was shot in the head,' Vic said. 'Maybe you could ask around, find out if anyone on the street has been talking about it. Was he killed by Drury because he wanted to quit? Or was he killed by McBride, to fuck up Drury's meq business?'

The idea had come to him while he'd been talking to Skip: the man who'd killed the cook probably didn't have the ray gun that killed Redway. McBride would have used it on the cook to send a message to Drury; Drury would have used it to put the murder on McBride. Find who'd done the one murder, you'd know who was up for the other.

He said, 'I'm also wondering how this new man, Drury, has been enforcing his crews. Has he been dumping bodies we don't know about?'

Dodger thumbed the last of the second doughnut into his mouth. A rime of powdered sugar clung to his beard. 'Are you short of work, Mr Gayle?'

'Is that supposed to be a joke, Dodger?'

Dodger shrugged.

Vic said, 'How much is his crew charging for a bag of their weak shit?'

Dodger hesitated. 'Twenty. Around that.'

Vic stared at him.

Dodger looked away, looked back. 'Sometimes they go as low as ten.'

Vic held out a twenty-euro note. 'Hang out on one of their corners, pick up any chatter. Anything about the way Drury runs his crews. Does he show up at the corners himself or does he have someone else do it? Who did he get rid of when he took over from McBride, and where were the bodies dumped? Does he have a beef with any drug crews, and especially, does he have a beef with McBride? And see what you can find out about that poor dead cook, too. It's a sorry day when we can't make someone answer for something like that.'

'That's a lot of work for twenty, Mr Gayle. Especially if I'm supposed to use it to buy their weak shit.'

'I'll come find you in a day or so. If you have something new and interesting to tell me, you'll be handsomely rewarded. You need a lift back?'

'I'll walk.' Dodger paused, then added, 'Can I show you something?'

'I didn't have you down as a weenie wagger, Dodger.'

'This is serious shit, Mr Gayle,' Dodger said. He cupped his hands together, studied them with a frown of concentration. After a moment something flickered there. A blue flame, elongating into a spiral that turned on its axis.

Vic stared at it. 'That's a neat trick.'

'You can see it,' Dodger said, with obvious relief. Points of light were reflected in his eyes. 'I call it the blue fairy. It started a couple of days ago. I wondered if it was just meq heads who could see it. I don't know anyone straight. Except the corner boys, and you can't ask them anything. But if you can see it, I guess it's real . . .'

The spiral flame was about five centimetres high now, slowly turning. More detail resolved as Vic stared at it, sinuous waves running along the edges of its turns, ghostly lines multiplying out into the air.

Dodger opened his palms and the flame vanished. Vic blinked away after-images and said, 'Can any of your friends do tricks like that?'

'If they can, they didn't show me. But I've been doing meq longer than anyone else I know,' Dodger said, 'so maybe it's just a matter of time.'

19. Avatar

A sea mist had rolled in overnight. It softened the edges of every-thing, thickened into a white wall above low waves that collapsed in foaming fans on the beach where Chloe walked, barefoot on rippled sand. The beach fading into the mist ahead of her, a chain of footprints lengthening behind her. No one else about apart from a couple of dog-walkers and a woman in a white tracksuit ghosting out of the mist, passing Chloe, ghosting away.

It was unreasonably early, a little past six, but Chloe had lain awake a long time thinking about Jack Baines and the trap that she and Henry Harris had chosen to walk into. And when she did sink into sleep she was trying to find her way through narrow crowded streets, searching for her mother. A sense of unbearable urgency, of the air thickening and walls closing in. She'd woken with a start, the dream's anxiety clinging to her like tar. The first dream about her mother in a long time. On edge, old fears stirring in her blood, she'd pulled on her clothes and gone out into the cold misty morning and the clean smell of the sea to clear her head.

Now she saw a shadow moving through the mist that hung over the sea. Someone wading through breaking waves towards her.

Wait. It wasn't a person.

A chill clamped her from head to foot. It was as if a tiger or a unicorn had emerged from this ordinary English daybreak.

The Jackaroo avatar sloshed through receding drifts of foam and walked up the wet sand and stopped a couple of metres from Chloe. It was naked, its skin golden. Male but unsexed. Its eyes were white shells in a gold mask. Its mouth formed a smile and the smile parted and moved.

'Pardon the intrusion. But I did not get the chance to thank you properly.'

Chloe swallowed what felt like a stone. 'You're Bob Smith?'

The avatar bowed low, so smoothly and elegantly that it did not seem at all like mockery.

Chloe said, 'What I did . . . It was too little, too late.'

'It was the thought that counted. The gesture. The symbolism. One of the things we like about you is that you risk your lives for those not of your species. It gives us great hope. And besides, as you can see, I have risen again. You cannot destroy the message by burning the paper on which it is written, although I understand why the attempt was made. An example of your bicameral nature. Love and hate. Phobia and agape. All that jazz. You're afraid, but you are also fascinated. You wonder if I came here simply to thank you. Well, I did want to thank you, but I also wanted to warn you. To tell you that you stand at a place where small actions may have large and unintended consequences.'

'. . . This is a warning?'

'Call it a heads-up. A pause in the game while you receive suggestions about your quest, or are rewarded with extra hit points. Is that a good metaphor? Does it help? Oh, but you're still confused. Listen: I'm not going to tell you what to do. We cannot make decisions for you. We came to help, but we do not want to interfere. We gave you a gift, yours to do with as you will. But you've heard all that before. We're happy to talk. To answer questions about why we don't stop war and suffering, cure cancer, end poverty, point the way to heaven or point out that there is no heaven. Ask us anything. We don't mind. We try our best to be candid, but there is an inevitable degree of mutual incomprehension. Because your qualia aren't our qualia. Because we're running models of who you think you are and what you think you know, but they're just models. Because the map isn't the territory. Because we aren't gods. We aren't even close. You know? At best, we're pipers at the gates of dawn. Who have come to this little blue planet to help. Just that. But there are others here, with their own agenda. Be careful of them.'

Be careful of who? Chloe started to say, but the avatar was leaving.

It didn't turn and walk away, walk back to the sea. It simply thinned. Quietly and without any fuss dissolved into the misty air. Its smile and the white stones of its eyes were the last to vanish. If not for its waterlogged footprints in the wet sand, Chloe might have dreamed it.

20 · The Leshy

Mangala | 26 July

Skip was late coming in the next day, entering the busy lobby of the UN building just as Vic was heading out. The boy detective was carrying a cardboard tray loaded with pastries and two go-cups from the food van in the building's car park, saying, 'I was doing a follow-up—'

'We can walk and talk,' Vic said. 'Start by asking me where we're going.'

'So where are we going?'

'To the aftermath of a perfect example of the mindless violence we usually have to deal with. You can tell me about your freelance Sherlock Holmes shit on the way there.'

'Matter of fact, I was doing some follow-up work,' Skip said. 'On my own time.'

'You know that you should check with me before you so much as fart, what with being on probation and all. And I know you know, because of that guilty little peace offering you're carrying. You drive. I want to enjoy this coffee while it's still hot.'

As Skip drove, Vic told him that he'd asked one of his CIs to find out what he could about Drury's drug business. He didn't mention his idea that the person who'd killed that meq cook probably didn't own the ray gun, and vice versa. It was the kind of long shot that only looked good if it came off. 'Any dirt he digs up, we can use against the man,' he said.

'Okay.'

'This is good shit, paid for out of my own pocket, and all you can say is okay? That follow-up work of yours had better be pure gold, Investigator Williams.'

Skip explained that he'd ticked off the rest of the motels on his list, no luck there, and had done a little research on McBride's girlfriend. 'Eva Winkler, Austrian, came up two years ago. An accountant, started to work for McBride's company a month ago.'

'He's a fast worker, our Mr McBride.'

'She's also thirty years younger than him, and a good twenty centimetres taller,' Skip said. 'She seems straight. A civilian. Should be easy to talk to.'

'If it comes to it.'

'Right. Of course. I also looked into McBride's business affairs,' Skip said. 'First off, his old company, the one Drury took over, had a piece of the construction work on the Petra Carlton. Actually, it has a piece of every construction project, because it has a piece of the construction workers' union. McBride has been using that suite without paying a cent ever since the place was open for business. So I reckon he still has some kind of influence with the management, which may explain the collective bad memory of the restaurant staff.'

'McBride paid them off.'

'Or threatened them.'

'But you can't prove it.'

'I sort of wondered if this had anything to do with Elder Culture artefacts. Drury was getting ready for some kind of expedition. And McBride mentioned an interest in the artefact business. So I did a bit of checking,' Skip said. 'It turns out that while McBride was still in charge of it, Sky Edge Holdings took out three licences to excavate Elder Culture sites. Standard two-year jobs; the last expired while he was in jail. But it's possible, isn't it, that he's still digging stuff up, and trying to smuggle it out illegally.'

'Like in the sting that put him away? That's not a bad idea,' Vic said. 'But how does it tie in with Redway?'

'Maybe Drury and McBride are fighting over some valuable Elder Culture stuff. One wants to smuggle it out, brought Redway and Parsons to help. The other lured them into an ambush out by the terminal.'

'You're speculating again, Investigator Williams. Still, you might want to pull copies of those licences. Find out where the sites are. There should be details of any finds, too. Licence holders are supposed to declare them.'

'I also checked with vehicle records. Sky Edge Holdings owns several white vans. Maybe we could take a look at them. Check for vegetation or dirt from the scene that got caught in the tyres and bodywork.'

'Dirt is dirt, and there's nothing special about the vegetation. And I can guarantee that you won't get a warrant to inspect those vans because – once again – all you have is speculation.'

'You're telling me I've been wasting my time.'

'You're the primary on this case,' Vic said. 'And it's bugging you because it isn't a free shot at the goal mouth. I get that. If I were you, it would be bugging me too. But you need to cultivate patience, youngling. And you need to listen to my words of wisdom, because as far as you are concerned, I am Obi-Wan fucking Kenobi. Okay?'

Skip was quiet, driving, digesting this. Eventually, he said, 'I guess your advice would be to concentrate on the search for Parsons.'

'Right now, we have a good old-fashioned murder to deal with. And this one, we know who did it.'

They drove to the bar in Junktown, a wooden shack pinched between two newer three-storey buildings clad in native red stone. A patrol car was parked outside, its light bar flashing. The senior of the two uniforms, Sergeant Karen Jørgensen, gave them the low-down.

A pair of tomb robbers had fallen out, and one had stabbed the other in the heart. The doer hadn't run off: he was too drunk. The bar owner had called the police and given him another sinker, a shot of red whisky dropped into half a litre of beer. Karen Jørgensen had found him hunched over it at the bar.

'He was crying,' she said. 'He said that he did not mean to do it, but his leshy made him.'

Skip said, 'His leshy?'

'Like a kind of woodland spirit,' Jørgensen said. 'He says that he picked it up in the necropolis up in the Holland Hills. Ever since then, it has been at his back. He calls it Vlad.'

139

Vic smiled. 'Like Vlad the Impaler?'

'That he did not say,' Jørgensen said, straight-faced.

'And what's his name? The doer.'

'Martin Benešová.'

'What's that? Polish?'

'Czech.'

'Any witnesses? Or were they all suddenly and inexplicably answering the call of nature when it happened?'

'We are holding three people. Plus the owner. She volunteered a statement.'

'We'll talk to her, but first we'll talk to Martin. He speaks English?'

'More or less. Although I should warn you, he is still drunk.'

Martin Benešová was in the back of Jørgensen's patrol car, a whip-thin white guy, bare-chested in a denim jacket and filthy jeans. Looking wall-eyed at Vic when he opened the door and squatted down, Skip standing behind him.

Vic said, 'So what's this all about, Martin?'

'Karlus said he don't want to work with me no more. On account of Vlad. Karlus don't like him, don't want anything to do with him. So Vlad, he stabbed him.'

'How did he do that?'

'He use my arm.'

'Let me get this straight, Martin. You're saying your fairy-tale friend did it?'

'My what?'

'Your leshy.'

'He protect me.'

'Is Vlad here now, Martin?'

'He always is here. I drink, it mostly shut him up. But this time I don't drink enough,' Martin Benešová said, and hung his head and started to cry.

Vic and Skip talked to the owner of the bar, a forthright woman who said that she hadn't seen Martin Benešová before. He had been drinking quietly and steadily when his friend had walked in, she said. They'd got into an argument, and Martin Benešová had raised up and stabbed him.

140

By this time the crime-scene techs had turned up and confirmed that it looked like the dead man had been killed by a single knife thrust.

'I don't see how you boys can tell,' Vic said, 'what with the knife still in his chest.'

They would have to wait until Martin Benešová blew clean on the breathalyser before they could take his statement. Vic told Skip that he would ride back to the UN building in the patrol car with their suspect. Skip, he suggested, could usefully spend the rest of the day looking for David Parsons in Junktown.

'There are all kinds of unlicensed hostels, rooming houses and the like around here,' Vic said. 'If you don't know where to start, give Rita Smith over in Vice a call. She'll know some good spots.'

Skip said that he knew of a few from his foot-patrol days.

'Well then, start there. If the people know and trust you, they might point you in the right direction. Don't try to bribe them. They'll take your money and lie. Find a violation and promise to overlook it as long as they cooperate.'

Back at the UN building, Vic secured Martin Benešová in the holding pen and found that the man's dead friend had recently been released on probation after doing time, working on one of the city farms, for assault. A quick call to the probation office established that he didn't have a wife, husband, or partner: there'd be no need for a death knock. Vic wrote it up, then buttonholed Jerzy Buzek about the murdered meq cook. Jerzy, an amiable young guy, said that it was currently on the back-burner. Forensics hadn't turned up anything useful, suggesting it was a professional hit, and although Jerzy had a very strong feeling that it had something to do with internal discipline in Drury's crew he hadn't been able to get anyone to talk about it.

'Did you talk to Drury?'

'I don't have enough to bring him in yet. But sooner or later one of his crew will come in with some serious shit hanging over them, and maybe I can use that as leverage to get some information. There had to be at least three people involved. Two to hold him up while the other nail-gunned him to the wall. And there were marks on the floor,' Jerzy said, 'suggesting a tripod.'

'They videoed it? That's sick, man.'

'As I said, a professional job. *Pour encourager les autres*, as the captain would say.'

'Who owned the apartment buildings?'

'Prometheus Developments. They're clean, no link to Drury.'

'How about to Cal McBride?' Vic said, and explained about the Redway murder and the ray-gun connection.

Jerzy thanked him for the heads-up, said that he'd let Vic know if he turned up anything else. Vic was back at his desk, working on papers for a case that was due to go to trial the next day, when Skip called him.

'We need to run over to the shuttle terminal. I reckon I know why Redway and Parsons were out there that night.'

21. Unexpected Guest

Norfolk | 9 July

Chloe decided at once that she wouldn't tell Henry Harris about her encounter with Bob Smith. She needed to process it, work out what it meant. It wasn't every day that you had a personal visit from a Jackaroo avatar. It was something you definitely had to pay attention to. Crazy and frightening and deeply significant. But of what?

There was no point, she thought, trying to work out why the avatar had chosen to speak to her. Why it had chosen to intervene. It would be easier to get inside the mind of a lion. But the avatar seemed to think that she was at the centre of something it considered to be important or dangerous, and it had given her a clear warning. Be careful about other people, with their own agenda. Whatever that agenda was. Whoever those others were. The Hazard Police? Fahad Chauhan, and the algorithm or eidolon that had affected him? Henry Harris and Ada Morange? No, until she'd figured that out, she'd keep the visitation secret. Keep it close to her heart.

When she found Henry in the pub, working his way through a Full English breakfast, he had news of his own. He pushed his phone towards her, said, 'Read this.'

It was a brief article on the *Guardian* website about the quarantine of employees of Disruption Theory after several of them had begun to display symptoms possibly associated with exposure to alien nanotechnology. It mentioned her name, said that she was being sought by the Hazard Police. A link led to another piece. It seemed that the man who had attacked the Jackaroo avatar, Richard Lyonds, had been a long-time user of the Last Five Minutes wiki;

there was speculation that he and Chloe could have communicated via its message boards. A police spokesperson appealed for her to come forward so that they could eliminate her from their inquiries.

Chloe read this with an airy feeling of falling. She said, 'This is total bullshit. All of it. The only connection I have with Lyonds is the pitcher of water I threw over him. No one has ever been infected by the avatars, and what about the other people in the room? Have they been quarantined? I bet they haven't.'

But she remembered Ram Varma snapping on vinyl gloves before scooping up those fragments.

'Classic stitch-up,' Henry said, and forked a section of sausage into his mouth. 'Your firm's website is 404'd, by the way.'

'Adam Nevers,' Chloe said. 'He threatened to take us down. And now he has.'

'Looks like it, doesn't it?' Henry said. 'He wants to contain this thing. Which is what the Hazard Police do. Locate a problem, assess the situation, isolate the people involved. The question is, what does he think he's trying to contain?'

'Boys' games,' Chloe said. 'Played by people who hate the idea of losing control, hate the idea that ordinary people might find some use for alien technologies. Who think they can control a universal principle by slapping a D-notice on it and arresting bystanders.'

'I don't disagree with you.'

'Nevers will be looking for Fahad, too.'

'And we'll do our best to make sure he doesn't succeed,' Henry said. 'We'll take care of your friends, too. The Prof has good lawyers. They'll be out before we get back to London.'

'And what about me?'

She was like Patient Zero, Chloe thought. Spreading contagion wherever she went.

'We'll look after you, too. You and the kid. We're on the same side, Chloe. We both want to do the right thing by him.'

'Whatever that is,' Chloe said, wondering what Ada Morange's idea of the right thing could be, seeing a teenage kid strapped to a table surrounded by machines, probes and whatnot, men and women in white coats telling him it wouldn't hurt, taking notes as he writhed under strange lightnings . . .

'Whatever it takes,' Henry said, giving her that bland unreadable stare. 'You look pale. Finding out that you're wanted by the police is never the best way to start the day. Eat something. Have a nip of brandy if you need it. We've a long day ahead of us. Unless you'd rather sit it out. If you do, I'll understand.'

'I'm ready,' Chloe said.

'Attagirl.'

The slice of wholewheat toast that Chloe had nibbled while Henry packed away his Full English sat like a cannonball under her ribs as they walked past motor cruisers and sail boats, past a beautiful old two-masted yacht with oiled teak decking and brass portholes. Her messenger bag was slung over her shoulder; she was dressed in her sweater and black jeans, and a hooded jacket her ex had given her two birthdays ago, currently blotched grey and white by the biomimetic camouflage baked into its Tyvek/nylon fabric.

Sea mist muffled the little harbour, the little town. Crab cages stacked waist-high, orange nets draped on racks, neat coils of rope. Small boats gently rocking on the rising tide. Oyster boats, crab boats . . .

Chloe's heart gave a kick when Jack Baines hailed them. His airboat floated toylike between two fishing boats, a rectangular skiff with a tall fan in a cage at the rear, the pilot's seat raised above a bench for passengers, big halogen spotlights either side of it.

'Nice ride,' Henry said.

Baines said that he'd built it himself. It had a hull of smart plastic with a retractable keel that could fold flat for navigating shallow channels in the marshes, had originally been powered by a supercharged 6.2 litre engine and high-octane petrol boosted with a home-made nitro mix, but he'd swapped in an electric motor and a pair of LEAF batteries a couple of years ago and hadn't looked back.

'Longer range, higher speed, and very much quieter. The low profile means that it hardly raises a blip on radar, which is exactly what I need for my sneakier errands. Although if I ever rebuild her, I'll go with a fan made from that fullerene composite they use on the new jet planes. Then she won't show at all.'

He seemed slightly wired, speaking fast, his gaze twitchy. He was wearing a heavy roll-neck pullover and oil-stained blue jeans; a peaked canvas cap was jammed over his blond hair. He said, 'We're just waiting for a pal I thought I'd bring along. He knows those two old girls better than me, can make introductions.'

'Why not?' Henry said. 'You know, I rode in one of these in the Florida Everglades. Years back, when I took my kids on a trip to Disney World. Before everything changed.' He smiled at Chloe. 'I bet you can't picture me with kids.'

'Actually, I'm having a hard time picturing you in Disney World,' Chloe said.

'Henry can be quite the sweetie,' someone else said. It was the woman in the white tracksuit, walking towards them out of the mist.

Baines said, 'Who's this?'

'An unexpected guest,' Henry Harris said. 'Sandra, meet Mr Jack Baines. Our tour guide for today. I wouldn't, Jack.'

Baines raised his hands chest-high, palms out. Because, Chloe saw with a little shock, Henry had produced his little revolver.

She said, 'I'd like to know who she is, too.'

'Sandra Hamilton,' the woman said. 'A colleague of Henry's. Pleased to meet you at last.'

Her blonde hair was pulled back in a tight ponytail. There was a Bluetooth earpiece plugged into her right ear. A long torch hung swordlike from the webbing belt buckled around her waist; a clunky yellow pistol – a taser – rode on her left hip.

'She's the coordinator of the infiltration crew,' Henry said.

'What crew? What else haven't you told me?' Chloe was wondering if the woman had been spying on her, at the beach. If she'd seen the Jackaroo avatar walking out of the sea . . .

Henry said, not unkindly, 'Did you really think this was all about you? Sandra and her boys will help us get this thing done with minimum fuss.'

Baines said, trying to sound cool, 'If your friend is interested in the sea devils, I'll take her along at no extra charge.'

'You know we aren't interested in your ghosts, Mr Baines,' Henry said. 'Did you really think I wouldn't check out you and your boss? Who won't, by the way, be joining us this morning.'

Baines said, 'I don't know what you mean.'

'There aren't any sisters. Or any sea devils, either,' Henry said. 'You and your boss were going to take us somewhere quiet so you could find out if we were working for a rival gang. Don't even bother to deny it. He told Sandra everything.'

'We should get going,' Sandra Hamilton said.

'Oh, that's right,' Henry said, still looking at Baines. 'We have people waiting for us out at the fort. Yes, we know about that too.'

'If you've hurt her—'

'We're business people, Mr Baines,' Sandra said. 'We're not interested in your criminal enterprise. As long as you cooperate with us there won't any blowback.'

Baines said, 'You're making a big mistake.'

Sandra ignored him, looked down at the airboat. 'Can you handle this, Henry?'

'I'll give it a go,' Henry said. 'Chloe, why don't you climb aboard and sit up front. You too, Mr Baines.'

Chloe felt angry and stupid and humiliated. Stung by Henry's remark that this wasn't all about her. She said, 'Suppose I don't want to go?'

'I think you do,' Sandra said, with a bright friendly smile. 'We need your opinion about something we found.'

22. In The Can

Mangala | 26 July

The shipping container, painted a light blue that reminded Vic of Earth's sky, sat in front of a short row of flat-roofed modular offices. The doors at its end were closed, with a crime-scene notice papered over the joint.

'Finn Bergmann spotted the broken seal,' the freight yard's security manager told Vic and Skip. 'After we looked inside, we hauled it out of the stacks, and your friends in drug enforcement took over. You ask me, it's a clear case of people-smuggling, but anything funny happens here, it's always drug enforcement comes in and causes me headaches.'

The manager, Barry Moon, was a short, barrel-chested English guy in his fifties, hair shaven to disguise his receding hairline, sleeves of his checked shirt rolled back from tattooed forearms, a high-vis vest in a fluorescent orange that left after-images, a white hard hat. Vic and Skip were wearing hard hats too, and temporary passes on lanyards around their necks. The vast yard bustled and clanged around them. Shipping containers were stacked five or six high in long rows, like Lego walls built by an inept giant. Ribbed steel boxes painted red oxide, painted white, painted yellow or blue. Familiar logos from a small blue planet twenty thousand light years across the Milky Way. Men and women shouting. Tall cranes rolling on rubber tyres straddled shipping containers, cans, and hoisted them effortlessly. Trucks beeped as they backed up to receive their loads. Little yellow forklifts scooted about, orange flashers whirling. A long low beast of a machine locked the cradle at the end of its hydraulic arm onto the top of a container and effortlessly hoisted it into the air.

Beyond the rows of shipping containers were stacks of construction materials, plastic-wrapped machinery on pallets, and neat grids of new cars and trucks that stretched towards the perimeter fence. The skyscraper bulk of the shuttle loomed above all of this, blocking out half the sky, hung in an invisible cradle created by manipulating space-time's sub-quantum foam or some such bullshit, using technology that had to be taken on trust because, like most of the Jackaroo's gifts, no one understood it. The shuttle had a human crew, and a human captain who was nominally in charge, although all she did, apart from dining with VIPs while the shuttle manoeuvred from Earth to the wormhole mouth fixed in L5 orbit and then drove in from the wormhole exit that orbited Mangala's star, was supervise the loading and unloading of passengers and cargo. The shuttles to the fifteen worlds arrived and departed on schedules fixed by the Jackaroo, and carried out their manoeuvres and transits without any human intervention.

Vehicles negotiated massive concrete access ramps that curved a hundred metres in the air to the big round door in the skin of the shuttle. Crawling in and out like ants busy around a nest. Vic remembered that he and the other passengers of the second shuttle flight had clambered down rope nets to the ground after the door had dilated, and had unloaded cargo using improvised cranes. Laborious, back-breaking work. Half of their stuff had still been aboard when the door had closed and without any fuss the shuttle had fallen away into the sky, leaving them lonely and bereft in their strange new world.

Barry Moon said, 'We unloaded over two hundred thousand metric tonnes of cargo this go-round. Including more than a thousand cans. Now we're loading stuff for export. Marble from Broken Hill, fresh vegetables and herbs from Idunn's Valley, sheets of reclaimed Boxbuilder shit, electronics from Mitsubishi's new factory, glacial ice from the polar edgelands. You name it. After the shutdown over Landing Day we're working 24/7 to catch up. Finn did good, spotting this one.'

Dust was blowing off the playa, skirling past the parked vehicles and skittering across concrete. Vic turned his back to the blustery wind, itchy and exasperated. As far as he was concerned, the day had gone to hell. On the way over, his ex had called him about those damn boxes in the garage; to get her off his back, Vic had to promise her, cross his heart and hope to die, that he'd come by for them on Saturday. Meanwhile, the boy detective had been bending his ear about the shipping container, believing this was another clue to be added to the unlikely structure of guesswork and conjecture he'd woven around his whodunnit. Now he was asking the security manager where Finn Bergmann, the Transport Police officer who'd spotted the broken Customs sticker, was at.

'He finished his shift and went home,' Barry Moon said. 'If you want a statement, you'll have to catch him there.'

'What kind of Mickey Mouse police do you have here, working to the clock when a crime's been discovered?' Vic said.

'By the time the drug enforcement people were done, it was a good four hours past the end of Finn's shift,' the security manager said. 'I should have finished for the day also, but I stuck around to help you.'

Vic slit the crime-scene notice with his pocket knife; the security manager cracked open the doors to reveal stacks of cardboard boxes containing TVs. Twenty or thirty had been removed to create a narrow passageway that ran back to a steel bulkhead. There was an oval door with a heavy-duty latching system. The long narrow space beyond was padded with quilted cotton and lit by clusters of bright LEDs. Three low, narrow couches were lined along one wall, black padding, straps, nylon privacy curtains. They reminded Vic of his journey on the shuttle, thirteen years ago. Rows of couches in a low-ceilinged compartment jerry-built from plywood and steel I-beams. The pressure of acceleration, as the huge craft had risen away from Earth. The stark reality of it. Some people crying. Some throwing up during a brief interval of free fall. Most, like Vic, lying still and quiet. He remembered that the woman on one side of his couch had been mumbling what might have been a prayer, eyes squeezed shut, hands tremblingly pressed together. The man on the other side had been plugged into his tablet, had stayed plugged in for most of the trip; Vic hadn't learned his name until they'd run into each other a year later.

The security manager was pointing out the air-conditioning plant, a microwave, plastic crates of freeze-dried army rations, a water-recycling set-up, a hi-tech toilet. It was hot and close in there, and it smelled about the way you would expect it to smell after three people had been living inside it for four days.

'This is a fifty-three-foot High Cube, the biggest can we use,' Barry Moon said. 'But it isn't my idea of luxury accommodation.'

Skip said, 'The shuttle's hold is pressurised, right? They could have got out, walked around.'

'Yeah, but it's freezing cold. Like forty below zero. The refrig units that transport perishables are warmer. Only the passenger accommodation is heated. And there are CCTV cameras so the crew can keep an eye on the cargo, make sure it doesn't shift. If I was riding this can, I would have stayed inside the whole trip.'

Vic said, 'Did you find any personal belongings?'

'Your friends took some stuff. Old clothes mostly. Whatever else they found, you should ask them. They took DNA samples from me and Finn, too. Like we were criminals.'

'That was just to eliminate any contamination,' Skip said.

'They downloaded video from the security cameras, too,' Barry Moon said.

'And I bet they won't find anything,' Vic said. 'Because it's a funny thing about all the cameras here, they never seem to see anything. Like the people in the Terminal Authority, they don't notice the clandestine shit that goes back with legitimate cargos.'

'That's Customs' department, not mine,' the security manager said.

'We're really only interested in these stowaways,' Skip told him, shooting a look at Vic. 'You've never had an incident like this before?'

'This is the first we found.'

Vic said, 'Are you certain? Because we're going to check the records anyway.'

'These people were loaded onto the shuttle at Earth,' Barry Moon said. 'You want to find out how they got on board without being detected, you should go back there.'

Outside, after Skip had soothed the security manager, as they were walking towards their cars, Vic told him that it was interesting, but he couldn't see any connection with Redway and Parsons.

'You have the two guys riding here on tickets,' Skip said. 'One is killed just outside the terminal. And now we find that three people smuggled themselves up here in a shipping container. On the same shuttle. So I reckon it would be a bit weird if there wasn't some kind of link. I should ask the guys in drug enforcement, see what they think.'

'Not much, probably,' Vic said. 'I mean, what crime has been committed here? I don't think we even have a statute about what I suppose you'd have to call illegal aliens. If anyone knows anything about this, it's that security manager, so-called.'

Skip said, 'You were riding that bloke pretty hard. What was that about?'

'The woman who had the job before him was involved with a gang smuggling vintage wines. She took bribes to look the other way. You think your friend Barry Moon doesn't know what's going on in his yard?'

'It doesn't mean he had anything to do with this. And he called it in.'

'The Mickey Mouse cop called it in. And I bet the people who rode inside that can knew this place is porous. Knew they had a good chance of getting through.'

'I'm wondering exactly how they got out,' Skip said. 'Was it through the gate, or through a hole in the fence? And who was waiting for them on the other side?'

Vic said, 'You want to hear my advice?'

'Do I have a choice?'

'No, you don't. My advice, make a note, stick it in the case file, move on. This is down to drug enforcement and Customs, and they won't thank you for trying to get inside their thing. But if you attach a note to the file, you're covered if there's any link to the murder. Meanwhile, you still have the friend of the dead guy in the wind. That's what you should be working. This foolishness, it's a distraction.'

'Even so, I have a feeling about it,' Skip said, meeting Vic's gaze with a stubborn look, a muscle knotted at the hinge of his jaw.

Later, Vic would think that this was the moment when he lost his authority. The moment he made an assertion that would quickly be proven wrong, and Skip decided that he knew better. Looking back, he wished he'd cut the kid more slack.

But all he said at the time was, 'Stick to what you know. Don't make up stories to cover what you don't.'

23. The Chapel

Norfolk | 9 July

The airboat was fast and surprisingly quiet, cutting through the mist that hung over the water, passing the headland of the island and a clutch of half-drowned roofless houses, entering a channel between stands of tall reeds. A maze of gravel shoals, mudbanks and salt marsh where there'd once been open water, created by shifts in tides and currents that had transported material eroded from the flooded margins of the coast and deposited it here.

Henry Harris perched in the chair in front of the airboat's fan, using a lever to steer the little craft. Sandra Hamilton, on the bench seat with Chloe and Jack Baines, called out directions to him and told Chloe about the drug business.

'It's a small-time operation. They grow Cthulhu's claw out here, process it at the shrimp farm, send it on to their bosses in London. We're going out to the centre of their plantations.'

It was an old sea fort, Sandra said, built in the Second World War to defend the east coast from German mine-laying aircraft. It had been decommissioned in the late 1950s, and sold to an eccentric property developer. He had rented it to a series of pirate radio stations in the 1960s and 70s, and later it had been used as a film set, the location for a reality TV programme, and a platform for servers of a website that enabled peer-to-peer sharing of every kind of data. After the death of its owner in the first decade of the new century the government had seized it in lieu of payment of inheritance tax; it was now rented to a group of Flemish nuns, *Les Recluses Missionaires*, a renegade contemplative order which had quit Belgium during the civil war.

There had been eight of them once; now there were only two, Sandra said. 'Or at least, that's what our friend would like the authorities to believe.'

Chloe said, 'Two sisters. You didn't look very far for your cover story, Mr Baines. Do they really see sea devils?'

Baines shrugged. He was hunched at one end of the bench, handcuffed to its handrest.

'Mr Baines and his wife are the caretakers of the sea fort,' Sandra said. 'But their real business is growing patches of Cthulhu's claw in various spots in the marsh.'

Baines started to say something, then thought better of it. Chloe felt a little sorry for him.

She said, 'Sahar Chauhan was their cook, wasn't he?'

Sandra said, 'He lost his wife, got a bad gambling habit, lost his job. The people who run the London end of this thing bought his debt and sent him out here to cook shine. Call it a kind of apprenticeship. He passed with flying colours, and was sent to Mangala. Probably to help out with their meq business. You can manufacture shine here, because Cthulhu's claw grows in saltwater marshes, but to synthesise meq you need fresh biochine blood and a skilled biochemist. Isn't that right, Mr Baines?'

'I didn't have anything to do with it,' Jack Baines said.

'Of course not,' Sandra said. 'You just grow a psychotropic alien plant, and smuggle cigarettes on the side.'

'Sahar must be a hell of a chemist,' Chloe said.

She remembered a TED talk that Daniel Rosenblaum had once given. He'd argued that human consciousness could be enlarged and transformed by alien drugs. Many users would be killed, yes, but evolution was neither kind nor cruel. Individual fates did not figure in it. According to Daniel, those who survived the new psychotrophs would become the first astronauts of a new kind of inner space, and their explorations would slowly but surely turn humanity into something beyond ordinary imagination. Chloe had never taken Daniel's ideas seriously. The man came up with this wicked mad stuff because he liked to provoke – liked being the maverick, the outsider, a wizard conjuring outrageous theories. If ideas about the Jackaroo and the Elder

155

Cultures don't seem crazy, he liked to say, they can't be right. But now she wondered if Fahad Chauhan's visionary pictures might have been inspired by something glimpsed when he'd used some kind of drug supplied by his father. Something new and even weirder than shine or meq. And she also wondered if she had become involved in a turf war between Sahar's employers and Ada Morange. It was not a good thought.

At last a shadow loomed out of the mist. Henry throttled back the fan and turned the airboat towards it. Chloe leaned forward on the bench seat, straining to see details as the shadow resolved into a rectangular platform supported by two fat, rust-stained concrete pillars. It stood at one end of a long mudbank crested with marram grass. Up on the platform, flat-roofed buildings huddled inside a low perimeter wall of raw breeze-block. Several wind turbines reared into the streaming mist, blades turning slowly.

The airboat nosed towards a landing stage at the foot of one of the pillars. Sandra jumped out and made the little craft secure; Henry told Jack Baines to be a good boy, and unlocked the hand-cuffs that fastened him to the bench.

Chloe was the last to climb the rusty ladder to the fort's plat-form. A man was waiting there, tall and young and alert, dressed in tunic and trousers in grey and white camo that matched her jacket. He was cradling a matte-black shotgun with a pistol grip and a wide bore: a riot gun that fired non-lethal beanbag rounds. Chloe had been shot by one once, years ago, when she had been part of a protest against building a shopping mall at the edge of the memorial zone in central London. It had hurt like hell, and the resulting bruise, across her hip and half her back, had been spectacular.

The young man, Leo Halifax, led them through a junkyard clutter of coiled steel hawsers, oil drums, packing crates and rusting machine parts, everything dripping wet in the mist, to the cluster of buildings. Prefabricated huts and shipping containers jammed together, raised on footings of crudely mortared concrete blocks, heavy tarpaulins lashed over flat roofs with spiderwebs of ropes.

A warped plywood door opened onto a square room with a floor of pale driftwood carefully fitted together and mortared with black tar. A second man in camo clothing was sitting on a kitchen chair, watching a screen tiled with windows that showed different views of the fort's platform and the misty marshland around it. As they crowded inside, he turned around and said, 'Nothing showing.'

'Any trouble getting in?' Henry said.

'Their security system was full of holes,' the man said. 'The drone took it down without breaking a sweat.'

A dumpy woman in her fifties sat on an old brass bed in the corner of the room, under a framed picture of the Virgin Mary rolling her eyes and clutching her chest like the 'before' picture of an antacid ad. The woman wore a moth-eaten cardigan and a headscarf; her sandals didn't quite touch the floor. A pectoral cross crudely welded from steel hung around her neck. For a moment, Chloe wondered if she was one of the nuns, then saw that her wrists were fastened with plastic strip. Jack Baines stepped towards her, asked if she was all right.

'You had to get involved,' she said. She had a heavy accent, German or Dutch or Flemish.

'And you had to tell them everything.'

'You expect me to keep quiet? This is not one of your stupid films.'

'Gert was very cooperative,' the first young man, Leo, said.

'Sit by your wife,' Henry told Jack Baines. 'We won't take up much more of your time.'

The man sat down slowly, staring at Henry with a mixture of unease and defiance; Henry, Sandra and the two young men held a brief conference, their backs turned to Chloe, who failed to not feel excluded.

On a desk made of a length of plywood and a couple of trestles, a big monitor was showing the ancient starfield screensaver, triggering a memory of her mother's study. For the longest time, she and Neil had kept the room as their mother had left it. Chloe had liked to sit in there, sometimes, when she couldn't sleep. A narrow fourth bedroom with a wooden clerk's desk and her mother's ancient desk computer under the window, a chaise longue with lumpy upholstery, two steel filing cabinets and shelves of books, posters for old exhibitions in cheap frames, hundreds of photos and clippings Blu-tacked to one wall. Neil sat in there sometimes, too. It was the guest bedroom now. Chloe and Neil had cleared it out over a hot summer's weekend a couple of months before he married. Had taken down the collage and packed the books and the old posters in plastic boxes they'd stacked in the roof space, loaded everything else into a hired van and taken it to the recycling centre. It had been liberating, actually. Not from their mother's memory, never that, but from the hopeless weight of their own past.

Chloe stepped over to the desk and moved the mouse. The screensaver vanished and the monitor filled with icons tiled over an image of Sylvester Stallone, bare-chested and toting an unfeasibly big gun.

'Don't touch that,' Jack Baines said.

Chloe smiled at him, said, 'You're a film fan. Me too.'

She totally didn't go for those old films full of explosions and macho posturing, but the first thing you did in an interview was try to establish some common ground. The ploy didn't work on Jack Baines, though. He ignored her, returned his attention to Henry Harris and the others, huddled in their private conflab.

Chloe studied the small tapestries hung on the wall over the desk: a sleeping cat, a dolphin caught in mid-leap, a starburst of lines stitched in different lengths and colours on black velvet. She said to the woman, 'Are these yours?'

The woman's gaze was dark and suspicious. 'What if they are?'

'Don't talk to her,' Jack Baines said. 'She's trying to play good cop.'

'I'm not a cop,' Chloe said.

'Oh really? Because I saw what you did, when that bloke knocked off that avatar.'

'Did you also see the police arresting me afterwards? I'm a civilian,' Chloe said. 'A researcher concerned about two missing kids. You were looking after them, I bet you're concerned about them too.'

'I'm concerned you lot want to use them like lab rats.'

The little huddle broke up. Henry dragged a chair across, sat close to Jack Baines and the woman. 'You're in a corner, Jack. You and your charming wife. Your bosses can't help you now. Only I can. So how about telling me why they are so keen to find the kid.'

'And if I don't, you'll what? Hurt me?'

'How about this. Tell me what I need to know, and I won't tell anyone about the nuns.'

'I don't know what you mean.'

Henry looked over at Sandra. She said, 'We used infra-red imaging to check out this place, Mr Baines. It showed your wife, no one else.'

Henry said, 'What happened to them, Jack?'

Baines looked at his wife. 'You told them, didn't you?'

'They already knew,' she said.

Henry said, 'Your wife claims that they died of natural causes: that you buried them in the marshes. I'm prepared to believe that if you cooperate. Look at me, Jack. Look at me so I can see if you're telling the truth. Why do your bosses want the kid?'

'She told you everything, I bet,' Baines said, staring at his wife, who stared right back.

'And now I want to hear the story from you,' Henry said. 'To see how your version tallies with your wife's. If they do, we'll let you get on with your lives. Such as they are. If not, we'll let the police know about those two poor holy women. And when your bosses find out you've been talking to the police . . .'

'It's nothing,' Gert Baines said.

'It means something to your bosses,' Henry said. 'That's why the kid ran away from this place, isn't it? And why he ran off again, when my friend Chloe found out about his pictures. So, and this is the last time I'll ask nicely, what does he have that your bosses want?'

'Don't say anything,' Baines told his wife.

'I already tell them,' she said. 'I tell them it is nothing. A worthless little trinket.'

'What kind of trinket?' Chloe said.

'Why don't you tell her, Jack?' Henry said.

'What's the point, if you already know?'

'The point is, I'll know if you and your wife are telling the truth.'

'It's just this little bead,' Baines said. 'Okay?'

'Where did she get this bead? And don't lie, because I'll know.'

'Her father sent it to her.'

'From Mangala.'

Baines nodded, a tight jerk of his head.

'What kind of bead? Describe it.'

'Small,' Baines said, holding this thumb and forefinger less than a centimetre apart. 'Sort of like green glass.'

'I've seen it,' Chloe said, remembering with a quick spark of excitement Rana Chauhan's bracelet.

Henry looked over at her, asked if she thought it could be the source of Fahad's inspiration.

'There are plenty of Elder Culture artefacts that look a little like stones or beads. Tesserae from tombs in the City of the Dead on First Foot and elsewhere. Sea glass from the factories on Yanos. Fragments of the shadow mosaics on Tian or Syurga . . .'

Chloe was remembering the red string and its green bead, remembering the little girl mentioning what might have been an imaginary friend or a favourite toy, might have been something else. *Ugly Chicken says she's nice.*

'And it might contain one of your alien ghosts.'

'An eidolon. Yes, why not?'

Henry thought about that for a moment, then turned back to Gert and Jack Baines and asked them how Sahar had managed to smuggle it back to Earth. Gert said that Sahar had bribed one of his fellow employees to post letters and presents to his son and daughter.

'So Sahar sent this Elder Culture bead,' Henry said. 'The kid, Fahad, started painting these pictures . . . What then?'

'You think you know everything,' Jack Baines said.

'I need you to tell me what happened.'

'Fuck you.'

Sandra said, 'You were looking after Fahad and Rana. Keeping them here.'

'So?'

'Be patient with me, Mr Baines. I'm trying to understand the situation.'

Gert Baines said, 'They couldn't go with their father. Too expensive. And anyway, the little girl, she was far too young.'

'Because no one under sixteen is allowed to go up and out,' Sandra said. 'But didn't they have family? Uncles, aunts, grandparents?'

'We were told to look after them,' Gert Baines said. 'Make sure they don't talk to people. So that's what we do.'

Henry said, 'They were kept as hostages.'

'We treat them good.'

'Too good,' Jack Baines said.

'Because they escaped,' Henry said. 'A couple of kids got the better of you.'

Baines shrugged.

Chloe said, 'You let the kids keep stuff that Sahar sent, didn't you? Letters and little presents and so on.'

Gert Baines said, 'Why not? We are not monsters. We do the right thing by these kids.'

Chloe said, 'And you didn't tell your bosses about it.'

Jack Baines said, 'Like Gert said, we did the right thing by them. Let them keep in contact with their old man.'

Henry, catching on, said, 'Out of the goodness of your heart? Bullshit. Sahar bribed someone to send this stuff, and he bribed you, too.'

'Sahar was my friend,' Baines said, looking offended. 'So I helped him out a little.'

Chloe said, 'He sent this bead. What else?'

Baines shrugged. 'Scraps, mostly. A pebble. Shards of some kind of plastic stuff. Something that looked a bit like a feather.'

Henry said, 'Is any of this stuff still around?'

'The kids took it all.'

'Or you sold it,' Henry said.

'Think what you like.'

'So why, if you were so nice to the kids, did they run off?'

'If you find them, you can ask them.'

Sandra said, 'We found the video clip, Mr Baines. We know what your bosses did to Sahar Chauhan.'

'Them up there aren't my bosses.'

161

'But they sent the clip to show you what happened to people who stepped out of line,' Henry said. 'Am I right? How did Sahar step out of line? Why was he killed?'

'Maybe you should ask his bosses.'

'Maybe I should tell the police about those two nuns,' Henry said.

Baines looked at his wife, who gave a fractional nod.

'Sahar was a good cook,' Baines said. 'The best. But there was a problem up there. His boss was put away on some bullshit charge. And meanwhile, Sahar was involved with these other people, smuggling things out. The stuff he sent the kids was only half the story. I think he was trying to earn enough to buy a ticket home. I don't know the details. But the guy that was sent up to sort things out found out about it. And yeah, I saw what happened to him, afterwards. I saw it and I deleted it.'

'You put it in your browser's recycling bin,' Sandra said. 'Not quite the same thing.'

Chloe felt something cold grip her from head to foot. She said, 'What did they do to him? To Sahar?'

Sandra hesitated. Henry said, 'They crucified him, basically. They nailed him to a wall and they shot him in the head. And they videoed it.'

Chloe looked at Jack and Gert Baines. 'When was Fahad's father killed?'

'About three months ago,' Sandra said. 'That's the date of the video, although it could have been altered. We can check it out more thoroughly when we get back.'

Chloe said, 'Fahad saw it. He saw it, and he realised that he might be in danger too, and he took off with his sister.'

Gert Baines said, 'The computer we have here, it is a piece of shit. The boy knows something about these things, and my husband is cheap, won't pay anyone to fix it. So he lets the boy. I told him, no. But he doesn't listen. And now look what happens. They steal our money and run away, and bring all this trouble on our heads.'

'I fucking deleted it,' her husband said.

Henry said, 'Dragging it to the recycling bin doesn't delete it. Even I know that. The kid found out about his father, didn't he,

162

and he ran away. Him and his little sister. Because they were scared they might be next.'

'We wouldn't have done anything,' Jack Baines said.

'Like you didn't do anything to those two nuns,' Henry said.

'We didn't tell anyone when they died, that's all. And fuck you for thinking otherwise.'

Baines's anger seemed genuine.

Henry said, 'Are your bosses looking for Fahad and Rana?'

'Why should they? Sahar's dead, they don't give a shit about two kids.'

'And they don't know about the Elder Culture stuff and Fahad's pictures because you didn't tell them. Because if you did, they'd know you'd been taking backhanders for delivering the mail.'

'You try to be nice,' Baines said. 'And look what it gets you.'

'Your idea of "nice" being to keep two kids prisoner,' Henry said.

'We fed and clothed them,' Gert Baines said. 'We made sure they went to school.'

'I hope you find them,' her husband said, with sudden force. 'You fucking deserve to find them. And good luck when you do. Because you're meddling in things you have no idea how bad they are.'

Henry said, 'Oh, we'll find them. Count on it. And we'll take better care of them than you and your charming wife.'

Sandra said, 'You've been very helpful, Mr and Mrs Baines. Chloe, I said there was something you needed to see. Henry, why don't you go with her while I wrap things up?'

The young man, Leo, led Chloe and Henry Harris through a kitchen and storage space fitted into a shipping container, down a narrow corridor walled with unpainted plywood.

'It would appear that each of the nuns had their own chapel,' Leo said, opening one of the doors at the end. 'They took Mass separately, never saw each other. Mad. There's a light switch here. Wait . . .'

A rack of fluorescent lights flickered on. The room was small, maybe three metres by two. There was a plain altar draped in white cloth with a crucified Christ hung over it and a kneeling stool in front. But that wasn't what Chloe saw at first. The walls of the little room were lined with wood panelling, and every square centimetre had been painted over. A diorama of red rocks and red sand and a dark blue sky wrapped around the room. Cliffs, distant hills. The orange splash of a fat sun high in one corner of the ceiling. And along one wall were the spires, throwing short shadows across a stretch of ground where grey vegetation coiled around boulders and shelves of rock.

Chloe stepped close to study the fretwork of the spires, their thorny projections. Something crouched at the very tip of one, a bag-like body and several ropy limbs knotted around a spar.

She could see brush marks. She could see dribbles of paint. She could see paint spatters. A thickness or rim of pinkish paint outlined the rocky horizon. Rough stippling suggested shadows. But when she stepped back the imperfections and blemishes and exposed technique blended into a totality that plucked a wire inside her.

Leo said, 'Gert Baines said that Fahad painted it just before he ran away. He used ordinary emulsion paint. The cans and brushes are over there, in the corner. Did it in two days, according to her. Barely ate, barely slept. It was like he was possessed, she said.'

'I need a record of this,' Chloe said.

'I'm already all over that,' Leo said. 'Used our drone to take a three-hundred-and-sixty-degree hi-def panorama.'

His camo suit had taken on the red tones of the painted land-scape; so had Chloe's jacket. As if they were both blushing.

Chloe thought of a severe old woman kneeling here, dressed in a habit and the kind of winged wimple that Belgian nuns wore in old films, surrounded by this wild alien beauty. An image with its own strangeness. Then she remembered that the two nuns were dead, buried somewhere out in the marshes.

'We have to tell the police about the nuns,' she said. 'I don't care what you promised Jack Baines. He and his wife might have killed them. And their families should know what happened to them.'

Henry and Leo exchanged glances. Henry said, 'We're operating in a semi-legal area right now. And Baines and his wife and their little down-home drug-growing thing are a side issue. The kid who did this,' he said, gesturing at the diorama that surrounded them, 'is in danger. He could end up like his father if we don't find him first.'

Leo said, 'Sandra said that you should see everything? There's stuff in the kids' bedroom, too.'

It was a small square room with a high window blinded by dried sea-salt. Bunk beds, a wardrobe with oak-finish veneer splitting from its MCF carcass, a musty odour of damp and mould. And plasterboard walls densely covered with black lines and loops from floor to ceiling. Even the door was covered. Chloe thought of the thorny scribbles in Fahad's tumblr, wondered if he had tried to reproduce the interior of one of his spires. Tried to imagine sleeping here . . .

There were drawings taped to the plasterboard walls. Sketches in red and black crayon of the spires and the desert landscape. A collage of images of cage fighters in outlandish sci-fi gear, pumped-up muscles glistening, faces contorted into snarls to show fangs or serrated shark teeth. Masks, body mods. And a poster, a fighter in silver shorts and a broad gold belt with a sunburst buckle that really worked its pulp sci-fi vibe, bare chest ridged with dermal armour, spikes jutting from elbows and wrists, standing with a bubble helmet tucked under one arm against a starry sky dominated by a ringed planet striped with Day-Glo orange and green. The fighter's cheesy *nom de combat*, Max Predator, was scrawled in thick silver felt-tip across the lower left-hand corner.

'Kid liked wrestling,' Henry said, perhaps missing this major clue, or perhaps pretending not to see it.

'We tossed the room,' Leo said. 'We didn't find any artefacts—'

'Because Jack Baines eBayed them,' Henry said. 'Or threw them out, when he found what happened to Sahar.'

'—but we did find this.'

Leo unfolded a square of paper. A childish scribble, wobbly crayoned lines in a rainbow of colours raying out from a central point.

Chloe remembered Rana Chauhan, holding up a drawing for her to inspect. She thought of Gert Baines's tapestry.

Leo's walkie-talkie crackled. Sandra Hamilton's voice said, 'We have visitors.'

165

24. Ease Up

Mangala | 27 July

Sergeant Mikkel Madsen was waiting for Vic when he came into the squad room. 'You have a bounce in your step, Investigator Gayle. Would I be correct in thinking that the trial went in our favour?'

'Man's been sent off to make fertiliser for the next fifteen years.'

Vic had been in court for most of the day, giving evidence in the morning, staying on to hear the jury's verdict. It had been a simple domestic murder. Two men had been cohabiting with a woman, all three of them shiners, and one of the men had decided to make the relationship more exclusive by strangling the other. He'd left the body wrapped in a length of carpet in the back garden of their house, and after a couple of weeks a neighbour had complained about an invasion of scrabs, little armoured scavengers as pestilent as rats. Vic had taken the call after a city health inspector had discovered the body; the prime suspect had confessed after a brief interrogation. An open-and-shut case that shouldn't even have gone to trial, but the defence lawyer had argued that the doer's confession was invalid because he had been undergoing cold turkey for his shine addiction, and the woman in the triangular relationship, initially a witness for the prosecution, had changed her testimony just before the initial hearing, had flat-out denied seeing anything, said that she had no idea how the dead man had managed to roll himself up in that carpet, but he was always doing weird shit like that. And because the scrabs had destroyed any forensic evidence there might have been, in the end it had come down to Vic's word against hers.

'For a change,' he told Mikkel, 'twelve upstanding citizens chose to believe the police.'

'You do look persuasive in that suit,' Mikkel said. He was a tall skinny man with pockmarked cheeks and a bushy moustache, fifteen years in the Norwegian police force and recently widowed when he'd won the lottery and come up. He took a noisy sip from his mug of coffee. 'Remind me. How many cases do you have outstanding?'

'Are you trying to take down my good feeling already? Have a heart.'

'I don't want you thinking that putting away the doer in a squalid little domestic is the highlight of your career. Especially as you have . . . How many open cases?'

'You know how many there are, and you know I'm working them.'

'Would I be wrong if I said sixteen?'

'I have a warrant out on one. Issued it last week.'

'But it stays open unless the doer turns up. Are you comfortable that the friends and relatives of sixteen victims are still waiting for justice?'

'If I promise to feel bad, will you get off my case?'

'I remember when the Jackaroo first announced their little gift,' Mikkel said. 'A lot of people said that it was a brand-new start. A chance to build fifteen different utopias on fifteen different worlds. A chance to redeem ourselves. But after all the fine talk about how we were going to do better, how we were going to realise the true potential of the human race, and so on, what did we get? It turns out that we brought every kind of human foolishness with us, and invented new ways to fuck up. Shine, meq, all the other new drugs. New ways of killing addicts slowly, while dealers and manufacturers kill each other quickly. Not to mention innocent bystanders.'

'If this is about the anti-drugs initiative,' Vic said, 'the case I just put away definitely counts.'

'We lead by example, Investigator Gayle. You look like a lawyer in that suit. Almost respectable. You up on the stand, me in the jury box? I'd believe everything you said. But like all of us you need to do better. Where is your apprentice, by the way? He hasn't been in all day. He should have been in court with you, learning how to put a bad guy away. But clearly not.'

Vic, who had no idea where Skip was or what he was up to, said, 'I'm keeping him busy. Helping him learn new skills, giving him a thorough grounding in custom and practice.'

'I hear,' Mikkel said, 'that he thinks he has a new lead in the Redway case.'

'Yeah. A possible link with the people who smuggled themselves inside that shipping container. Drug enforcement checked the waste tank of its toilet, found what was left of a bunch of torn-up papers. They weren't exactly in the best condition, as you can imagine, but the techs were able to piece together a few fragments. Turns out they were drawings of an Elder Culture site. According to the kid, these drawings resemble the layout of Site 326, one of the Elder Culture sites licensed to Cal McBride's company, Sky Edge Holdings. His *former* company, because Danny Drury is in charge of it now.'

Skip had called Vic that morning, talking a mile a minute. Vic had been forced to hang up on him because the trial had been about to start and he'd been in the middle of a conversation with the prosecution lawyer, but he believed that he'd caught the gist.

'That's what the kid told me,' Mikkel said. 'But I'm not hearing any actual evidence of any kind of link with the Redway thing.'

'I admit it's a stretch,' Vic said. 'But the drawing connects the people in the shipping container with that site, and Sky Edge Holdings. And Skip thinks Redway and his associate, David Parsons, were connected to the stowaways. That's why, he thinks, Redway and Parsons were out by the shuttle terminal when they were jumped, and Redway was zapped in the head.'

'But you don't know who these stowaways are,' Mikkel said.

'Not yet.'

'Or who killed Redway.'

'We're pretty sure it was either McBride or Drury. Both of them claim to have been elsewhere when Redway was killed. We checked their alibis, and both have holes, but yeah, so far we don't have anything that puts either one at the scene. Which is why I told Skip to concentrate on finding the friend of the dead guy, David Parsons. He was there when his friend was killed, and maybe he can tell us something about these stowaways, too. There's a watch notice out on him, and Skip has been checking out hotels and motels, flop houses and the like.'

'That's not all he has been checking,' Mikkel said. 'It seems that when he went over to the land-registry department to take a copy of that excavation licence, he found out that two other parties had also requested copies. A biologist who works for a company in France, and the British consulate. I see that this is news to you.'

That must have been the part that Vic had hung up on. He said, starting to get a bad feeling, 'I've been out of the loop, what with being in court most of the day.'

'The kid went to look for this biologist,' Mikkel said, 'but her place is closed up. Her neighbours think she's gone on one of her field trips. So then he went to the British consulate, wanting to know why they were interested in that licence, if they'd taken a copy on behalf of Redway and Parsons.'

'Oh man.'

'Exactly. The consul called City Hall, City Hall called the seventh floor, seventh floor called the captain, and she tore a strip off the kid.'

'What can I say? He's young and eager, this is his first case—'

'You're his partner. I don't want to have to step between the two of you.'

'I appreciate your tact, sergeant.'

'But if you cannot control your apprentice's wayward tendencies and teach him how we put down murders, that's exactly what I'm going to do. Tell me about the kid. Is he getting laid on a regular basis?'

'I've seen his partner. And since the kid isn't a damn fool, I'd say yes.'

Vic had met her just once, soon after Skip had started work in violent crimes. She'd come in one evening to collect the boy detective for a concert they were going to. Classical music, out in the park. A knockout blonde with an athletic figure, unselfconscious in a clingy grey dress, telling Vic, after Skip had introduced them, to look after her man.

169

'If that department is taken care of, show your apprentice how we relax around here. Take him somewhere convivial, engage in some male bonding over a drink or three, and explain to him that he should ease up on this whodunnit. It has been three days now, he has no hard proof that his two suspects had anything to do with it, and the only witness is missing. Probably buried by now somewhere in the back country. He should keep it active, follow up any new leads that present themselves, but meanwhile other cases are stacking up. Tell him all that,' Mikkel said, 'and then tattoo the chain of command on the insides of his fucking eyelids.'

25. Max Predator

Sandra said that two small boats were approaching from different directions, impossible to tell whether they were police or Jack Baines's friends. Maybe both.

'We'll keep them distracted while you and the asset make your escape,' she told Henry Harris.

'The asset?' Chloe said, as she followed Henry through the misty junkyard.

'It's like being a VIP.'

'In your world, maybe.'

'This is my world. Stay close, do what I tell you, and we'll be fine.'

They had almost reached the ladder to the landing stage when two men stepped out from behind a dinghy upturned on railway sleepers. One young and muscular, a baseball bat cocked on his shoulder; the other about Henry's age, long grey hair tied back with a red bandana, raising a shotgun and saying, 'Stay right where you fucking are.'

Chloe raised her hands out of stupid instinct.

'And who might you be?' Henry said.

'I own this place,' the man said. He had a wall-eyed glare that radiated pure black menace. 'Who the fuck might *you* be?'

'Pirates, matey,' Henry said. 'If I were you, I'd put down that gun.'

'I don't reckon I will,' the man said, and there was a sudden sharp bang and he spun halfway around.

Chloe flinched, thinking that the man had shot Henry, and Leo stepped up beside them and fired his riot gun again and the man slammed against the handrail by the ladder and dropped his shotgun. Henry stepped forward and in a single smooth

171

move scooped up the shotgun and gave the man a hard shove that flipped him over the rail. Henry looked down, then slung the shotgun far out into the misty air and turned and said, 'Thanks, Leo.'

'What about this one?' Leo said. He was aiming his riot gun at the young man, who had dropped his baseball bat and spread his hands.

'Let me guess,' Henry said to the young man. 'You work for the people Jack Baines was supposed to deliver us to.'

'If you think you can get away with this you're fucked,' the man said. He had the sullen look of a schoolboy caught trespassing.

'If I were you,' Henry told him, 'I'd think long and hard about the life choices that brought you here. Can you handle this, Leo?'

'Not a problem. What about the people in the other boat?'

'We'll give them a run for their money,' Henry said, and grabbed Chloe's arm and pulled her towards the ladder. As she climbed down she saw the grey-haired man struggling to extract himself from hip-deep mud. He was beslimed from head to foot, the whites of his eyes flashing when Henry gave him a cheerful little wave.

'Buckle up,' Henry told Chloe. 'We're in for a bumpy ride.'

Chloe was still strapping herself into the bench seat when the airboat shot away from the landing stage and skimmed past a speedboat that suddenly appeared out of the mist. A quick glimpse of two men in the boat, one of them yelling something, a throaty roar as the speedboat's motors revved up. Henry shouted 'Hold on!' and the airboat swerved hard. A ridge of marram grass rushed towards them. Chloe locked her arms around the back of the bench and with a jouncing rush the airboat was suddenly airborne, launched from the top of the ridge and skimming across the back slope in a long arc. Her messenger bag flipped up and walloped her in the face, and the airboat landed on water with a jolting impact, swerving at a sharp tilt between two wings of spray. For a moment, she thought that it would tip over, but then its hull slapped down and it was off again, smashing through a reed bed.

'Pure James Bond,' Henry yelled happily.

Chloe had bitten her tongue. She spat blood, told him that he was a crazy fool.

'That's what they said to the Wright brothers.'

'I think you can slow down now.'

After a minute he did. The rattle of reed stalks died back to a soft hiss. He said, 'We should be all right. The mist's too thick for them to put up a drone. If those losers even have a drone.'

'Are we going back to Martham?'

The airboat reached a long channel and Henry steered into it. 'We'll head for civilisation and call for a pickup.'

'Just how many people are involved in this?'

'As many as necessary. The Prof is taking it very seriously. She wants to make sure we do our best by you and those runaway kids.'

It didn't comfort Chloe. Ada Morange had a reputation for getting what she wanted. Chloe, caught up in the gears of her machine, had a bad feeling that she had made the wrong decision, that she was running into trouble instead of away from it. She felt that she had been shanghaied. Kidnapped. The steady progress of the airboat deeper into mist and uncharted marshes didn't help.

She and Henry talked about what they knew. Sahar Chauhan had gone up to Mangala, sent artefacts back, had been killed because of obscure drug-gang politics. Fahad had found out about his father's death and had run off with his little sister, both of them infected by something. An eidolon that had also got inside Gert Baines's head, Chloe told Henry.

'One of her tapestries was the spit of the drawing that Leo found,' she said. 'And Rana Chauhan showed me a similar drawing when I met her and her brother in the DP camp. She mentioned something she called Ugly Chicken, too. I think that's what she thought the eidolon looked like. It got inside her head, her brother's, Gert's, and it did something to Mr Archer and his followers, too.'

'That's how it started for you, didn't it?' Henry said. 'Their breakout.'

'I think Fahad took off again because he was scared the breakout would attract the wrong kind of attention,' Chloe said. 'And in a way he was right.'

173

'It gives me a funny feeling inside my skull, thinking about these alien ghosts. Like an itch I can't scratch. How come,' Henry said, 'it affects people differently? The kid did these pictures, but the people in that cult were all happy-clappy and babbling in tongues.'

'Eidolons try to communicate with us, but we can't understand or comprehend what they're trying to say. So when we try to channel it, translate it, it comes out in different ways. Often manifesting in obsessive-compulsive activity.'

'Meaning this kid can't stop making those pictures.'

'He thinks he's saying something important. Something urgent. Something people need to know,' Chloe said.

She was channelling Daniel Rosenblaum, and wondered where Daniel was now. She hoped that he and Jen and the rest of the crew were safe, sent up a little prayer.

'So we just have to look for more paintings or whatever.'

'And graffiti, pavement art, that kind of thing.' Chloe was thinking of the poster. She'd wanted very badly to ask Jack and Gert Baines about it, but there hadn't been time. She said, 'Also, there's the guy who turned up at the breakout. Who has a client who is interested in Fahad's stuff.'

'Eddie Ackroyd. Yes, I would definitely like to have a little chat with him. If the Hazard Police haven't found him first. And if they haven't,' Henry said, 'the first thing I'll ask him is why not.'

The mist lifted long before they reached Norwich. They left the airboat in the harbour and found a coffee shop on the bustling waterfront. Dehydrated and slightly dizzy from too much sun, Chloe drank a bottle of water straight down, and while Henry phoned his contact she excused herself and in the bathroom stall called Gail Ann Jones. She used the phone that she hadn't told Henry about, the phone she hadn't been using because reporters had glommed on to it. And possibly the police too, if Henry was right, but needs must.

'I thought you were going to call the phone you gave me,' Gail Ann said.

'I don't want to compromise it – I've had to use my old phone. I shouldn't even be calling you . . .'

'But you need backup. Are you okay? What can I do?'

Chloe gave her friend a quick recap of her adventure at the sea fort. Realising as she talked how totally Gothic it sounded. Dead nuns, drug dealers, a madly obsessed artist held prisoner with his little sister . . . And she hadn't even mentioned the appearance of the Jackaroo avatar.

Gail Ann said that it sounded like she'd been having a high old time. Chloe said that it really wasn't all that. She'd seen herself in the mirror over the bathroom sink: dishevelled and sunburned, her camo jacket spattered with dried mud.

She said, 'But I did learn some useful stuff about Fahad's family. And I found something that might help me find him. It looks like he's a fan of cage fighters. He had a poster of one. A guy named Max Predator.'

Gail Ann said, 'For real?'

'I guess it's like a stage name. I was wondering if you could find out who he is, where he works.'

'Ask him if he knows the kid you're looking for? That's a long shot, sweetie.'

'The poster was signed. And this guy has all kinds of body mods. Plates of armour on his shoulders, his upper arms, devil horns in his forehead. A lot of that stuff is Elder Culture tech. And a lot of people in that world do drugs, too. Stuff that enhances their neural responses.'

Daniel Rosenblaum had once written an article about the cage-fighting scene; Chloe had skim-read it when she'd started out with Disruption Theory.

Gail Ann said, 'So this cage fighter might have bought his drugs from the bad guys who were keeping your kids prisoner.'

'I think there could be a strong link. It's a genuine subculture, cage fighting,' Chloe said, wishing she'd paid more attention to Daniel's article. 'A sort of cross between transhumanism and showbiz.'

'Are there girl fighters?'

'Why not?' Chloe said, even though she wasn't sure.

'Because I'm trying to think out a line of attack.'

'You don't have to *write* the article, just introduce yourself, say you're thinking of doing a piece. Say you happen to know Fahad Chauhan, or drop his name somehow.'

'Ask if they have a current address for him? Why would they?'

'I'm wondering what else Fahad's father sent back from Mangala. Whether Fahad ever sold this Max Predator anything, did he hang around the place, is he part of a fan base, and so on.'

Chloe's hand was sweating on the phone. She was worried that Henry Harris would burst in and find her. Worried that the police or some reporter would get a fix on her. But she couldn't pass up this chance to get ahead of Ada Morange's machine, to give herself an edge, something she could use to negotiate a better deal. The quip about being an asset had stung hard.

Gail Ann said, 'I'm looking at Maxie's website right now. Ew.'

'I'm not asking you to date him.'

'According to this,' Gail Ann said, 'he's part of a stable based at a gym in the Reef. Like he's a racehorse.'

'I know it isn't much of a lead,' Chloe said, 'but it's all I have right now. And listen, can you do this as soon as possible?'

'Are you in trouble?'

'I'm not sure. A little, maybe. I'm definitely kind of on the run. And there are other people looking for Fahad. Bad guys.'

'I'll get my Girl Reporter act over there now,' Gail Ann said.

'Be careful. If there are any suspicious characters hanging around, anyone who looks like the police, forget about it. Bail.'

'Don't worry about me. I'm having fun. And when this is over,' Gail Ann said, 'I'm going to sell the hell out this story. Try and stop me.'

26. Official Drunk

Vic took the boy detective to a joint everyone called the Belgian Pub, even though it was run by a Dutch couple. A small dark wood-panelled place that served all kinds of imported beers. They worked their way through several bottles of Lion Heart Stout and something called Feral Hop Hog that Skip championed, and Vic told the boy detective exactly why he'd fucked up with the consulate.

'It's politics. The UN and City Hall know the consulates are into all kinds of undercover shit. They're looking out for the interests of their countries, various companies . . . The UN turns a blind eye to all that because it can't keep the shuttle operations running without international cooperation. And City Hall doesn't want to jeopardise the export market and piss off companies that have established factories here, bring in income and keep citizens in gainful employment. I know why you wanted to chase down that line of inquiry, but you're going to have to forget about it.'

Skip was subdued after his run-in with the captain, but he wouldn't let it go. 'Look, I know I fucked up, but I also know that there's a connection between Redway and those stowaways. Redway was zapped by a weapon known to have been used by McBride. The British consulate checked out the licence that McBride took out for an Elder Culture site, and a drawing of the site was found in that can. It could be, couldn't it, that Parsons is hiding out in the consulate.'

'If he is, you won't be able to talk to him.'

'A man was killed. Aren't we supposed to find out who did it?'

177

'Not if he died in the service of his country. The captain told you to ease up on the case, didn't she? Well, that's exactly what you're going to do. And from now on, everything you do, you're going to check with me first. You want to piss, you hold it in until I give you permission.'

But Skip wasn't going to let it go easily. 'I talked to drug enforcement about the shipping container. It was supposed to go to an address in Idunn's Valley, but the address doesn't exist. Someone sent it all the way from Earth to a place that isn't on the map, and someone in the terminal checked it off. I was kind of hoping to sit in on interviews with the checkers, the people who track the containers from the point of unloading to their place in the stacks, and then onto the trucks that take them to their final destination. One of them was in on this thing for sure.'

The boy detective had a ragged, distracted look that Vic recognised: someone whose case was eating their life. He tried to explain how it worked, how some cases fell open at a touch, how others were real headbangers that refused to give up their secrets.

'But the thing is, there are always more cases. We had more than six hundred murders in the city last year. Not to mention attempted murders, violent assaults, kidnapping, extortion . . . People come up, they think it's the Wild West. Or the place drives them crazy. Six hundred murders, and we have fourteen investigators in the squad, basically doing triage. So when things don't work out with one case, you don't keep banging your head against it. You move on to the next. But that doesn't mean we forget about the ones that got away. Sometimes, a year or two later, the doer will get drunk and confess to their partner. Or get religion and turn themselves in. Or they'll get banged up for something else, boast about how they got away with murder to someone on their work gang who dibs them in exchange for a reduced sentence. Ask anyone on the squad,' Vic said, 'we all have a story like that. So here's how it is with this one. While you're waiting for Parsons to turn up, you need to be doing something else instead of getting into other people's business.'

But he could see that Skip wasn't listening. His second year on Mangala, Vic had been out on the playa and come across a research team that had trapped a stalker. A thin angular bio-machine like a praying mantis crossed with a gazelle. It had rushed to and fro in the cage, battering against bars. Never letting up, never giving in. Skip was a little like that. He wasn't ever going to give up on his whodunnit.

So Vic ordered another round and changed the topic. He talked about his time as a police constable in Birmingham back on Earth, walking the beat in a pointy helmet and carrying a truncheon instead of a gun – well, most of the time, there had been some serious riots in the long economic stagnation before the Spasm. Skip asked him if that was why he didn't carry a gun now.

'I carried a gun before I became a murder police. It really was like the Wild West in Petra, back in the day. But on this job the worst has already happened when we roll up. It's about reading the scene. It's about understanding people, not exchanging shots with them.'

'You've been on the job a while, I guess.'

'I'm seven years shy of my twenty, let's put it that way.'

They got into talking about what they'd do after they retired. Vic told Skip that there were plenty of good security jobs for retired investigators. 'I'm not talking about foot patrol in shopping malls. I have a good friend at the university, campus police,' Vic said, and with a pang thought of his partner, Chris Okupe. Skip told him about his plan to do his twenty and buy a spread in Idunn's Valley and raise sheep, finally said it was time to head home. Vic had a haphazard memory of moving on to another bar, of dancing with a woman to a jukebox playing Bruce Springsteen, but he woke alone in his bed in his bachelor efficiency, and had to drink about three litres of water and stand under a shower alternating between hot and cold until he felt even halfway human. He was getting old, was what it was. His aunties would be scandalised that he was approaching fifty and still lacked a family. Scandalised, but also righteously pleased that their prediction that no good would come of flying off to another world had proven to be absolutely correct.

He managed to get into work more or less on time, and found Mikkel Madsen doing his helicopter thing again. Saying, 'I am grievously displeased with you, Investigator Gayle.'

'If this is about the kid, I talked to him. Gave him the full benefit of my wisdom,' Vic said. 'So if he's gone and done something stupid, I don't want to know. I intend to eat as many painkillers as I can stand, throw up as and when necessary, and otherwise sit in a quiet corner and do paperwork.'

'You tied one on with him.'

'We went on an official drunk, as ordered.'

'Yet he comes in here hours before the shift starts, fighting fit and happy. You know why?'

'You're going to tell me, aren't you?'

'He had a busy morning while you were sleeping off your official drunk. He checked in on both Drury and McBride. And it seems that both are in the wind. What the kid wants to do is go to Idunn's Valley. That is where the excavation site is located, and that is where he thinks Drury and McBride are headed. Also that biologist who took a copy of that excavation licence. The captain had to give him a little lesson on the facts of life, how we don't trespass lightly on other jurisdictions, proper procedures, the difference between hard and circumstantial evidence et cetera. The kind of lesson that I believe I asked you to deliver.'

'He's stubborn, but I'll get him straightened out. Where is he?'

'He is working a case I gave him,' Mikkel said. 'Two guys went at it in a do-it-yourself place. People are stripping the shelves because they think the dust storm is going to be Armageddon. One accused the other of queue jumping and stabbed him with a chisel. Assault with intent. The kid has about fifty witnesses to interview. Trying to iron out the kinks in all the conflicting stories should keep him out of mischief for a couple of days. More than long enough for you to find him something else that will usefully occupy his keen mind.'

'I'll do my best. Meanwhile, do you have any aspirin?'

27. Seriously Strange Shit

London | 10 July

Chloe and Henry spent the night in a hotel hard by the M25. The kind of blandly anonymous place where salesmen meet their clients and companies hold away days. Generic toiletries, triple-glazed windows that couldn't be opened, a restaurant with rattan screens, bamboo stems in glass tumblers as table centrepieces, and the choice between watching a TV screen tuned to a sports channel up in one corner or a view across the motorway to fields of oilseed rape while you enjoyed the 'eclectic' menu of micro-waved Indian and Thai food.

They'd driven there from Norwich after picking up a Nissan people carrier at the station car park, delivered by an extremely polite young man in chinos and a blue windbreaker.

'I want you to make sure my old motor is recovered,' Henry said, as he signed for the vehicle. 'It's parked in the long-term car park by Acle harbour. The police might be looking out for it by now – the Disruption Theory crew have probably given up everything they know. So whoever picks it up should watch their step.'

'I'll take care of it personally, Mr Harris,' the young man said.

He exchanged sets of keys with Henry and handed him a new phone, then lifted a folding bicycle from the back of the people carrier and pedalled off.

The stuff they'd left behind at the pub in Martham was waiting for them when they arrived at the hotel. Chloe imagined a cadre of smart young men and women operating out of some kind of Acme distribution centre, supporting clandestine operations with every service and necessity. A thought both absurd and chilling.

While she picked at soggy spring rolls and an insipid vegetable stir-fry, Henry fielded several calls on his new phone, told her that Sandra and her people had extracted themselves without difficulty, said that the Prof's lawyers were working on getting Daniel and the others released on bail.

'It shouldn't be a problem. They aren't really the target.'

'Meaning that I am.'

'The others are a way of getting close to you. You may be the way to getting close to the kid. But we're still good. We're off the map, and Sandra's people have set up a false trail.'

There was a moment when Chloe could have told him about sending Gail Ann to check out the gym where Max Predator trained, but she let it pass. She wanted to know what Gail Ann had found out first, and she still wasn't certain that Ada Morange's plans coincided with the best interests of Fahad and his sister.

She slept surprisingly well, woke to an alarm call at six, showered, and, sitting at the edge of the bed wrapped in a towel, used the room's phone to call Gail Ann.

It rang a long time, long enough for Chloe to become worried.

'Now you're calling the new phone,' Gail Ann said, when at last she answered. 'Took me an age to find it.'

'Did it go okay yesterday?'

'I didn't even know this time of day existed,' Gail Ann said. 'Before I even try to answer that, let me at least start making coffee.'

'I kind of need to know if you found out anything useful,' Chloe said.

'Didn't you get my messages?'

'I'm in a hotel. Using the room phone.'

'They still have phones, in hotel rooms?'

'It controls the TV, the air conditioning . . . I think this call is costing like two pounds a minute, but I can't be sure my phone isn't bugged or something. I used it to call you yesterday because it was all I had. How did it go at the gym?'

'It was interesting in all kinds of ways. But first, did you hear about Disruption Theory's offices?'

A fire had broken out in the offices late last night. There'd been a brief mention about it on BBC London's news feed; Gail Ann had found several references on Twitter and Facebook, including a photo taken from a neighbouring block of flats. A long-distance shot and a little blurry, she said, but it was definitely Disruption Theory's building, the top floor lit up by flames.

Chloe felt hot and then cold. She said, 'This is my fault.'

'Section 808 claims to have firebombed it,' Gail Ann said. 'They said that the place was harbouring dangerous alien technology.'

Section 808 was an extremist group which had broken away from the Human Dignity League after it had entered the political mainstream.

Chloe said, 'Was anyone hurt?'

'Not according to the BBC.'

'That's right. Everyone was arrested.' Chloe wondered if Henry knew about this. Of course he did. She said, 'This is all down to me.'

'You can't hold yourself responsible for what extremists do. Let me tell you about my little adventure at the cage-fighter gym,' Gail Ann said. 'I know it will make you feel better.'

'Did you find Max Predator's manager? Did you talk to him?'

'It was a her, actually. Just a sec. There. Now I have coffee.' Gail Ann slurped some, said, 'Oh my.'

'Does she know Fahad? Does he hang at the gym?'

'We're getting ahead of ourselves,' Gail Ann said. 'Let me start at the beginning. So the gym? It was sort of tacky and sad. These bodybuilders grimly working away at their machines, lifting weights, whatever. And all these mirrors so they can admire their gross mods. Horns and fangs are popular. Also claws, and these hooks, they call them spurs, at wrists and elbows. There was one guy with little horns growing out of his forehead. There was another guy with bright red skin and a kind of spiny ruff. Sort of like a lizard. And tattoos like you've never seen. One guy had tattooed eyeballs. It's some kind of Jamaican thing, apparently.'

'What about Max Predator?'

'He wasn't there. So I hung around until the gym's owner turned up. She's also Max's manager. Judith Elborough, this tough old broad with a posh accent, sounds and looks like a racehorse trainer from the Home Counties. I checked her background afterwards. She inherited the business from her husband, who skipped out of the country when his investment company turned out to be a Ponzi scheme. He'd bought a share in the cage-fighting business, put in their son's name, and she took it over—'

Chloe said, 'But does she know Fahad?'

'She knew Fahad's father. But I didn't get that from her. She wouldn't talk to me. I said that I was working for Ada Morange. Which isn't a total lie, seeing as you do. And she said that Professor Morange's people had already seen her. I said I was doing a follow-up, thinking on my feet—'

'Wait. She talked to Ada Morange's people?'

'They beat me to it. I suppose they noticed that poster too.'

'What did they ask her?'

Chloe was wondering what else Henry hadn't told her. She knew that she would have to confront him; also knew that he would tell her only as much as he thought she needed to know.

Gail Ann said, 'I don't know. The Elborough woman called my bluff.'

'Shit.'

Gail Ann said, 'Luckily, I'd already talked to some of her fighters while I was waiting for her to show up. They aren't fighters, by the way. They're, get this, *warriors*. One of them, a big hairy guy who calls himself the Warewolf, asked me out. Told me that he was going up against his big rival in a couple of days, said I should sit ringside and bring him luck. Only it isn't a ring, of course. It's an actual cage. Once you're inside it, you don't get out until you win or you're down. Wolfie has some amazing scars. And fur all over his body. Grey, with a vee of white on his chest.'

'Sounds like you had fun,' Chloe said.

'It was definitely interesting. I might even go see him fight. There's a story in it. Not my usual thing, but it's good to be stretched. Anyway, I told him about your runaway artist. Explained why you wanted to get in contact with him, and so forth. And it turns out that Wolfie knew his father. You know how mods work?'

'I know it's Elder Culture tech,' Chloe said, beginning to wonder when Gail Ann was going to get to the point.

'They're derived from these like alien creatures, biochines. You take fragments from their hides – proteins, collagen, or whatever – and treat them in various ways and stick them under your skin. Different ones grow different mods.'

'And Fahad's father was involved in this.'

'He supplied antagonists that suppress side effects, and stop the mods growing when they've grown enough. Wolfie told me some gross horror stories about mods going bad.'

'So Sahar Chauhan worked for Judith Elborough at some point. Making these antagonists.'

'According to Wolfie, he worked for these tasty geezers—'

'Tasty geezers? He really said that?'

'Really. He's an East End boy, his parents have a café in Poplar they've owned for like fifty years? Anyway, Sahar Chauhan treated people who'd been given new mods. He'd do blood tests, use them to work up the right mix of antagonists.'

'And did Sahar ever bring Fahad with him?'

'Now we're getting to the good part,' Gail Ann said. 'Wolfie said that Sahar used to come to the fights, visited backstage several times with his son. Who was a huge fan of Max Predator. Wolfie claims that the names are deliberately cheesy. The punters love it. So I guess that's where Fahad got the signed poster you told me about.'

Chloe said, 'Has Fahad visited the gym recently? Looking for work. Trying to sell some of his art . . .'

'Wolfie said he doesn't know. I think he was telling the truth, too. But here's the really good part. Are you sitting down?'

'Why don't you just tell me?'

'After I left the gym, a couple of hours later, I got a message from someone who not only claims to know Fahad, but says that Fahad wants to meet up.'

'With you?'

'No, sweetie. With you.'

*

185

Henry was in the hotel's restaurant, looking up from his plate of sausage and beans as Chloe sat down. 'Here's someone who got out of the wrong side of the bed.'

'We need to talk,' Chloe said. 'Get everything in the open.'

'Would this be about the fire at Disruption Theory, or your friend's visit to the gym?'

'We could start by talking about everything you haven't been telling me.'

'We both saw that poster in the fort. We both followed it up. After Sandra and her boys got out, they went to the place where Mr Predator works out and talked to the woman who manages him. Meanwhile, you asked your journalist friend to snoop around. Did she find anything interesting?'

'I know that Sahar Chauhan was making stuff, antagonists, which cage fighters use. I know he took Fahad to the fights.'

'And Fahad came into the gym a couple of months ago, looking for work. Janet Elborough told us that she gave him some cash and got rid of him, because she knew that his father's employers were looking for him. Did your reporter friend tell you about them?'

'Not yet.'

'The McBride family,' Henry said. 'A long-established criminal firm. They own the shrimp farm in Martham, and the company that sent Sahar Chauhan to Mangala. And now they're looking for Fahad. The Elborough woman says that she didn't tell them about his visit to her place. Maybe she's telling the truth, maybe not. She relies on them for those antagonists, and they might be into her for other stuff.'

'But she talked to your people,' Chloe said.

'Sandra can be very persuasive. You should be flattered, really,' Henry said. 'This thing you started has the Prof's full attention.'

'Then why do I feel that I'm being sidelined?'

'If you were being sidelined, you wouldn't be here with me,' Henry said. 'Listen. The Prof has a profiler working for her. The kind of shrink who works out the home lives of serial killers from the way they operate. He says that you and the kid are a complementary pair. You both lost your mothers, have absent fathers. You have a reputation – the wiki, that move you made trying to protect the Jackaroo avatar. And now you're actually wanted by the Hazard Police. You're on the run, just like him. This profiler thinks you can use all of that to get the kid's trust. So you're still in this, for as long as you want to be.'

'But no more secrets. No more withholding information.'

'Didn't I just tell you what we found out? And listen, I'm impressed that you were able to find out about that kid's connection to that gym so quickly, but no more stunts like that, okay? You could have put this thing of ours at risk. Not to mention your friend.'

Chloe said, 'I found out something else. One of Fahad's friends has been trying to get in touch with me.'

She explained that the friend had sent a text message to Gail Ann after she visited the gym. 'She left her contact details with some of the fighters. Either this friend is one of them, or they work there and heard Gail Ann asking about Fahad, heard her mention my name. They sent her a message, asking her to ask me to check my messages.'

'They sent you a message?'

'Two days ago. I didn't see it because my phone has been turned off. Mostly turned off. When I checked, there were about two hundred messages in my inbox. Almost all of them were from reporters, but there was one sent anonymously, asking me to reply to it if I wanted to talk to Mangala Cowboy. That's the name—'

'The tumblr thing. How did they know your phone number?'

'Apart from the fact that just about everyone in the world seems to know it? I left my card in Fahad's door when I visited the displaced-persons village.'

She watched Henry think about this. He said, 'I hope you didn't reply. Your phone is compromised.'

'I was hoping I could use yours,' Chloe said.

Henry thought about that, saying at last, 'But it might spook them if your reply came from a different number. Give me your phone.'

She handed it over. He thumbed through the phone's inbox, aimed its screen towards Chloe. 'This is the message?'

'That's it.'

'It could be a con. A game run by the Hazard Police.'

'How would they know about Gail Ann?'

'Because they've probably made it their business to find out about everyone you've called with this damn thing.'

'I used it yesterday,' Chloe confessed, 'because you threw the other one away. And I used the room phone to call Gail Ann this morning.'

'By which time her phone might have been compromised.'

'I called her other phone. A new one I gave her when all this started.'

Henry smiled. 'That's almost smart.'

'That's almost a compliment.'

Henry weighed the phone in his hand, then tapped out something with his thumbs and set it on the table. 'Done. Have you eaten yet?'

'What did you say?'

'That you wanted to talk. Get some breakfast inside you. We have an appointment.'

'What kind of appointment?'

'A hospital appointment. Your friend Eddie Ackroyd got himself beaten up.'

Chloe was working her way through a latte and a bowl of fruit and yoghurt when her phone started to buzz. She and Henry looked at it; Henry picked it up.

'Four o'clock, the Reef's free market,' he said, reading off the screen. 'Does that mean anything to you?'

'I know where the Reef is. I used to hang out there a lot when I was freelancing. Is that it?'

'Short and sweet,' Henry said, and switched off the phone and pocketed it. 'Eat up. We'll visit your friend Eddie first, then work out how to play this.'

They drove to London, to the Whittington hospital. Another polite young man in a blue windbreaker was waiting for them in the car park, told Henry that so far no one had been to visit Mr Ackroyd. 'The police interviewed him when he was admitted to casualty, but they haven't been back.'

Henry said, 'The local police?'

The young man nodded. 'Mr Ackroyd suffered a ruptured spleen. He was operated on yesterday. Now he's in a recovery ward, awaiting discharge. Apparently there is some dispute about the bill. So far there is no indication that the Hazard Police know his whereabouts.'

'Good to know,' Henry said. He handed Chloe's phone to the young man and said that he wanted the message from Fahad's friend traced, then told Chloe, 'Let's get this done. I'll do the talking. You look sympathetic.'

'It won't be easy,' Chloe said.

But she did feel a small and unexpected pang when she saw Eddie Ackroyd in his raised bed, looking smaller and older in a hospital gown, grey hair neatly combed back from his bruised and bandaged face. His eyes were swollen and his nose was taped; one arm was in a cast from elbow to wrist. He was sitting up and reading a paperback book, looking up from it at Chloe with a kind of dull resignation. Perhaps it was fear, or perhaps he'd been fed some kind of elephant tranquilliser, but he lacked his usual sarcastic edge.

While Henry fetched two chairs, Eddie said to Chloe, 'Who's your friend?'

His mouth was bruised too; at least two of his teeth were missing.

'He works for Ada Morange.'

Eddie took a moment, lifting a paper cup, spitting into it. There was blood in his saliva. 'He looks like police.'

'We're here to help, Eddie. Listen to what he has to say.'

Henry got straight to the point, telling Eddie that he knew about his interest in Fahad Chauhan and the client who left mysterious clues in a folder in the editors' board of the LFM wiki, but wanted to hear his side of the story.

'Why should I tell you anything?' Eddie said.

Henry took out his phone, dialled a number and told the person at the other end to go ahead with the payment, and said to Eddie, 'For a start, we've taken care of your hospital bill. Check it out.'

Eddie took the phone as if suspecting a trick. 'Who is this? I see. I see. No, I suppose that's all right . . .'

Henry took the phone back. 'You've got yourself in a bit of a pickle, Mr Ackroyd. But we're willing to help you if you help us. We'll make sure you aren't disturbed here. No unexpected visitors. We'll pay all your medical expenses, including reconstructive dentistry. And we'll pay a finder's fee, too.'

They dickered about the price, but Eddie's heart wasn't in it. After a couple of minutes he agreed on about half what Chloe had expected him to demand. It wasn't much of a story, he said. He was only trying to make a living, like everyone else.

'Why don't you tell us about the people who beat you up,' Henry said. 'Was it in the street, or did they pull you into a car and take you somewhere?'

Eddie said that they had been waiting for him in his house. 'Two of them. One about your age, the other younger. They tied me to a chair, and they started to snap records in half. I collect early opera records. 78 rpm.'

'Really? I still have some of my dad's old LPs,' Henry said.

He was, Chloe could tell, having fun.

He and Eddie discussed the merits and demerits of digital v. analogue for a couple of minutes, Henry expressing interest when Eddie explained how he used steel needles to play his records, then steering the conversation back to the main topic.

Eddie said, 'Luckily, they didn't know which ones were valuable. I have several early Carusos, recorded before his voice changed, including Trimarchi's "Un Bacio Ancora". I have a near-mint copy of Alessandro Moreschi on G and T singing "Ave Maria". One of the last castratis, the only one ever recorded.' He paused to spit into his cup. 'They missed those, but they broke twenty-two others, right in front of me. I told them I would answer their questions, but they broke them anyway. Because they could. And then, after we talked, they beat me up.'

He said that he'd told them everything he knew.

'I mentioned my client to you,' he said to Chloe. 'That's who they were mostly interested in. I explained that I'd never met him. That he feeds me tips and I follow them up, interview the people involved, get their stories. That's what he's interested in. Their stories.'

Eddie said that he'd done it seven times now. Always the same, he said. First a clue to send him to the general area. When he found the people who were getting ready to break out, he'd document them as fully as possible. After he uploaded everything, he'd be paid in shellcoin, the African digital currency. Completely untraceable.

'The one in Dagenham, I noticed the flyer, followed it up. The boy, Fahad, wouldn't give me the time of day, but I knew he was the focus of the breakout,' Eddie said, and delicately spat into his cup again. 'And I knew he was holding out on me, that he had a potent artefact, or had been exposed to one. You noticed it too, that's why you're here. But I saw him first.'

Chloe said, 'I guess I'm losing my edge.'

She felt a little sorry for Eddie, punished because he'd been caught up in something he didn't understand.

Henry went over the business with the client. Eddie stuck to his story, saying, 'I'm telling you what I told them. He always contacted me. Afterwards, I'd send the video clips and the interviews, always to a different email address.'

He didn't have the addresses. The thugs had taken his tablet and his phone.

Henry asked Eddie if he knew who they worked for. 'Are you certain they weren't police?'

Eddie said, 'I know police. I was part of the Occupy movement when I was a student. I marched against breaking up the health service, privatising universities . . . It seems foolish now, but at the time we really thought we could change things. I know police. And they weren't police.'

Chloe said, 'How did they find you?'

Eddie shrugged, one hairy shoulder bare in his hospital gown.

Henry said, 'He put some of Fahad's pictures up for sale on eBay.'

'They're mine, fair and square,' Eddie said.

Chloe said, 'You bought them off Mr Archer, didn't you?'

'Just doing what I do,' Eddie said. 'Trying to make a living any way I can.'

'You beat me on that hustle, Eddie,' Chloe said. 'I'll give you that.'

'And look where it got me.' Eddie spat into his cup, looked at Chloe. His eyes were bloodshot, the bruised flesh around them beginning to take on a yellow tint. He said, 'Be careful out there. What we've walked into, it's some seriously strange shit.'

28. The Worst Thing

Mangala | 30 July

Vic was woken by the scratchy rhythm of his phone's ringtone and groped for it half asleep, the terrible shadow of a hangover looming at the edge of his consciousness. He couldn't find the bedside table or the damn phone, wincingly opened his eyes. An unfamiliar bedroom, pink pillowcases and pink sheets and some kind of patchwork quilt, the naked curve of a woman's back close to him.

It had been his day off yesterday. A Saturday. He'd gone into Junktown and found Dodger, who'd told him that he hadn't been able to find out much about Danny Drury.

'From what I heard, he doesn't represent on the streets. But I did hear that he recently hired some tasty geezers. Former soldiers. Serious muscle. Word is he's looking to rumble with someone.'

'With Cal McBride?'

Vic was thinking of Skip's idea that Drury and McBride were headed for that Elder Culture site in Idunn's Valley.

'That was one of the names mentioned.'

Vic gave Dodger another forty and told him to find out who Drury had a beef with, and headed over to his ex's place to pick up the last of his stuff. Halfway there, he became stuck in an epic traffic jam on the ring road. A juvenile plainswalker had wandered onto the carriageway and there'd been a pile-up when a truck skidding around it had ploughed into half a dozen other vehicles. Vic glimpsed the biochine in the distance, sails semaphoring sunlight as it scampered away, pursued by the round-up crew. Way back, when Petra had been nothing more than huts and tents strung along half a dozen streets bulldozed out of the playa, biochines had wandered all over the place, innocently curious about the new arrivals. These days, they were rarely spotted inside the city limits: they had learned what humans could do, and kept well away.

It took more than an hour to round up the biochine and reopen the ring road. And when Vic arrived at what used to be his home, late and exasperated, his ex, Janet, straight away told him that she had a new boyfriend, and they were getting serious.

'He's moving in, actually. So I appreciate you finding the time to come over and take away your things.'

'Because he was poking about in the back of the garage, taking an inventory of your old paint cans, and got upset, finding my shit?'

'He's a lovely man. A surgeon at the hospital, came up just a year ago. You might even like him.'

'I'm not ready for double dating, but hey, I'm pleased for you. Really. Have he and Poppy hit it off?'

Poppy was Janet's daughter from her previous marriage. Nine years old, bright, energetic, and possessed of an infallible bullshit detector when it came to grown-ups. And presently – Vic was certain it wasn't a coincidence – at a friend's house on a playdate. He still missed her, missed their walks along the rim trails in the hills above the lake. Poppy was a fiend for natural history, loved to take photos of biochines and to collect bugs. Hoppers, mirror flies, army beetles, blinkies, web worms, Goliath grubs, and all the other weird insects that weren't really insects.

Janet said, 'She and Aldo get along just fine. How are you doing, Vic?'

'You know. Making out.'

They were talking in the big kitchen, with its work island surfaced in polished pink marble, the sweep of glass that looked out over the rock garden and the view of the blue expanse of Lake Europa, the reservoir that stored the city's water. It was a minimalist house, Janet's previous husband having been an architect. Cantilevered levels of concrete and glass, clean white spaces, carefully selected pieces of imported furniture. Vic had never felt comfortable there. He'd felt exposed in all that light. There'd been no corner he could claim as his own.

Janet was a tall energetic redhead, the owner of a 3D printing company, on the board of the city's hospital and a founding member of the city's eighteen-hole golf club. They'd met at a police charity ball, lust at first sight, love a little later. But Janet had always wanted his full attention, had always resented his work, the unpredictability and the long hours, the fact that he was never really off duty. The usual grief. After two years she'd told Vic it wasn't working, and that was that. She knew what she wanted, knew when to give up on something. He didn't much like her ruthlessness – as far as he was concerned, it was selfishness masked by pragmatism – but he had to respect her honesty.

She offered him lunch, but he noticed that she kept glancing at her watch and knew from her pinched look that she wanted to be elsewhere, with her new boyfriend or out on the links. So he stuck the plastic crates of his stuff into his car – an old pair of hiking boots, a Kindle loaded with history books, clothes that Janet had bought him, the aftershave and lotions she'd given him as birthday and Christmas presents – and to celebrate this last tick mark in the dissolution of his marriage he tied one on in the Irish pub, drinking until last orders.

He couldn't recall the woman's name; he must have picked her up in the pub. Or no, he remembered now, he'd tried to walk back to the municipal apartment building, one in the morning, the sun burning on the glass fronts of office buildings. One of the downsides of thirty-one days of sunlight was coming out of some dim cosy pub or bar long past midnight and being blasted by atomic radiance. As if you were some vampire about to explode into dust. He'd stopped at the diner on the corner of Hope and Esperance, ordered a mac and cheese to settle his stomach, the waitress had just been coming off shift, and here he was.

The phone still doing its thing.

It was in his jacket, strewn with the rest of his clothes on the floor. The caller was Mikkel Madsen, saying, 'I need you to come in, Vic.' Refusing to explain what it was about, saying again, 'Come in. As soon as you can.'

Vic felt a tremor of foreboding pass through the heavy gravity of his hangover, and although there was nothing he wanted more than to collapse back into bed and sleep until noon, he started to gather up his scattered clothing. The woman on the bed – Joni, he remembered, *Hi I'm Joni* written in ornate red lettering on her name badge, a perky thirtysomething who'd been impressed to meet an actual murder police she'd seen on the local news – rolled over and looked at him through the spill of her hair and said so that was how it was with the resignation of someone this had happened to before.

Vic's head thumped full of blood when he sat down on the edge of the bed to pull on his trousers; he swallowed a mouthful of saliva. 'Something's come up,' he said. And without knowing why he added, 'I'm really sorry.'

Joni turned out to live in one of the blocks of system-built flats that could be erected inside a week using stacks of components shipped from Earth, everything from framework steels to door-knobs and taps. Vic called a cab but baled out halfway to the UN Building and in a Starbucks threw up in the toilet and drank half a litre of chocolate milk that he immediately regretted. It wasn't just the usual feeling that he'd been badly beaten and cast onto the deck of a wildly pitching ship: there was also a terrible sense of existential doom, as if he'd become a wretched ghost haunting his own life.

'I hope you feel as bad as you look,' Mikkel said, when Vic at last arrived in the squad room. Only a couple of investigators were working on this Sunday morning, both of them looking at Vic and then looking away, deepening his feeling that something truly dreadful was rushing towards him.

He said, 'The kid fucked up, didn't he? How bad?'

'The skipper wants to talk to you,' Mikkel said, and there she was at the doorway of her office, Captain Lucille Colombier, giving Vic a look of pity and tender concern, and he knew at once it was the worst thing.

29. The Reef

'Fahad and his friends knew what they were doing when they chose this place,' Sandra Hamilton said. 'Plenty of foot traffic, half a dozen public exit points and an unknown number through shops and workshops . . . And then there's the composition of the coral itself, the way it grows. The place is a regular Swiss cheese. I can't guarantee that I'll be able to keep track if things go sideways.'

Henry Harris said, 'What about other interested parties?'

'My spotters haven't seen any sign that anyone else is keeping watch. But I can't rule anything out,' Sandra said. 'The police could have intercepted every message sent to Chloe's phone. And they've had a presence in the Reef ever since people moved in. They're *embedded*.'

They were in the back of a sweltering van in the ruined lorry park next to the Reef, studying views of its exterior and interior. One of Sandra's young men was controlling drones that patrolled the perimeter; two more were keeping watch inside, transmitting images from their spex. Sandra was dressed in her white track-suit; Henry had changed into cargo shorts and a long green shirt printed with parrots, an attempt to disguise himself as a sightseer.

He looked at Chloe and said, 'As long as you stick to the plan you'll be fine. We'll keep watch and run interference. We'll have your back at all times. All you have to do is sit tight and wait for Fahad to make contact. If everything works out, we'll take things from there. If things look as if they're about to go pear-shaped, I'll tell you to walk away. And that's exactly what'll you'll do. Walk and don't look back.'

Sandra said, 'We have just enough time to go over the script once more.'

'Let's just do it,' Chloe said, but she felt far from ready as she walked towards the looming bulk of the Reef, a fluttering sense of precarious insecurity that reminded her of her first day in big school. She was wearing her spex, transmitting everything she saw to Sandra and her crew, and to Henry, who had gone on ahead of her, had already disappeared into the Reef's maw.

Its swollen, thundercloud-coloured lobes bulged up five or six storeys high: an early experiment in growing flood defences with construction coral that had run wild and spread halfway across the Thames before the commensal organisms that fabricated it, several hundred types of alien bacterioforms, had been brought under control with hormone sprays developed by one of Ada Morange's companies. Chloe crossed a kind of apron that had been bulldozed out of a tongue of coral and sealed with a translucent polymer that showed the complex three-dimensional web of stony branches beneath, their purple and indigo shades spreading across her camo jacket. There was a small bus station, a line of tour coaches. Before he'd left the van Henry had put on a name badge: *Hi! I'm Henry from Springfield IL.* Chloe was hoping that he wouldn't try to make some kind of move on Fahad, attempt to snatch him.

She passed through the shadows of spiky buttresses, followed a wide passageway illuminated by shafts of sunlight that dropped through the latticework ceiling at irregular intervals. The circular openings to tunnels that led deeper into the Reef loomed ahead. There were entire buildings buried in there, penetrated and invaded and overtopped by the exuberant growth. There were workshops and factories, mazes of passageways, voids, and veins, and the homes of five thousand people. Climate refugees, plain old-fashioned illegal immigrants, and a variety of crews of tribes, biohackers and pirates who wanted to live off-grid in a self-declared semi-autonomous free zone. The authorities generally left them alone because the Reef was one of the places that the Jackaroo claimed to find very interesting, and no one knew how they would respond to an attempt to regulate it or shut it down.

Chloe hadn't spent much time in the Reef after starting work with Disruption Theory, but the free market was the same as it ever was. It was housed in a small shopping mall that had been flooded by the river and then swallowed by the Reef. The coral's growth held back the river's flood now, and pumps kept the mall dry. Its retail units had been excavated and subdivided, and a bustling maze of tiny shops, tattoo and body-mod parlours, cafés, bars and food stalls had colonised the broad walkway and food court. Coral bulged overhead, strung with webs of fairy lights.

Henry's voice buzzed in the earpiece of Chloe's spex. 'I see you. No, don't look for me. We should assume that the kid and his friends are watching. Find a place to sit. Make yourself comfortable and be prepared for a long wait. These things never run to schedule.'

But Chloe had already seen the person she'd been looking for, turning away from her, walking unhurriedly across her line of sight towards the public toilets. 'I have to pee – nerves, I guess,' she told Henry, and switched off her spex and ducked inside the toilets, an egg-shaped space saturated with a hallucinogenic ultraviolet glow.

Gail Ann was standing at the sink, touching up her lipstick. She was dressed in a denim jacket and roomy shorts and big hiking boots. An antique People's Liberation Army cap was tilted over one eye. Her gaze met Chloe's in the mirror and she grinned and said, 'I feel like a spy in a spy film.'

Chloe had made a quick call to her friend when she'd returned to her hotel room to collect her stuff. She said now, 'This is going to sound insanely inadequate, but thanks for coming.'

'I'm not going to miss an important chapter in my exclusive. Is it safe to talk?'

'I'm with some people, but they won't follow me in here.' She described Sandra's young men and Henry's costume, and said, 'I'm supposed to talk to Fahad, persuade him to come with me. While I'm doing that, you could try to get close to his friends. They probably know who you are, from the gym. Find out how they know Fahad, what they know about his situation . . . And you should tell them about me. Answer any questions they ask.'

Gail Ann capped her lipstick and blew a kiss at her reflection. She looked confident and unflappable, up for anything. 'Make friends. I can do that.'

'I told myself this was for Fahad,' Chloe said. 'That I can help him negotiate the best price for whatever it is that's infected him and his little sister. Make sure that they'll be given a chance to live a normal life afterwards. And I do want to help him, but I have to admit that I'm also scared that when this is over, when I've persuaded him to come in, that'll be that as far as I'm concerned. So long and thanks for all the fish.'

'Which wouldn't be good, for the story.'

'Anything you find out, I can use it to stay in the game. Also I want Fahad's friends to know that it's safe to get in contact with me again, if things go wrong.'

'Do you expect this to go wrong?'

Gail Ann's gaze was serious under the bill of her cap.

'My friend does,' Chloe said. 'The police are looking for Fahad, and his father's employers have an interest too, it turns out.'

'If it helps, I brought Noah's car. He thinks I'm helping a friend move. So if you need to get out of here in a hurry . . .'

'Like in the films?'

'It would make a great scene, wouldn't it?'

'If anything does happen, the police or whatever turn up, get out as quickly and quietly as possible. Walk away and don't look back. My friend will take care of me.'

'And if I happen to give one of Fahad's friends a lift?'

'Don't even think about it. If they have any sense, they'll have an escape route. Probably more than one.'

'How are you holding up?'

'I'm a bag of nerves, frankly.'

'You don't look nervous,' Gail Ann said. 'You look . . . eager.'

'I really want this to work out.'

Gail Ann smiled. 'He put a hook in you, didn't he? Cute Pakistani boy, those soulful eyes they have, eyelashes to die for.'

'Something put a hook in me all right,' Chloe said.

*

She circled the free market, sat at the counter of a stall that sold churros and paper cones of muscular café au lait, Cuban style. She perched sideways on her stool, watching passers-by, trying and failing to spot Sandra's operatives. Henry's voice buzzed in the earpiece of her spex. She couldn't see him, either, but she knew he was close by because he was commenting on people walking past her.

Saying, 'How does that guy eat, with those fangs?' Or, 'That's barely human.' Or, 'Is that supposed to be a !Cha tank she's trundling along there? Because she clearly hasn't ever seen a real one.'

Chloe raised the cone of coffee to her lips. 'And you have.'

'The Prof has one as a house guest,' Henry said. 'Damn thing calls itself Unlikely Worlds. It claims to be interested in the Prof. Says that she is a potential catalyst. You can imagine how much she loves that.'

'I met it,' Chloe said. 'Him. All !Cha, the ones on Earth, are male. Ada Morange held a party after she bought a majority share in Disruption Theory.'

Henry said, 'I was there.'

'I don't remember you.'

'I was walking perimeter security. The idea being that you and the other guests didn't see me.'

'Is this your way of telling me that you aren't really a freelance investigator?'

'I do all kinds of work,' Henry said.

'That old Range Rover. Is that even yours?'

'I like to use it for surveillance work. What would you have done if you were met by a couple of beefcakes in black suits, mirrorshades and curly-wire earpieces? No, I figured the down-at-heel junkyard look was the way to go.'

'You played me.'

'I tailored my look to your expectations.'

'You profiled me and you played me.'

'The Prof likes you, as much as she likes anyone. She's interested in you, in a good way. I'm an expression of that interest.'

It was half past four.

200

'They're late,' Chloe said.

'They're always late. They like to check the venue one last time, have to psych themselves up . . . Know what this reminds me of? Camden Market, back in the day.'

'That's for daytrippers and poseurs who like the alienist look but don't want to live the life,' Chloe said. 'This is where people who live the life live the life.'

'You have it too,' Henry said. 'The obsession with the alien and the weird. But you don't have the look. No mods. Not even a tattoo that I can see.'

'It affects different people in different ways,' Chloe said.

She thought of Fahad and his little sister, Rana. Both of them responding to something. Both touched, infiltrated, possessed.

Henry said, 'I used to hang out in Camden Market just about every weekend. Me and my mates. Like this, watching the world go by, the different tribes.'

'Which tribe did you belong to?'

'Indie rock, mostly. My little gang wore Fred Perry shirts and skinny jeans and Converse hi-tops, and Camden was our home, our turf. Everyone else in the market, no matter how hip they liked to think they were, they were just passing through. They were, like you said, daytrippers. So we have that in common at least. We're both observers. We like to watch. We see things from the outside . . . Look sharp. I think we're on.'

A young man ordered a coffee to go and pushed a sheet of paper across the counter to Chloe. One of Mr Archer's flyers.

'He sees only you,' the young man said, looking straight ahead. He was eighteen or nineteen, tall and thin and jittery, dark skin and high cheekbones, dressed in an oversized T-shirt screen-printed with the Max Predator poster, black ribbed leggings. Turning now, slouching away with his paper cone of coffee.

'Stay cool. Remember that I have your back,' Henry said, and Chloe followed the kid around the pool and down one of the narrow passages between storefronts.

She felt an airy sense of excitement. Closing in on her prize, hyper-aware of passers-by, a woman working at a sewing machine in a narrow plate-glass window, a couple of men gossiping in a storefront that sold Jackaroo masks and Jackaroo sunglasses and Jackaroo bobbleheads, rows of them staring blankly as she went past. Remembering, with a shiver in her blood, the Jackaroo avatar wading out of the sea. Remembering its warning.

The young man stopped at a shop window where alien stones and minerals glittered on a ladder of transparent shelves, and told Chloe, 'Wait here. If it's all clear he'll be with you.'

And then he was gone, leaving Chloe to study the stones. Lumps of red sandstone, chunks of marble, pebbles, a big geode like a broken egg with purplish crystals inside. Test tubes half-filled with sand, different colours. Sheets of slate each with a fossil or fragment of a fossil, like pages from some strange and deeply ancient book . . . She felt a sudden ache, like the nostalgia from looking at old family photographs, people and places in times before she was born, before the aliens came, before the Spasm. A yearning for a place she'd never seen.

'There he is,' Henry's voice said in her ear, and Fahad was standing beside her, his reflection beside hers in the gleaming glass. Rana clutched his hand, peeking around him at Chloe, who smiled and asked how she was.

The little girl ducked her head away, looked back. Chloe had a sense, suddenly, of the watchful presence that had followed her out of the displaced-persons camp. It was right there, at her back. She had to fight the urge to look around.

'You caused us a lot of trouble,' Fahad said.

'I know. And I'm sorry for it. But I came here because I want to help you. You and Rana.'

Rana tugged at her brother's hand. 'Tell her what Ugly Chicken says.'

Fahad said, 'Not now, Rana.'

Rana said to Chloe, 'He likes you.'

Chloe said, 'Is he your special friend?'

The little girl nodded.

'I think I can feel him watching me.'

'He won't hurt you.'

'That's good to know.'

Fahad said, 'The place where you work got firebombed, and the police are looking for you. If you're in so much trouble, how can you help me?'

'The place where I work, Disruption Theory, is owned by Dr Ada Morange. She's rich and smart. She has a lot of resources. She helped me, and she wants to help you too. You and Rana. But I bet you already know that. I bet that's why you asked me to come here. You think she can help you, but you aren't sure that you can trust her. You want me to tell you that you can.'

Henry said in her ear, 'You better wind this up, Sandra's picking up—'

His voice cut off with a little click. Chloe wondered what she was supposed to do, he hadn't told her to walk . . .

Fahad was saying, 'Her people came to the gym yesterday, asking about me. And then your friend turned up. How come, if you're working for her?'

'I wasn't sure her people would ask the right questions.'

'Meaning you don't exactly trust her,' Fahad said.

'Dr Morange is interested in your drawings, Fahad. She wants to know why you draw them, what they mean to you. So do I. I came here because I really think she can help you. And if you come with me, right now, you'll see—'

Shop doors slammed open on either side; police in uniform and plainclothes barged out, crowding the passageway. Fahad clutched Rana to him, glaring with fright and anger, and Chief Inspector Adam Nevers smiled down at Chloe. 'Actually,' he said, 'I think you should come with me.'

'You've fallen in with some bad people,' Nevers told Chloe, as they hustled down the grimy service corridor behind the shops. 'And you've put yourself in serious danger. The kids too. But if you help me I think I can find a way of clearing all this up.'

His hand was on her shoulder, steering her. Unpainted plasterboard on one side, pipes and swags of cable running along a rough wall of dark purple coral on the other, widely spaced low-watt lights. He'd taken her spex, dropped them on the ground and stepped on them. Ahead, Fahad and Rana were sandwiched between two uniformed policewomen; two more police, burly young men in T-shirts and jeans, brought up the rear.

'The kids were already in danger,' Chloe said.

'Did you really think that Ada Morange could help them?'

'I thought *I* could help them.'

She was trying to stay calm. She was wondering where Henry and the others were. Wondering if they would challenge the police, if they'd been arrested.

'You're out of your depth,' Nevers said. 'Dr Morange was using you, Chloe. And she wants to use the kids, too. She isn't interested in their welfare. She's interested in whatever it is that's infected them with peculiar ideas.'

'And why are you interested in them, Chief Inspector? Is it pure charity on your part?'

Chloe felt peculiarly calm, but her mouth was dry and her heart was going like crazy.

'The thing that's infected these kids could be dangerous. As you well know. It has to be contained. Think carefully, Chloe. Think about which side you want to be on. And don't expect any help from your friend Henry Harris. We have his surveillance team and pretty soon we'll have him.'

They pushed through a narrow door into the free market. People staring, whistles and catcalls echoing under webs of fairy lights, no sign of Henry or Sandra's young men. Down the wide passageway, out into sunlight and the fresh smell of rain, puddles shining everywhere on the translucent surface of the broad tongue of coral. Three Range Rovers with tinted windows were drawn up in front of the line of tour buses, light bars flashing. Knots of police in uniform and men and women in suits and skirt suits, pistols and tasers at their hips. A big drone with a blue and white chequered paint job tilted in the air, its amplified voice telling people to disperse. And beyond all this, beyond ragged rows of parked cars, on the far side of acres of weedy tarmac, Sandra's surveillance van was on fire, tossing flames and billows of black smoke high into the air.

Rana began to struggle, trying to free herself from the grip of the policewoman who held her. The woman told her to be quiet, they were going for a ride in a police car, it would be a lot of fun. 'I don't want to,' Rana wailed, upset beyond reason.

Fahad bucked between the two police holding his arms. 'Leave her alone!'

'Let's keep moving,' Nevers said, and the policewoman hoisted Rana up, the little girl kicking and screaming, and the awful thing happened.

Chloe was overwhelmed by a tidal surge of unreasoning panic, and something sharp and bright she couldn't look at loomed overhead. She had the impression of the air splintering apart and raw sun-stuff lancing out, a seethe of activity boiling off it. The sense of a voracious inhuman intelligence turning its attention towards her, bigger and brighter than any eidolon she'd ever seen or heard about, pushing into her head.

And then there was a moment of sickening eversion, as if her mind was a glove that had been pulled inside out, and the world came back. The seething raw light was gone, but everyone around her was flinching away from some private horror show. Nevers had drawn his pistol and was pointing it in different directions, face twisted into a desperate grimace. The policewoman dropped Rana and fell to her knees and wrapped her arms around her head. A policeman doubled over and vomited. Another policeman screwed the heels of his hands into his eyes, his mouth stretched wide in a red scream. And Rana was running. Knees and elbows splayed, running past the police and the police vehicles. Chloe chased after the little girl as she dodged between parked cars. Behind her, Fahad was shouting something.

There was no sign of Rana. Chloe looked around, then dropped to her hands and knees, peered under the cars on either side.

The little girl was pressed against a wheel, knees tucked into her chest, arms wrapped around her shins.

'It's okay,' Chloe said, trying her best to smile. 'It's okay now. You can come out.'

'I don't like the bad people.'

'Nor do I. Let's make sure they don't catch us.'

'Ugly Chicken doesn't like them either,' the little girl said.

'I know.'

'He made everyone see things. Were you scared?'

'Very scared.'

Chloe remembered seeing, in some disaster-porn documentary, a robot sent in to inspect the burning heart of a nuclear reactor smashed open by an earthquake. She felt that she'd been given a glimpse of something like that: an elemental devouring light that could boil a person's brain in her skull. And with a horrible lurch of association she thought of the Trafalgar Square bomb, the incandescent flare of her mother's last moment, and wondered if that was what Ugly Chicken had tapped into.

Rana said, 'It wasn't meant for you. He mostly aimed it at the bad people.'

'Can you scoot out, sweetheart?' Chloe said. 'We need to get going.'

Footsteps behind her: Fahad, breathless and sweating, squatting down to look at his sister. 'You did good,' he told her, and said to Chloe, 'I don't even know why I wanted to meet you. We can take care of ourselves.'

'Let's get out of here. Find somewhere to talk.'

Fahad picked up Rana and cradled her to his chest, and he and Chloe scurried across the lorry park. Chloe's camo jacket flickered, trying to imitate the candy colours of cars, a stretch of weedy tarmac. Her heart was beating quick and high and she had only one thought in her head: get as far away from the Reef as possible.

They were close to the ragged hedge of buddleias at the edge of the lot when she heard the whine of an engine behind her. Fahad stopped and turned around, but she couldn't look. If she did, she might see Ugly Chicken again, might turn into a pillar of salt. She grabbed Fahad's arm, shook him, told him to keep going.

He said, 'It isn't the police.'

A tinny horn beeped, and a bright yellow runabout swerved towards them through crackling weed stalks, braked with a hard squeal. Its passenger door popped open and Gail Ann said, 'Hey girlfriend. Need a lift?'

30. Death Knock

Skip Williams and his partner Corinda Summerville lived in a suburban development on the eastern side of the city, built on the alkali pan where Vic and his friends had held motorbike races back in the day. Now hundreds of prefab bungalows were strung along a skewed grid of curved roads that he had trouble navigating. Eucalyptus saplings shivering in the wind, tidy gardens of rock and gravel and cactus, a few lawns of the new half-life turf, a green too vivid to be natural.

He drove past the same shopping centre twice before he realised he should turn left instead of right at the Y-junction dominated by a gull-winged church. Skip's bungalow was at the edge of the development, on a street that ran out into the empty playa. No trees here, drifts of sand along the gutters. There was a police cruiser in the driveway. Vic parked and walked over to it, feeling about two hundred years old in gravity that seemed to have doubled, leaned at the window and asked the uniform if there had been any specific threats or anyone suspicious driving by.

'I chased off a couple of journalists,' the uniform said. 'Otherwise it's been quiet. I heard it was something to do with a drug crew.'

'Not everything in this town is drug-related,' Vic said. 'It only seems that way. And this is one of our own, so don't go spreading rumours.'

Lucille Colombier had sat him down and given it to him straight. According to Skip's partner, Skip had worked late on Friday evening, writing up his assault-with-intent and trying to find out why Danny Drury and Cal McBride had both left town. He'd gone into work on Saturday, too, and come back a few hours

207

later, agitated and excited. He'd packed, kissed his partner and told her he would be back in a couple of days, and left.

According to Lucille, the trigger had been a report of a multiple homicide outside Winnetou, a small town in Idunn's Valley. Skip hadn't asked for permission to check it out; instead, he'd booked two personal days and flown straight there. He'd talked to the constable handling the case, had been seen in a café in town. A few hours later, his hire car had been found burning behind a produce-storage shed. Skip's body was in the boot.

'It was badly burned, and they aren't set up for DNA analysis down there, but they found Skip's wallet and badge, and pulled prints off two of his fingers,' Lucille said. 'The county constable believes that either he ran into some bad people, or he was involved with them and had a falling-out. I told him that Skip was an upstanding officer. I hope I'm right, because internal affairs will be going deep into his background. The people of the seventh floor are already looking for someone to blame for this, and who better than a dead man?'

'The kid was clean. A Boy Scout. If anyone thinks differently let me talk to them. I'll change their minds,' Vic said, and meant it.

He asked about the multiple murder. Lucille said that she didn't have much information. 'It was on a farm several kilometres west of the town. A serious shootout, vehicles set on fire, five dead. A witness claimed that some kind of laser was involved.'

Vic felt a sudden chill. 'The ray gun.'

'My thought exactly. Skip wanted to go out there when he found that the chief suspects in this murder had left town. He told me that they had some quarrel over an Elder Culture site. But it was outside our jurisdiction and he had no evidence, so of course I turned down his request. But then he heard about this shootout.'

'And thought it had to be something to do with McBride and Drury. I should have known the kid wouldn't give up on the case,' Vic said. 'I should have seen this coming.'

'We can apportion blame later,' Lucille said. 'Right now, we have a man down, and I want his body back before the dust storm hits. Which means in the next couple of days.'

'Yes, chief.'

It was a punishment. It was a reprieve.

'No doubt the county constable will want to interview you about Skip's investigation,' Lucille said. 'When he does, you will be polite and cooperative, no more, no less. Remember that it's his case. Do not get involved. Do not offer assistance. You are going there only to confirm the identity of a fallen officer and to bring him home. Am I understood?'

'Loud and clear,' Vic said, knowing that he had every intention of disobeying his captain's orders.

Now, outside Skip's home, he asked the uniform who was inside.

'The girlfriend, one of her friends, the family liaison officer. There was a neighbour, too, but she just left.'

'What about the CS techs?'

'They came, they went. This is fucked up, uh?'

'Beyond fucked,' Vic said, and with his heart gathering weight in his chest walked up the flagstone path and rang the bell. Feeling the same awful foreboding of every death knock, every interview with raw grieving wives and husbands and partners.

Corinda Summerville was in the living room, curled up in a corner of a sofa. Her friend, another blonde woman around her age and about six months pregnant, sat at the other end. The TV was on, sound muted. TVs were often on at times like this. The anaesthetic quality of television for once being actually useful. Vic sat on an armchair across from the two women. The family liaison officer, an anxiously cheerful young man, offered to make tea and drifted out when no one responded.

Vic got past the awkward bit about how sorry he was. Corinda said, 'They won't tell me when they're bringing him back.'

There were three kinds of bereaved, in Vic's experience. The angry and baffled. The complete meltdowns. The numbly brisk. Corinda was the third kind, more or less. Haunted and red-eyed but determined, holding it together with a frail dignity.

He said, 'I'm going down there to sort that out. And I'm going to do my best to find out what happened, too.'

'I'll have to tell his parents,' Corinda said. 'I can't decide whether to write a letter or rent time on a q-phone.'

209

Her friend reached over and squeezed her hand and told her that she didn't have to worry about any of that now.

She was the self-appointed guardian angel, and didn't bother to hide her resentment over Vic's intrusion. He ignored her. He needed to ask some delicate questions, and he had another piece of business to deal with before he flew to Idunn's Valley.

He said, 'It would help if I could ask a few questions.'

'This is all about that ray-gun thing of his,' Corinda said.

'I'm afraid so.'

'She's already talked about that,' the friend said.

Corinda said, 'I'll do anything if it'll help find who did it.'

Vic led her through it as gently as possible. What Skip had told her before he left. What his mood had been. What he'd said when he called to tell her that he'd arrived. It didn't give him much and made him feel like a wasteman, and all the while Corinda's friend was staring at him like a mastiff wondering which limb to rip off first.

He clicked his card on the coffee table, amongst scrunched tissues and tea cups. 'Anything you remember, even if you don't think it's important, you can call me. Any time.'

'All right.'

'Or even if you just want to talk.'

'Bring him home.' Corinda's stare was bright and fierce. She was hugging a cushion to death. 'Do that for me. Bring him home.'

Vic broke his rule of never promising something he wasn't certain he could deliver.

'I won't come back without him.'

31. Ugly Chicken

England—France |
10—11 July

'I still don't know if I made the right decision,' Fahad said. 'But Rana says that *he's* happy with it. So there's that.'

Rana had consulted Ugly Chicken in a Burger King on the A13, after Chloe had called the emergency number that Sandra Hamilton had given her, and had been told to sit tight and wait for pickup. The little girl had mumbled into the microphone of her fist and cocked her head as if listening to a reply, sometimes with a grave expression, sometimes smiling and nodding. 'It's private,' she'd said, when Chloe had wondered what they were talking about. And, 'He'll tell me if he has anything to say to you.'

Chloe asked Fahad if Ugly Chicken ever spoke to him, but he ignored the question, saying, 'Maybe it'll come good in the end.'

They were sitting at a pine table in the kitchen of a safe house somewhere in Kent. Fahad was absent-mindedly sketching on a pad of paper that Sandra had supplied. Rough outlines of the usual landscape done in swift confident lines with red and black Sharpies, each image torn from the pad and crumpled when it was done. He was left-handed.

He told Chloe that the need to draw came over him like a fierce hunger. The first time, he'd stayed up all night, growing ever more frustrated because he couldn't get down on paper what pressed inside his head. The raw urgent need had frightened him, but he'd learned by trial and error which drawings eased its grip.

He was scribbling with the black Sharpie now, outlining the shape of the alien space he'd tried to reproduce in the squalid bedroom at the sea fort. Chloe asked him if it was the interior of one of the spires; he said he wasn't sure.

'I call it the black room, but I don't know if it's really a room. Rana shows her drawings to Ugly Chicken, but he won't talk to her about my stuff. He won't say what they are, or why he makes me draw them. Maybe he doesn't know how he affects other people.'

'I think he had a pretty good idea about what he was doing, at the Reef.'

'We can't control it. It just happens.'

Fahad hadn't seen the manifestation at the Reef: he'd never seen Ugly Chicken in any guise. And although Rana drew her starburst pictures over and over, she wouldn't ever draw her imaginary friend. It was one of the things he didn't like, according to her. After showing her pictures of all kinds of birds, Fahad believed that Ugly Chicken looked a little like a cross between a pelican and a turkey vulture. Sort of squashed and mostly naked, patched with bright colours. A big crooked beak for a mouth, eyes of different sizes and number, not all of them on its head. He spoke directly to Rana and they had created a world of rules and customs, things that had to be done in a particular way, things that were forbidden. Fahad said that she'd always liked to order her family of dolls and stuffed animals and robots about, explaining their relationships to each other, refereeing their squabbles. She had incorporated Ugly Chicken into those games; it used those games to communicate with her. And it put pictures in Fahad's head, and he felt that he had to get them down on paper or die.

He ripped out the half-completed sketch of the black room and smoothed the next sheet of paper and picked up the red Sharpie, drew the outline of a spire in two swift strokes, dashed lines on either side to indicate the rounded hills at the horizon. Looking up at Chloe, smiling. 'At first, I thought I had gone crazy. Now I know it has a purpose.'

Chloe picked up one of his crumpled sketches, flattened it on the table, and said, 'You know what this is, where this is?'

'Do you believe in fate?'

Fahad had a way of abruptly changing the subject when she asked him a question he didn't want to answer.

Chloe said, 'That depends on what you mean by fate, I guess.'

'I mean, do you believe that we were supposed to meet? That something ordered the world so that our paths would cross?'

Chloe took his questions seriously. She thought of how she'd walked out of the rehearsals for the select-committee appearance. How she'd decided to justify it by chasing up Mr Archer's Facebook announcement. Had it been no more than a whim, or had she unconsciously responded to the background landscape of that announcement?

She said, 'You think Ugly Chicken makes you draw that stuff because it knew I'd see it?'

'You found me, didn't you?' Fahad said.

He had a nice smile, but rarely used it. He was serious and suspicious, with that mix of vulnerability and arrogance particular to teenage boys. He'd barely said more than a dozen words while they'd been waiting for Sandra Hamilton. Even Gail Ann hadn't been able to crack his shell. And now that he was talking, it was clear that he wanted to steer the conversation in particular directions, to reveal only what he chose to reveal.

Chloe played along, saying, 'Mr Archer's meeting just happened to be taking place when I needed an excuse to be somewhere else. And anyone could have seen that announcement. Some other scout could have decided to check it out.'

'But you did,' Fahad said.

'Me and Eddie Ackroyd.'

She thought of Eddie's mysterious client. If he had been aimed towards that breakout, why not her? A shivery thought.

'But he isn't here, and you are.' Fahad had sketched the intricate latticework of the spire; now he began to add the little spurs that ornamented its flanks. Quick precise tick marks. His tongue pressed into a corner of his mouth. When he was finished, he looked at Chloe and said, 'I expect you think you rescued me. Me and Rana. But suppose we didn't need to be rescued?'

'I know you can look after yourself, that you can take care of your little sister. But there are some bad people looking for you, Fahad. Not just the police.'

'We *escaped* from the bad people. All on our own. I found a place to live, got a job stacking shelves in a supermarket, Rana was back in school . . . But then Mr Archer started up his thing, and it seemed like a good idea to help him. Even though I sort of knew it wasn't my idea. You found us, because of that, and then that weird sweaty guy in black . . . And I thought, maybe the bad guys could find us too.'

'That's why you ran away again.'

'I didn't run away. Rana and me moved in with some people I know. Friends, sort of, from the cage-fighting scene. And then you found us again. Maybe you could call it fate, but I don't think so. I think he wanted it to happen.'

'And what does he want now? What do you want?'

Fahad didn't reply at once, but bent over the pad again, using the black Sharpie to cross-hatch the spire's shadow across rocky ground evoked by spare dashes and scribbles of red ink. At last he said, 'I suppose you know that my father is dead. Killed by the people he was working for.'

Chloe nodded. 'I'm sorry.'

'He wasn't a good man. He wasn't even there for me most of the time. But he was trying to be good. When I was very young, in Pakistan, the government decided that intellectuals were enemies of the people. Both my father and mother worked in the University of the Punjab. She was a mathematician; he was a pharmaceutical engineer. There were pogroms, riots, against people like them. People were murdered. I had a sister, two years older than me. She was killed. One of my aunts had taken her shopping with our cousins, and they were all killed by a car bomb.'

Fahad had stopped drawing. He spoke quietly and precisely, as if reciting from memory. Retelling a story he'd been told many times.

'A few days later, after the funerals, people shot at our house. So my father decided that it was no longer safe for us, in our country. He used his connections to send my mother and me to England. The university had been closed down by then, but he had a consultancy with a pharmaceutical company, and he stayed on so that he could send us money. You need a lot of money to come to England and live here. Six months later, my father was denounced by one of his former students and thrown in prison. Along with many of his colleagues.

'He was in prison for eight years. Meanwhile, my mother brought me up. We lived in Oxford. She worked in the university, as a secretary. And then there was an amnesty, and my father was released. He went to Germany, as a political refugee, and then he came here. You can imagine how it was for me. This man, this stranger, claiming to be my father. Coming between me and my mother, who collaborated in the charade. But my father worked hard to win my affections, and he got a job with GlaxoSmithKline and we moved to Uxbridge. We had a nice house. My mother made a lovely garden, and Rana came along. I remember that we were very happy.

'My mother went back to work after Rana was born, with an insurance company in Wembley. One night she stayed late because a colleague was leaving and there was a party. She was driving home, it was raining, and a lorry ploughed into her car and killed her. My father took it badly. He believed that my mother's death was a judgement. There was a payment from my mother's life insurance. My father called it blood money. By then, he had begun to drink heavily. He fell in with some bad people and started to gamble. Cards, high stakes. He lost all of the insurance money, and then he lost everything else. He owed a lot of money to the wrong people, and to cover the debt he started to steal from his job. He was found out, and fired. And his gambling debt was bought by the McBride family, and he was told he would cook drugs for them, to pay it off. He refused, and Rana and I were kidnapped. Held as hostages until my father gave in.

'So we moved to a little town in East Anglia, on the Flood. You saw what it was like. My father cooked shine. He was so good at it he was sent to Mangala, to cook meq. Rana and I stayed behind. We were hostages again. We weren't treated badly, but the man and woman who looked after us were crooks. Thieves. My father got into the Elder Culture artefact business. He wanted to make enough money to buy a ticket to Earth. He sent things back to us, too. Things we could sell to make a little money. The people looking after us stole most of the stuff, but they let us keep a few things, including a little bead. And perhaps,' Fahad said, 'that was also fate. And perhaps it wasn't.'

'This was Ugly Chicken's bead,' Chloe said.

'Who can say if it found its way to us by choice or by accident? You might say that it doesn't matter, because by whichever path it arrived the destination was the same. But I think that it matters a great deal whether our lives are shaped by the choices we make, or whether they are shaped by the choices of something that stands outside of our ordinary experience.'

'You've thought about this a lot.'

'Wouldn't you, if you were in my situation? Our guardians thought that the bead had no value, and gave it to Rana. I believe that the thought wasn't their own. And I don't think it was my father's decision to send it to us, either. I began to draw my pictures. Rana began to talk to her new imaginary friend. And a few weeks later I found out that my father had been killed.

'I saw how he died,' Fahad said, his gaze dark and steady. 'Rana and I escaped. That was the first time Ugly Chicken showed itself to other people. I stole some money, but it wasn't enough. I was still wondering how I could buy a ticket to Mangala when you found us. Do you see now how it all works out? You saw my pictures and wanted to know what they mean. And they led you to me, and maybe you will help me get what I want.'

Chloe said, 'If you want Ada Morange to help you find the people who killed your father, to bring them to justice, you'll have to ask her yourself.'

'I don't want them "brought to justice",' Fahad said. 'I don't want them handed over to the police. I was brought up to believe that we should forgive those who trespass against us. But you and I know that it isn't enough, don't we?'

He was right about one thing, Chloe thought. She had been like him once upon a time, back when she had helped to set up the LFM wiki, when she had been looking for the truth about what had happened to her mother. When she had been looking for someone to blame. When she had been trying to make sense of the horror show that had knocked her life completely off course.

216

Yes, Fahad was very like she had been, back then. Scared and angry, boastful and defiant. She understood his bitterness and his hurt, and wished that she could tell him that it would heal, in time. That you live all your life in the presence of your parents, and they're suddenly gone, and it's like a raw wound in the heart of your being. You can't imagine going forward without them, but you do. And, gradually, the wound heals. A poem she had once found spoke of a tree falling in a wood, and the gap it leaves. And into the gap falls sunlight and new life. But she knew that Fahad wouldn't care to hear that. He was still too raw, too angry. He wanted justice. An eye for an eye, and all that Biblical shit.

She said, 'If Ada Morange agrees to help you, you'll have to give something in return. That's how it usually works. You'll have to tell us about the pictures, where they are, what they show. You'll have to tell us what Ugly Chicken really is, and what it can do.'

Fahad turned the pad so that the spire was, for her, the right way round.

'This is on Mangala,' he said. 'It was made by the people who made Ugly Chicken. He was asleep a long time. And now he is awake, and wants to go home. He wants to show us where he belongs and what he can do. But if you want to know more than that, you'll have to take me to Dr Morange.'

Early the next morning a courier delivered Chloe's passport, taken from her flat, and brand-new passports for Fahad and Rana. They were driven to a private airfield and boarded a little prop plane that hopped across the Channel to Normandy and landed on a strip mown into a meadow of a farm owned by Karyotech Pharma. Ada Morange and Henry Harris were waiting with a stout middle-aged woman: Rimsha Batti, one of Fahad and Rana's aunts. She had been found by Ada Morange's people in Pakistan, and they'd brought her to France to chaperone her niece and nephew.

Rana was shy with this strange woman; Fahad suspected some kind of trick, glancing indifferently at the pictures of his mother and her many relatives that Rimsha displayed on her phone, which she also used as a translator because she had very little English. She said that she had come of her own free will to help her nephew and niece; she had left behind her husband and her own children, her work as a librarian. 'Dr Morange paid for my air fare, nothing else.'

Chloe was suspicious too. Not of Rimsha, who seemed like a sensible independent woman, but of the way this little family reunion had been arranged. Henry said it was mostly a legal precaution. Fahad was Rana's brother, but as far as the authorities in Britain were concerned he wasn't her guardian. Rimsha was prepared to intercede on their behalf, if it came to a battle in the courts.

Henry had evaded the police during the confusion created by Ugly Chicken, and had made his way to France after supervising a little distraction – dispatching lookalikes on a private jet to Shanghai and leaking to a friendly media outlet blurry CCTV of them boarding the plane.

'It won't fool Nevers for long, but it might give us a bit of breathing space,' he told Chloe. 'Time for you to decide what you want to do next.'

But Chloe already knew what was coming. She'd known ever since she'd seen, as the plane had come in to land, the Mangala shuttle balanced at the horizon.

'What about you?' she said. 'Are you done yet?'

They were sitting in the dappled shade of a grape arbour while Ada Morange talked with Fahad and Rana inside the farmhouse. Henry had shed his down-at-heel private-eye impersonation, was clean-shaven and dressed in black jeans and a white short-sleeved shirt. He looked older. He looked his age.

'You may be disappointed to know that I'm going all the way,' he said. 'If young Fahad agrees to our plan, that is.'

'As if he has a choice.'

'Of course he has a choice. We aren't monsters. We're trying to do our best for those kids.'

At last, Fahad and Rana came out of the French doors, past the wiry alert man who escorted Ada Morange everywhere. Ex-Foreign Legion, according to Henry. Rana ran off down a slope of glass towards the old apple orchard, arms extended airplane style; Fahad smiled at Chloe and said, 'She wants to talk to you.'

Ada Morange sat straight-backed in her black wheelchair by the room's stone fireplace. Heavy oak furniture, oriental rugs on the stone-flag floor, lilies pale as ghosts in a big Chinese vase on a side table. A grandfather clock ticking in a corner. The old woman thanked Chloe for her help, asked her opinion of Fahad.

'He talked to you openly and willingly. Do you believe him? Do you believe this eidolon can lead us to something interesting, or is the boy spinning a story to get me to take him to Mangala?'

Ada Morange wore a black pencil dress with gauzy sleeves. Classic Chanel. Her white hair was brushed straight back from her forehead. A line taped to the back of her bony hand looped up to a pouch of clear liquid hung on a rod at the back of her wheelchair. A choker of red pearls gleamed like drops of blood against the corded tendons of her neck. In the wreckage of her health she was formidably elegant and commanding.

'Fahad's paintings and drawings, his obsession with that landscape . . . All of that is very real to him. And Ugly Chicken is real, too. No question about that. I saw it,' Chloe said, with a tingling sensation of remembered panic. 'A small part of it, anyway.'

'Yes, when you escaped from the Hazard Police. We examined such CCTV footage as we could obtain, of course, but found nothing. The eidolon must operate directly on the optical nerves. Perhaps also the limbic system, where emotions and memory are regulated.'

'I think it helped Fahad and Rana escape from their guardians in Norfolk, too,' Chloe said. 'Fahad said that it wanted to be found. That's why, he said, it got inside the heads of Mr Archer and the others in that little cult. That's why he let them use his pictures, even though he knew it might attract the attention of the wrong people.'

'He told me that the eidolon wanted to attract your attention,' Ada Morange said.

'And yours too, perhaps,' Chloe said.

'Indeed. It may have a deeper agenda than we can know. We believe that eidolons like Ugly Chicken are fragments of something much larger. That they're broken, damaged. But suppose they only appear to be damaged because we don't really understand them?

Suppose we don't see them for what they really are? Suppose we don't realise they are manipulating us in ways we can't see or comprehend? But even if it is not some broken thing, even if it has potency, agency, it is quite possible that it is feeding the boy and his sister fantasies of a place that no longer exists except in its memory.'

'We can't know until we go there, can we?'

'Yes. That's exactly the problem.'

Ada Morange's dark gaze reminded Chloe of a chimpanzee she'd once seen in London Zoo. Her eleventh birthday, just before things started to go bad, before chimpanzees had been wiped out by Texas flu. A different kind of intelligence, recognisable but unreadable.

She said, 'Can your special friend help us?'

'I have already asked him. Unfortunately, while Unlikely Worlds is not as wilfully enigmatic as the Jackaroo, on this matter he offers no opinion. I fear that there will be no neat ending to this, in the manner of the old Greek plays. Where the Gods descend, and all is explained, and tidied away. No, if we want to know more, we must discover it for ourselves.'

'Fahad told you what those spires are, didn't he? What he thinks they are.'

'Yes, he did. He claims that they are the equivalent of a shuttle terminal, used by the spaceships of the Elder Culture that built it. If that is true, if any trace of them still exists, it will be a wonder. We are utterly dependent on the shuttles to reach the worlds the Jackaroo gave us, and have no control over their schedules or flight plans. And apart from a few disputed fragments around what might be the craters of crash sites, we have never found anything resembling a space vehicle, nor any depiction of space travel, anywhere in the fifteen worlds. We assume that either the Elder Cultures lacked the technology, or that it was as primitive as ours and was abandoned after contact with the Jackaroo. Or that if any Elder Culture once possessed the means for independent travel between the fifteen worlds, all traces have been erased by time. Most ruins are very old, after all, and little more than mineralised traces compressed in layers of rock.

'That is why,' Ada Morange said, 'this will be in the nature of a preliminary investigation. I have rebuilt my company, but its resources are not what they once were. I must test the boy's claims thoroughly before I mount a full-blown expedition. And Rana will stay here, of course, in the care of her aunt. We will talk to her, let her play games, and in general get to know her and her special friend. She is very charming, is she not? She has not been damaged by her guest. She is herself. That she sees it as a separate entity is very good. Very hopeful. But we cannot let her go with her brother. It would not be right to put her life at risk.'

'I want to go,' Chloe said. 'I want to help Fahad and Rana. I want to see this thing through.'

It burst out of her. It was as if, yes, something else had spoken. But it was also what she wanted.

'That's good,' Ada Morange said. 'Fahad will help us to find where Ugly Chicken came from, but he has certain conditions. Very bold, that boy. I admire it. One of them you already know about: he wants us to help him find the people who killed his father. The other is that you must accompany him to Mangala.'

32. Little Dave

When Vic drew up outside Danny Drury's house, Alain Bodin and Maria Espinosa got out of the unmarked Ford Victory that blocked the gate, and told him that there was no sign of Drury. 'Just the husband and wife who do the cooking and cleaning, look after the garden,' Alain said. 'And the guy who answered our knock.'

Little Dave was sitting in the back of the unmarked car, his wrists cuffed behind his back. Looking up when Vic tapped on the window, looking away.

Vic said, 'I guess he isn't in the mood to talk.'

'The piece of shit didn't even ask us what it was about,' Alain said, with a spasm of anger and disgust. 'Because, of course, he already knows.'

Maria said, 'How are you, Vic?'

'After I deal with this, I'm heading out to Idunn's Valley to pick up the body. The stupid fucking kid,' Vic said. 'Trying to play that boy-detective shit. Thinking he was in his own personal action film.'

'You must not blame yourself,' Maria said. 'He did what he thought he had to do.'

'Kid fucked up, is what it is,' Alain said.

'He didn't say one word about what he was planning,' Vic said. 'If he'd told me, I could have done something, stopped it . . .'

The three investigators shared a quiet moment.

Vic said, 'What about the other two? The husband and wife?'

'We talked to them,' Maria said. 'They claim that they don't know anything.'

'They told us that Drury and the others rolled out a couple of days ago,' Alain said. 'They don't know where they went or when they will be back. Your friend claims to know even less. You want to talk to him here or in the squad room?'

'I want to take him for a drive,' Vic said.

Alain and Marie extracted Little Dave from their car and walked him over to Vic's. The man was nervous, avoiding Vic's gaze.

As Little Dave stooped to wedge himself into the back seat, Alain put his hand on the stubbly boulder of the man's head, gripping it like a bowling ball, and banged it against the sill. 'Oops. I forget to tell you to be careful how you get in when you are handcuffed.'

Little Dave had the sense not to reply or complain. Sitting on his hands in the back seat, staring ahead, trying not to flinch when Alain slammed the door, almost succeeding.

When Marie handed him the handcuff key, Vic said, 'I'm not going to do anything stupid. I'm just going to put him on the spot.'

Alain said, 'Why are you telling us? We aren't even here.'

In the car, Vic adjusted the rear-view mirror and stared into it until he had Little Dave's attention. The fucker looking like a child who knows he's been caught but is trying to tough it out. Piggy eyes smouldering with resentment, lips clamped tight.

Vic said, 'Don't ask me what this is about, because I know you know. In fact, I don't want to hear one word from you until we get to where we're going. If I do, I'll pull over and haul you out and shoot you in the face and send a photo of it to your fucking mother.'

Part of it was his tough-cop act, a role he could put on and take off. Part of it, surprising him, was for real.

He drove north and east out of the city, past the airport and into the hills beyond, following the road to the quarries that supplied much of the construction stone for the city. He overtook flatbed trucks, tipper trucks, and about five kilometres out turned down a track that dipped into a valley where a small swift river ran between tumbled rocks, and parked on a flat ridge near the stark frame of a burned-out wooden house.

Vic got out and opened the passenger door and told Little Dave to get out too. He made the man assume the position against the side of the car, unlocked the handcuffs. 'Let's go for a little walk.'

Little Dave followed him to the edge of the rise. Fans of scree fell to the river. A herd of biochines, jointed six-legged things, was grazing amongst stiff bushes up on the far side. In the distance something was making a nagging whine that sounded exactly like a plane saw, rising and falling in the cold breeze.

Vic said, 'Way back when, people tried to raise goats here. The goats didn't make it past the first year. All of them got eaten. But we should be safe enough for a little bit.'

The biochines were harmless herbivores, but Vic was pretty sure that Little Dave didn't know that.

Little Dave took out an ecig. Trying to look casual, although his gaze kept going back to the biochines. He was in shirtsleeves, hunched against the cold clean wind. He said, 'I'm dying for a puff. All right?'

'Best not. It can drive biochines crazy.'

'If you're trying to put the fear in me, it isn't going to work,' Little Dave said, but he put the ecig away.

'You came up five years ago,' Vic said. 'Ever been outside the city before?'

'What's the point? It all looks like this.'

The man was uncertain, sullen and suspicious. Watching the distant biochines rather than Vic.

'You come all the way to a wild alien planet, but you aren't interested in what it's really like, or in making a new life for yourself . . .'

Little Dave shrugged.

'So why not stay at home?'

'I was born in Romford. You ever been in Romford?'

'I bet you were in and out of jail, back in Romford.'

'That's all in the past, innit. Doesn't count here.'

'Is that why you came up? Because you were running away from the consequences of a serious crime?'

Little Dave shrugged again.

'Did you meet up with Cal McBride's people in prison, or afterwards?'

'I told your friends I don't know where he is.'

'You told them you don't know where Danny Drury is. But what about your old boss? Where is he? The reason I ask,' Vic said, 'is because he hasn't been seen at his hotel. The Petra Carlton, where he has a suite. He hasn't been at the construction site for his pleasure dome, either. I have to confess, I'm a little concerned about his safety. If he's had an accident, ended up at the bottom of a foundation trench or in a shallow grave out on the playa, you'd be doing yourself a big favour by telling me about it now.'

'I don't have nothing to do with him no more.'

'That's right. The new boss came up while McBride was in prison, and you switched sides. Just like that. As if three years of working for the man meant nothing at all.'

'I didn't switch anything. I'm still in exactly the same job.'

'And what job is that, exactly?'

'I look after the house, don't I?'

The man sounding plaintive.

Vic said, 'Doing what? Mopping floors, emptying wastebins . . .'

'Security and such.'

'You like to think you're a badman, don't you?'

A shrug.

'There was a Big Dave once upon a time, wasn't there? Cal McBride's right-hand man, killed in a traffic accident. If it was an accident.'

Little Dave shrugged again, pretending to be interested in something way beyond Vic.

'I just realised why Danny Drury and his goons still call you Little Dave, long after Big Dave copped it. Because you're small-time. A minnow amongst sharks. You're their pet. They let you stay on after they kicked out Cal McBride because you're harmless. A joke. And now they've left you here to face the fucking music, while they're somewhere out there playing Cowboys and Indians.'

'I just look after the house. I don't know nothing about any of that.'

Vic unsnapped his shoulder holster and pulled out his gun, the Colt .45 he kept locked in the bottom drawer of his desk. The gun he'd never worn on an investigation until now. It got Little Dave's attention straight away.

'Someone killed a cop. Not just any cop. My partner. My friend. Tell me again you don't know anything about anything,' Vic said, 'and I'll shoot you in the fucking kneecaps and leave you here.'

Little Dave stared at him, and plainly saw something he didn't like. 'All right,' he said. 'All right! They went back to Idunn's Valley. And that's all I know, I swear.'

'This is Danny Drury and his goons.'

'Yeah.'

'What about Cal McBride?'

'I told you. I don't have nothing to do with him no more.'

'Don't lie to me, or I swear I'll shoot you and drive you over to that pack of biochines and kick you out of the car.'

In that moment Vic knew that he could shoot the little fuck dead if he had to. He could see himself doing it: it rose up from some deep part of himself.

Little Dave flinched from his gaze, saying, 'You're fucking crazy.'

'You bet I am. You bet your life. Cal McBride. Is he alive or dead?'

'Alive, last time I knew.'

'Meaning Danny Drury didn't kill him, or have him killed.'

'Drury wouldn't dare.'

'Where is he now? Cal McBride.'

'I might have heard he went to Idunn's Valley.'

'And that's why Danny Drury went back there. Yes or no?'

'Yes!'

'Back to that Elder Culture site. Site 326.'

'Yes.'

'They're both looking for the same thing, aren't they?'

'I think so.'

'Yes or no?'

'Yes. Jesus, stop pointing that fucking gun at me. I'm telling you, aren't I?'

'What are they looking for? And don't tell me you don't know. I bet you spend most of your time in that house with your ear pressed against keyholes.'

'I don't know what it is, exactly, but it got someone haunted.'

'Who would that be? Name names, or it's a short ride to the local wildlife.'

'Someone on Earth. I think it was something someone sent back. As a present, a souvenir.'

'Something from Site 326.'

'I suppose so. Danny, Mr Drury, he went to check it out. But I don't think he found anything.'

'And how did he hear about it?'

'They have contacts back home. Bent coppers, clerks, IT people. Not Mr Drury, the people he works for.'

'The McBride family.'

'They're an old firm. One of the best.'

Vic had a sudden epiphany. He said, 'They sent people here, didn't they? The McBride family. They sent people to look for this thing when Drury couldn't find it. Three people, smuggled up here in a shipping container. Don't tell me you didn't hear anything about that.'

'Not about any shipping container.'

'What, then?'

Little Dave's Adam's apple bobbed when he swallowed, and he looked away.

'We've come this far,' Vic said. 'You know you have to go the distance.'

'As long as you understand I didn't have nothing to do with it.'

'As long as you didn't, that won't be a problem.'

'And this is just between you and me. I won't stand up in court for it.'

'Have I read you your rights? Is your lawyer present? We're just having a little chat, completely off the record.'

'Because if anyone finds out I told you this, I'm dead.'

'Anything you tell me here, it's as my confidential informant. Strictly between you and me.'

'You swear?'

'What are we, kids in a playground? Just tell me, or you're walking home.'

'All it was, Mr Drury heard that two police were coming up on the shuttle. Something to do with this artefact, back on Earth. The one that got someone haunted.'

'Let me guess. Two police by the names Redway and Parsons.'

'They came here to look for the source of the artefact. Mr Drury was having them followed. He wanted to find out who they were seeing here, where they were going. He thought they might cause him all kinds of inconvenience if they got too interested in his business.'

'Because this artefact had been found in that site in Idunn's Valley.'

'If you know all this, why are you asking me?'

'Did Redway and Parsons get too close to Drury's business? Is that why he ambushed them?'

'That wasn't Mr Drury,' Little Dave said. 'All he was doing was having them followed. Discreet like. They went out to the shuttle terminal and someone jumped them. One went down, the other took off, disappeared . . . Mr Drury had his street crews looking for him, and then I suppose he must have heard he was out in Idunn's Valley.'

'And Drury and his goons went after him,' Vic said, thinking of the gun battle out at Winnetou.

'I wouldn't know about that, would I?'

'And I don't suppose you know who killed John Redway, either.'

'I heard it was Mr McBride, but I couldn't swear to it. I suppose he had contacts too.'

'I suppose he did. What about the three people in the shipping container?'

'I don't know anything about them, Mr Gayle. On my mother's life I don't.'

They went over it again, but either Little Dave really didn't know anything else, or he had given up all he was willing to give up. Vic believed it was the former: Drury probably didn't trust Little Dave with anything important.

Vic put his Colt away and said, 'One more thing. Tell me about the ray gun.'

'The what?'

Little Dave trying to look as innocent as a schoolboy.

Vic said, 'The thing Cal McBride used to scramble the brains of people he didn't like.'

'Oh, that.'

'Yes, that. Who has it now? McBride or Drury?'

'Mr Drury turned the house upside down when he took over, looking for business records, all kinds of shit. And he didn't find everything he was looking for. Mr McBride knew he was going down, and he squirrelled stuff away before he did.'

'Is that your way of telling me McBride has it?'

'All I know is that Mr Drury doesn't. So,' Little Dave said, 'what about me?'

'What about you?'

'What do I get for being your confidential informant?'

'I'll give you a pass on this, and some advice, too. Think long and hard about the course of your life, and start making some changes.'

'What else is someone like me supposed to do?' Little Dave said. Now he thought this was over, he'd regained something of his confidence. Probably believing that he'd got away with something, because that was how people like him justified what they did. 'First thing they do when you arrive here is shove you in a camp, expect you to do work for free. I thought, fuck that, and took off. But you need an ID card to get work, and you can't get an ID card until you've finished working for the city. What choice did I have?'

'You should have done your piece in the Orientation Camp, like everyone else,' Vic said. 'Contribute something to the community, help build this new world, and learn something about it.'

'I was never cut out for that shit. Too much like school. I got out of that when I was thirteen, and never looked back.'

'And how's that working out for you?'

Little Dave didn't reply.

'What I want you to do now,' Vic said, 'is clasp your hands behind your head and fix your eyes on the horizon. No, don't fucking look at me. At the horizon. And don't you dare turn around.'

Little Dave protested, but did as he was told. Vic got in the car, saw in the side mirror Little Dave look around when he started the motor. Little Dave running after the car as Vic floored it, dwindling in the red dust. At the junction with the road, the Ford Victory parked there flashed its headlights. Vic returned the signal and drove past, turning towards the city and the airport. Alain and Maria would pick up Little Dave and take him in for questioning, put his story on the record. Meanwhile, Vic had a flight to catch, and some hard questions to ask the police in Idunn's Valley.

33. Anomalous Patterns Of Brain Activity

France | 12–18 July

'I can't tell you where I'm going or what I need to do,' Chloe said. 'But I promise that you'll be the first to hear everything when I come back. Swear you won't write it up until then. Until this is finished, one way or another.'

'I'm already writing it up,' Gail Ann said. 'But if you think it'll put you in danger, I won't show it to anyone just yet.'

'I was thinking of Fahad and Rana,' Chloe said. 'And you, too.'

She was using a throwaway phone that one of Ada Morange's people had given her. Standing amongst gnarled apple trees in the old orchard, looking south. The meadow with its mown airstrip, a file of poplars marking the course of a small river, a patchwork of fields and woods stretching away towards the Mangala shuttle. A huge alien spaceship thumbprinted against the blue summer sky.

She'd already had a painful conversation with Neil, telling him that she had to go away for a while, promising that she would explain everything as soon as she could. She'd also had a brief chat with Rosa Jenners, who said that one of her regulars had told her a story about a scout, based in Rome, who was pointed towards breakouts by pictures of nearby churches sent via an anonymising network, and like Eddie Ackroyd was paid for his work in shellcoin.

'Although it might just be a story,' Rosa said. 'You know how it is in the trade. Someone tells you a story that a friend of a friend heard from someone they met in a pub . . .'

And now Chloe was saying goodbye to Gail Ann for the second time – the first had been when they'd parted at the Burger King after Sandra Hamilton had caught up with them – and trying to explain why she had to do what she was going to do without giving too much away. Not because she didn't trust her friend, but because she didn't know who might be listening in at Gail Ann's end.

'Don't worry about me,' Gail Ann said. 'One of Ada Morange's lawyers emailed a phone number I can call if I get into trouble with the police.'

'A freebie from my sponsor,' Chloe said. 'I'm told it doesn't have an expiry date. If you don't need it for this thing we fell into, you can use it later.'

'Actually,' Gail Ann said, 'I've just had an off-the-record chat, so-called, with this very intense chief inspector who came to my flat this morning.'

'Adam Nevers,' Chloe said, with a feeling of falling.

'He told me you were old acquaintances.'

'I bet. Did he threaten you? If he did, call that number.'

Gail Ann said, 'Oh, he wasn't really interested in me. He told me that he knows where you are, and what you're planning to do.'

'Did he go into details? No, don't tell me,' Chloe said. 'I don't want to have to lie about it.'

'He wouldn't tell me. He did say that you were putting yourself and the Chauhans in direct danger. And that you were putting national security at risk. I guess he's pissed off because he can't reach out to you.'

'He just did. I'm sorry you got dragged into this mess.'

'Oh, a person could get a taste for this kind of front-line gonzo journalism. And Chief Inspector Nevers isn't half as fearsome as some of the creatures I've run into during London Fashion Week. I suppose I should wish you bon voyage.'

'We're going to find something. Something wonderful.'

'I hope so. I need a good capper for my story. Take care, sweetie.'

'You too,' Chloe said, and prised out the phone's card and snapped it in two, dropped the fragments in the long grass, and walked up through the trees towards the farmhouse.

It was her last full day on Earth. She seemed to be saying goodbye to everything.

Over the past week, she and Fahad and Rana had been subjected to batteries of tests that attempted to quantify the influence of Ugly Chicken. EEG, MEG, a trip to the hospital in Caen, where they'd put on plastic helmets and been fed into the rumbling, beeping doughnut of a scanner that produced high-resolution atlases of the neurological highways in their brains. There'd also been visual-perception tests, a session with a psychologist who'd questioned Chloe about her childhood and showed her those inkblot patterns. An extrasensory perception test where she had to guess whether the symbols on a series of playing cards were circles, squares, crosses, wave lines or stars; a questionnaire in which she had to agree or disagree with a long series of statements.

I have to shut my mouth when I am in trouble.

Evil spirits possess me at times.

The tests showed that both Fahad and Rana exhibited anomalous patterns of brain activity, presumably due to the influence of Ugly Chicken. Odd spikes in the visual dorsal stream and between the temporal lobe and Broca's area, the region responsible for language processing and control of speech; periodic slow waves across the entire cerebral cortex, too, the kind normally associated with deep sleep. Chloe was relieved to learn that she hadn't been affected. At least, not in any way that the scientists could detect.

Fahad was scornful. He said that he didn't need a bunch of machines to tell him that he and his sister had been chosen by the eidolon, said that it would communicate with them and no one else. He had endured the tests with thinly stretched patience. He wanted to prove himself but was wary of the scientists, seemed to think that they were trying to trick him, find an excuse that Ada Morange could use to row back on the deal they'd made.

Rana basked in the attention, ordering the scientists about, explaining what they were doing wrong, borrowing bits and pieces of equipment to do her own tests on Chloe and Fahad. She especially liked a little camera linked by a fibre-optic cable to a flatscreen. Liked to point it at her eye and study the close-up on the screen. Liked to point it at her brother's eye, at Chloe's. Chloe asked her if she was looking for Ugly Chicken; Rana laughed and said he didn't live in people's heads.

'Is he here now?'

'He's always here,' Rana said, folding her fingers around the bracelet on her wrist.

'I mean is he awake or asleep?'

A crease dented Rana's forehead while she gave that some serious thought. She said, 'He was asleep a long, long time. Like Snow White. He's happy to be awake.'

She was comically bossy and forthright. The scientists treated her with a respectful deference, and terminated the tests as soon as she showed signs of becoming tired or fractious. Not only because of her age; they didn't want to inadvertently trigger Ugly Chicken's defences.

The tests were carried out in an ancient barn that contained a laboratory with a black resin floor, gleaming workstations, and racks of equipment. The farm was Ada Morange's country retreat, and it was also a research lab. The shuttle was very old, haunted by the imprints of a hundred Elder Cultures that manifested as visions, highly localised aberrant weather patterns, 'transitory events', and abnormal behaviour in people and animals in the countryside around the port. One of the ongoing projects was analysis of the behaviour of a supercolony of red ants that extended across several square kilometres and appeared to be developing a kind of symbolic language.

One of the scientists, Fatou Ndoye, told Chloe that analysis of the bead in Rana's bracelet showed that it was a form of cat's-eye apatite.

'So it's an alien crystal?' Chloe said, thinking of cheesy old sci-fi programmes. 'A *sentient* alien crystal?'

'We don't yet know if it's truly self-aware or a sophisticated computer emulating a degree of self-awareness,' Fatou Ndoye said. 'But it is a marvellously strange artefact.'

She was about Chloe's age, elegant and scary-smart. She had been seconded to the Ugly Chicken project from research into organic photon-plasmon emitters, something to do with quantum-information processing in the nervous systems of a clade of biochines. She explained that, like cat's-eye apatites on Earth, Rana's bead contained parallel fibres that produced a chatoyance, a luminous streak of reflected light like the pupil in a cat's eye.

'It is possible that information is stored in the quantum fields of those fibres,' Fatou said. 'Several of the Elder Cultures were able to pack vast amounts of data into small ordered matrices – quantum dust, minerals, even biological materials. There has been some interesting work on this in CERN and the Institute of High Energy Physics in Beijing, but there is much we do not yet know.'

There were briefing sessions on the clandestine accommodation in which they would ride to Mangala, from the shuttle's flight profile to the operation of the high-tech toilet. They couldn't travel up and out on tickets bought on the free market because the British government had issued a stop notice to the UN Commission on Planetary Settlement, so they were being smuggled aboard. It wasn't the first time Karyotech Pharma had done this, according to Henry. Back in the early days, before controls had been applied to the market in tickets sold to third parties by lottery winners, companies in the Elder Culture biz had resorted to all kinds of tactics to undercut or outwit their competitors.

The British government had also issued an Interpol Red Notice for the arrest of Chloe, Fahad and Henry but, because the French government had yet to forgive the 'English perfidy' that had almost caused the collapse of the EU, its police were reluctant to cooperate. 'For once, the intransigence of French bureaucracy will work in our favour,' Henry said. 'And our own lawyers are throwing tons of sand into the gears of justice too. By the time Adam Nevers turns up with a warrant, we'll have been to Mangala and back.'

There were briefings given by Michel Charpentier, a raffish archaeologist who had worked on Mangala eight years ago. He was coming with them, travelling in what he called cattle class rather than their clandestine accommodation. He told them about his work on Mangala, about its Elder Culture sites and its capital city, Petra, and gave them a brief lesson about walking surveys and shovel test pits. 'If we are fortunate, we should not have to sift a gram of dirt,' he said. 'We are only looking for one thing at this time: whether or not the site interests the eidolon.'

Ada Morange's agent on Mangala had discovered that a company formerly owned by Cal McBride had taken out licences to excavate several Elder Culture sites. According to Michel, one of them, Site 326, was especially promising. The company hadn't yet filed a detailed report of its finds, but Michel had worked up a 3D topographical model from the contour map of the initial landscape survey. A cluster of mounds each about thirty metres across, low truncated cones with flat tops and sloping sides. He rotated the model, tipped it up and down, then brought up an overlay of spires rising from the footprints of the mounds and asked Fahad if it looked familiar.

'Of course it looks familiar. You used my pictures.'

'What about the relationship of the spires to each other? Take your time.'

Fahad bent over the tablet, used his forefinger to spin the image around. He said, 'Is that a river?'

'Along the eastern edge? Yes, a big one.'

'There shouldn't be a river.'

'The mounds are many thousands of years old. The river probably changed its course several times. And your spires collapsed, left these mounds of rubble. We tried to match them with your drawings, but you drew different numbers of spires, sometimes standing close to each other, sometimes not. We'd like to know if you think that seems to be the right number of spires, in the right pattern.'

Michel was languidly patient, but Fahad refused to commit to a definite answer. He didn't know the exact number of spires, or their size. He drew whatever was in his head at the time. It flowed down his arm onto the paper. The reconstruction looked familiar, but he wasn't sure if it was where Ugly Chicken had come from.

'I'll know when I get there,' he said at last. 'Ugly Chicken will lead me to the right place.'

Later, Henry said to Chloe, 'I can't figure out if he's hiding something because he doesn't trust us, or he really doesn't know.'

'If he didn't trust you, he wouldn't be here,' Chloe said. 'Where is that site?'

'A big valley about a thousand kilometres south and west of Petra. There are more than four hundred known Elder Culture sites on Mangala, but I have a good feeling about this one. Those mounds look right, and the licence was issued three years ago, which fits with the time frame.'

'His father stole artefacts from the site, his boss found out . . .'

'Our person on the ground gave us some info on the boss. Cal McBride. Soon after the excavation licence was issued, he went to prison over some smuggling scam. He lost control of his company while he was inside, came out about six months ago, maybe looking for people to blame. Or maybe the new boss of the company found out about Sahar Chauhan's little sideline in purloined artefacts. Like the kid said, we'll know when we get there.'

Ada Morange was absent during the days of lab tests and briefing sessions. She returned on the last afternoon, the afternoon when Chloe said her farewells to Neil and Gail Ann, bringing with her the !Cha, Unlikely Worlds, and Daniel Rosenblaum, freshly sprung from detention along with the rest of Disruption Theory's crew. They dined together that evening on the terrace of the farmhouse, under the grape arbour. The old woman sat at the head of the long table; Chloe on her left, Daniel on her right, the tank of Unlikely Worlds standing next to her wheelchair, its black cylinder balanced on a tripod of three skeletal legs like a miniature Martian fighting machine. A shot glass of apple brandy sat on its flat top. Unlikely Worlds explained that a demon 'smaller than one of your bacteria' was inflating the vanishingly small chance that certain molecules would be somewhere other than inside the glass. Not molecules of alcohol, but the congeners that gave the apple brandy its unique flavour.

'It's my only vice.'

According to the !Cha, their tanks each contained a school of tiny shrimp-like creatures that housed various aspects of their personalities. In the oceans of their home world, they said, males of their ancestral species had constructed elaborate nests decorated with weed and shells to attract a mate. The strongest, those most likely to produce the fittest offspring, made the biggest and most elaborate nests, and attracted the strongest, most fertile females. Although they had left their home world a long time ago, male !Cha still advertised their sexual prowess by collecting Elder Culture artefacts, ghosts and eidolons, and stories. Stories most of all. That was why they followed the Jackaroo, they said. The Jackaroo's interactions with other species created all kinds of deep, rich tales.

Some people believed that the !Cha were the power behind the Jackaroo. Others that the !Cha were another kind of Jackaroo avatar. Their tanks were sealed, impervious to X-rays, microwaves, radar, and ultrasound. Anything might be inside, or nothing at all. Schools of shrimp, monstrous nightmares, machine intelligences, magic crystals inhabited by ghosts or eidolons, like Rana's cat's-eye bead.

The Jackaroo, of course, had only ever made vague, enigmatic comments about their fellow travellers.

'We are friends with all we find,' they said.

Unlikely Worlds told Chloe that human stories were especially fine – their effect on female !Cha was rather like the buzz he got from the congeners in his glass of apple brandy.

'Your own story is not without interest,' he said. His voice, a mellow baritone, was modelled on an old movie star who'd several times played God. Richly paternal and reassuring, it hummed in the air somewhere above the table. 'I took the liberty of studying your entries on the Last Five Minutes wiki. A tragedy rooted in the foolishness of your species.'

Chloe, unsettled and provoked, said, 'I would have thought you would be more interested in Fahad and Rana. Their story is way weirder than mine.'

'I prefer to work in miniature,' Unlikely Worlds said. 'And besides, yours is more purely human.'

This was after dessert and coffee. Rana had been excused from the table, and she and her brother were chasing fireflies on the lawn. She ran through the little constellations of green and red and blue flashes, laughing with innocent delight. Before dinner, she had given her bracelet to her brother in a touchingly simple ceremony. She didn't seem at all upset to part with the bead and her imaginary friend. She was happy that Ugly Chicken was going home. Happy because Ugly Chicken was happy.

Now Unlikely Worlds said that the LFM wiki was an interesting attempt to overcome the shortcomings of human memory.

'Perhaps you excel at storytelling because your memories are stories you tell yourselves. The truth recedes into the past and becomes a different truth. You select some facts and discard others. You exaggerate certain things, make up other things out of whole cloth, and from this patchwork create glorious fabrications.'

'Are we really so interesting to you?' Chloe said.

Ada Morange said, 'They are interested in certain people, most definitely. We have had many discussions about history, he and I.'

'The concept of *hero* is very interesting to us,' Unlikely Worlds said. 'We are composites. No one component is worth more than any other. Your minds are in some ways similar. Your so-called "self" is a composite superimposed on the activity of many competing subpersonalities or agents. What you perceive as your consciousness is a string of temporary heroes rising above those they have defeated. And so you seek out heroes in the common story of your race.'

'Heroes are mostly fiction,' Daniel Rosenblaum said. 'The idea that certain men or women have a disproportionate effect on history has been largely discredited.'

He'd been subdued all through the evening, greeting Chloe with an unsettling formality and showing no interest in her adventures, most of his attention on the alien in their midst.

'Yet Dr Morange thinks herself one such,' Unlikely Worlds said.

'Is that not why you are here?' Ada Morange said. She appeared to be amused.

'Interesting things happen around you,' Unlikely Worlds said. 'You attract stories. I wonder, Chloe, if Ada is using you, or if you are using her. Who is the hero, and who the shield-carrier? I cannot say. Not yet. It is all so delightfully entangled.'

'Perhaps the bead in Rana's bracelet is the hero,' Chloe said.

Later, she had a brief reconciliation with Daniel.

'I was angry with you,' he said. He was a little drunk, sipping a glass of brandy and smoking a cigar. She'd never seen him smoke before. 'I'm still angry, just a little. You blundered into something you didn't understand, and I was caught in the blowback. Everyone was. First everyone was arrested. And then the office was fire-bombed. And now, I've just been told, Ada Morange is going to shut down Disruption Theory.'

'I'm sorry.'

Daniel shrugged.

'How are Jen and the others?'

'As if you really care.'

'Self-pity doesn't suit you, Daniel.'

'I have a lot to feel sorry about,' he said, but relented a little. 'Actually, I want to give you a bit of advice, if you'll let me. Ada has rebuilt her company to a certain point, but now she needs to find something game-changing that will take her to the next level. That's why she bought into Disruption Theory, and I took her shilling with the full knowledge that she would exploit anything we found. And now, well, she hopes that this thing of yours, this Ugly Chicken, is the game-changer. And if it is, she'll do every-thing in her power to keep hold of it. So what I'm trying to say, Chloe, is be careful. Don't get caught in any crossfire.'

'I can't let this go,' Chloe said.

'That's my girl. That's what makes you such a good scout.'

'What about you? What will you do now?'

'Ada has offered positions elsewhere to everyone who works – who used to work – for Disruption Theory. She offered me a position, too. Here, as a matter of fact. That's partly why I came. Mostly.'

'This place is definitely full of spooks and weirdness.'

'I turned her down. I'm thinking,' Daniel said, 'of writing another book. I need to get Ada's permission, confidentiality clause and all that, but I think she'll like the idea.'

He paused, no doubt expecting Chloe to ask the obvious ques-tion. When she didn't, he added, 'You'll be in it of course. We all will.'

Chloe said, 'Good luck with it. But I already have someone covering that beat.'

*

Departure day dawned grey and cool, the sky sheeted edge to edge with cloud. One of the discreet, infallibly polite staff had laid out coveralls for Chloe. Thanks but no thanks: she pulled on zebra-striped leggings and a plain white oversized T-shirt and went out to find breakfast.

And discovered that Ada Morange, Unlikely Worlds and Daniel Rosenblaum had left in the night.

'It doesn't mean anything,' Henry said.

'Dr Morange has a hundred different affairs to attend to,' Michel Charpentier said. He was wearing a blue shirt and had a pale yellow sweater draped over his shoulders in the way that only the French can pull off. 'That she spent an entire evening with us last night is an enormous sign of her confidence.'

Fahad wouldn't be reassured. He was growing jittery, wondering aloud if he was doing the right thing, fretting about Rana.

'I wish I could trust that woman,' he said, nodding towards Rimsha Bhatti, who sat at the far end of the table with several of the scientists.

'If you want to do right by your father this is the right thing to do,' Chloe said, and immediately realised she was being a bit harsh. She was on edge, humming with the unsettling mix of anticipation and mild dread that she remembered from childhood holidays. She said, '*I* wouldn't be here if I didn't think we were doing the right thing.'

She tried her best to eat a bowl of granola while Henry ploughed through his usual Full English breakfast, Michel sipped from a bowl of coffee, and Fahad nibbled at a slice of toast and fed Rana with fruit and yogurt, making helicopter noises as he aimed each spoonful at her mouth. The bead gleamed greenly on his wrist. At last, Rana tired of the game and grabbed the spoon and said that she knew how to eat, thank you very much, and Fahad gave her a look that just about broke Chloe's heart.

Rana told Chloe that she'd had a dream about Ugly Chicken.

'What was he doing?'

'He took me into the sky,' Rana said. There was a dab of yogurt on her nose. Her glossy black hair was gathered into two short pigtails that stuck out from the back of her head.

'It doesn't mean anything,' Fahad said. 'She has dreams like that all the time.'

'We flew past stars and planets and all kinds of things,' Rana said.

'And then what happened?'

Rana shrugged. 'And then I woke up.'

She seemed to be unaffected by Fahad's nervous impatience and the fuss of preparing for departure, listened with placid acceptance as Fahad explained that he'd soon be back. But when Chloe and Fahad and Henry were about to climb into the people carrier, she broke away from Rimsha Batti and ran towards her brother.

'Take me, take me, take me!'

Fahad gathered up his sister and hugged her, then carried her back to their aunt and set her down and told her to be brave, said that she should be happy because their friend was going home. But Rana blubbered with inconsolable distress, and Chloe noticed Henry and the driver of the people carrier watching with narrow attention, as if, like her, they were half-expecting Ugly Chicken to show itself. When Fahad walked back to the people carrier he avoided everyone's gaze because he was crying too.

Michel shook hands with them and said that he would see them on the other side, and they drove off, joined a thin but constant stream of traffic on the autoroute towards the port. The shuttle leaned into the sky, huge as a mountain. Fahad pressed against the passenger window, looking up at it and turning Rana's bracelet around and around on his wrist. Chloe felt a flutter in her stomach. This was this. No turning back.

The people carrier left the autoroute at a slip road and drove past warehouses and an industrial estate and pulled up in a lay-by behind an articulated truck with a blue shipping container on its trailer. Chloe and the others got out and the driver of the truck swung down from his cab. It was the wiry ex-Foreign Legion guy. He climbed onto the trailer and cracked open the doors of the container, revealing a wall of cardboard cartons, said that as soon as they were inside he'd repack the cartons and they'd be on their way.

'You will be on board in two, three hours. The last to go on, the first to be unloaded.'

Henry led Chloe and Fahad through the stacks of cartons to an oval hatch in a bulkhead. Chloe turned to catch a last sight of Earth, trees and cloudy sky framed by the open doors of the container, and then she ducked through the hatch and that was it: she was committed.

34. The Cloud Tree

Mangala | 30 July

Fighting a headwind all the way, the little Cessna crawled low over the vast red playa and scrub-covered plains, flew out above the forested slopes at the edge of Idunn's Valley. The sky was tinted a hard cold pink. The sun hung low above what looked like a hazy brown band stretched across half the horizon. The leading edge of the dust storm, according to the pilot.

'Man, it's big,' Vic said. Dressed in a microlight down jacket, jeans and hiking boots, strapped in the seat next to the pilot, he was the only passenger on the plane.

'More than two thousand kilometres across, and getting bigger all the time,' the pilot, a laconic Finn with buzz-cut grey hair, said.

Idunn's Valley was a crooked verdant scar that ran from the edge of the sprawling northern ice cap to the ring sea that girdled the equator. Glaciers fed a slow, wide river that meandered through it; little towns and farming settlements were spreading along a narrow belt pinched between the river and the alien veldt and forests, the latest in a long succession of civilisations that had risen and fallen along the river banks long before the first hominins had walked out across the plains of Africa, the ruins each left behind cannibalised by succeeding Elder Cultures or erased by changes in the river's course or by dust and sand blown in from the deserts on either side of the valley. So far, prospectors had mapped the outlines of more than three hundred ancient sites along the river, excavating the fossilised remains of alien technology and architecture, uncovering a number of still-active artefacts, eidolons, and other revenants, and novel polymers and metamaterials. Room-temperature superconductors, quantum

244

dust, solar paint, the proton-exchange membranes that were the basis for LEAF batteries and cheap desalination, and half a hundred other prizes.

It was good to get out of Petra, Vic thought, good to be reminded that there was so much more to Mangala than the housing developments and shopping malls, schools and hospitals, office blocks and industrial estates that were spreading from the city centre like the pulsing growth of a bacterial colony, to escape the deepening grip of multinational corporations and the Coca-colonisation of the weird. Out here, you could still have your mind eaten by an alien phantom, stumble upon a lost city, or discover a fraying thread of some kind of weird quantumised metamaterial that could kick-start a new industrial revolution and make you a billionaire. Out here were places not yet mapped. Old dreams and deep mysteries. A world wild and strange and still mostly unknown. And he was a lone avenger, arrowing through the raging weather of this strange planet, ready to speak for his dead.

Static lightning flickered in the air. Dust devils dipped and swayed across the yellow veldt like eccentric dancers. Once, the pilot tapped Vic's shoulder and pointed off to the left. A cloud tree set alight by a lightning strike was burning in a shroud of blue hydrogen flame and shedding flurries of sparks: clouds of microscopic sporelings that would rise high on the fire's updraught and seed new life across hundreds of square kilometres.

This vivid portent set an atavistic thrill fizzing in Vic's blood, triggered memories of his first days on Mangala: the first days of human colonisation. He'd brought a motorcycle with him, and in his free time would choose a random direction and ride out into the playa until all traces of the hand of man were lost in a dry sea of red rock and red sand. Try that now, you'd have to travel a long fucking way to find a place where someone hadn't set up a campfire, or scrawled graffiti on a rock, or shot up a needle tree, or left behind a litter of fast-food wrappers and soft-drink cans. But back then you didn't have to go far to find places where no human being had ever before trod. Where you could lie down in the warm light of the fat sun or the steely glitter of

245

the alien stars and lose yourself in the profound silence of the desert, where the only noise was the beating of your heart and the sigh of your lungs, where you could feel your mind unravel into the ancient unknown.

A bend of the broad river gleamed below and the plane turned sharply to follow it. On the far side, ranges of low hills clad in red and orange forest stretched into a dim haze and the turbulent base of the mountainous dust storm. The plane flew low over a patchwork of fields. Acres of fast-growing strains of alfalfa and mustard, gleaming seas of polytunnels, a cluster of grain-storage tanks, a scatter of buildings around a crossroads.

'Winnetou,' the pilot said.

The little town where Skip had been murdered.

And then the plane was descending in a sudden swoop towards a dirt runway, bumping down and taxiing towards the Portakabin that served as flight control, administrative offices and waiting room.

The pilot cut the engine and said, 'This could be my last flight for a while. That monster is advancing faster than predicted. If I can't return tomorrow, how will you get back?'

'I haven't thought that far ahead,' Vic said.

35. A Different Sun

The Shuttle | 18—22 July

Space travel turned out to be as tedious and cramped as a long-haul plane trip. Canned air, microwaved food, close quarters, the nagging low-level fear of some catastrophic accident. A video link to a spyhole camera bolted to a corner of the shipping container gave a view of the outside, but after the container had been loaded onto the shuttle with airy swoops and alarming clangs and shudders there was little to see. A few glimpses of men and forklift trucks moving about stacks of containers tented with orange webbing. A line of small yellow excavators tethered with cables. Three hours passed. Four. The passengers were boarding, Henry said. First the winners of the emigration lottery, then government and UN officials, and finally Michel Charpentier and the other corporate passengers.

Henry, Chloe and Fahad explored the nooks and crannies of their narrow rectangular living quarters. Three couches. Pop-up screens and pull-out keyboards, the forbidding control panel of the toilet. Lockers under the couches contained caches of clothing and microwaveable meals, bags of fruit, pouches of soup. There was a little refrigerator stuffed with bottles of mineral water and fruit juices and yogurt. They ate lunch: cheese and salami, fresh bread and olives. Chloe tried to read, but the sense of the paragraphs and sentences kept slipping away.

At last, the lights began to blink and a calm, friendly woman's voice told them to prepare for take-off. They strapped themselves into their couches. It reminded Chloe of lying on a hospital stretcher bed when she'd been a kid, waiting for the operation to remove her appendix. The same dread, the same helplessness.

The same dry metallic taste in her mouth. And then, without so much as a premonitory tremor, the force of the smooth and steady acceleration of the alien craft began to press down. The voice told them that it would last eight minutes, told them to breathe slowly and steadily and stay as still as possible. As if Chloe had any choice, crushed by a giant's fist into the couch. She told herself that millions of people had taken the shuttles to the Jackaroo worlds, that it was about as dangerous as riding a lift, tried not to think of the weird forces that were flattening the fabric of space and squeezing the shuttle into space.

She knew the itinerary by heart. Up into orbit, a single loop around the Earth and then the fall to the L5 point in the Moon's orbit, where the combined gravitational pull of Earth and Moon provided a stable equilibrium point which the bracelet of wormhole mouths orbited. The wormholes were shortcuts through the hidden dimensions of space-time; the usual explanation was to imagine space as a flat piece of paper, draw two dots on it, and fold it so that the dots kissed. They'd fall through one of those dots and emerge from its twin, balanced at the L5 point between Mangala and its star. Twenty thousand light years traversed in a moment outside time. And then they'd fall to Mangala.

Nothing to it.

There was a stomach-swooping interval of free fall as the shuttle swung around the Earth, and then a little weight returned again. The voice, which reminded Chloe of a kindly teacher she'd had in primary school, said that the shuttle was on its way to the wormhole mouth and that it was safe to move around.

This part of the trip took a little less than a day. Fahad spent most of the time on his couch playing video games and occasionally scribbling on his sketch pad. Pictures of the spires as they might once have been, different angles of Michel's 3D reconstruction of the site as it was now, densely hatched sketches of the black room. He was losing the itch to draw, he said, now that they were going where Ugly Chicken wanted to go.

Henry exercised, using a system of elastic cords, told Chloe and Fahad that if the body stayed fit the mind would follow. He played three games of chess with Chloe and because his only strategy was to force a way up the centre with his most powerful pieces he quickly lost every time, and that was the end of chess.

As they picked over a dinner of various microwaved curries and rice, he revealed that he'd ridden on a shuttle once before, to Yanos. He'd gone out to supervise security at a research camp. 'Mostly developing ways to keep out the megafauna rather than dealing with rivals and troublesome locals.'

Unlike Mangala, Yanos was tidally locked to its star. One side was mostly desert scorched by permanent sunlight, with a vast permanent rainstorm at the substellar point; the other was a dark ice cap, bordered by a habitable twilight strip where islands of tangled forest were interwoven with skinny seas and marshes. Henry told Chloe and Farad about the sun fixed at one spot at the horizon, the constant gale that blew from light side to dark, lashing through tangled forests. He told them about spin trees that generated electricity from the wind, spike trees that snapped with lightning when the gale strengthened into a storm, the stupid blundering beasts that staggered up from the shallow seas to fight and mate. He told them about the portion of ruined factory that Karyotech Pharma had been exploring, the helical ramps spiralling past subterranean levels that were mostly collapsed or flooded. The weird clockwork critters that infested the place, and the tinkertoys and ghost plastics and other enigmas spawned by half-ruined hives of nanomachinery.

'I was there for six months when the company had its little financial hiccup and we had to pull out. We'd barely scratched the surface.'

'So you don't know much about the world you went to, and you don't know anything about the world we're going to,' Fahad said.

'Michel and the field agent will take care of that part,' Henry said. 'I'm here to take care of you.'

They pulled their privacy curtains around their couches and dialled down the lights and slept. Chloe woke to bright light and the woman's voice announcing that they were approaching the wormhole. A little later, the voice began to count down from sixty seconds. They lay on their couches and watched the yellow dot of the shuttle creep the last millimetres towards the red dot of the wormhole's mouth. Chloe reflexively closed her eyes at zero. They had just passed through a circular black mirror a little over a kilometre across, flanged up from weird physics and impossible materials by aliens and embedded in the flat end of a rock sculpted into the shape of an ice-cream cone. Now they were falling across billions of kilometres of vacuum towards Mangala. They had crossed twenty thousand light years in less than an eye-blink, and she had felt nothing.

Fahad and Henry hadn't felt anything either.

'So much for the romance of space travel,' Henry said.

The gravity cut off while the shuttle made a cumbersome manoeuvre, came back again. They were three days from planetfall. Mangala didn't possess a moon, so the wormhole exit hung at the L5 point sixty degrees behind the planet, where its gravity and the gravity of its star achieved equilibrium – a far greater distance than the Earth–Moon L5 point.

Fahad sat on his couch in spex and gloves, twitching as he slaughtered hordes of pissed-off Elder Culture revenants or whatever.

Henry strained at his bungee cords, flicked impatiently through crime novels. He declared that video games were no preparation for the real thing, showed Fahad and Chloe a selection of unarmed combat moves. Chloe demonstrated a couple of good ones from a self-defence class she'd once taken. Fahad wanted to know why they hadn't brought any guns.

'We won't need them because we aren't going to get into a fight,' Henry said. 'We aren't going to get into a fight because the bad guys don't know that we're coming. That's our advantage, kid. Surprise. Much better than any gun. If we're lucky, they won't even know what they discovered. We can just walk in there and take it.'

'When we know what it is,' Chloe said.

'Don't worry,' Fahad said. 'When I see it, Ugly Chicken will tell me what to do.'

As far as he was concerned Henry and Chloe were working for him now. That was the deal, in exchange for his cooperation.

'Let the kid think what he wants for now,' Henry told Chloe. 'When we hit dirt, he'll soon learn how things really are.'

Men and their stupid dominance games.

Chloe studied maps of Mangala. The empty land around Site 326, in Idunn's Valley. Other sites where significant Elder Culture ruins had been uncovered. The capital, Petra, the playa around it, the arcs of low hills that were actually the remnants of the rim of an ancient crater that had been flooded and mostly buried in sediment when Mangala had been warmer and wetter. Craters and hills, salt lakes and tablelands, canyons and rivers running south towards the band of the equatorial sea.

She slept a lot, too, the privacy curtain pulled around her couch. She had complicated dreams and couldn't remember anything about them when she woke, only a claustrophobic sense of unfocused urgency.

She discovered that it was hard to stay fresh using only wet-wipes and bottled water.

At last, the voice warned them that the shuttle was about to enter orbit around Mangala. They climbed onto their couches and buckled themselves in. Gravity cut off for twenty minutes, then returned, growing relentlessly, pressing down on them.

According to the voice, the shuttle was decelerating, leaving orbit and entering the atmosphere of the planet. The pressure on Chloe's chest began to ease, decreasing until what seemed to be her normal weight returned. Although Mangala's gravity was a little over three-quarters that of Earth's, it felt much stronger after the days in the feather-light pull of the shuttle.

Henry switched on the external camera. Presently, lights flickered on in the vast hold and men and women appeared, moving amongst stacks of shipping containers. Several hours passed, an agony of uncertainty, until at last a big front loader loomed into the camera's field of view and with a jolt they were lifted up and trundled out into the light of a different sun.

36 · Cold Store

Mangala | 30 July

The constable of the county, Karl Schweda, was waiting for Vic at the airfield. As they drove towards Winnetou in his powder-blue Land Rover, Karl told Vic that he'd taken Skip to the site of the shootout and to the morgue where the bodies were laid out, and then had driven him back to his motel.

'I have witnesses who saw him in the café at about six, six-thirty in the evening, but what he did after that I do not know,' Karl said. He was a lean blond young man with a brisk competent manner, trim in his olive-green uniform. 'I know now that I should not have left him on his own, but did not think he would be in any danger.'

'He shouldn't have come out here alone,' Vic said. 'And that's partly my fault. So I'd say we've even on that score.'

'First the shootout, and now this,' Karl said. 'I could never imagine such a thing could happen here.'

'You had five killed in the shootout.'

'Five that I know about. Five that were left behind. Your partner told me it was two gangs fighting over an Elder Culture site.'

'Site 326. You know it?'

'It is a long way downriver. Nothing but wild country between here and there. I supposed that was where the people who won that shootout had gone. To claim their prize. It did not occur to me that they would come back so soon.'

'Maybe some of them never left.'

'I thought of that too.'

'And they might still be here.'

'Yes. It is not a good thought.'

252

They drove past a couple of Quonset huts hunched under a tall wind turbine, the old kind, its three blades spinning at full tilt, drove past houses – clapboard shacks, really – strung alongside the road. Washing streaming out on a line. Two women hammering a sheet of plywood over a window. At the crossroads in the middle of town, a dozen trucks and articulated lorries parked nose to tail on the road to the docks, waiting for the ferry.

'Farmers have been stripping their fields and greenhouses of produce ahead of the storm, sending it upriver to Babylonia,' Karl said. 'The forecasters say that the edge of the storm won't reach that far.'

'A lot of people passing through town.'

'Exactly. I don't mean it as an excuse, but it is perhaps why we did not see trouble coming.'

Karl said that his husband, Chris, was out in the country, finding out who had left and who was staying, checking that they had sufficient supplies and a working radio. 'The front is only a day or two away, and soon the night-year begins. If there is anything you need to do here, you should do it before then.'

The No Tell Motel, where Skip had checked in and never checked out, was a single-storey string of rooms with a few pickup trucks and 4x4s parked in front, a white-painted cabin with a vacancy sign lit behind its plate-glass window. The motel's owner, Derla Ragahaven, told Vic that Investigator Williams had checked in and had almost immediately driven off, said that she'd thought nothing of it. She hadn't seen anyone lurking round the motel, or a car or truck that wasn't registered to any of her guests, either.

'I already tell Constable Karl this. My night clerk has already run off, and also his wife, who was my maid,' she said. 'So I must do everything myself. How long did you say you were going to be here?'

'I didn't. Do you have a spare key for Investigator Williams's room?'

'Constable Karl has it. You might ask him when I can have it back, and when I can start renting the room again.'

Karl Schweda stood with his back to the closed door, watching patiently as Vic prowled around Skip's motel room, opening and closing the drawers of the chest of drawers, looking under the bed, checking the bathroom. Vic didn't expect to find anything. He was trying to get a feel, a psychic trace, of where Skip had been and what he had been doing.

'I put his clothes and travel bag in storage,' Karl said.

'His phone and spex, too?'

'His phone was found with him. If he had a pair of spex I didn't find them. Here or in the car.'

'So either Skip was carrying them and the bad guys took them, or the bad guys came back here to check out Skip's stuff, and found them.'

It would be nice to put either Danny Drury or Cal McBride in the room, but Vic was pretty sure they would have sent one of their goons to toss the place.

'I look for footprints and fingerprints, and vacuum for hair and other traces,' Karl said, 'but what can I tell you, it's a motel room. We have not yet attempted DNA analysis. Our budget is unfortunately quite small, and unless we know what to look for it is not worth it.'

'My department can help you out, if you need it. I've seen everything I need to see here. Perhaps you could take me to my partner.'

They drove to the cold store in Karl's Land Rover and were met by Winnetou's general practitioner, who was also the town's coroner. The bodies lay in green rubber bags on the floor of the bare windowless room. Six of them. One was Skip; the others were from the shootout, all but one burned beyond recognition. The doctor knelt and unzipped the bag containing the unburned body, a man found shot dead near Winnetou's docks. Vic had been hoping it would be either Danny Drury or Cal McBride, but he didn't recognise the dead man. There was a tattoo on his right shoulder: wings backing a balloon, with a crown and a lion above it. Two gunshot wounds in his chest.

Karl said, 'We have not yet done DNA, but we check fingerprints against the central database. No hits.'

Vic didn't ask to look at Skip's body. According to Karl, he had been shot in the face and was badly burned. The shape of him curled up in the green bag, like an alien embryo in an egg sac. Horrible to see. Vic signed off the paperwork that would allow the release and transport of Skip's body back to Petra, and said, 'Show me where my partner was killed.'

37. Little Hiccups

Mangala | 22–24 July

Getting out of the terminal's freight yard turned out to be a lot harder than smuggling themselves aboard an alien spacecraft and riding it across twenty thousand light years to another world under a different star. They'd been told that Dr Hanna Babbel, Karyotech Pharma's field agent on Mangala, would organise a way of sneaking them out, but after exchanging texts with the woman Henry said that there'd been a couple of little hiccups.

'First up, Michel didn't make it. He was involved in a smash on the way to the shuttle. A car shot out of a slip road, clipped his people carrier and spun it into the crash barrier, and sped off. No one was killed, but Michel was bashed up pretty badly. A fractured leg, a broken collarbone, concussion. Local police found the car a couple of hours later. Burned-out. And stolen, needless to say.'

'Nevers,' Chloe said, with a dipping feeling.

'Probably. The son of a bitch is sneakier than I thought.'

'Michel was supposed to be our guide,' Fahad said. 'How will we get to the site now?'

'Don't worry about it,' Henry said. 'Dr Babbel is a native. She knows everything there is to know.'

'But she isn't an archaeologist. She can't help us find what we need to find.'

'As you keep telling us, your friend will do that. And if we have to dig anything up, I know how to handle a spade. But before we get to that, here's the other little problem: Dr Babbel says she didn't have time to sort out a truck that can shift our container.

And we can't walk out because there's too much activity in the terminal yard. They work around the clock to shift cargo off the shuttle and load it up before it departs.

'So what we're going to do,' Henry said, 'is sit tight for two days. There's a big holiday coming up, the annual celebration of the first footfall on the planet. The yard will shut down then, and we can sneak out.'

'Bullshit,' Fahad said. 'We have to get *out* of here. We have to get *going*.'

Chloe shared that impatience. The need to get moving. It was a tightness in her belly, a wire in her brain.

Henry said, 'If yard security or the local police arrest you, how will that help us find what we came here for? Sit tight and stay cool, Fahad. Like my old mum used to say, all good things come to those who wait.'

'Suppose I leave now?' Fahad said.

'I have the code to unlock the hatch. You don't.'

'Suppose you tell me what that is,' Fahad said.

'Suppose you calm down,' Henry said, giving Fahad a flat unforgiving look.

Fahad glared back, hands knotted into fists. The two of them like little boys facing off in a playground.

Chloe said, 'I think both of you should calm down.'

'That's it. Take his side,' Fahad said.

'I really, really don't want to spend any more time in this stinky little can with you two. But Henry's right. We have to sit tight until it's safe to leave.'

'Look on the bright side, kid,' Henry said. 'We only have to wait two days. It could have been a lot longer. We caught a lucky break with this holiday. Some of the people we smuggled up and out had to wait far longer before they could break out. Two days? It isn't anything.'

Fahad started to say something, and Henry held up his hand. 'No more discussion. The Prof paid for this trip; you agreed to go along with her plan. This is part of it.'

Chloe said, 'If you can send text messages, I bet you can connect to the local internet, too. Give us that, at least.'

'Good idea,' Fahad said. 'We can do some research on the local web.'

Henry held up his phone. 'All this does is send and receive encrypted text messages via an HF rig in the chassis of the can. No voice transmissions, no email or web browsing . . . If you want to see what kind of porn Mangala offers, kid, you'll have to wait until you can buy an actual phone.'

They could look out at the new world through the spyhole camera, at least. A view of stacks of shipping containers mostly, glimpses of men and women in high-vis vests and hard hats, cranes and big forklift trucks. The clanging sounds of containers being shifted, the deep vibrations of heavy vehicles going past. An arc of sky the colour of evening, trains of high thin clouds, unvarying light and shadows. Daylight here lasted as long as the planet's year, thirty-one days, and the night was another year.

Fahad pulled out his sketch pad and drew the black room, tore off the page, drew it again. And again. He told Chloe that he was beginning to think it was important. 'We have to find the spires. Where they were. And then we have to find this.'

Henry studied one of the cast-off drawings. 'If this black room is inside a spire, then what's inside the black room?'

'I don't even know if it's a room,' Fahad said.

Henry turned the sketch upside down. 'Perhaps it's a view of the inside of Pandora's box. Or the inside of your head. A mess of tangled lines leading nowhere in particular.'

'Perhaps it is the kind of thing where each person sees what they want to see,' Fahad said.

Later, after Henry had drawn the curtain around his couch and gone to sleep, Fahad brought Chloe a cup of tea: a peace offering. They sat together, whispering. Fahad asked her if she trusted Henry.

'He knows what he's doing.'

'I don't mean can he do his job. I mean can we trust him?'

'We both made a deal with Dr Morange,' Chloe said. 'And we both believe that she would keep to it, or we wouldn't be here.'

'But the thing is, she's not here to make sure the bargain is kept. And if Mr Harris thinks that what I need to do will get in the way of what he has to do . . . You see?'

There it was again. His unappeasable need to avenge his father's death. Henry had told him that when this was all over, after they'd found whatever it was that Ugly Chicken wanted them to find, he could go to the local police and tell them everything he knew. And when Fahad had shrugged, said that the English police had already let him down and the police on Mangala probably wouldn't be any different, and besides, they'd probably arrest *him*, for being some kind of illegal immigrant, Henry had said that the Prof would make sure the bad guys stood up in court for what they'd done. 'If the police blow you off, she'll hire lawyers, private investigators. Whatever it takes.'

Fahad said now, to Chloe, 'Besides the question of trust, I have doubts about this so-called plan. Dr Morange promises to help, but it turns out that she cannot protect Michel, and this Dr Babbel person cannot even organise a truck. And now we have to sit here and hope we aren't found . . .'

'It's just a little hiccup,' Chloe said. 'And what you want to do, you can't do it on your own.'

'I am not crazy or foolish. I know what the people my father worked for are like. And even if I did not care about my own life, I must think of Rana. Who I had to leave behind, like a hostage. So don't worry, okay? I'm not going to do something dumb. But the people who killed my father, they're going to pay for it. I won't give that up.'

His bristling toughness and naive vulnerability turned Chloe's heart. Like Neil, like her, he'd had to grow up fast.

She said, 'You need Henry and you don't like it. But don't forget that he needs you, too. If he could find this place without your help, you wouldn't be here. Me neither. We'll do the one thing, and then the other. I'll make sure that Henry sticks to the deal. That's why you asked me to come, isn't it?'

'Yes, but was that me, or was it Ugly Chicken? And did you agree to come because you wanted to, or because he wanted you to?'

'The scientists couldn't find him in my head, so I guess it's me.'

'Just because they couldn't find him doesn't mean he isn't there,' Fahad said. 'I thought I was using him to get what I want. That it was like a deal we had made. He used me; I used him. But now

259

I'm beginning to wonder if you can bargain with something so old and clever and strange.'

Chloe asked him if he felt any different, now he was wearing the bead.

Fahad shook his head. 'But that's okay. Rana says that he'd been asleep when she found him, that she woke him up. Dr Morange told me that it was possible that he became imprinted on her. Like chicks – the first thing they see after they hatch, they think it's their mother because that's what they expect to see first. And if it's something else, a person, a dog, they follow them around anyway. Or it could be that he was able to make a direct connection with Rana, her nervous system, her brain, because she wore him against her skin. She showed me, the doctor, differences in our brain scans, said that if I wore the bead all the time it was possible that he'd find a way to speak to me, too. She's very smart, but even she doesn't really know anything about him. Just guesses. I wonder what else he has done, how much he has changed me . . . But how could I ever know? How can I know which thoughts are mine, and which aren't?'

The poor kid.

Chloe said, 'One thing we do know, he's making us itchy and impatient. Eager to get going, now we've brought him home. Angry and frustrated because of this delay.'

Fahad smiled. 'So I should be patient, because it is a way of resisting him.'

'I think we should make this thing our thing. We should do it because we want to do it.'

Fahad said, 'Do you think he affects Henry, too?'

It was a good question. Chloe hadn't thought about it before. Henry was a stubborn old geezer, practical, direct. She imagined that even his dreams were austere. Technical drawings of machine parts, battle plans with clashing arrows.

The day crawled by. Fahad retreated into his video games again. Henry woke up, did a hundred push-ups using his left arm, a hundred using his right. Chloe found it hard to sleep. The constant noise and vibration of heavy machinery outside; her thoughts racing around and around the same grooves.

The next morning, Henry used his phone and said that they would be out in a few hours. A little later he said, 'Hear that?'

Fahad frowned. 'I don't hear anything.'

'Exactly. The shift is over. It's the holiday. Everyone in the city will be partying.'

They had already packed their go bags. They ate a last meal, tidied up and checked that they'd left nothing behind that could identify themselves. Henry tore up Fahad's drawings and fed the pieces into the toilet.

And then there was nothing left to do but wait. At last, Henry's phone beeped. He punched the code into the hatch's lock, turned the wheel, swung it open. The cardboard cartons had shifted and toppled during the voyage; they had to restack them to clear a path to the doors of the container. Henry inserted a thin strip of aluminium in the gap between the doors, worked it up to the top and twisted, worked it to the bottom and twisted again. Something gave with a metallic snap, and Henry put his shoulder to one of the doors.

Cold air blew in, the air of another world. It smelled of iron and electricity.

38. The Shooter

Mangala | 30 July

Skip's body had been found behind a boxy steel-framed storage shed at the edge of a ploughed field. Red dust scudded over the field, silting between the furrows, drifting across the service road. Long shadows everywhere, the crimson glare of the low sun.

Vic examined the splash of char where Skip's hire car had been set alight. He hoped that his partner had been dead before he'd been tipped into the boot. It was a lousy way to go any way you cut it.

He said, 'Where's the car now?'

'We store it behind the station,' Karl said. 'These electric cars do not burn as badly as those with petrol engines, but there was nothing left for forensics.'

'Except the body.'

'Well, yes. Of course.'

'Any tyre tracks?'

'The ground is too dry. There has been no rain here for more than ten days. The strange thing is,' Karl said, 'your friend was shot twice in the head at close range. We found both casings near the car: .38 Smith and Wesson Special. We also found some .45 ACP casings, and two .45 rounds recovered from the wall of the storage shed. The rounds lacked rifling marks. They were fired from a generic printed gun, perhaps.'

'Perhaps.'

'I hear there is a glut of them in Petra. Our local criminals mostly favour hunting rifles.'

Vic knocked that one right back. 'You'd think someone visiting from the city to do a murder would stand out amongst the right-eous farmers around here.'

'Ordinarily, perhaps. But because of the storm all kinds of people have been passing through.'

'That's all you found, .45 ACPs and the two .38s? No nine-millimetre casings?'

Skip had been carrying a police-issue Glock 17, firing nine-millimetre Parabellum recoilless rounds.

Karl said, 'You think perhaps your friend shot at his attackers? We did a grid search, and Chris swept the area with his metal detector. We found only what I told you. I'm sorry.'

'Show me where you found these .45 ACPs.'

They walked along the access road to a spot by the ditch between the road and the edge of the field. Vic studied the ground, looked back towards the storage shed squatting under the mad red sky.

He said, 'You found just the two rounds in the wall?'

'As I said.'

'And how many casings?'

'Thirteen. The shooter fired off a full clip.'

'I wonder what else he hit, apart from the side of that shed.'

'I do not know what or who he hit,' Karl said, 'but I think someone hit him. We found blood spatter here, and a thin trail of it back towards those greasewood bushes. And someone broke into Doc Demirkan's on the night your friend was killed.'

'A medical surgery?'

'Doc Demirkan is a veterinarian.'

'Someone wanted to fix themselves up without troubling the medical authorities.'

'I think so. One other thing you must know,' Karl said, 'is that we found a thumbprint on one of the casings. No one local. Or at least, no one local in our records.'

'Did Skip mention that he was going to meet anyone?'

Karl shook his head. 'No one called him while he was with me. According to the owner of the café, he ate alone and left alone. That was the last time anyone saw him.'

'Apart from the bad guys, and this mysterious shooter. Maybe he arranged to meet Skip here, but the bad guys got to Skip first.'

Vic was thinking of John Redway's friend. David Parsons. He saw Skip waiting in his car, saw him stepping out when another vehicle came along the service road, thinking it was the person he was supposed to meet. But it was the bad guys, shooting him as he came towards their car, then dumping his body in the boot of his car, setting fire to it. And meanwhile the man who had set up the meet, creeping along the ditch to get a view of what was going on, saw the bad guys climb into their vehicle, and raised up and shot at them as they went past . . .

He said, 'There's only one motel in town. It could be that the bad guys were watching it, saw Skip check in and recognised him, and decided they wanted to find out what he was up to.'

'Or perhaps they were watching me, and saw me meet with your friend,' Karl said. 'I confess that I do not like that thought, but we must consider it.'

'Because they could be watching us now.'

'Of course.'

'If they are,' Vic said, 'we might have a chance of finding them.'

They drove through town, west along the river to the location of the shootout, at the edge of a flat and empty field, near a copse of spiky white trees. The vehicles involved had been towed away, but Karl walked Vic through the scene. A Suzuki jeep had been badly shot up, windscreen starred and smashed; two RVs burned to charred frames squatting on tyre rims. They had still been burning when Karl and his husband and Winnetou's volunteer fire team had arrived. Nothing they could do but let them burn out, Karl said.

One of the trees had burned, too. Standing stark black amongst its pale neighbours, shedding skirls of fine black ash into the wind. The river curved beyond the trees. There was a low building about a kilometre away in the other direction, nothing else but fields and patches of native vegetation fading into a brown haze.

'There are two boats beyond the trees, at the edge of the river,' Karl said. 'Someone shot them up.'

'It sounds like they shot everything up,' Vic said.

'Pretty much,' Karl said. 'We find nine-millimetre, .38 and .45 casings. And a good deal of 5.56 millimetre casings – at least one person had an assault rifle.'

264

'And someone used the ray gun.'

'Yes. That is what your partner called it. It set fire to one of the trees, and a little later was used to set fire to the RVs. We find four bodies in one,' Karl said. 'The fifth man we found later, at the docks.'

'Is your witness reliable?'

'Ove Lassen. Yes, of course.'

'Is that a Swedish name?'

'Danish. I know him well. A good man.'

'He owns this place?'

'He's a neighbour. The owner and his wife have eight children, all under the age of ten. They drove upriver three days ago, after they harvested their produce. But they keep a few pigs, and Ove stopped by to feed and water them. He saw the vehicles in the fields, heard gunshots, and called it in.'

'And he saw the ray gun in action.'

'He said it was like a flash of intense blue light,' Karl said.

'Did he see who fired it?'

Karl shook his head. 'He was about a kilometre away, and did not care to get any closer.'

'Sensible man.'

Vic looked all around. A bleak, empty place. Someone had set up here, and someone else had got the jump on them. Drury v. McBride. Or McBride v. Drury.

They drove to Karl's office and Vic fired up his tablet and brought up the image of the fingerprint card for David Parsons. The right thumbprint scored a ten-point match with the print pulled off the cartridge.

'So this shooter is some kind of spy?' Karl Schweda said, after Vic had explained about the two so-called businessmen. 'He followed your friend down here?'

Vic said, 'Or he followed the bad guys, then spotted Skip.'

They were sitting in the kitchen of the little apartment above the office and the two-cell jail now, eating Karl's five-alarm chilli.

'So where do you want to take this, Investigator?'

Vic forked up some chilli. Man it was hot, but in a good way. 'It looks like we have two ways to go. There's the shooter, David

265

Parsons. And there are the people who killed my partner. Either they're amongst the dead you pulled out of those RVs, or they're long gone.'

'You think downriver, to this Site 326.'

'Possibly. Probably. But Parsons, if he's hurt, might still be around. And it's possible a couple of the bad guys are still here, too. Waiting to see who else turns up.' Vic thought of the two women he'd seen boarding up a house, said, 'How many empty properties are there, in and around town?'

'Forty, more or less,' Karl said. 'Chris has made a list.'

'Plenty of hiding places,' Vic said. 'Maybe you could print out that list. And a map would be good, too.'

39. Drive-Through McDonald's

Mangala | 24 July

One by one they stepped out onto the surface of the planet: ordinary poured concrete, a bright yellow feathery weed caught in a crack, shivering in the chill breeze. The shuttle loomed above them, casting a vast shadow across container stacks and low buildings.

Chloe wondered if she should say something, some kind of small step/giant leap shit, but Henry was already leading Fahad to the far end of an aisle between two stacks, and she hurried after them. Her jacket turned red, then blue, then red again as she walked past different containers. A stocky man in a high-vis vest and a hard hat was waiting by a low-slung vehicle. John Cerdan, according to the ID badge clipped to his vest. Fahad hung back, saying he thought the contact was a woman; Cerdan said, 'You mean the Doc? She waits outside. I take you to her, but you must do everything I tell you. For a start, put on these.'

They donned the vests and hard hats that he handed them, hung visitor badges strung on lanyards around their necks, and climbed into the vehicle. Cerdan drove at a good clip past row after row of containers, past a crane perched on four struts that each terminated in pairs of wheels with tyres taller than a man. Fahad wanted to know if their driver worked for Dr Morange?

'I'm a friend of the Doc,' Cerdan said. 'And I don't care who you are, or why you're here. All I do is get you out while everyone enjoys the holiday.'

They drove across an expanse of bare concrete to a pole gate in the perimeter fence. Cerdan slowed the vehicle, raised a hand to a woman sitting in a glass booth, the pole jerked up, and they were outside.

Warehouses on one side of the road and a slope of scrub rising on the other, a distant glitter beyond the edge of the shuttle's shadow that must be the city. Petra.

The electric cart drew up beside a filthy Subaru Outback parked on the shoulder of the road. A grey-haired woman climbed out and shook hands and exchanged a few words with Cerdan and cast a shrewd gaze over Chloe and Fahad, like a farmer assessing new stock.

'The very definition of a motley crew,' she said. She was in her fifties, with a broad face and small dark suspicious eyes, dressed in baggy blue jeans and a moth-eaten roll-neck sweater. 'I am Hanna. Dr Hanna Babbel. Where is your equipment?'

'You're supposed to supply everything we need,' Henry said.

'We'll see about that. I've had little warning and even less information. You better get in before someone wonders what we are up to.'

As she drove them away from the terminal, Hanna Babbel told Henry that she knew this was something to do with the Elder Culture sites she'd checked out, no more than that. 'They tell me, my bosses on Earth, that you will explain.'

'It's in the nature of a treasure hunt,' Henry said. He was riding in the passenger seat; Chloe and Fahad were on the bench seat behind. Fahad leaning forward, saying, 'Are those fireworks?'

Clusters of coloured stars were flowering and fading in the dark blue sky above the city.

'Landing Day nonsense,' Hanna said dismissively. She was driving fast and erratically, square hands clamped on the wheel. Her fingernails were clipped short; the little finger on her left hand was missing. 'An excuse for people to stop work and get drunk. So you are looking for some type of Elder Culture artefact, no doubt. Or perhaps you search for one of the so-called lost cities.'

'Something like that,' Henry said.

'You need my help but you do not trust me with the truth.'

'The truth is, we don't really know what we'll find,' Henry said.

'I see. What it is, I get two phone calls from Earth, first time in many weeks. The first tells me to look for excavation sites licensed by a company called Sky Edge Holdings. The second

268

tells me to expect guests and give them any help they ask for. Even though I have my own work to do, and it is not the kind of work you can stop, just like that.'

Fahad looked at Chloe, eyebrows raised. As if to say, see what we get, instead of what we were promised?

Chloe asked Hanna Babbel about her work.

'They didn't tell me about you. So I suppose I should not be surprised they didn't tell you about me.'

'They said you are a biologist. They didn't go into much detail, but I'm sure it must be interesting, working out here,' Chloe said, trying to find a way to get past this woman's bristling suspicion.

Hanna said, 'I have been here for eleven years. I was part of the crew that Karyotech Pharma sent to study the biota. We were preparing an expedition to the southern hemisphere when the funding dries up and the others go home. I still collect plants and animals, samples of soil and rock, and send them back to Earth. What they do with it I do not know because they do not tell. And I have my own work, on biochines. Mangala has more kinds than anywhere else, at least three distinct clades.'

'You also report on the work of the Prof's rivals,' Henry said. 'You're well paid for it. And you'll be well paid for this, too. We need your help to find out where an artefact came from. You'll help us get equipped, and if it comes to it you'll ride along with us. So no more sob stories about your work being interrupted. Because this is your work, right now.'

'I will of course do my best to help,' Hanna said stiffly.

'I know you will.' Henry was pointing again. 'What's that? A McDonald's?'

'Yes. Drive-through. Very new.'

'This place is a lot more civilised than I thought it would be,' Henry said.

'The city is,' Hanna Babbel said. 'Outside it, not so much.'

'Here be dragons,' Chloe said.

'Things far stranger than dragons.'

They were driving through the city's outskirts now, along an elevated four-lane highway. Hanna Babbel commented on places wheeling by. A shopping mall. 'The biggest on the planet, for what it's worth.' Factories where electronics were assembled, where clothes and shoes were made.

'We have thousands of new immigrants with every shuttle,' Hanna said. 'We have to find work for all of them. We also have a big problem with crime. Too many people who don't want to work to earn a living come up here looking for a free ride. The Jackaroo imposed the lottery system on the UN, and we suffer the fallout. See that glass tower? That's the UN building. The tallest in the city. Where our Lords and Masters live.'

It was twenty, twenty-five storeys high, standing above a clutter of roofs like a lighthouse above the sea. The city was mostly a low-rise sprawl, a little like the old part of Marrakesh, where Chloe and Dave had gone on their first and last holiday together. Yet amongst the mundane buildings were clusters of tree-like things, skinny stalks terminating in dark, fluffy puffballs, actual alien plants, and in the hazy distance a scalloped range of hills glowed in the level orange sunlight.

They left the ring road and drove past factory buildings, down a long street lined with bars and shops, cafés and small businesses. Lawyers, assayers, pawnshops, laboratories offering carbon dating, neutron bombardment, gas chromatography, MRI . . . A busy traffic of scooters and trucks and battered cars. People at a bus stop. A small cinema advertising a film that Chloe had seen last year.

Narrow streets spalled off on either side of this main drag, twisting around clusters of pitch-roofed shacks and compounds walled with roughly mortared concrete blocks or fenced with corrugated iron. Hanna lived in one of these compounds, at the end of a deeply rutted track. An electric gate topped with barbed wire rolled back to reveal a big square of red dirt, with a trailer home and a long wooden shed on one side, raised beds of vegetables and a polytunnel on the other, a cluster of cages at the far end. Angular things paced or sprawled inside the bars and wire mesh of the cages. Alien critters. Biochines.

Fahad walked towards them. Chloe went after him.

There were a couple of dozen of the things, rat-sized, cat-sized, wolf-sized. It was difficult not to see them as mutated versions of Earthly creatures. Weird giant insects. Clockwork armadillos. Some had six legs, some four. Some had armoured plates on their shoulders or hindquarters, shaped into articulated helmets around their heads. Clusters of tiny black eyes, mouths like sphincters, or complicated mouthparts that folded back to reveal drill-bit tongues, or combs armed with hooks and spines.

The biochines stirred as Fahad approached. Whining and chittering and squealing. Cheap horror-film sound effects. A tall skinny armoured thing a little like a giant praying mantis reared against the bars of its cage, screeching like a saw cutting metal, clawed forelimbs raking the air.

Fahad turned to Chloe. 'I can feel him! I can feel him trying to speak to them!'

Chloe felt a touch of Fahad's excitement. It was the first time that Ugly Chicken had manifested itself since they'd climbed into the shipping container. 'What does he want?'

Fahad looked at the mantis thing. It was thrusting its tiny head back and forth between the bars. A thick yellow froth dripped from squirming mouthparts. 'I don't know . . .'

Now Henry Harris and Hanna Babbel bustled up, the biologist telling them to leave her biochines alone, grabbing Fahad's arm when he didn't move, saying, 'Can't you see you're upsetting them?'

Fahad tried and failed to get free. His face was flushed with anger and excitement. 'Let me go! This is important!'

Chloe said, 'Fahad is carrying an artefact with an embedded eidolon. It wants to talk to your monsters.'

'They are biochines, not monsters,' Hanna said. 'And they are mine. Whatever you are doing, it is hurting them.'

'She's right,' Henry said. 'Fahad, you've proved your point, whatever it is. Now let's get something to eat, and we can all introduce ourselves properly.'

They sat around a roughly carpentered picnic table. Hanna dished up a couple of frozen pizzas carelessly heated in a microwave, cheese half-melted, crusts spongy and damp. Chloe picked at her food, feeling as though she had jumped out of a plane and hadn't yet pulled on the ripcord of her chute and didn't know if she could trust it.

She kept noticing odd details. A scatter of fossil-bearing stones set into the rough plaster of the compound's wall. A skinny spar of what looked like translucent half-melted plastic standing in the middle of the vegetable garden. A tall, sharply pointed cone of polished black rock planted near the door of the long shed like an old-fashioned rocket ship ready for take-off. Clumps of yellow feathers stuck here and there in the red dirt.

Fahad told Hanna about Rana's bead and Ugly Chicken, showed her some of his pictures. He didn't tell her about his father.

'They are not common, beads like that,' Hanna said. 'But they aren't especially rare, either. I never knew of one harbouring an eidolon before, but why not?'

'It sort of talks to me,' Fahad said, ever-so-casually. 'And it was trying to talk to those things. Your animals.'

'Since they reacted to it, I must suppose it is real,' Hanna said. 'So. You think it makes you draw the place where it was found, and you come all this way to look around. I have heard crazier things, but not many.'

'We need to get to one of those sites you researched, as soon as possible,' Henry said. 'Site 326, in Idunn's Valley.'

He pulled up the map on his tablet. Hanna studied it and said that it would not be a difficult trip; at least, in theory.

'It is about a thousand kilometres from here, and the roads are mostly good. As far as Winnetou, anyway. After that you will have to travel on the river, or hire a small plane. But there are some problems you must consider,' she said, with the gloomy relish of someone who loves to impart bad news. 'First, it will soon be night. Thirty-one days of night. Second, a big dust storm is about to roll over the area. And a little after that, it rolls over the city.'

'And you didn't bother to tell anyone about that until now?'

'As I have said, no one told me why you are coming,' Hanna said. 'You want to do what you need to do, you must get out there quick. Soon, nothing will be moving.'

Chloe said, 'How long will it last?'

'The storm? Who can say? People already strip the super-markets here, thinking it might be like the Big Blow that hit in the second year. That one lasted three months. And if you get in trouble in the middle of it, out there in the back country, no one will come to help you.'

'I don't know about anyone else, but I want to get this thing done and go home,' Henry said.

'If we wait in the city until it blows over, we can plan and prepare properly,' Fahad said. 'We could even look for the people my father worked for—'

'And if we hang around here the bad guys could find out about us. Or get there ahead of us. We want to find this thing, and they do too. No,' Henry said, 'we'll go as soon and as fast as possible.'

'I will help you buy what you need,' Hanna said. 'But that is all. It is crazy to go out into the storm, and I have work here.'

'The Prof wants you to help, so you're in,' Henry said.

Hanna was good at the slow-burn silences and imperious stares of someone who believes that she lives in a world where everyone else is slightly retarded. She aimed that stare now at Henry's stone face.

He said, 'I work for the Prof and so do you. You do what I tell you to do, or the UN and the local police will find out about your little fossil-smuggling enterprise. The guy at the yard, Cerdan, he's your contact, isn't he? Loads your stuff on the sly so you don't have to pay Customs, or inspection taxes. Oh, don't pretend to be surprised. Of course we know about it.'

'I need the money for my research,' Hanna said. 'The Prof, she does not pay me enough.'

'She pays you plenty. And she'll pay for whatever we need, which you'll get to keep when this is over. Meanwhile, why don't we work up a list of what we need, what you already have and what we need to buy?'

40. A Long Way Off Your Beat

Mangala | 30 July

Karl Schweda drove Vic back to the motel and told him he'd stop by with a list of empty properties in the morning.

'I appreciate the help,' Vic said.

'I swore an oath to protect the people of this county,' Karl said. 'How I see it, Investigator Gayle, you are assisting me.'

The cold wind had strengthened; Vic kept his head down as he crossed the short distance from the Land Rover to the door of his room. When he switched on the light, the man sitting on the edge of the bed said, 'I think you should stay right where you are.'

Vic recognised him from the Hotel California's CCTV footage: white, athletic build, cropped hair. He was dressed in tan slacks and a blue denim shirt, the left sleeve torn off. His bare arm was in a sling fashioned from the knotted sleeve; the bandage above his elbow was spotted with blood. He was holding a pistol in his right hand, some kind of Colt knock-off. It was the colour of old soap and it was aimed at Vic's chest.

'So what should I call you?' Vic said. 'David Parsons? Or are you going to tell me your real name?'

The man smiled. 'I'll ask the questions, if you don't mind.'

Vic ignored that. 'The guys who shot you – did you hit any of them?'

The man's eyes widened slightly. Gotcha.

Vic said, 'The local police found a bunch of cartridge cases near the place where the body of my partner was found. And don't tell me you don't know what I'm talking about.'

'Before we get into that, I need you to lose your gun.'

The man seemed very calm, but he had sweated through his shirt and the pistol's muzzle was making small circles.

Vic took two steps into the room. 'Why don't I show you my ID, prove I'm one of the good guys?'

'First lose the gun,' the man said, and raised his pistol, re-centring it on Vic. They were just two metres apart now.

Vic used his thumb and forefinger to pull his pistol from the slide holster on his belt, laid it on the floor. He said, 'I have to unzip my jacket to reach my badge, so don't shoot me, okay?'

The man's smile was there and gone. 'I'll do my best.'

Vic skimmed his badge case at the man's face. The man reflexively batted at it with his gun hand, and Vic stepped sideways and caught the man's wrist and bent it up and back. The man half-rose from the bed as he fought against the pressure, but he was one-handed and off-balance, and Vic had better leverage. The man fell back on the bed and dropped the pistol. Vic kicked it under the bed and stepped back and scooped up his own gun.

The man stared at him, white-faced, breathing hard. 'That was quite a risk you took.'

'You weren't going to shoot me. You came here because you need my help.'

The man picked up the badge case and flipped it open. 'How long have you been on the job, Investigator Gayle?'

'Just about all my life. Why don't you tell me who you are and why you're here?'

'Chief Inspector Adam Nevers, Alien Technology Investigation Squad,' the man said. 'I can't show you any ID, so I'm afraid you'll have to take my word for it.'

'Because you're travelling under a false name. Like the guy killed near the shuttle terminal. Your friend John Redway.'

Nevers didn't show any surprise. 'His real name was Ellis Sinclair.'

'Was he a policeman too?'

'We have both lost our partners, Investigator Gayle.'

Vic sat in the armchair by the window, the gun resting in his lap. It had been a long day and it didn't look like it was going to be over any time soon. 'My partner, Skip Williams, was the primary in the investigation into Ellis Sinclair's murder. He came here because he was following the prime suspects, Cal McBride and Danny Drury. Yeah, I can see those names mean something to you. I know you were there when Skip was killed. So why don't you tell me what went down?'

'Before we get into that, Investigator Gayle, I think we should discuss how we can help each other.'

'You think I'm going to help you?'

'We're both chasing after the same people. I know things you need to know, you have resources I lack . . . Of course we can help each other.'

Nevers had the same air of natural-born superiority as Danny Drury. Private education, Oxbridge, fast-track promotions, the unexamined assumption that foot soldiers like Vic would knuckle their foreheads and jump when he said jump. Well screw that.

Vic said, 'You're a long way off your beat, Chief Inspector. You're wounded and shit out of luck, which is why you came to me. You need my help to find the bad guys, but I don't need yours. I know this is about three stowaways who smuggled themselves here in a shipping container, and an Elder Culture site excavated a while back by Sky Edge Holdings. A company once owned by Cal McBride, now run by Danny Drury. The two of them had a set-to outside town, and whoever was left standing has gone downriver, to that site. So here's how it is. If you tell me what you know, maybe we can help each other out. But if you don't, I'll have the local law lock you up.'

'On what charge?'

'To begin with, you're an accessory to two murders. I'm sure I can turn up some other stuff. Threatening a police officer, possession of an illegal firearm . . . I guarantee that you won't be going back to Earth with whatever it is you came here to find. You'll be in a prison work gang, making roads or picking fruit, for the next twenty years.'

'That's an impressive threat,' Nevers said.

'If you think any part of it isn't true, now's your chance to tell me.'

In the silence, Vic could hear the wind hunting at the window behind him.

Nevers said, 'You don't know who killed your partner, do you?'

'I know it was either Cal McBride or Danny Drury. And I know where I can find them.'

'I'll give you an eyewitness statement, and I'll help you catch them, too.'

'You're still trying to make a deal, but you can't.'

'I'm talking as one police officer to another. As someone who's also lost his partner.'

'Don't you try to use that against me.'

'We both want the same thing.'

'I won't bargain over my partner's body to get it.'

Nevers didn't say anything.

'I want to do this the right way,' Vic said. 'So what I'm going to do now is call my friend Karl Schweda. The constable of this county. This mess has landed in his lap, and he deserves to know about it. We'll get your gunshot wound treated, and you can tell us everything you know. The whole sorry story from beginning to end. And then, and only then, I'll think about whether I need your help.'

'That's the best you can do?'

'As far as you're concerned? That's it. If you don't like it, you don't have to tell me anything and you can stay here, in jail. Karl's a good guy. I'm sure he'll make you comfortable.'

'Where you might leave me anyway, even if I tell you everything.'

'It's up to you. But, one police officer to another, I think you know that telling me everything is the right thing to do.'

41. Through The Mirror

Mangala | 25 July

The three travellers dossed down in cheap sleeping bags in the squalid living room of Hanna Babbel's trailer: the kind of worn grey carpet found in rented offices, a greasy couch and a coffee table piled with used trays of microwaved meals, papers and books, blades of sunlight slicing through cheap plastic blinds and falling on a photograph of a scowling man with a bushy moustache. The former Mr Babbel, according to Hanna. 'To remind me why I never go back to Earth.'

Chloe had a hard time getting to sleep, woke to find Henry snoring and Fahad's sleeping bag unzipped and empty. He was outside, standing in front of the cage of the mantis-like biochine. The thing was pressed against the bars, its small triangular head angled towards him. It was making a low buzzing sound, like a fridge motor ticking over.

Fahad smiled at Chloe and said, 'Ugly Chicken has made a friend.'

His right hand was gripping his left wrist and Rana's bracelet.

Chloe said, 'Is that what he's telling you?'

'He isn't talking to me. Not yet. But I can feel him, in my head. He's awake, Chloe. Ready to go.'

'That's beyond cool, Fahad. Seriously.'

'Because it means you have not come all this way for nothing.'

'Because the risk we all took is paying off.'

'Yes. It will all work out. You'll see.'

Hanna Babbel scowled when Fahad explained about befriending the biochine and what it meant, told him to keep away from her valuable specimens and find something else to play games with.

Henry pretended to be sanguine, saying that it was nice that Fahad and Ugly Chicken were getting along so well, but wasn't it time that the thing explained what it wanted them to find?

'Even if it did, we'd still have to go and look for it,' Chloe said. 'But at least we should know what it is when we see it.'

'I feel good about it,' Fahad said, looking around at the others, his smile like sunshine breaking through clouds. 'I feel this is right.'

They spent most of the day driving around the city and picking up supplies. Stopping first at a dealership, where Henry bought an aluminium-hulled skiff and a ridiculously oversized outboard motor, and a trailer that they hitched to Hanna's Subaru.

'You pay far too much,' she said.

'So what? It isn't my money,' Henry said. He had a credit card that drew on an account in a local bank, pumped up with funds transferred via the shuttle. Just for today, he said, he was Santa Claus.

They towed the boat to the compound and went out again. The ordinary streets and buildings, the ordinary cars and buzzing swarms of scooters deepened Chloe's dreamlike feeling that she hadn't travelled across twenty thousand light years at all, but instead had fallen through a mirror into an alternate Earth, or the kind of fictional country where action films and shoot-'em-up video games were staged. Only the low, soft orange sun and the pinkish sky suggested otherwise.

They staged a swift raid for basic clothing on a Gap in a shopping centre, but finding essentials for their expedition took most of the rest of the day because outdoor sports shops and hardware shops had been stripped by people anxious about the oncoming storm. There was a drought of bottled water, hardly any food left on the shelves. Most of their supplies consisted of cereals, dried pasta, power bars, odd combinations of fruit juices – strawberry and orange, mango and ginger – and a kilo of Jamaican Blue Mountain coffee beans that cost more than everything else put together.

'If the worst comes to the worst, we'll have to live off the land,' Henry said. 'Some of these alien critters must be edible. I mean, if we can suck down a McFlurry we can eat pretty much anything.'

They had stopped in the drive-through McDonald's they'd seen yesterday, to regroup and work out if they'd forgotten anything, for a last taste of the Earth before they headed off into the great unknown. In the restaurant, Chloe felt a fresh wave of the odd feeling that she hadn't really left Earth: the familiar pod-like furniture and playschool colours, the familiar odours and perky staff in familiar uniforms, the familiar menu. She was picking at a clammy salad served in a plastic shell. Henry was washing down his double cheeseburger with a big glass of red wine. They served wine and beer here, and there was a café section for coffee and pastries. It was a Continental version of McDonald's.

Hanna explained that few of the plants and animals on Petra could be eaten by human beings or the animals they had brought with them.

'The musculature of biochines is based on various polymers. Plastics. As for other animals, and plants too, they are mostly inedible or poisonous. You would not expect otherwise. They were brought here by Elder Cultures from their homeworlds. It is not a true integrated ecology, but patchworks of competing clades. In the early days, people had to sterilise the soil with chemical treatments or by steam injection before any crops would grow.'

'Maybe we should order a couple of dozen cheeseburgers to go,' Henry said. 'They never go off. Leave one on a shelf for a year, it's still edible.'

Fahad was quiet, hunched in his brand-new blue Helly Hansen parka. He hadn't once complained during the long march of their supply run, but he'd lost the shine of his enthusiasm, and had given up on his Chicken McNuggets and strawberry milkshake. Now he pushed back from the table and excused himself.

'Kid is getting nervous,' Henry said, watching Fahad thread his way past tables and booths to the toilets.

'So am I,' Chloe said. 'This is a giant step into the unknown.'

'It's mostly desert,' Henry said. 'I know deserts.'

'Do not make the mistake of thinking this is like Earth,' Hanna said.

'Yet here we are in a McDonald's.'

Henry was definitely happier than Chloe had ever seen him. Henry Harris, man of action.

He said, 'This isn't a full-blown expedition. It's a quick raid, in and out before the storm hits. So we don't need to take much in the way of supplies. And this place is on a river, so we won't lack for water. If the worst comes to the worst, aren't there farms out there? Farms, orchards . . . We can buy food, scrump apples.'

'We will be a long way from any farm,' Hanna said.

They pulled up the maps again, reviewed the route they would take to Idunn's Valley and the settlement closest to the site, the winding path of the river. After a few minutes, Chloe said, 'Where's Fahad?'

He wasn't in the toilets. He wasn't anywhere in the busy restaurant. He wasn't in Hanna's Outback, wasn't anywhere in the car park.

'Split up,' Henry said, all business. 'You go left, Chloe, I'll go right. You,' he told Hanna, 'stay by your vehicle. Don't fucking move.'

'This is my fault? You blame me, who helps you without thanks? Who works hard out here, on her own, for so many years?'

But Henry was already jogging away.

Chloe went in the opposite direction, walking along the road in the traffic's buffeting slipstream. There was no pavement, so she kept to the shoulder, treading amongst patches of grey furze, black spikes like spearheads pushing up from red dirt. Passing the edge of the car park of a giant Ikea shed.

She felt an airy apprehension, felt as if this strange world had revealed itself to be tissue-thin. She was pretty sure that she knew where Fahad was headed, what he'd been planning all along, and hoped she was wrong.

She was going past an Aldi supermarket now, with a construction site on the other side of the busy road. And saw him, saw Fahad in his blue parka weaving across four lanes of traffic. Horns, brake squeals. Fahad reached the far side, was running across a sloping lot of bare dirt when a white van cut out of the traffic and barrelled towards him. He glanced over his shoulder and put on a spurt of speed, but the van overtook him and cut in hard, and as he changed direction a man jumped out of the back and grabbed him and hauled him backwards, struggling and kicking. The man lifted Fahad into the van and jumped in after him and the van took off, banging down the slope.

Chloe, stranded on the far side of the busy road, saw a red 4x4 swerve out of the traffic and follow the van. She thought she recognised the driver, and thought that if she was right she really had gone through the mirror.

42. Shit Becoming Real

Mangala | 30 July

'I am happy to keep him locked up here,' Karl Schweda said. 'He admits he was at the scene of the shootout and also your partner's murder. He possesses a firearm which he acquired illegally. He admits to using it . . . It is more than enough to detain him.'

'I think he was telling the truth about what happened to my partner,' Vic said. 'He had no reason to kill him. If he did, he wouldn't have come to ask for my help. And if he's telling the truth about Skip, the rest of his story just might be true, too.'

They were sitting in Karl's office. Adam Nevers was in one of the cells downstairs, demolishing a burger sent over from a café in town. The local doctor had cleaned and rebandaged his wound, and he'd told his story to Vic and Karl, putting it on the official record.

He'd come out to Idunn's Valley, he'd said, because he had been following Danny Drury and his associates after they'd kidnapped one of the stowaways from the shipping container. And he'd followed the stowaways to Mangala because they possessed a potent artefact that came from an Elder Culture site excavated by Cal McBride's company and wanted to find more like it or find something larger and even more potent . . . Nevers hadn't been clear on that point. He'd said that Sahar Chauhan, the biochemist who'd cooked meq for the McBride family, had sent the artefact back to Earth, to his son and daughter. A little bead containing some form of eidolon that had affected the children. The son, Fahad, had begun to draw pictures of the same alien landscape, over and over. They had attracted the attention of a research group owned by Ada Morange, a biotech entrepreneur. Her company

283

had sent Fahad and two of her employees to Mangala, inside that shipping container; Nevers and his partner had ridden on the same shuttle on corporate tickets.

'If you had come to us about this thing instead of pulling this sneaky spy shit,' Vic said, 'my partner might still be alive. Yours too.'

Nevers didn't have anything to say about that.

'Tell me what happened outside the shuttle terminal,' Vic said.

'Ellis and I planned to keep watch on the traffic coming out of the terminal, hoping to intercept the stowaways,' Nevers said. 'But we were ambushed as soon as we turned off the main road. Ellis went in one direction; I went in the other. They chased down Ellis, and shot at me when I tried to go to his aid.'

'Did you see who killed your partner?'

According to Little Dave, Cal McBride owned the ray gun that had killed Ellis Peters, but it would be nice to get confirmation from an eyewitness.

But Nevers was shaking his head. 'I was too far away. I saw someone stoop over Ellis, saw a flash of blue light . . . '

'And then?'

'And then they came after me, and I got out of there. I didn't have a gun at the time. There was nothing else I could do.'

'No one's blaming you for taking off,' Vic said.

Nevers said, 'I was hoping, now that I've told you everything I know about the death of your partner, that you would be willing to share any information you have about the death of mine.'

'I don't have anything I can take to the prosecutor,' Vic said.

He wasn't going to open up his investigation to a man who'd been operating on the dark side. And he didn't like Nevers's weak attempt to justify himself. If you do something you know is wrong, you should own it, not try to explain it away.

'I'm not talking about facts,' Nevers said.

'Who do you think did it?'

'I'm certain that it was either Cal McBride or Danny Drury. The man who used to run the company that took out the licence on Site 326, or the man who runs the company now. Whoever it was knew who we were, why we'd come here. It's very likely that someone in the force back home has been feeding them information. Old-school criminal families like the McBrides always have an inside man. When I get back, I'm going to make it my first priority to find out who it is, and who they passed the information to.'

Vic thought it likely that the McBride family would have passed any inside information to Danny Drury, and McBride had found out because he had an informant in Drury's crew. Like, for instance, Little Dave.

He said, 'Someone killed your partner. You fled the scene. What did you do then?'

'I found Danny Drury's house. I found Cal McBride's construction site, and the hotel where he lived. I was planning to confront McBride first. It was easier to get to him. But then I found where the stowaways were hiding. A place owned by a so-called freelance biologist. She paid for a copy of the excavation licence of that Elder Culture site, and she exports material back to Earth, to Ada Morange's company. I'd just caught up with them when Drury's people snatched the boy, Fahad. I followed Drury here, and so did McBride. And that's where things started to go wrong.'

'Did you see the shootout?'

Nevers shook his head. 'I was watching Drury. He got into a speedboat, and took off downriver. By the time I heard about the shootout, it was all over.'

Nevers had been looking for a boat, trying and failing to buy or hire one because everyone was heading upriver, away from the dust storm, when he'd spotted three men Drury had left behind, presumably to look for any of their enemies who had escaped.

'It wasn't hard to keep track of what they were doing; there was always at least one of them keeping watch at the docks,' Nevers said. 'Sitting in a Range Rover. When all three headed out of town I followed them, saw them kidnap Skip.'

Vic said, 'They kidnapped him?'

'He drove out of town, towards the site of the shootout. They ran his car off the road, bundled him into the trunk of his car, took him out to a place behind a big storage shed. Perhaps they wanted to question him, but when they opened the trunk he came at them, they shot him . . .'

285

Vic felt something cold and heavy move through him. He said, 'You didn't intervene?'

'Of course I did. That's how I got shot,' Nevers said, staring straight at Vic as if daring him to deny it.

Karl stirred and said, 'How do you know these were Drury's men?'

'I staked out Drury's house after he snatched Fahad,' Nevers said. 'I recognised two of them.'

'He kept this kid in his house?' Vic felt a little chill, wondering if the kid could have been there when he and Skip had visited the place.

'I didn't see Fahad,' Nevers said. 'But when I saw Drury and half a dozen of his crew leave in a little convoy, I followed them. And that's how I ended up here.'

Karl said, 'And before that, you followed these stowaways all the way from Earth. This artefact must be very valuable.'

'It's very dangerous,' Nevers said. 'I saw what it can do. We caught up with Fahad and his little sister at one point, and the thing reared up . . .'

The man had a stricken, haunted look.

'Eidolons can definitely fuck with your head,' Vic said, thinking of the man who'd killed his partner in that Junktown bar.

'I'm certain that it influenced Fahad and the others. That it made them want to come here,' Alan Nevers said. 'Why, I don't know. But not for anything good. And right now the boy is heading downriver with Drury and his crew. Heading towards that site to do God knows what.'

The man was clearly anxious to prevent that happening. Genuinely believed that this artefact, the eidolon it contained, was dangerous and had warped the minds of everyone who had come into contact with it.

Now, up in the office, Vic told Karl, 'Everyone thinks there's something valuable to be found at this site, but it all comes down to this eidolon. It got inside this kid's head, and maybe it did a number on his friends, and on Nevers. I don't think he chased these stowaways here just because they broke a couple of laws back on Earth.'

Karl agreed. 'I have some experience of prospectors deranged by their finds. They believe that they have found the secret at the heart of the universe, or that they have acquired superpowers, and so on. Most of them are harmless, but a few can be actively dangerous. One woman, over at Hwyel's Crossing, was possessed by an eidolon from a tomb she uncovered on her farm. She kidnapped people and sewed machinery into their living bodies. To make them like the creatures she saw in dreams. Nevers is not that crazy, of course, but it is quite possible that what he and the others are chasing is nothing but a fever dream.'

'Drury and McBride clearly have inside information,' Vic said. 'That part of Nevers's story definitely rings true. Three years ago, Cal McBride's company took out a licence to excavate a site south of here. Then McBride went to jail, and Drury took over. And when Skip and I interviewed Drury about the murder of Nevers's partner, he had a ton of camping gear in his house.'

'So he was getting ready to come here.'

'His people back on Earth tell him about this haunted bead Sahar Chauhan sent his kids. They tell him the son is coming here. So he snatches the kid and this bead, and heads off to the site. Cal McBride wants that bead too, and gives chase. If Nevers was telling the truth, that's what the shootout was about.'

'And McBride lost.'

'We don't know yet that he was killed. He might still be in the game,' Vic said, 'but Drury is definitely on his way to the prize.'

'If you are thinking of going after him, I cannot go with you,' Karl said. 'I have too many responsibilities here.'

'I understand. This one is on me,' Vic said.

There was a brief silence as Skip's death hung between them.

Karl said, 'You could wait here. Whatever happens downriver, Drury has to come back this way.'

'And he could head on past this town to some place further upriver. And when I catch up with him he'll have an explanation about why he couldn't possibly have been here, backed up with alibis and a swarm of lawyers. No, I have to catch him in the one place I know he'll be.'

'You will walk into the middle of his camp and ask him and his man to give themselves up?'

287

'Only in my dreams. I'm going to lay back with a camera and a humungous telescopic lens I happen to have brought along. I have a little drone, too.'

'You came prepared.'

'Well, I *was* a Boy Scout, even if it was a long time ago on another planet. Drury killed Skip and kidnapped these stowaways. I'm going to put him square in the frame, get probable cause to go through all his shit. And if McBride is still after the artefact too, I want to see what happens. So if you know someone who has a boat I can hire, or even buy . . .'

Karl said, 'Chris and I go fishing, on occasion. Strange fish you cannot eat, but Chris mounts them as trophies or sells them to agents for bioscience companies. I could perhaps lend you our skiff, small though it is. But even better, I know someone who might be able to fly you out there. Get you close enough to walk in, and pick you up again afterwards.'

Vic felt a wire twist in his stomach. Shit was becoming real. He said, 'That sounds dangerously like a plan.'

'Also, you will need camping equipment, in case the dust storm arrives early and you have to wait it out. I will give Able Ngomi a call. He owns the local dry-goods store. He can sort out what you need, and I will make sure he doesn't charge you too much.'

'Karl, my man, I'll be paying you back for the rest of my life.'

'I hope you will.'

'I came up on the second shuttle. I was here for the Big Blow. Planet hasn't killed me yet, and some little dust storm won't do the job either. And I have no intention of getting in a spot where Drury or anyone else can take a pop at me. This is strictly a reconnaissance mission,' Vic said, knowing it wasn't, knowing that if it came down to it he was going to have to step up to Danny Drury. Man kills your partner, you don't walk away from that.

Karl said, 'What about Nevers?'

'If you want to formally charge him, it's fine by me. But before you do, I'd like to talk to him again. Man's sitting there so quietly, it's like my grandmother used to say, dog don't howl if he has a bone. He knows more than he's told us. I want to find out what that is.'

43. Gone

'I really thought it was Nevers in that 4x4', Chloe said, 'but now . . .'

'Now you're trying to rationalise it away,' Henry said. 'Me, I can't think of any reason why not. Anyone with enough money can buy a ticket on a shuttle these days – and think of all the publicity the Met would get for the first interplanetary arrest. If he did follow us, though, it means someone must have leaked our travel plans. Maybe I should phone home, ask them to look into that.'

They were cruising the area on the far side of the construction site where Fahad had been snatched – blocks of warehouses and factories, silos and empty lots – looking for white vans while they tried to work out what had just happened. The nature and extent of the disaster.

'If he knew we were coming here,' Chloe said slowly, thinking it through, 'then it's possible that the McBride family knew too.'

'It's possible that everyone knows more than we do,' Henry said.

'So it's possible that they snatched Fahad. They were following us, they saw him break away . . .'

'The kid played us,' Henry said. 'Strung us along with bullshit about ancient ruins while all the time he was working on his own agenda, waiting for the moment when he could make a run for it. It was very nicely done. The only problem is that when he broke away to go looking for the people who killed his father, they found him instead.'

'The ruins are real,' Chloe said.

'But are they really what he says they are? Let's hope the people who snatched him think so. Otherwise he's going to be in real trouble. Turn here,' Henry told Hanna Babbel. 'We'll do one more block.'

Hanna made the turn. She'd hardly said a word since Chloe had come running back to the car park of the McDonald's. Distancing herself from this monumental fuck-up.

A long road between two chemical plants. Rows of squat tanks. Pipes lagged in dirty white insulation. A chimney feathered brown fumes into the clean sky: a human stain on the clean breast of this new world. Hanna slowed when Henry pointed to two men unloading a white van behind a chain-link fence, but it was the wrong kind of white van, smaller than the one Chloe had seen.

At last, they gave up on the search and drove back to the compound. Chloe raised the possibility of calling the police; Henry shot it down at once.

'We have no evidence that the kid was kidnapped, who kidnapped him, or why. And before they do anything else, the police would check our backgrounds, find out we have fake IDs . . . At least we know that Nevers hasn't talked to them. Otherwise they'd already be all over us.'

'If it was Nevers.'

'I believe you saw what you saw, even if you don't,' Henry said.

He asked Hanna about Cal McBride, where he lived, what business interests he had.

'How should I know?' Hanna said. 'I have never heard of him before you ask me to check out that site.'

'There has to be the equivalent of Companies House. A place where businesses and their directors are registered. Also an electoral register. Or don't you have elections here?'

'Of course we do. For the mayor and the city council, and so on.'

'Give me your phone,' Henry said to her. 'I need to start searching for this Cal McBride.'

He poked at it, muttering, holding it up at one point to show Chloe an image of an old bruiser with white hair and a face like a fist, dressed in a white tux and a shirt that was mostly yellow and blue, a beautiful young woman on his arm.

'Mr Cal McBride,' Henry said. 'At some charity do. Despite his shady business dealings and his spell in prison he's quite the man about town. Love the Hawaiian shirt.'

'It's Versace,' Chloe said. 'A Hawaiian shirt would be better, but not by much.'

Henry poked and prodded some more, saying at last, 'Sky Edge Holdings, the company that took out that excavation licence, is into property development. Should be some leads to uncover there. And here's Mr McBride's address, on Rue du Alain Blanchet. I'm looking at a map. This little district with lots of greenery in it, all the streets have French names. You know where that is, Hanna? If you don't, I can show you.'

'Is Bel Air. Very rich neighbourhood.'

Chloe said, 'Are we going there? Seriously?'

'Just to eyeball it,' Henry said casually. Too casually for Chloe's liking. 'When you need to find out about someone,' he said, 'start with where they live.'

It was on a street of large detached properties, a long low house set in a green garden behind a wall. Hanna parked opposite the arched gate and Henry studied the place with a monocular screwed to his right eye, turning the focus ring this way and that. Saying, 'No white van, but that doesn't mean anything. If I'd just snatched a kid off the street I wouldn't bring him back to the place where I live. Security cameras, strands of razor wire on top of the walls . . . A warning that they're electrified. And check out that watchtower. Mr McBride likes his privacy.'

'There's someone at the gate,' Chloe said. 'Watching us.'

'So there is.' Henry rolled down the window and gave the guy a cheerful wave, told Hanna they could leave. 'Now they know we know. Which they probably already knew, but still.'

He seemed grimly pleased. Beads containing alien eidolons that got inside people's heads and gave them visions of ancient wonders were the stuff of fantasy stories. Dealing with bad men who did bad things was something he understood. Something he could deal with.

It deepened Chloe's sliding feeling that they were moving inexorably towards some kind of bullshit macho confrontation. She said, 'Do you think you can rescue Fahad single-handed? Deal with these kidnappers and Nevers on your own?'

'Of course not. I'm going to hire some help. A couple of local soldiers who know the country. But first, I need to gear up. Hanna, do you have a gun?'

'Of course. A hunting rifle. You need protection, in the back country. And not just from biochines and other fauna.'

'I need something a little more inconspicuous. Something I can carry in a pocket or stick in my waistband. A Glock 17 for preference, but any semi-automatic will do in a pinch.'

'You will need ID and a licence to buy it,' Hanna said. 'And it takes two weeks to get the licence, after you apply.'

'But I bet someone like you knows someone who can help speed things through. Someone who deals in guns, or someone who prints them. Explosives would be good too. C-4 if you can get it. Gelignite or plain old blasting powder if you can't.'

'I will ask,' Hanna said. 'But you must be patient. People who deal in such things are suspicious of strangers.'

Back at the compound, Hanna made several phone calls, told Henry again that he must be patient, and went off to feed and water her pets. Henry used her tablet to do more research on Cal McBride, telling Chloe that he had been implicated in several murders.

'Men found with burn marks, scrambled brains . . . Two of them, quote, known associates of notorious businessman Cal McBride, unquote. A reporter asked him if he had an Elder Culture weapon; he said that if he did, he'd sell it and retire on the proceeds. Cute guy, our Mr McBride,' Henry said, clicking on a sidebar link and looking thoughtful.

'What is it?'

'A report of a body found near the shuttle terminal yesterday, an unidentified man apparently with his brains burned out.'

'You think it has something to do with us?'

'The story implies it was something to do with McBride. It's definitely something I'd like to ask him about. Police won't confirm the manner of death, say they are making good progress, blah, blah, blah . . .'

'And now McBride has Fahad.'

'If he took the kid, it's because he needs him. Fahad's safe for now, and we're going to find him.'

Hanna came back after an hour or so, saying that the boy had taken a knife and her bolt pistol from the laboratory.

'I thought you only had a hunting rifle,' Henry said.

'It is not a pistol as such,' Hanna said. 'It uses compressed air to fire a length of metal into the brain of a biochine. Those that have brains.'

'The crafty beggar,' Henry said. 'He went equipped.'

'He escaped the sea fort with his sister,' Chloe said. 'He stayed hidden for several months before I came along. He's resourceful. A survivor.'

'I hope so. Because we need him and that bead to find what we came here to find.'

'I have other news,' Hanna said, and told them that someone, a friend of a friend, was willing to sell Henry a pistol.

'It's always a friend of a friend,' Henry said. 'Well, no point hanging around. You come too, Chloe. We'll stick together for now, in case the bad people have another pop at us.'

They drove out of the city into the low hills. It was a hair past midnight, but the sun shone as it had done ever since they'd arrived. A long day getting steadily worse . . .

Hanna turned off the blacktop and the Subaru wallowed up a dirt road that snaked beside a dry river, climbing past a string of shacks and trailer homes to a chicken farm in a clearing hacked out of native vegetation that grew in thickets of stout white zigzags. There was a big prefab barn, a mud-brick shack with a pitched roof of corrugated iron. A wind turbine reared above the tops of the zigzags, one of the new vaneless types: it looked like a giant Polo mint on a stick.

They climbed out into silence and cold dry air. And as they walked towards the shack men came out of the barn, cutting them off from the Subaru, and the door to the shack opened and a man with a shock of white hair came out, walking up to them with his hands in the pockets of his quilted gilet, surveying them like a farmer assessing new stock.

'Mr McBride,' Henry said, standing still with his arms folded, giving the man his best deadeye stare.

'Mr Harris. And Ms Millar. A pleasure to meet you at last.'

Chloe said, 'Where is Fahad?'

'We need to talk about that,' Cal McBride said. 'We need to talk about a lot of things. Not you,' he told Hanna. 'I don't need you any more.'

'She sold us out,' Henry said, sounding philosophical. 'I was wondering about that.'

'I am doing you a favour,' Hanna said. 'Mr McBride will help you. You will see.'

'Then why don't you fuck off,' Henry said pleasantly, 'so Mr McBride can explain himself.'

Cal McBride stepped up, pulling a torch from the pocket of his gilet, saying, 'Before you do, here's your reward. Hold her still, boys.'

Two men grabbed Hanna's arms and as she struggled Cal McBride raised his torch and jammed it against the side of her head. There was a flash of blue light and Hanna collapsed in the men's grip, her head crowned in flame.

44. Wire

Mangala | 30 July

'You're making a bad mistake,' Adam Nevers told Vic.

'How so, Mr Nevers?'

'Because you haven't come to release me. You want to pump me for more information instead.'

'There is this one thing I'd like to get straight,' Vic said.

He was sitting on a plastic chair outside the steel bars of Nevers's cell. Nevers perched on the edge of his cot in T-shirt and jeans, a bulky new bandage around his left arm.

'And while we waste time with this nonsense, Drury is getting closer to his goal,' he said.

Vic ignored that. 'All it is, I was wondering how you knew that the people in the shipping container were coming to Mangala.'

'I told you. I had inside knowledge.'

'Buying shuttle tickets on the open market isn't cheap. Even if it is government money, you committed a lot of resources to this. I think you needed more than the word of an informer.'

'It's a very special informer.'

'I have a couple of CIs myself, but I wouldn't take off for another world purely on the basis of something one of them said.'

'You're planning to go to Site 326. And if you go without me, you probably won't come back,' Nevers said.

Vic ignored that. 'You came out all this way, and you can't be sure the people you're chasing will find anything useful. It's Elder Culture stuff. Most of it junk. Ruins. And even if it's functional, most of the time no one can work out what it does. But here you are. If you don't mind me saying so, it's as if you're working off a personal grudge.'

295

'You know the old cliché from horror movies? "Meddling in things Man wasn't supposed to understand"? That's what these people are doing. Meddling with a very powerful and dangerous alien artefact. I have personal experience of that.'

'They want to find Elder Culture tech that'll help conquer the world. And you're – what? Their nemesis?'

'I'm doing my job.'

'And look where it got you,' Vic said.

It was a cheap shot, but he wanted to rattle the man. Get him angry, and see what popped out.

Instead, Nevers looked away, as if examining something in his head, then looked back. 'You searched my gear.'

'Of course we did.'

'And you found the wire?'

'The wire?'

'It looks like a crumpled Christmas ornament.'

'We may have found something like that.'

'I hoped that I wouldn't have to resort to using it, but it will explain everything,' Nevers said.

'And how will it do that?'

'I need a place where I can raise eidolons. Your friend the constable must know of somewhere like that. From what I understand, this world is basically one big haunted house.'

Karl Schweda drove Vic and Adam Nevers north along the riverbank. He wasn't happy about it, even with Nevers handcuffed on the back seat, behind the wire screen of the cruiser.

'We could be driving into an ambush.'

'No one is following us. And he doesn't know where you're taking him.'

'The people involved in that shootout had drones,' Karl said.

'You think he's on their side?'

'I know he is not on yours.'

Behind them, Nevers said, 'I'm going to prove to Investigator Gayle that he needs my help.'

Five kilometres north of the town there were limestone cliffs along the edge of the river, where it had cut through stratified deposits that had formed at the bottom of an ancient, long-vanished sea. An Elder Culture had built tombs inside a deep shelf close to the river's edge, where a friable seam had been eroded by rain and floodwater. Karl led Vic and Nevers to a narrow path that slanted down the face of the cliffs, said he'd keep watch, and handed Vic a walkie-talkie.

'Any sign of trouble, I'll give you a call,' the constable said. 'You had better come at once, because I will not wait.'

Vic had Nevers take the lead as they crabbed their way down the glassy thread of the path. Nevers favoured his left arm, but descended at a sprightly clip. Vic had trouble keeping up with him. Waves driven by the razor wind dashed on fallen rocks below; Vic felt horribly exposed, and kept his hand on his pistol.

The shelf was sheltered beneath an overhang and slanted down at the rear. The tombs were scattered along its length, small things like half-melted beehives constructed from some kind of dark glistening stone. Water seeping through the stone ceiling had created clusters of stalactites; water fell drop by drop into clear pools cupped in fringes of lime accretions, and had deposited irregular caps of bone-coloured lime on many of the tombs.

Vic, watching Nevers wander amongst the tombs and water pools, felt a shiver as a shadow detached from other shadows and drifted after the man.

There was a cluster of tombs in Petra that was haunted by eidolons. The Indian Burial Grounds. A park had been laid out around them and school parties visited, little kids learning about Elder Cultures, but Vic remembered that it had been a pretty damn frightening place when it had been first discovered, when no one knew what eidolons were, what they could do. A couple of women, one a psychologist in her former life, the other a librarian, had been amongst the first to try to communicate with them. Talking to them, showing them images on tablets, simple arithmetic and geometry. Nothing doing. The eidolons had a trophism for anything that disturbed their tombs – they'd follow a biochine as soon as follow a person – but they ignored every attempt to talk to them or snag their attention. It was like trying to talk back to a TV, the librarian had told Vic. Rachel Sweeting. They'd been sleeping together at the time, a brief fling, Vic's second on Mangala. Back in the day, when their hold on the world seemed so tenuous that hardly anyone formed permanent relationships.

These were smaller than the eidolons in the Indian Burial Grounds, and there were a lot more of them. Twists of smoke wavering through the half-light like the ghosts of bats. Translucent projections from caches of quantum memory. Some briefly whirled around each other, like dancers in a waltz, before catching up with the others, gathering around Nevers, trailing after him as he walked back to Vic.

'Don't think you're anything special,' Vic said. 'They'll follow anyone.'

But he felt an edge of anticipation and alarm. He had never seen so many eidolons before.

Nevers took out a Ziploc bag and pulled out the twist of wire it contained and tossed it to the floor, stepping back as the eidolons spun around it like a pack of dogs disputing a morsel of food. The wire twisted and jiggled, one end drawing into a circle on the ground, a footing from which the other end rose like a snake, a metre of stiff wire that suddenly kindled a sharp blue incandescence that burned through the shadows whirling around it.

And something stood up. A man-shape rising out of shadow, faint and transparent, dressed in a black tracksuit and wearing sunglasses. Looking at Vic and saying, 'Well now. Who's this?'

45. Honour And Revenge

Mangala | 27-28 July

The road's straight line unreeled across the flat desert. Red dirt, red rocks. Drifts of grey vegetation. Stands of spiky lattices, like charred cacti. Small fleets of scalloped dunes drifted across salt flats. This had once been the floor of a shallow sea, Cal McBride said. A pinkish tint in the sky. The fat sun sat in a kind of shawl of red haze near the horizon, casting long shadows everywhere.

The RV drove for hour after hour at a steady one hundred and ten kilometres per hour. The road. The desert. The big sky. Traffic scurried past in the opposite direction, heading towards the city. Pickups, cars and 4x4s fleeing the dust storm. Road trains with tractor units hauling eight or nine trailers. A convoy of motorcycles, mostly Harleys, their riders in outlaw leathers. Now and then a low building or a cluster of trailer homes swung past, preceded by big signs advertising petrol, food, a café or a bar.

It was how Chloe had imagined driving across America. The size of it. The emptiness of it.

McBride, chirpy as a tour guide, pointed out alien ruins. Strings of cubical, roofless enclosures shimmering in the sunlight, mostly running along ridges. A tall slender black column stood in the distance – a fascination stone, according to McBride, that could hold unwary travellers in a trance until they died of thirst or were killed and eaten by animals or biochines.

'You're kidding,' Henry said.

'No, I'm not. There all kinds of traps out here. All kinds of things that can kill you if you aren't careful,' McBride said.

He pointed to a salt flat off in the distance, where fossilised vehicle tracks a million years old had been found. 'Big machines,

299

wide as a city block. Tracked like tanks. Imagine what they must have looked like, trundling around.'

He told Chloe and Henry about the ring sea at the equator, bordered by thousands of kilometres of salt dunes and alkali lagoons. He told them about a permanent waterspout climbing more than two kilometres before topping out in a long feathering of spray, constructed by who knew which Elder Culture for who knew what purpose. He told them about sliding stones the size of cars that drifted across salt flats a thousand kilometres to the south, moving singly or in flocks, never stopping. They were no more than thin shells of crystalline iron that trapped and heated air, yet appeared to possess a certain intelligence and purpose.

'You remember that old tourist trap on Shaftesbury Avenue? Ripley's Believe It or Not? That has nothing on this world. It's fucking magic,' McBride said.

He was wearing a belted khaki jacket, a black kerchief salted with tiny skull-and-crossbones knotted at his neck. The hems of his khaki trousers were tucked into calf-length brown leather boots. He sat on the sectional couch at the rear of the RV with Chloe and Henry, pointing out marvels as they rolled past. Three burly men, construction-worker or biker types with beards and bushy moustaches, sat up front, pistols holstered on their hips. McBride's weapon was clipped to his belt. He'd shown them how it worked on the first day of their captivity. Opened it up to show a regular LEAF battery and a thumb-sized slug of grey quasi-metallic metamaterial capped by a crystal nipple. The slug turned an electrical current into a beam of coherent high-energy photons with an efficiency approaching one hundred per cent. At full power, McBride said, you could burn down a house. It was a genuine Elder Culture ray gun – one of a kind, according to him.

Henry shared a look with Chloe. She knew he was thinking about the dead man at the shuttle terminal.

McBride said, 'You're lucky you ran into me. I know how to get things done, and I know all there is to know about Elder Culture shit.'

After they'd been ambushed at the farm, Chloe and Henry had been confined in separate bedrooms of a suburban bungalow. McBride's goons had brought food at irregular intervals and escorted Chloe when she needed to use the bathroom, but had refused to answer any of her questions.

There was sheet metal over the window, sunlight burning at its edges day and night. A flatscreen TV on the wall, a mattress on the floor, no other furniture. Chloe watched TV and slept because there was nothing else to do and she didn't want to think too much about what might happen to her.

She tried knocking on the partition wall a couple of times, remembering how prisoners had communicated in a movie she'd once seen. Henry didn't reply.

McBride turned up in the afternoon of the second day, with the gear Chloe had bought in another lifetime. He stood outside the door of the bedroom while she changed, telling her in a loud cheerful voice that he had made a deal with her boss, and now she and Henry were going on a little trip. He said that he hadn't snatched her friend Fahad, but he knew who had: Danny Drury, a scheming little fucker who'd get what was coming to him soon enough. Told her, when she emerged from the bedroom, that she looked pretty good, asked her where she'd found her camo jacket.

'It was a present.'

She was wearing it over a thin black roll-neck sweater, Montane Terra pants, her New Balance hiking shoes.

'I could import them, use you as a model in an ad campaign, sell a fucking ton of them,' McBride said. 'I don't know what they told you about me, but what I really am is a businessman. An entrepreneur, like your boss.'

'Henry isn't my boss.'

'Not him. Dr Morange. Yes,' McBride said, clearly enjoying Chloe's surprise, 'we had a nice chat, she and I, over the q-phone. A very useful chat. What it boils down to is that we're partners in this enterprise now. I help you and Henry; you and Henry help me. Anything we find we share. Straight down the middle.

I help you find the goods; Dr Morange provides the expertise to work out what it can do and how to market it.'

'What about Fahad?'

'If you're worried that I'll punish him because he ran away from my family back home, I could care less. They fucked me over. They're dead to me,' McBride said.

For a moment a hard light entered his gaze and Chloe saw what lurked behind the cheerful cockney-geezer facade.

'Fuck them,' McBride said. 'And fuck Danny Drury too. He killed Sahar, the kid's father. Did you know that? Sahar had developed a little sideline, dealing in Elder Culture stuff, and he was also going to come back and work for me, after I got over my little trouble with the legal authorities. Well, Drury got wind of all that, and he did Sahar. And not in a nice way, I can tell you. Not because he had it in for Sahar especially, but to teach me a lesson. To show me what I could and couldn't do. To show me who was boss now. As if he ever could be. I liked Sahar. I really did. He had his problems, he was a gambling fiend, but he was a good man. And skilled. Better than anyone I've ever known. I like to think of him as my friend, and he did not deserve to die like that. So I swear to you, Chloe, I will do the right thing by his son. If the kid finds what he promised to find, he'll go free, and so will you. And you'll get a cut. Everyone will make on this deal, I promise you that.'

It was hard to tell how much of that was sincere and how much was put on. Chloe suspected that even McBride couldn't tell. But his deal with Ada Morange was for real. Henry had been allowed to speak to her.

'She isn't happy about it, but she's pragmatic,' he told Chloe. 'And if this is the only way to get what she wants . . .'

'So he's our friend now.'

'Think of him as an unreliable ally. We don't have to trust him, but he has resources we can use. We'll go along with his plans, and see what shakes out. Let's face it, the alternative is much worse.'

'No kidding,' Chloe said, remembering Hanna Babbel collapsing with her hair on fire.

*

They passed a small settlement: huts buried in mounds of red dirt, a prefab industrial building squatting near a great tumble of white blocks, sharp-edged despite millennia of wind-blown dust. Some kind of plastic as hard as diamond, according to McBride. People cut them up using welding gear or lasers, and glued the blocks into storm walls. He pointed to one such wall at the far edge of the next settlement they passed. A snow-white curve that sheltered the huddle of trailers and shacks from winds that mostly blew from the west.

That was where the dust storm was coming from; that was where they were headed. The west. Idunn's Valley. And that was where the people who had taken Fahad were headed, too. A little convoy about twenty kilometres ahead. McBride said that he could take them down any time he wanted, but couldn't guarantee the kid's safety. So his plan was to let them get to the site and find what there was to find, and then he'd pounce.

'Never mind all that nonsense about the licence expiring a year ago. I found the site; I excavated it. And the bead in question, it came from there, on my watch. Danny Drury had no interest in it until he was given his orders, so fuck him and his crew. They can do the dirty work, and then I'm moving in to take what's rightfully mine.'

Chloe thought it was typical bluster, but Henry said that it wasn't a bad plan. He was dressed in a green hunting vest over a black hoodie, grey cargo pants made of some kind of nanotech material with a slippery sheen, and heavy boots. He seemed relaxed, bantering with McBride, generally behaving as if they really were equal partners.

Right now, they were talking about films. Henry liked black-and-white noirs from the 1940s and '50s. McBride preferred products of the auteur school of the 1970s, and later homages. Both agreed that Altman's *The Long Goodbye* had something going for it. 'But if I had to pick an all-time favourite,' McBride said, 'it's a no-brainer. *Revolver*. You know it? London gangsters. Hard men making hard choices. Honour and revenge. Danger and redemption. *Revolver*. It's a mind-fucker, Henry. When we get back we'll watch it together. You'll fucking love it, I guarantee.'

The RV stopped and another man took over from the driver and they went on. It was past midnight, but the sun still sat at the horizon in its permanent sunset. Stretches of concrete alternated with longer stretches of compacted dirt sealed with a polymer derived from Boxbuilder ruins. Chloe lay on the couch and dozed off, woke with a shudder and saw that a range of rounded hills had heaved up from the horizon.

Breakfast was a banana and a pot of strawberry yogurt.

A pass cut through the hills and the road descended in tight switchback loops. A long, long valley stretched below. Sometimes the RV had to pull over on the shoulder, nothing but empty air next to it, to allow articulated lorries and road trains to swing around the tight curves. They crossed a kind of grassland, descended through a strange forest towards a broad river.

Sandwiches and bottles of water were passed around for lunch.

The sky darkened; the sun was a bleary red eye peering above a brown haze that stretched across the horizon. The edge of the dust storm, according to McBride.

There were fields, and then houses and barns and storage sheds at intervals. A busy crossroads with lorries and pickup trucks and 4x4s parked along the streets. Winnetou, the last town on the river, according to McBride. Henry straightened up on the couch, suddenly alert. Chloe felt a quickening in her blood. They were closing in on Site 326.

The RV turned off the road and bucked down a track beside the river, pulled up beside another RV and a jeep with big all-terrain tyres and a rack of floodlights, parked in the lee of a copse of pale, tree-sized things that looked like inverted lightning strikes with feather webs billowing and straining around them. Everyone climbed out into a cold wind choked with scuds of dust. Chloe felt its iron grit between her teeth.

McBride pointed to a wire tether dwindling away into the hazy sky, said there was a balloon up there.

'For comms. We're operating a drone, a stealthed quadcopter, keeping watch on Drury. When he sets off downriver, we're going to follow right behind. Come inside, check it out,' he said, ushering them into the other RV, where a man nursing a joystick was hunched at a screen that showed a view of wooden docks. Telling McBride that he was just in time, it looked like they were getting ready to go.

The image on the screen zoomed towards two men sitting inside a sleek speedboat; the operator pointed to one of them. 'That's Drury, right there.'

McBride peered at the screen. 'But where's the kid? Where's the rest of his crew?'

'There were three vehicles,' the operator said. 'Two pickups towing boats, and a Range Rover. They dropped off the one boat and Drury and the other guy, and left. I guess they took the kid with them.'

'There's something wrong here,' McBride said. 'The kid is supposed to be going downriver. And what about the pickups and the Range Rover? Not to mention the other boat.'

'I thought you wanted me to keep watch on Drury,' the operator said.

'Fuck. He's just sitting there.'

'Maybe he's waiting for his crew to come back.'

'Maybe his fucking crew have already slipped past us. Where's Sammie?'

'Down by the docks, like you asked.'

'Call him. Tell him to start looking for Drury's crew.'

While the operator used his phone, Henry said, 'If you know where they're going, why don't we get ahead of them and set up an ambush at their destination?'

'You're a soldier, aren't you?'

'Once upon a time.'

'Then you should know, soldier boy, that you shouldn't make plans until you have all the facts. And the fact is,' McBride said, 'that sneaky fucker Drury came out here a couple of weeks ago, after he heard that something potent had been found at my site. He was hoping to find more of the same, but he didn't, of course. He isn't as smart as he thinks he is. He left a party behind, and they've been working away ever since. So if I did like you said, I'd have to deal with them first, and that would tip him off as to what I was up to.'

'Tricky,' Henry said.

'We'll follow him and keep close eyes on him. We'll let him do the work, and when we're ready—'

McBride smacked his fist into his palm, smiled at Chloe and Henry.

Behind him, the operator said, 'The speedboat's leaving.'

'Keep the drone on it,' McBride said. 'The fucker's up to something.'

The two men bent close to the screen. Henry leaned towards Chloe and said quietly, 'Stay alert. We might have to make a move of our own.'

Chloe felt her heart beat high and light. 'Okay.'

'Are you scared?'

'Of course I am.'

'Me too,' Henry said, although he didn't look it. He was his usual self, possessed by a confidence that Chloe hoped she could trust.

The drone operator said, 'They'll be going past us in a few minutes, boss. What do you want us to do?'

A moment later, before McBride could answer, the screen went black.

46. We're Here To Help

Mangala | 30 July

Vic had never before seen a Jackaroo avatar in real life. The aliens had made contact because humanity had been about to fail and fall short of their full potential, as so many other intelligent species had failed and fallen, but they did not want to control or direct what people did with their gifts. It was not their thing, they said, to interfere. Kind of like the prime directive in that old TV show. They kept their presence on Earth to a minimum and had no contact at all with the people on the fifteen worlds they had gifted to humanity. They had even written it into the treaty with the UN.

Nevertheless, most people on Mangala believed that the Jackaroo were watching them. After the aliens had made themselves known, the conspiracy theorists and the UFO nuts had gained a new lease of life. They'd gone mainstream, elaborating ideas that Mangala and the other worlds were Petri dishes in some galactic experiment. Skinner boxes. Rat mazes. It was possible, some said, that eidolons weren't the ghosts or memories or imprints of former tenants, but were instead part of a covert monitoring process that nudged and guided people in certain directions.

And here was proof of those paranoid theories, hissing and fizzing and swaying in front of Vic, conjured from some kind of memory wire and parasitising the quantum dust and algorithms that generated the eidolons in this ancient necropolis.

He stood his ground, feeling a prickling across his body, every hair trying to stand up, as the ghostly man-shape turned towards him. Its attention had the weight and warmth of summer sunlight.

Nevers was saying something, saying that it was all right, that this was a friend.

'I am a friend,' the avatar said.

Its voice came from nowhere and everywhere. It was the wind hunting in the crevices of the long dark ledge. It was the gentle clap of waves washing along the river's edge. It was Vic's breath and heartbeat.

'We're here to help,' it said. 'But we do not want to shape you. We give you the tools, but we let you make from them what you will. As is right. As it always has been. But there are others. Fellow travellers. Who do not share our scruples. Who plunge into your lives. Who plunder your stories. And if your stories are not pleasing, they reshape them.'

'He means the !Cha,' Nevers said.

'They are young . . .'

The avatar's voice faded into a dismal hiss; its body rippled like a heatwave mirage. Rogue eidolons fluttered away like scraps of mist, and the avatar stretched like a whip and gathered them into itself and slowly regained its shape and definition.

'They have no patience,' it said. 'They like to accelerate change. They want to see what comes next.'

'That's what this is about,' Nevers said. 'The !Cha trade stories. And they create them or make them more interesting by directly interfering. By aiming people in certain directions.'

Vic said, 'So the people we're chasing, they're working for the !Cha?'

'They are being manipulated,' Nevers said.

'We changed you when we first contacted you,' the avatar said. 'It was unavoidable. Perhaps you will change further. Or perhaps you will dwindle, or destroy yourselves. But whatever happens, it should be your choice.'

Vic said, 'Why involve me? Doesn't that go against your principles?'

The avatar hummed and swayed. It said, 'The !Cha are part of us. We are part of them.'

'The !Cha are pointing people towards something dangerous,' Nevers said.

'They love stories,' the avatar said.

'And we have to give this one the right ending,' Nevers said.

His smile was fierce and eager and hungry. The poor guy not realising that he was being manipulated – or knowing and not caring.

And Vic was in this too, in over his head. He had a sliding feeling that he was in the wrong place, heading in the wrong direction. Like one of those frustrating dreams.

He said, as calmly as he could, 'I'm a murder police. I'm here because I want to find the people who killed my partner. And yours, too. This other stuff is way beyond my pay grade.'

'It's all part of the same thing,' Nevers said. 'The people you want are the people I want.'

Vic thought about that. He didn't trust Nevers, let alone the avatar, but he'd seen the aftermath of the shootout, knew he was outgunned by the bad guys. And the avatar would definitely give him an edge.

He said, 'So how can your friend here help us do the right thing?'

47. Run

Chloe and Henry stood back while Cal McBride harangued the drone operator, telling him to get the fucking thing back on line right now. 'And give me the phone. Let me talk to Sammie.'

Chloe said to Henry, 'Drury is coming after us, isn't he?'

'There's a good chance of it. Can you run?'

'I won the four-hundred-metre race in school one time.'

'When I say run, run. Run for your life.'

McBride said that Sammie wasn't answering.

'He's watching Drury's crew, like you asked,' the operator said.

'Well he's not fucking picking up. And why haven't you fixed the fucking drone?'

'There's nothing I can fix. It's all good here. Either the drone is down, or something is blocking the signal.'

'Play the last minute of footage again,' McBride said.

The screen blinked, showed the two men in the speedboat.

'There,' McBride said. 'Stop.'

He pointed at the screen. One of the men was turned in his seat, looking straight at the drone's camera, one hand raised.

'Waving hello, the cheeky fucker. Oh, and now he's giving us the finger. Well, fuck you too, Mr Danny Drury.' McBride was suddenly all business, telling two of his men to move up the track, find what cover they could. 'Rolls, you stay with me. Tommy, Dean, pack up this shit. Fast as you can, bring what you can carry to the boats, burn the rest. It's time to go,' he said, and turned to Chloe and Henry, pulling his ray gun from its loop, telling them they were coming with him.

Then they were outside, hustling towards the jags of the lightning trees. Chloe, breathless and excited and scared, half-ran,

310

half-walked as she tried to keep up with the men. The ground was ploughed but barren, pale ridges studded with reddish stones. She remembered that Hanna had said that the soil had to be steam-cleaned, sterilised, before plants would grow in it. She stumbled when dust whirled up around her, and Rolls, a big man in a denim jacket, its sleeves ripped off to display his muscular arms, caught her and hauled her along.

She protested, tried to shake off his grip, but he was implacable. They were almost at the trees. And then Rolls seemed to trip, his feet tangling together in an awkward pirouette, and he let go of Chloe's wrist and clapped his hand to his neck. Blood oozed between his fingers. A hard crack echoed out across the field. Chloe realised it was a gunshot, realised that it was the second one she'd heard, as Rolls grunted and collapsed at her feet.

McBride shouted, a raw wordless sound, and turned and aimed his ray gun. For a moment, a thread of intense blue light seared across the ploughed ridges of the field. Then Henry grabbed McBride's arm and twisted it up and back. Blue light split the air above their heads, bending towards one of the lightning trees and setting its fluttering clouds aflame. The light winked out; McBride had dropped the ray gun. As Chloe darted forward and scooped it up, Henry stepped back, a pistol in his hand. He must have snatched it from McBride, but it seemed like a magic trick.

'No,' McBride said, and put up one hand like a traffic cop as Henry swung the pistol and whacked him on the side of his head. McBride staggered, half-raised a hand to fend off Henry's second blow, and fell in a heap.

'Run!' Henry said, and Chloe ran, chasing him towards the tree-things. The one touched by the ray-gun beam was burning fiercely now. An acrid smell like scorched plastic scraped her throat.

She heard shots behind her, quick sustained bursts, and glanced around. One of the RVs was on fire from stem to stern and two men were silhouetted against the flames, firing into them. Other shots sounded far off, an erratic *pop pop pop* blowing on the wind.

Henry ran into a space between two lightning trees and Chloe followed, dodging around clumps of stuff like stiff string, coming out of the other side of the copse and seeing the river, seeing boats drawn up at the edge of the water, one of them the speedboat that the drone had been watching, seeing two men turning towards them. Henry swung his pistol up and one of the men fired at him, a hard clatter and a flash of yellow flame. Henry fell and Chloe yelled and ran to him, rolled him over. There were bloody rips in his hunting vest and she couldn't find a pulse when she laid a finger on the angle of his jaw, couldn't find a pulse in his wrist.

She locked her hands together and pressed on his chest, and something rattled in his throat as if he was trying to breathe and she pressed again and his mouth opened and a smooth glossy bubble of blood rose out of it and spilled over his chin. Then someone grabbed her and lifted her up and pulled her away. Another man stooped and picked up the ray gun and Henry's pistol. A tall man in a quilted white coat, wearing a face mask and goggles, long black hair in a loose ponytail, turning the ray gun in his hands, saying to Chloe, 'This is McBride's secret weapon?'

Chloe nodded dumbly in the iron grip of the man who'd grabbed her.

'How does it work . . . ? Aha.' Chloe flinched as the tall man pointed it at her. Then he shrugged inside his coat and said, 'You can let her go, Billy.'

She almost fell to her knees. Henry lying dead at her feet. Her hand on the sleeve of her camo jacket, feeling the shape in the sheath at her wrist. Her attention on the tall man, who said to the man who'd let her go, Billy, 'I thought I told you I wanted both of them alive.'

'It was him or me,' Billy said.

'Did I hear you give a warning? Did you fire a warning shot? Did you shoot to wound?'

The tall man's voice rising to a shout at the last sentence.

Billy stood his ground. 'He was armed, Mr Drury. He was going to shoot. So I shot him.'

'Because it was either him or you.'

'Like I said.'

'How about him *and* you,' the tall man said, and raised the ray gun.

48. Downriver

The plane was a sturdy banana-yellow four-seater with blunt wings cantilevered above its cabin. It flew low, bouncing in sudden air pockets, rising and dipping alarmingly but always pressing on against the buffeting headwind, its prop burring like an angry hairdryer.

The pilot, a young Italian guy dressed like a WW2 air ace in a leather jacket with a fleece collar, said it was hairy weather and getting worse. 'Part of the storm must have pushed ahead of the rest.'

'But you can fly in it. You can get us there,' Vic said. He was strapped in beside the pilot; Nevers was on the bench seat behind, crammed in amongst camping equipment that Vic hoped they wouldn't need.

'I can get you there, no problem,' the pilot said. 'But maybe I can't wait around as long as you'd like.'

The plane followed the river as it ribboned across the red and grey landscape. The pilot navigated by landmarks, now and then consulting a map displayed on the tablet on his knees. The horizon all around was obscured by a deep ochre haze in which fugitive whips of light flickered. Static discharges, according to the pilot.

'Fucks up the instrumentation, but as long as we can see the river we'll be fine.'

Vic wished that he could share the young man's optimism. He was heading into the unknown, looking for who knew what, in the company of someone he couldn't trust. It was some kind of plan, but definitely not the kind he'd imagined.

At last the plane flew over a curved range of hills and dropped towards a wide basin floored with a chaotic terrain of broken blocks and narrow canyons: an ancient impact crater bisected by the course of the river. The pilot pointed down, jabbing his forefinger three times for emphasis, said they were going in.

'Where do we land?'

'On hills on the far side. Don't worry. We use the headwind to brake us.'

Vic's stomach airily lifted as the plane bucked in conflicting currents of air. A range of hills resolved out of the haze, barren slopes suddenly looming in the windscreen. The plane's nose pitched up and the prop roared and with a sudden bang they were down, rolling uphill towards a crest, crunching over stones and turning sideways, lurching to a halt.

The engine cut off and the blurred disc of the prop resolved into three spinning blades, stopped. In the quiet cabin, Vic could hear his heartbeat and the whine of wind outside. Behind him, Nevers said calmly, 'Not bad.'

They unloaded quickly, wearing goggles and face masks because of the dust, hunched in the chilly gale. The heavy roll of the inflatable boat, a tent, food and water. It made a small mound that they covered with a ground sheet, pegging its flapping margins firmly into the hard dry ground.

'How long can you wait?' Vic asked the pilot. 'A day? Two?'

'Not even a day, in this,' the pilot said. He shook hands with Vic like an executioner measuring him for the drop, Vic slung the rifle he'd borrowed from Karl Schweda over one shoulder and his kitbag over the other, and he and Nevers set off.

They descended into a long draw and crossed a dry stream bed and climbed the slope beyond. The bleary unsleeping eye of the sun was fixed at the horizon, cold and red and huge in the dun sky. Jagged black tufts bent in the wuthering wind. The abrasive hiss of dust. The slope topped out and they started across a rough tableland. Irregular slabs of rock set in drifts of sand; dry gulches packed with leathery vegetation. They cut around the smaller gulches, scrambled down into the larger ones and climbed back up. Navigating by the fixed point of the sun because they had lost sight of the river.

Vic was sweating under his layers of clothing, couldn't quite get his breath inside the mask clamped over his mouth and nose. Grit chafed his elbows and knees. He stopped every so often to swap the strap of his heavy kitbag from one shoulder to the other, wiped dust from his goggles. He was definitely out of condition. Too old for this Boy Scout shit.

Nevers waited patiently each time Vic halted, calmly scanning the empty landscape that faded into reddish-brown haze in every direction. He had jammed his left hand in the pocket of his jacket, which gave him a slight list as he walked, but otherwise he seemed unencumbered by his gunshot wound.

Vic looked all around too. He had the uneasy feeling that someone was following them, just out of sight.

They passed through a field of stacks of flat rocks piled higher than a man, like figures in some long-abandoned game. The feeling of being followed grew stronger. Once Vic thought he saw something flicker at the edge of his vision and spun around and walked backwards for a few paces, seeing only rock stacks fading into the diesel haze.

They climbed into a gulch too big to navigate around, pushing through presses of stiff leathery vegetation, splashing through a trickle of water at the bottom, scaled the other side. Vic hauled himself up using the vegetation as handholds. His arms and legs ached. The strap of the kitbag cut into his shoulder and its weight unbalanced him; once he fell to his knees and stayed there, helpless with fatigue, until Nevers came back and hauled him to his feet.

There was a short string of Boxbuilder ruins at the top of the slope. Vic unhitched the kitbag and flopped down on a flat stone in their lee, unable to do anything but breathe.

Nevers stood a little way off, looking towards a faint smudged glow at the horizon. After a little while he came over and squatted beside Vic and asked him what he thought the weird light was.

'The pilot said it was some kind of static discharge.'

'Perhaps.'

'Is your friend telling you different?'

'I don't have a spooky connection with him, if that's what you're thinking. It doesn't work like that.'

315

'Right. Powered by eidolons.'

'I believe he'll find plenty of those where we're heading.'

'He'd better. Because if there's any trouble, he'll have to do most of the heavy lifting. I haven't ever fired a gun in anger, not even back in the good old Wild West days.'

'My friend is ready to help in any way he can,' Nevers said. 'As am I.'

The cold of the stone was seeping into Vic's behind, but he was too tired to care. He could sit here and let Nevers and the Jackaroo avatar do their thing. Whatever it was. Nothing good, that was for sure. Vic had confiscated the wire that generated the avatar and zipped it into the inner pocket of his jacket, and he was pretty sure that it had something to do with the feeling that something was following them. He was in control right now, but his rifle and pistol wouldn't do much good against an alien ghost, and he suspected that Nevers would do anything to stop the bad guys getting hold of whatever it was they were hunting, and that he'd take Vic down too, if it came to it.

'Don't forget that we're here only to collect evidence,' Vic said. 'We sneak in and we see what's what and document it and we get out. That's it. We can deal with the bad guys later.'

That was what he'd told Nevers before they'd set out, but even he didn't really believe it now. Truth was, he'd never really believed it.

Nevers shook a couple of tablets into his palm and dry-swallowed them.

Vic said, 'Is your arm giving you trouble?'

'It's fine. Why don't you let me carry that kitbag for a while? We can't have far to go now.'

'I can manage. Well, maybe I need a hand to get to my feet . . .'

They went on. Nevers was keyed up, getting ahead of Vic and waiting impatiently for him to catch up. Vic plodded on, remembering how light he'd felt when he'd first arrived. He had long ago grown accustomed to Mangala's gravity, but Nevers had an eager bounce in his step. It made Vic uneasy.

They passed through another regiment of stacked stones, some in close clusters, others spaced in long lines. Vic's feeling that he was being stalked returned; when a shadow appeared in the haze, off to the left, a bolt of panic snapped through him and he stupidly unslung his rifle. He stood his ground as the shape grew larger and more distinct: a low-slung biochine the size of a large dog stumping along on three pairs of legs, a stiff spiky tail stuck out behind. It was mostly yellow, blotched with triangles of deep orange and rust.

Vic tracked it with his rifle as it went past and vanished into the haze.

'An actual alien beast,' Nevers said. The bastard sounded delighted.

'They're mostly harmless,' Vic said, although he wasn't sure what kind of biochine it was. Nothing he'd seen before, but he was a long way from home . . .

He slung his rifle on his shoulder and they walked on. Hazy glimpses of more biochines moving through the murk. Disturbed by the oncoming storm perhaps, except they seemed to be headed into it, moving in the same direction as Vic and Nevers, towards the smudge of skyglow. Once, a swarm of rat-sized things chittered past on long angular legs, scrambling over rocks, gone before Vic had properly registered their presence.

And then Nevers suddenly stopped and crouched down. Vic plodded up to him, discovered the abrupt edge of a low cliff that curved away on either side as if some giant had taken a bite from the land. Another impact crater, maybe.

The cliffs were footed in fans of fallen rocks. Beyond, level ground stretched into the haze beneath silky ribbons of frozen light. Vic scanned the scene with his field glasses. The dim shapes of a couple of flat-topped mounds. A biochine as big as a car trundling towards them. The rocky margin of the river, and there, yes, a cluster of tents. Vanishing as a scud of dust blew past, reappearing. Orange and blue in the sere landscape.

A flicker of movement off to his left: three bright red spiny footballs rolled over the edge and fell to the rocks below.

'Something is drawing those things here,' Nevers said.

'I see tents, but I can't see any people. Then again, I can hardly see anything in this shit.'

'If we aren't going to move closer, perhaps my friend can find out something.'

'We'll try something else first,' Vic said, and unbuckled the kitbag and drew out an aluminium case and snapped it open.

The quadcopter nested in black foam padding was the shape of a flying saucer and the size of a dinner plate, with four fans caged beneath it and a pair of stereoscopic cameras in a fixed housing. Vic unpacked the joystick control and tablet display and switched on the little machine. It rose up, hovering at eye level and transmitting an image of himself and Nevers to the tablet in his lap.

'I need you to spot for me,' Vic said, and handed Nevers his pair of binoculars. 'Guide me in towards those tents, out at about eleven o'clock. Tell me if I get too low to the ground or too close to some rock.'

He rubbed his hands together, took a breath, and sent the little quadcopter out above the edge of the cliff. An updraught caught it and knocked it sideways; it tilted and spun before its autogyro routine kicked in and stabilised it.

'Try not to fly it into the ground,' Nevers said.

'Just point me at those tents,' Vic said. 'I'll do the rest.'

He flew high at first, yo-yoing in the gusty wind, views of the ground pitching and spinning on the screen, half the time showing only sky. It was a lot harder than he remembered, back when he'd used drones to stake out drug corners. Beside him, Nevers gave terse instructions, and at last the orange and blue blooms of the tents appeared on the tablet's screen.

Vic painstakingly edged the drone towards them.

'No sign of anyone at home,' he said, after a couple of minutes spent trawling about.

'You might want to head to the left,' Nevers said. 'I thought I saw some activity around one of those mounds.'

Vic kicked the drone higher and spun it around, saw what Nevers meant.

Things were stalking and crawling and humping around the perimeter of the mound as if on patrol. Things were standing here and there like sentries – Vic was reminded of a documentary he'd seen about meerkats, although these dark spiky sentries were in no way cute. He saw a shallow trench and guided the quadcopter towards it, saw a small opening in the side of the mound.

'Looks like someone has been busy,' he said.

'Perhaps the bad guys are trapped inside,' Nevers said. 'Can you get the drone any closer?'

'I don't want to get too low, in case one of those biochines takes a swipe at it,' Vic said.

And someone else said, 'You can stop wanking around with that toy, lads. Time to get real.'

Vic rolled over and sat up. Three men stood there. Two were aiming rifles at him and Nevers. The third was Cal McBride.

49. Downriver
Mangala | 28-29 July

'No need to thank me for dealing with the man who killed your friend,' the tall man with the ponytail, Danny Drury, told Chloe. 'Billy had it coming. He had an attitude. Thought that because he'd been in the Paras he knew better than his boss. If you don't make the same mistake, we'll get along fine. Okay?'

Chloe stupidly nodded. She was the numb centre of a ringing calm.

'Okay,' Drury said, and spoke into a walkie-talkie, telling someone that he had secured the woman but that the man, Harris, was dead. 'Billy bought it too.'

The voice crackling out of the walkie-talkie said something about not finding McBride.

'Come on back,' Drury said. 'There's some tidying-up to do.'

He handed Chloe goggles and a mask. After she'd fitted them over her eyes and mouth he fastened her wrists with a cable tie and with an oddly delicate courtesy helped her climb onto the bench seat of his speedboat.

'As long as you don't give me a reason to shoot you, we'll get along fine,' he said.

'Where are you taking me?' Chloe said.

'I think you know where.'

A Range Rover roared up; four men tumbled out. While they carried the bodies of Billy and Henry away, Drury spoke with the driver, a bearded man with a piratical eyepatch. The men came back and two climbed into the Range Rover; it executed a three-point turn and sped away.

Drury went off through the stand of lightning trees. One of the men who'd stayed behind inspected Chloe with a cold direct stare; the other pulled down his face mask and lit a cigarette and said something that made them both laugh. They wore red quilted jackets and desert camo pants, were armed with small sub-machine guns with blunt barrels, slung carelessly over their shoulders. Chloe looked away. That jolt of alarm when a crew of big noisy young men came barrelling up onto the top deck of the night bus: it was nothing to what she felt now. Shock had numbed her to the bone and one of her shoes had filled with water when she had climbed into the boat. A fine spray of Henry's blood dotted her hands.

There was a flash of blue light beyond the trees; Drury came back at a run. He told one of the men to give him his sub-machine gun and a spare clip, and walked over to the other boats, two aluminium-hulled skiffs with big outboard engines. Gunfire hammered holes low in the hull of the nearest, the hard percussion echoing out across the river, and Drury pulled out the empty clip and jammed in the spare and shot up the second skiff. He tossed the sub-machine gun back to its owner and the three men crowded into the speedboat.

As they swerved out into the brown flood, heading downriver, Chloe turned to watch the funeral pyres of the burning RVs as they dwindled and faded into the murk. Thinking of Henry, trying to formulate a prayer or a promise. He had children somewhere, she thought, and remembered the empty coffin at her mother's funeral and vowed that she'd make sure that he went home. If she survived this she'd make sure he went home.

The speedboat slammed down the middle of the wide cold river, following its lazy loops through stony land hazed by dust. It was way past midnight. Chloe hunched in a corner of the bench seat she shared with Drury, remembering the trip down the Thames from Freedom Tower after the Jackaroo avatar had been assassinated. An age ago. Another world.

Drury and the two men up front said little to each other and completely ignored Chloe. Which was fine by her. Drury was a rival of McBride's, but he was no friend of hers. He had kidnapped Fahad. He had shot the man who had shot Henry. Shot him to see how the ray gun worked, what it did. Shot him because he could. And she was absolutely certain that if she and Fahad couldn't give him what he wanted he'd kill them. He'd probably kill them anyway. So she had to stay alert. Be ready to take any chance she could.

She fell asleep, woke as the boat nosed towards a gravel beach. The men cranked up a camping stove and boiled a pot of coffee. Drury handed her an aluminium mug and she held it between her bound hands and sipped while he fired up a chunky tactical radio with a whip aerial and a telephone handset. Telling the person at the other end that he couldn't hear one fucking word in three. Saying, 'He did what? Inside?' Looking at Chloe and slinging the radio's strap over his shoulder and walking off down the beach, talking at length out of earshot, coming back and telling her, 'Things are moving along nicely.'

She needed to pee. Another humiliation. Drury opened a folding knife and asked her if she was going to be good, shrugged when she didn't answer and cut the cable ties at her wrists.

'Run a hundred kilometres in any direction, there's nothing but river and rocks,' he said.

One of the men gave her a roll of toilet paper; she squatted behind a clump of grey wirewool, pretending that her captors weren't in earshot.

Drury insisted on tying her wrists when she came back. She was given a sleeping bag and lay amongst the others on the hard cold ground, trying not to see Henry dropping down after he'd been shot, nothing like the way it was in films, trying not to see the bubble of blood rising between his lips. She woke to the same dull light and the same cold wind. Her captors fried up bacon and eggs; she ate a leathery fried egg between two slices of spongy sliced white bread and washed it down with tea. The men pissed into the river; she went behind the clump of wirewool again.

Drury didn't bother to retie Chloe's wrists, this time. She followed him into the speedboat and they set off again. After a couple of hours they passed through a shoal of sandbanks. The largest were crested with what she supposed was vegetation. Shocks of blood-red filaments; stiff tangles of jointed, semi-translucent tubes; heaps of blue-green bubbles quivering in the cold wind; low stacks of stiff plates that glistened like wet leather. Monocultures of different plants from different biological clades passing by like exhibits in a botanical garden or special effects in a movie.

The goggles fastened over her eyes slightly distanced her from the world. Cold wind blew into her face. Dust scratched at the rim of her mask, settled in her hair and the creases of her clothes. She jammed her hands between her knees for warmth.

Things like bundles of knotted rope slid from a sandbank and lashed away into deeper water. More special effects. Then the speedboat cut past the last of the sandbanks and there was only the river again.

Lunch was a cheese and tomato sandwich and a bottle of water.

They were running close to the bank of the river now. Passing cliffs of banded sandstone, fluted and rounded into fantastic shapes by erosion. An arch stepped out into the flow of the river like a bridge; the speedboat steered around the far side and the river bent and there were fleets of small islands again, with blunt prows upstream and long tails of gravel downstream. Several were crowned with skinny towers clad in what looked like pitted porcelain. The wind keened and fluted around them as they spun by.

Chloe asked Drury if they were Elder Culture ruins; Drury said he had no idea.

'My expert in this alien shit told me they could be ruins or they could be nests. The kind wasps or termites make.'

A couple of hours later, Drury took out his radio and fiddled with it, talked briefly to someone, then leaned forward and told the two men in front that everything was good.

The dust haze thickened, blew aside to reveal a cliff or bluff of red rock bulging over the river, sloping down run-outs of rubble, and a rocky shore. There was something funny about the sky, a pearly gleam or shine like the reflected glow of spotlights.

The speedboat throttled back and turned, puttering into a sleeve of water pinched between tilted shelves of rock. The motor cut. The speedboat drifted past a small motor cruiser, grounded on a steep fan of pebbles.

The men stirred around Chloe. One of them helped her climb over the side of the speedboat and she followed them, splashing through icy ankle-deep water to the shore. Drury took her arm and steered her up a slope, pebbles rolling and turning underfoot, to its crest.

She stopped, gripped by freezing déjà vu.

There it was, unambiguous, absolute. The original of Michel Charpentier's 3D model; the landscape of Fahad's pictures. A bare bleak flatland, red stone and sand. A cluster of flat-topped mounds. Low cliffs ribboning away into the tawny haze towards the ghostly outline of rounded hills. All this sitting under a kind of dome or cap woven from faintly flickering light the colour of the inside of an oyster shell.

Drury was pointing towards one of the mounds. 'Your little friend says there's something in there.'

'Fahad is here? I thought he was with you.'

'That's what I wanted McBride to think. No, I sent your little friend on ahead a couple of days ago. He says that he's found something. And you're going to tell me if he's right.'

Drury dismissed the two men and led Chloe across a stretch of stony ground. Flat black stones like gravemarkers were embedded here and there, half-buried by sand and dust. Elder Culture stuff. Chloe didn't like to look at them too closely. They had a faint but distinct aura, like radioactive openings into some other, utterly hostile dimension.

Several tents were pitched behind a half-buried shelf of ordinary sandstone, shivering in the rip of the wind. Drury unzipped a flap in the largest and Chloe followed him into a blue space with three sleeping compartments down one side. A man in a canvas director's chair looked up from the tablet in his lap; a big, shaven-headed man in a red quilted jacket, squatting on his heels near a space heater, stood up.

Drury and his two men pulled down their masks and stripped off their goggles; Chloe followed their example. They made a crowd under the slanting membrane of the tent's roof. The air was warm and stale. There was a strong sharp tingling odour, like the taste of a battery on her tongue.

'I thought there were two of them,' the man with the tablet said.

He wore a baseball cap pulled low, blue jeans, a black leather jacket. Amusement flickered in his sharp gaze.

'Her boyfriend had an accident,' Drury said. 'What's cooking, Tommy? Give me some good news.'

'We extended an exploratory tunnel into that mound the kid fell in love with. Found a void he got very excited about. It seems pretty much intact, but empty. No activity, as far as I can tell.'

'As far as you can tell. What about the kid?'

'He's out there now. You can't keep him away. Luke is looking after him; Riley and Logan are patrolling the perimeter; Niles and Patrice are making the tunnel safe. We had a roof fall. The mudstone is as friable as old cat shit.'

'And you're doing what? Apart from sitting on your arse in this cosy tent.'

'Keeping an eye on the general situation,' Tommy said. 'The magnetic anomalies are stable, but something's definitely coming online. You saw the light effects. Plus this fucking dust is getting thicker.'

'The edge of the storm?'

'That's still maybe fifty or sixty kilometres away,' Tommy said. 'Call this a local intensification of pre-existing conditions.'

'There have been more critters checking in,' the shaven-headed man said. He had a tattoo of two praying hands on his neck, *Believe* written across them in cursive script. 'We took down a bunch this morning. Like turkeys in a shooting gallery.'

'Something's bringing them here,' Tommy said. 'The lights, maybe.'

'Some actual hard facts would be good,' Drury said.

'About this weird shit? I'm just a humble archaeologist. I don't do weird shit.'

'Everything you dig up on this planet is weird shit.' Drury held out his hand; Tommy gave him the tablet. Drury flicked through images, now and then showing one to Tommy and asking him what it was or what it meant. None of Tommy's answers seemed to satisfy him; at last Drury held the tablet towards Chloe. 'See this?'

Some kind of map: different shades of greens, white contour lines. After a moment, she realised that the contours were the mounds.

'Magnetic anomalies,' Drury said. 'Remnants of some kind of machinery under the mounds. Spaceships, maybe, if this really is a space port. If the kid really is telling the truth.'

'You've seen it, haven't you?' Tommy said to Chloe. 'The kid's familiar. Ugly Chicken.'

'It's real,' Chloe said.

'I don't doubt that, given what's been going on here. What does it look like?'

'Like your worst nightmare. I hope you get to see it soon.'

Tommy smiled, looked at Drury. 'Love the attitude. Do I get to keep her, afterwards?'

'We'll talk about after when there's an after.' Drury pointed at the shaven-headed man. 'Take me to this mound. Chloe, you come too. You can tell me if it feels right.'

He seemed calmer, almost happy. Chloe felt a small measure of relief. As long as he was happy, she thought, he wouldn't do anything bad. And thought then that she was beginning to get a touch of Stockholm syndrome, sympathy for the people who had kidnapped her and would almost certainly kill her when they didn't have any more use for her. She had to remember that. She had to make herself valuable. Play this out any way she could.

Out in the whip of the wind and dust, trying to keep up with Drury and the shaven-headed man as they strode across the uneven ground to the nearest mound. A narrow trench three metres deep had been dug halfway around its circumference, exposing a close-woven lattice. She felt another dizzy wash of déjà vu. Remembering the mural in the nun's chapel. The basket-weave struts of the spire, and something indistinct crawling through or over them . . .

Drury was saying something about broken towers. He was shouting through his mask, shouting to be heard over the whine of the wind, telling her that the river had flooded the area many times, depositing alluvial material and burying the towers that had stood here.

'Tommy surveyed it when we first came out,' he said. 'Those magnetic anomalies I showed you weren't there then. Something somewhere has been switched on. Something is waking up.'

'I think I can feel it,' Chloe said, although she couldn't. But if Drury thought she was some kind of clairvoyant or human dowsing rod, channelling alien energy patterns, she might be able to win a little wriggle room.

'Yeah . . . ?' He was staring at her through the goggles of his mask.

She said, 'When I first met Fahad, I felt as if someone else was there. This is like that, only much stronger.'

'You mean this Ugly Chicken.'

'Maybe.'

She was glad she was wearing the goggles and mask; she'd always been hopeless at lying.

Drury studied her, then said, 'Come with me,' and he was off again, striding towards the neighbouring mound.

There was another trench, with a generator standing at its edge and air hoses snaking into the maw of a low tunnel. The noise of jackhammers came out from it. Two men stood in the lee of a solitary boulder, both wearing red quilted jackets. Drury must have bought a job lot. One of the men was burly, a rifle slung at his shoulder; the other was slender and unarmed. With a jolt, Chloe realised that it was Fahad. While Drury talked to the burly man, she told Fahad how glad she was to see him, asked him how he was.

'We found it! The black room! We found it, and he's in there now.'

'Ugly Chicken? What is he doing, Fahad? Is he talking to you?'

'They took the bead from me. Rana's bead.' Fahad was happy and excited. Talking quickly, jiggling from foot to foot. 'But it doesn't matter. He isn't in it any more. He's in the black room. He's inside the system. He's fixing things so he can go home.'

'I thought this was his home.'

Fahad looked at her, eyes dark and serious behind his dusty goggles. 'It's complicated.'

'What's he doing, Fahad? What are you doing?'

'It will be wonderful. You'll see.'

'I mean, what are you doing, helping these men?'

'As if I have a choice. As if *we* have a choice.'

'Did Drury hurt you?'

'No, no. He was very kind. He told me about McBride, my father . . .' Fahad paused, then said, 'Mr Harris. He is here too?'

'He's dead, Fahad. Shot and killed by one of Drury's men.'

The words tasted like old coins on her tongue.

'I'm sorry,' Fahad said. 'Truly. But I'm glad you're here. I want you to see.'

For a moment, Chloe thought he was going to explain everything, but then he looked past her and she turned, saw Drury coming towards them. She stepped forward and hugged Fahad, said quietly, 'Drury killed your father. If he told you any different he was lying.'

'He said you'd say that,' Fahad said, and disengaged himself.

Drury's hand fell on Chloe's shoulder. 'You can come with me,' he said. 'It isn't safe to leave the two of you together.'

50 · Deal

Cal McBride's goons took Vic's rifle and pistol, patted him and Adam Nevers down. One of them found the crumpled nest of gold wire in Vic's breast pocket and handed it to McBride, who weighed it in his palm and asked Vic what it was. McBride was sitting on a slab of rock, wearing a safari jacket and a sheepskin gilet, not quite aiming his pistol at Vic and Nevers. His head was bandaged and, under the dusty lenses of his goggles, his eyes were puffy and bruised.

'It's a gift from a friend of Mr Nevers,' Vic said.

'It's some kind of Elder Culture shit, isn't it?'

'You tell me. You're the one who has an interest in the artefact business.'

'What does it do?'

'I'd be happy to give you a demonstration,' Nevers said.

'I bet you would.'

McBride joggled the wire again, then stuffed it into the breast pocket of his safari jacket. 'You're here because you're chasing people who have fallen under the spell of some kind of Elder Culture eidolon. You think it's leading them to some kind of dangerous artefact. And I'm here because I'm after Danny Drury, who snatched those people and put them to work, looking for that artefact in the site I excavated. So the thing of it is, we're both on the same side.'

Vic said, 'Was it Drury who gave you the bang on the head and those two shiners?'

'He ambushed me outside that little shithole of a town, and he killed three of my people,' McBride said. 'He has some muscle

329

down there with him, ex-Army types, but me and my boys have been scouting the lie of the land, and I reckon that if we join forces we can take them down. You get Drury, Mr Nevers gets the people he chased halfway across the galaxy, and I get back the company Drury stole from me while I was in jail. How does that sound?'

'I'm not going to agree to anything while there are guns pointed at me,' Vic said.

'You agree to help me, the guns are put away,' McBride said, and stood up and held out his hand. 'Why don't we shake on it, like gentlemen?'

'I've got a better idea,' Vic said. 'Hand over your weapons and sit tight while I wake up my drone. Something's going on down there. I want to know what it is.'

'What's going on, Drury is digging up something that belongs to me,' McBride said. 'And if we don't stop him, he's going to load it into his fucking speedboat and take off back to civilisation. And then what are you going to do?'

'I can arrest him when he gets back to Petra.'

'And what about the people who led him to this shit? The people haunted by that eidolon. You think he's going to take them back with him?'

'He has a point,' Nevers said. 'If Fahad Chauhan and the others are down there, Drury doesn't have any incentive to keep them alive once they've led him to the prize.'

'Oh, they're down there, all right,' McBride said. 'Drury couldn't find his own fucking arse without a map.'

'And if we help you, what happens to us once you get what you want?' Vic said.

'I told you,' McBride said. 'You get to arrest Drury, and save Fahad and his friends. You get to come out of this a hero. We all do.'

'I don't think so.'

'Why not? Pride? Principles? They won't save that kid and his friends.'

'I think you'd take the artefact and leave no witnesses,' Vic said.

'I admit, part of the reason I came here was for the artefact,' McBride said. 'But I can't get it without your help. So I'll settle for getting my company back, and making sure Danny Drury gets what's coming to him.'

The two of them stared at each other, standing in the dusty wind under the sky's frozen ghostlight.

Nevers said, 'I'll help you take Drury down. And as far as I'm concerned, you get to keep everything he took off you. You can even kill him, if you want. That's none of my business. But you don't get to keep what's down there. Because that's *my* business, and I intend to destroy it.'

'You really think it's powerful shit, don't you?'

'I know it is. And I know how to put a stop to it.'

McBride patted his breast pocket. 'With this thing of yours.'

'Exactly. I came here to put an end to something horribly dangerous. Something that controls and destroys everyone who tries to use it. If you help me, you'll get Drury, and everything he took from you. Do we have a deal?'

Vic couldn't read Nevers. Couldn't tell if he was making a play or if he really wanted to go in with McBride.

'What about your friend?' McBride said.

'You think we're friends because we're both police? Six hours ago I was locked up in a cell,' Nevers said. 'Gayle let me out only because he needed my help. And now I'm offering you that same help.'

Vic said, 'I suppose, Mr McBride, that in addition to getting your company back, you'll want to walk on the murder of Ellis Peters, too.'

McBride gave him a look of perfectly constructed innocence. 'Of who?'

'Mr Nevers's partner. The man you killed outside the shuttle terminal.'

'I don't know what you're talking about.'

'Yes you do. You killed him with your ray gun. Burned his brains out.'

McBride said, 'If I had this ray gun, we wouldn't be having this conversation, would we? Because I wouldn't need your help to take Drury down. *He's* the one who has it. He used it to kill your partner, Mr Nevers, and he'll use it to kill Fahad Chauhan and the others if we don't do something about it. So, do we have a deal?'

'I take care of the artefact,' Nevers said. 'And you take care of Drury.'

'Absolutely. Word of honour,' McBride said, and stuck out his hand again.

Nevers stepped forward and grasped it. Golden light flared around them.

51. The Black Room

Mangala | 29—30 July

Chloe was taken back to the tent and shepherded into one of its sleeping compartments. One of Drury's men gave her a bottle of water and a scalding container of microwaved lasagne. No point asking if he had something without meat in it. She peeled off her wet shoes and socks and ate a little of the cheese sauce and slippery pasta, discovered she didn't have an appetite, drank all of the water.

She tried to map out how she could survive this, but her thoughts kept dissolving into pointless fantasies of escape. Slitting a hole in the tent when her captors weren't looking. Somehow scooping up Fahad and stealing a boat and outrunning Drury on the river. And she kept seeing Henry, too. His blank look when he'd been shot. The bubble of blood rising in his mouth. His body hanging limp between the two men as they carried it off . . .

A man was standing over her, shaking her shoulder. She asked to use the toilet and was taken outside. The sky had darkened and the dust haze had thickened, obscuring the mounds and dimming the frozen scarves of light tangled overhead. The toilet was a plastic sentry-box exactly like the ones at music festivals. It had the same stink, too. Chloe squatted inside it and listened to the wind hoot and wail outside until the man who'd escorted her rapped on the door.

Drury and Tommy took her on a tour of the mounds. There were ten of them, and they walked all the way around each one, Drury asking her if she could feel anything while Tommy swept the air with a long boom wired into his tablet, taking readings

333

of local distortions in the magnetic field. Chloe said that only the mound they'd tunnelled into seemed active, and hoped that Fahad hadn't told them any different.

Fahad was sleeping, Drury said. After the tunnel had been cleared he had spent half the night inside the mound. 'He looked like one of those fairground fakirs, trying to summon spirits. He was about as successful, too.'

'We should have brought a crystal ball,' Tommy said.

'I should have brought a real fucking archaeologist,' Drury said.

He was tired and irritable. Chloe hoped that it was because things weren't going the way he planned.

She told him that Fahad needed time; Drury said that was what the kid had told him. 'His spirit guide is still fine-tuning the fucking machinery, or some such shit.'

'Let me talk to him,' Chloe said.

'No, I'll let him rest. Then we'll give it another go-around. And if that doesn't work,' Drury said, 'you'd bloody well better be able to find some way of motivating him.'

He wouldn't let her see Fahad's black room, either. They returned to the tent, and she sat in the sleeping compartment and tried to ignore the stray glances of the men. The oppressive claustrophobia reminded her of The World's Worst Holiday, a camping trip in Wales when her parents' marriage had been splitting open. Soon to be followed by The World's Worst Christmas, after her father walked out. It had rained every day, in Wales. Classic British holiday weather, as if global warming had never happened. Or perhaps because it had. Her father had sat under the awning of their tent drinking cheap red wine, or had disappeared on long solitary walks; her brother had mooned after some unobtainable girl; Chloe, aged seven, had been forced to accompany her mother on trips to local churches and chapels. While her mother sketched architectural details, she'd sit in a pew, reading, or sit in the church's porch and watch rain fall amongst gravestones and crooked crosses. Later, she would have given anything to have those long quiet hours back, but at the time she'd been bored and fractious, disturbed by the tension between her mother and father, the change in the family's emotional climate that she couldn't, at the time, understand.

She dozed, jerked awake with a little shock. There were more men in the tent now, big animals crowding the common space. She recognised the bearded, eyepatched driver of the Range Rover, one of the men who'd been left behind to search for McBride.

'There's a problem,' Drury told her. 'Get your mask. I need you outside.'

'What is it?'

'Your friend Fahad is trying to fuck me over.'

She was hustled to the trench cut around the nearest mound. Two men were standing guard there. One told Drury there was no change in the situation; the other handed him a pair of field glasses.

Drury pushed his goggles up to his forehead and leaned at the edge of the trench, studying something through the field glasses. Then he gave them to Chloe and told her to take a look.

She had to stand on a plastic crate. The field glasses laid reticles and several small stacks of numbers over a hazy view of things moving through blowing dust. Biochines, different sizes. Some as big as cows, or cars. A jostling crowd circling the neighbouring mound.

'They started to turn up after the kid arrived,' Drury said. 'One or two coming in at irregular intervals. My guys shot them. But a few hours ago a whole lot more came in out of the countryside, and they're still coming in. And when I sent two of my men to pull the kid out of his hidey-hole, his black room, a bunch of those monsters tore them to pieces.'

Chloe remembered the mantis-thing in Hanna's cage, purring like a contented cat. She said, 'You think Fahad called them here?'

'You're the expert on the kid and his eidolon.'

'You took him prisoner, he saw a chance to try to take control ... What would you have done, in his place?' Chloe said. She was angry and scared because she knew what was coming, could see it barrelling down the tracks towards her, massive and unstoppable.

'The question is, what's he doing in there?' Drury said. 'And why is it so fucking important to those biochines?'

Tommy said, 'The signal is steady. But who knows if that means anything?'

Chloe said, 'What signal?'

'A broad-spectrum radio pulse,' Tommy said, hefting something that looked like an antique mobile phone. A fat antenna protruded from its leather case. 'It started up a couple of hours ago. The kid said his Ugly Chicken has woken something. If he's done something else since then, it hasn't changed the signal, but it doesn't mean he *hasn't* done something else. Just that we can't detect it.'

'Because you didn't bring the right equipment,' Drury said.

'So sack me and send me home,' Tommy said.

'Maybe I should send you in there to get the kid,' Drury said.

Chloe said, 'I'll go.'

The two men looked at her.

She said, 'I mean, that's what you want me to do. So I'll do it.'

'I want you to bring him out,' Drury said. 'Tell him that I won't hurt him. Tell him that I'm not even angry with him. But also tell him that if he doesn't come out, I'll smash that precious bead of his to dust. And just in case you're thinking of trying any funny stuff...'

He snapped his fingers, and one of his men handed him a fat length of dull olive tubing. Drury pulled at it and it suddenly doubled in length; he unfolded a gunsight at one end and a trigger mechanism at the other.

'This is an M-80 rocket launcher,' he said. 'A one-shot handheld anti-tank weapon made in the Republic of Serbia. Fine piece of kit. We have six of them. And if you don't bring that kid out in the next thirty minutes we're going to fire every single one of them into that fucking tunnel.'

Chloe walked out into the dust and wind with a heavy feeling of inevitability. The feeling that everything in her life had led up to this point.

A little walkie-talkie was hooked to the collar of her jacket and plugged into her ear; she was carrying a torch and two bottles of water, a watch borrowed from one of Drury's men, an ugly thing with a ridiculous number of little dials. Drury had told her that if the biochines attacked her, he and his men would shoot the nearest, give her a sporting chance to make a run for it. He did not need to say what would happen to her if she returned alone.

With guns at her back she walked towards the pit, and the alien monsters that prowled its edge.

Several dead biochines were scattered across rippled sand and broken pavements of black stone. Then she saw the first live ones, long and low and segmented, scuttling over the irregular ground. She stood stock-still, holding her breath, as one of them coiled over itself and flowed towards her, moving on a multitude of stiff spikes. Tufts of hair bristled at the joints of its armour, a pair of black prongs jutting from its rear. It circled her twice, then reared up.

She cried out. She couldn't help it. A voice crackled on the walkie-talkie, asking her what had happened.

The biochine swayed snakelike, its head level with her face. Its underside was like a string of pale vertebrae, each bearing a pair of stiff spikes on prominent ball joints. Its head was small and complicated, with a ring of flexible whiskers twitching around a lamprey maw. It swayed back and forth, then struck with speed and precision, its mouth clamping around her left wrist, a stinging sensation, tugging, sudden release. She snatched her arm back, but the biochine was already flowing away. She remembered to breathe, and a deep trembling started in every muscle.

Her wrist throbbed.

She stripped off the camo jacket and pulled up the sleeve of her sweatshirt, discovered a mottled circle of small white blisters around her wrist, each tipped with a spot of blood. She said into the walkie-talkie, 'Are these things poisonous?'

'What happened?' Drury said.

'One bit me. Are they poisonous?'

'I guess you'll soon find out. Where is it now?'

'Gone.'

'Then why are you still standing there?'

Chloe shrugged into her jacket, zipped it up, and went on, hollow with fear and anticipation. Biochines resolved out of the blowing dust all around her. Tall, skinny black things that stalked about on two legs, with narrow heads that were mostly serrated jaws. Shelled things covered in fluorescent orange and green spines that flexed in pulsating waves. An elephantine boxy thing stumping past.

Monsters. Creatures whose logic confounded human experience.

Animated mops topped with writhing ribbons. Small hopping things that were here and suddenly *there*, hundreds of them seething around her. She froze, and they were gone, all at once, and she rubbed her legs and arms, wondering if she'd been bitten again.

The blisters circling her wrist warmly throbbed.

The mound loomed ahead. Biochines shifted away from her as she walked towards it. Treading carefully, her heart beating high, afraid that if she mis-stepped or tripped they might attack. She reached the shallow trench at the edge of the mound, squashed a foolish impulse to turn and wave to the men watching her.

She said into the walkie-talkie, 'Okay. I'm here.'

She could see the mouth of the tunnel that slanted down into the mound. Clusters of rat-sized things clung spiderwise to the flaking ochre mudstone around it. Shield-like bodies, splayed legs thin as wires, clusters of eyes – she supposed they were eyes – that glowed sharp and green. She clambered down an aluminium ladder into the trench, stepped towards the tunnel mouth. Froze when the rat-spider things shifted, scurrying around and over each other, green eyes flashing and blinking.

When they stopped moving, she called Fahad's name. No answer. She called again, said, 'I'm coming in,' and switched on the torch and ducked into the tunnel.

It was about a metre in diameter and roughly circular in cross section, mudstone walls sprayed with some kind of polymer or resin. Glistening like a gullet in the torchlight. Chloe crawled on hands and knees, clambered through a narrow slot between two dark straps. Beyond was a puckered opening in a dense weave of black wire. She scrambled head first into the hollow space beyond.

The black room. The oval print of the torch beam changed shape as it flowed over flat planes and sharp angles. A shadow crouched in a far corner.

Chloe pulled off her mask and said, 'I came alone.'

'He sent you, didn't he?' Fahad said. He was filthy with dust, clutching something in his left hand. A knife. No, a screwdriver . . .

'Of course he did. But we can talk without being overheard,' Chloe said.

She switched off the walkie-talkie, pulled one of the bottles of water from her pocket and tossed it to Fahad. He flinched when it smacked down, made to reach for it and then hesitated, as if suspecting a trick. Chloe unscrewed the top of the other bottle, drank. Cool water dissolved the parched taste of dust and fear. After a moment, Fahad reached out and snagged the fallen bottle and retreated.

Chloe sat on the slanting floor. One facet of an angular volume enclosed by walls of close-woven black wire. It was as chilly as metal but slightly resilient, like plastic or hard rubber. The individual strands were about the thickness of her thumb, knotted over and around each other in no obvious pattern.

She checked the borrowed watch – a little over fifteen minutes left – and told Fahad, 'One of the things outside bit me. Tasted me. And the others let me through. So I guess Ugly Chicken wants me here.'

Fahad took a long drink from his bottle of water. He said, 'You're protected because he's inside your head. A small piece of him, anyway.'

'He made me want to come all the way out here. I felt it when I first saw this place. Felt as if I'd come home. Is that what you feel?'

Fahad nodded.

'Did you call up all those monsters to keep you safe, or was it your friend?'

'He wants to keep this place safe.' Fahad paused, then said in a rush, 'It's happening, Chloe. It's begun.'

'This wonderful thing you told me about.'

'He called to his friends.'

'The biochines?'

Fahad shook his head. 'Ugly Chicken is a memory of someone or something that had used this place long long ago. After he woke up, he used us to get back here. But that isn't the end of it. He wants to go back to where his original came from. So he went inside the operating system of this place, and he called to his friends. Out there beyond the sky. In space. And one of them answered him.'

It took Chloe a moment to process that. She said, 'Ugly Chicken called to a shuttle?'

'To some kind of spaceship. He said it'll be here soon. Here to take him home. He'll help us, Chloe. He brought the biochines. And the spaceship he talked to will be here soon. Then it won't matter about what Drury wants.'

'Even if it's about to land, or whatever it does, you can't stay here any longer,' Chloe said. She explained about the rocket launchers, and Drury's ultimatum. She checked the watch again, said, 'We have just ten minutes to work out what to do.'

'He wouldn't blow up this place,' Fahad said.

'Don't bet on it. He has Rana's bead. And this isn't the only mound, the only spire.'

'I told you. Ugly Chicken isn't in the bead any more.'

'Drury doesn't know that,' Chloe said.

'And anyway, he still needs me. If he didn't, he would have already fired those rockets into the tunnel.'

Chloe scooted closer to Fahad. 'And what will he do when he doesn't need you any more? When this spaceship comes? You're hiding in here because you're scared of him. That's okay. I'm scared of him, too. Henry's dead: one of Drury's men killed him. And Drury killed your father, too. Wait,' Chloe said when Fahad started to say something. 'Let me finish. Drury took over McBride's business when McBride went to prison. Drury found out that your father was dealing in Elder Culture artefacts, and that he wanted to go to work for his old boss, who'd just been released from jail. So he killed him and made a video of it, to keep other people who worked for him in line.'

'But it was McBride who told you that.'

'Yes, it was. And I trust him about as much as I trust Drury. But I think he was telling the truth about your father.' Chloe paused. It was an ugly thing to ask, but necessary. She said, 'Did you see the video? The one Jack Baines's bosses sent?'

'Why do you think we ran away?'

'You saw what was done to your father. He was shot, wasn't he?'

Fahad didn't say anything.

'McBride had some kind of ray gun. Henry took it off him, and then Drury took it from Henry. But before that, McBride used it on Hanna Babbel. I saw him do it. He paid her to lead Henry and me into a trap, and then he killed her. Also, when we were trying to find who had taken you, Henry found news reports about murders of men associated with McBride, all of them killed like Hanna. So if McBride had killed your father, he would have used his ray gun. It's like his trademark. Drury lied to you, Fahad. He was scared that you wouldn't cooperate with him if you found out that he killed your father, so he told you it was McBride.'

She watched Fahad think about that.

She said, 'You wanted me to come with you, to Mangala. I guess that was because you trusted me. Trust me now.'

'What do you want to do?'

'The biochines are protecting you. Forming a cordon. But suppose they could be persuaded to do more than that?'

'I already tried,' Fahad said. 'I mean, I'm not stupid. I asked Ugly Chicken to chase away Drury and his men.'

Chloe said, 'Maybe you could ask him again. Only this time, tell him what I told you. Tell him that Drury killed your father. Tell him that Henry's dead. Tell him that we'll be killed too, if he doesn't help.'

Fahad said he would try again, and pressed the heels of his palms over his eyes, the tips of his fingers over his ears. Going inside himself, muttering prayer-wise, pausing, muttering again.

Chloe was watching him closely, willing him to get through to Ugly Chicken, when pure blue light shone briefly around her. It took her a moment to realise what it was. Not some new manifestation of the eidolon, but the ray gun, probably fired at its lowest setting. She checked the watch. Still five minutes to go. Either Drury was getting impatient, or he was worrying about what she and Fahad were doing. Probably both.

Fahad was still murmuring his appeal. Chloe watched two minutes tick by, something kinking tighter and tighter in her chest, and at last Fahad took his hands away from his eyes and said, 'I don't know if he heard me.'

'Did you tell him that Drury wants to kill us?'

'I tried. Okay? I tried. But I don't know if he is listening.'

'Let's hope he is. Because that's our only chance now.'

341

52. Local Grid

Vic saw it all. Saw Nevers grasp Cal McBride's hand and jerk him forward, saw Nevers place his left hand on McBride's breast pocket. A flare of light like a door opening onto summer sunshine; then three gunshots. McBride was down, twisting on the ground, and one of his goons was also down, two bloody holes ripped in the chest of his pea coat. Nevers was aiming the gun he'd grabbed from McBride at the second goon, who let his pistol drop and spread his hands.

'Take care of him,' Nevers told Vic. 'And be quick. We have an appointment with a ghost.'

Vic moved forward and scooped up the goon's pistol; when he stepped back, Nevers was gone. Vic searched the goon and hogtied him by cuffing his right ankle to his left wrist, checked the one Nevers had shot – no pulse, fixed dilated pupils – and tossed his pistol over the edge of the drop. McBride was clasping his knee, blood oozing around his fingers, face tight with pain. He wasn't going anywhere, poor guy. A glint of gold on the ground nearby. Vic scooped up the thread and took off downhill, after Nevers.

There was a kind of track winding down the steep slope, the bed of an old stream. Vic saw a fugitive gleam below: Nevers at the bottom of the slope, following a star that drifted through the air ahead of him. Vic pulled off his face mask and shouted Nevers's name, but his voice was torn away by the wind and Nevers didn't look around as he disappeared into the tumble of house-sized boulders at the base of the slope.

Vic picked his way down dry stone chutes, falling several times, once sliding a long way down a slant of wind-polished rock and

342

slamming against a boulder at the bottom. The impact bruised his hip and knocked the breath out of him. As he lay there, sweating inside his down jacket, one elbow throbbing where he'd banged it, he heard three gunshots, hard and distinct above the whine of the wind.

He pushed to his feet, danced down a gravel slope, and followed the stream bed's meandering path through the chaos of boulders, tracking bootprints and a muddle of small and large gouges he supposed had been made by biochines. He glimpsed two prone shapes through the blowing dust, raised his pistol and advanced cautiously, found two men in red quilted jackets, one on his back, one curled up, both dead.

An assault rifle lay nearby, a military model with a skeletal carbon-fibre stock and vents in its short barrel. Vic scooped it up and went on, climbing a sand dune that crossed the stream bed, following the deep bootprints in its concave surface. At the crest, he saw a cluster of little flat-topped hills ahead, ghostly in the haze and blowing clouds of dust. Mounds. The Elder Culture site.

Vic slid down the face of the dune in a welter of sand, sand in his pockets, in his boots, picked himself up, and saw someone crouched behind a shelf of rock about a hundred metres away.

It was Nevers, squatting on his haunches with an assault rifle laid across his thighs, field glasses in his right hand. As Vic came towards him, he looked up and said, 'The bad guys are definitely having a spot of bother with the local fauna. Biochines all over the shop.'

'Where's your friend?'

'In the local grid. We can put an end to this now,' Nevers said. He stuffed the field glasses into a pocket and stood, his right hand gripping the barrel of the assault rifle.

Vic eased off the safety of his own rifle. 'We're not going anywhere until you tell me exactly what's going down,' he said, and there was a flash in the distance, a lightning track leaping up into the sky, there and gone. Shazam. A fucking magic trick. He blinked searing green after-images from his eyes, saw a tiny spark falling.

The drone. He'd left it on autopilot and someone had spotted it and shot it down.

Nevers was running towards the mounds. Vic raised the rifle, sighted on his back. But he wasn't that kind of guy. The kind who shot down fleeing suspects. He took a deep breath and ran too.

53. Cavalry Charge

Mangala | 30 July

Chloe and Fahad crawled down the tunnel and tumbled into the trench. Cold wind, blowing dust, the shadows of monsters lurching past as they circled the mound. Individuals and loose groups travelling clockwise and anticlockwise, appearing out of the haze and going past and disappearing.

Fahad, crouching beside Chloe, asked her if she thought it had worked.

'There's only one way to find out,' she said, and switched on the walkie-talkie.

Drury said at once, 'You fucked with the comms.'

Chloe felt a freezing disappointment. She really had been hoping that Ugly Chicken would come through for them, that it would have aimed the biochines at Drury and his men. But there he was, unruffled, unharmed.

She said, 'Something in the black room must have blocked the signal.'

'You're outside now.'

'Of course.'

'Do you have the kid?'

'He agreed to come out.'

'Stand up so I can see you,' Drury said.

'Wait a sec. He's having last-minute nerves,' Chloe said. She switched off the walkie-talkie and told Fahad to crawl.

'This is your plan?'

'Ugly Chicken didn't send the biochines after Drury, but he can't get at us inside their cordon. We can slip away before he realises what's happening.'

Fahad shook his head. 'We bring him all this fucking way! We bring him home, and he won't do us one little favour!'

He sounded about half his age, his voice cracking with fury and frustration.

'It was always a long shot.' Chloe said. 'If we want to escape, we're going to have to do it on our own.'

They crawled to the end of the trench and clambered out and ran, bent low, following the curve of the mound. They passed something the size and shape of a fat woman sprawled in the dirt; it was coated in pale bristles that stirred with independent life. A heap of scaly pine cones scattered. A knee-high stool whirled by. It was like navigating a Disney animation of a Hieronymus Bosch painting. Chloe's heart kicked when clumps of scarlet spikes bounced away like demented jack-in-the-boxes, vanishing into a squall of dust.

No blue ray-gun flash. No rockets. Would she hear the bullet that hit her? Probably not.

When she judged that they had put the mound between themselves and Drury and his soldiers, she told Fahad that all they had to do now was circle back and steal one of the boats.

'Or we could find somewhere to hide,' Fahad said. 'The spaceship will be here soon. I know it.'

'How long can we hide from Drury and his goons, with no food and no water?' Chloe said. 'We have to go, Fahad. We have to get out of here. When this is over, you can come back. I promise. I'll come back with you.'

They dashed across an open space, dodging between monsters, and reached the shelter of another mound. Chloe got her bearings from the low red sun and told Fahad that all they had to do was work their way around it and head for the river.

They circled the mound, started across the open space beyond. The sun at their backs, the river ahead of them. Chloe clutched Fahad's arm when two shadows appeared in the haze ahead of them. Monsters, she thought. Please let it be only monsters.

She and Fahad knelt. The shadows faded and Chloe was beginning to think they could move on when footsteps crunched behind them and they were seized and pulled up and turned around.

The soldiers frogmarched Chloe and Fahad back to the trench and shoved them in. Chloe landed hard, and as soon as she got to her feet Drury was in her face, pushing her against the wall of the trench, pinning her with his weight, his hand at her throat, saying, 'What the fuck?'

His voice was high and hoarse with fury; dust stuck to a wet patch in the middle of his face mask.

Chloe met his angry gaze. 'We were trying to find a way back through the biochines.'

'No you weren't. You were trying to find your friends.'

'You shot my friend.'

'Don't you fucking lie,' Drury said. 'We spotted their drone. Up there. Look,' he said, and wrenched Chloe around, pointed.

Chloe sighted along his arm, saw something that might have been a bird, a black speck there and then not there as wind thickened the blowing dust.

'Quadcopter,' Drury said. 'Tommy picked up the C-Band signal; my guys pinpointed its infrared signature. Who does it belong to?'

'I have no idea. Really.'

'McBride. Cal McBride and his fucking drones.'

'He isn't a friend of mine.'

'You came here with him.'

'He took me prisoner. Me and Henry.'

Drury ignored that. 'I think he took down two of my men. Patrice and Niles, out on the northern perimeter. We can't fucking raise them. You talked to him, didn't you? You talked to McBride while you were in there with the kid.'

His face was close to hers again, blue eyes sharp behind his goggles. Chloe met his stare, said, 'How could I talk to anyone? All I have is the walkie-talkie you gave me.'

'You switched it off. And then tried to sneak out. Did you really think I wouldn't anticipate that? Frankly, I'm disappointed.'

'I did what you asked me to do. I persuaded Fahad to come with me.'

'I should shoot you dead,' Drury said, pulling the ray gun from his belt and pointing it at Chloe.

She flinched, turned her head from the black circle of its maw, and Drury shoved her away and aimed into the sky, bracing his right hand with his left.

A thread of intense blue light angled across the ochre sky; a swift parabola of sparks rained down and winked out.

'All right,' Drury said, with grim satisfaction.

'Now they know we know they're here,' Tommy said.

'They already know,' Drury said. 'But now the ball's in their court . . . What the fuck's that?'

Off in the distance, a clattering percussion had started up, and things were whooping and whining and hooting like a demented factory.

Tommy leaned at the lip of the trench and peered out. 'Looks like the monsters didn't like your fireworks.'

Drury turned to look, and someone sang out '*Incoming!*' and started firing, and then the other men were firing too, a fierce crackle of gunshots. Chloe found a foothold and boosted herself up, caught a glimpse of shapes trundling out of the murk before Drury pulled her away and sent her sprawling. He aimed the ray gun at something beyond the trench and nothing happened and he shook it and aimed it again. Nothing. He strode over to Fahad, who all this while had been sitting quiet and still, knees drawn up and arms wrapped around them, trying to make himself as small as possible. Shouting now in fear and surprise as Drury yanked him to his feet.

'You,' Drury said, shaking him, 'will explain exactly what you did.'

'You shouldn't have used Elder Culture tech,' Fahad said. He was trembling with fear and anger. 'Ugly Chicken didn't like it.'

'Bullshit. You called those fucking monsters down on our heads. Now you can make them go away.'

Gunfire on either side, the sudden thump of high explosive. A man laughed. Another man was shouting: 'Get some! Get some!'

Drury jammed the ray gun under Fahad's chin. 'You want to live, you'll find a way to unfuck this right now.'

Fahad struggled in his grip, managed to get a hand loose, tried to punch Drury's face. The man blocked it with his forearm and whacked Fahad with the ray gun. The kid sat down hard, blood running from his nose; Drury kicked him in the ribs and sent him sprawling. Stood over him with the sole of his boot on his neck, saying, 'You finally found your dick, kid. Shame it was too little and too late. Any last words?'

He wasn't even out of breath.

Fahad was choking, trying and failing to pry the boot away. Drury pulled his pistol from his belt and aimed it at Fahad's face, and Chloe ripped out the strip of memory plastic concealed in her cuff and shook it with a snap of her wrist to make it rigid and ran at Drury, springing onto his back, locking her left forearm under his jaw to force it up, sawing at his throat with the sharp-edged blade.

He clawed at her, then swung around and ran backwards, smashing her against the side of the trench. A terrific blow against the back of her head numbed and dazed her; she couldn't resist as Drury grabbed her collar and belt and swung her through the air. She flew across the trench and smacked into its wall. Drury was on his knees, hands pressed to his throat, blood spreading across the front of his white coat, blood pouring between his fingers and pattering on dry red dirt. He raised his pistol and something punched Chloe in the side, a hard blow echoed by the hard sound of the shot.

They looked at each other. Blood slicked the front of Drury's coat and he was having trouble breathing. He wrenched off his face mask, coughed a spray of blood and smiled redly at Chloe. Blood pulsed from the wound in his throat. He tried to raise the pistol again, and Fahad stepped up, clutching the ray gun. There was a flare of blue light and Drury fell forward, his coat and hair on fire. Fahad turned to Chloe, and Tommy loomed behind him and knocked him down.

Chloe tried to push to her feet. A weight shifted in her belly and a pure white moment of agony wiped her clean and she sat down. Tommy was shouting something lost in gunfire and the shouts of men and the howls of monsters. Something sleek and cat-shaped, a cat sculpted out of needles and spines, struck a man and he screamed and tried to bat it away and it bit off his fingers. Tommy loomed over Chloe. She stared at him, stared at his pistol, and then he was down, tearing at a crumpled leather bag fastened over his face.

Biochines were pouring into the trench. Chloe saw a man throw away his rifle and try to scramble out, saw black shapes swarm over him and drag him down. She tried to get up again, and another pure moment of pain blanked out the world.

Fahad was kneeling beside her. Blood drying under his nose, his gaze anxious. He said, 'He helped us after all. You see? He helped us.'

'I see.'

The biochines were gone. Ruined bodies lay scattered along the trench.

'Drury shot you.'

'Yes. Yes, he did.'

'Can you walk?'

'I don't think so. Find help, Fahad. Find the people who were flying that drone . . .'

A shadow fell across them. A man stood at the lip of the trench, aiming a combat rifle at them as he looked all around. Then he reached up and pulled off his face mask.

'Chloe Millar,' Adam Nevers said. 'What have you done now?'

54. Men and Monsters

Mangala | 30 July

Vic chased Nevers across stretches of sand and gravel, past shatterings of rock and clumps of ragged ribbons streaming in the wind, through veils of dust that swelled and slackened and swelled again. Always the dust and the wind. Vic was labouring against it, finding it hard to suck air through his mask. He was tempted to rip it off, but knew that if he did he'd choke on the dusty air. His bruised hip was stiffening and pain spiked it at every step, and sharp pains prised at his chest. He was too old for this foolishness. Old and out of shape, puffing like an old-fashioned steam engine, and Nevers was getting away, vanishing into haze and wind-blown dust.

It was really blowing hard now. Thickening clouds swirled around Vic as he jogged along, the rifle held at port arms. Everything but his immediate surroundings was lost in brown smog. The sun a low bloody smear.

Indistinct shapes flowing through the murk ahead of him. The hard rattle of gunfire. The blink of an explosion and the hard percussion of it coming afterwards, blown on the wind, blown past him.

Something bad going down. Men v. monsters. And Vic was running straight towards it, probably the worst idea in a life full of bad ideas. He told himself that he was doing it for Skip and knew that was only partly true. He was angry at himself for letting Nevers get away. He was angry because Nevers had faked him out so easily. He told himself that he was going to get himself killed out of stubborn pride, but he kept going because every alternative was worse.

For a moment, the dusty haze blew thin and he glimpsed Nevers way ahead of him, jogging along steadily, the son of a bitch. And then the dust thickened and swallowed him again.

Vic followed, limping and blowing, feeling a sudden sick urgency. Something whooped past him and he belatedly realised it was a stray round. He'd never been shot at before. Never before had to draw a gun in anger, either.

But the rattle of gunfire was dying away, fraying to stray shots. Vic limped past dead things sprawled on the ground. Past dead things splayed and shattered around starbursts of char, some still slowly writhing. Past something like the legless and headless torso of a man, crawling on its elbows and leaving a trail of blue slime.

A mound loomed ahead, a trench cut across the ground in front of it. Vic slowed to a walk and jacked the combat rifle under his armpit, sweeping it back and forth as he walked over broken black flagstones to the edge of the trench.

A young woman sat below, clutching her belly. Blood leaking over her fingers. A young man crouched nearby, watching as Nevers pawed through the pockets of a dead man burned hairless in a charred coat. Bodies were scattered on either side. Bodies and pieces of bodies. Men and monsters. And now Nevers was standing, turning, his rifle slung on his shoulder, a bracelet looped between the fingers of his right hand.

Vic raised his rifle and said, 'This is as far as it goes.'

'Yes, it is,' Nevers said, holding up the bracelet. 'The thing we came to find – it's in here. And we know how to deal with it.'

There was a faint envelope of light around him. As if he was standing in the glow of a spotlight.

'You're too late,' the young man said. His voice was muffled by his face mask and his long black hair was dishevelled and dusty, but his gaze burned with scorn. 'Ugly Chicken has already called to its friends. The spaceships are on their way.'

'They aren't here yet,' Nevers said. 'There's still time to undo things.'

Vic said to the young man, 'There are spaceships here?'

'They're coming,' the young man said.

'Seriously?'

'I swear on the life of my sister,' the young man said.

Nevers said, 'Take care of these prisoners, Investigator Gayle, while I root out the source of the infection.'

'No,' Vic said.

Nevers looked at him, ignoring the rifle. 'We're going to do the right thing.'

'Yes, we are. You can start by kneeling on the ground and clasping your hands on your head.'

'You're going to arrest me? I don't think so.'

'For the murders of three men back there.'

'I think you should take a moment, Investigator. Get your breath back before we get on with the job.'

'There is no job. You come out here to my world, you and that avatar, and expect me to dance to your tune. You promise to help me, and then you run off the first chance you get. You expect me to help you enforce laws that have no authority here, over something you don't own or even understand. No more. This is where your foolishness ends.'

'It's my job to make sure that disruptive technology is properly controlled,' Nevers said.

'Maybe on Earth. But out here we're free to do what we like. That's what this world is for.'

'Free to find stuff that could seriously fuck us up,' Nevers said, jiggling the bracelet. 'And this is exactly that kind of stuff.'

'Is that what your friend told you?'

'They want to help us. That's why they're here. And if they say something is dangerous, wrong, then we should listen to them.'

'Or perhaps we should make up our own minds,' Vic said. 'Drop that bracelet and your fucking rifle and assume the position.'

'If you want to arrest someone, Investigator Gayle, arrest Fahad Chauhan and Chloe Millar. They came here illegally. They interfered with Elder Culture technology—'

'Policing Elder Culture ruins isn't my business. But it isn't yours, either. Because you have no authority here. Assume the fucking position. And that's your last warning.'

Nevers stared at Vic, inscrutable in face mask and goggles. He said, 'Do you really think that arresting me will do any good?'

Something was definitely occupying the same space as him. His face glinted with a kind of golden glaze.

Vic steadied the rifle on his hip, pulled the tangle of wire from his pocket. 'You won't be able to do anything without this.'

The Jackaroo avatar stepped forward. 'Silly little man. I'm not there any more. I'm in the local grid.'

Behind its ghostly gleam, Nevers let the bracelet unspool between his fingers and fall to the dirt. He raised his boot, ground it down.

Later, Vic said that it was as if graves had opened all around him. The flagstones half-buried in the sand and gravel along the edge of the trench and scattered between the mounds seemed to invert and narrow beams of hard black light burned up from them, leaning away into the sky. As if an unbearable reality had punched through weak spots in the fabric of the world. And figures were struggling amongst the columns of black light: identical pairs of antagonists mirrored everywhere around him. Angels and devils battling in the dusty air.

Fahad said that it was as if a golden giant had loomed against the sky. An anime monster swatting at a swarm of fighter planes. The planes trailed black threads, swooping around and around the monster, wrapping it in a constricting net that immediately began to tighten, cutting into its substance. Slivers of furnace light burned in gaps between the threads, jetting into the air in every direction as the monster struggled and roared and diminished.

Chloe saw the world shift and change, as if everything had been replaced by a copy of itself. Everything the same; everything slightly different. She saw the image of the Jackaroo avatar explode like a stained-glass window, shattering into a thousand animated shards. Sharp and swift and burning, they swirled around Nevers, who screamed and dropped to his knees, and then whirled high into the air. A skinny column that grew thicker and brighter as it lengthened because the shards were multiplying. And suddenly there were other shapes in the air around it, flocks of small quick dark ghosts fluttering in the glare of the column, each plucking out a shard and wrapping around it and falling out of the air. A hard rain striking the ground all around and vanishing into it, while overhead the column diminished until it was no more than a stain fading into the dun sky.

A few fugitive ghosts fluttered here and there in widening gyres. One slanted low and swooped above the trench, turning to look at Chloe as it went past. She had the impression of a face like a shelled walnut randomly studded with black stones, or a drop of water swarming with black motes, or a ball of churning insects, or a clutch of busy clockworks. Something so unfamiliar that her mind couldn't make sense of it, a wrongness projected by a logic at right angles to everything she knew, a mask or shield that hid a fierce avid awareness that would shrivel her if she saw it entire. She felt the extreme edge of that attention pass through her mind, and then it was gone, and the last trace of the column was gone too.

The Jackaroo avatar had vanished. Nevers looked up cautiously, dazed and dishevelled, and the other man jumped into the trench and told him to stay exactly where he was. He was aiming his rifle at Nevers, glancing down at Chloe and asking her how she was doing.

'Not so good, to tell the truth.'

She had forgotten the heavy pain in her belly for a moment, but now it was back.

'You hang in there,' the man said. 'I'm going to call for help.'

Fahad was standing at the wall of the trench, staring towards the mound that cradled the black room at its centre. He tore off his face mask and goggles, turned to Chloe. He was crying. 'He's gone,' he said.

55· Some Kind of Connection

Mangala | 5 August—
10 September

The walls of the hospital room were painted a soothing green, with a long narrow window shuttered by a venetian blind. Chloe could glimpse slivers of a dusty night sky through the slanted blades. It was as if she was afloat in a planetary ocean of deep smog. The lights dimmed in the evening and the pulse of the hospital slowed and settled, although there was always the clatter of a trolley on its way to somewhere else, the squeak of shoes on polished floors, human voices, and at last the lights brightened and it was another day. But it was always night outside. The night-year of Mangala.

Tethered to drips and the beeping monitor, she drifted on slow deep morphine tides.

One day she woke and the policeman, Vic Gayle, was perched on the chair by her bed. A large middle-aged man in a brown suit with a pink check, looking tired and a little awkward.

There were flowers on her bedside cabinet. Yellow roses.

He asked her how she felt, and she said it was about what you'd expect after being shot.

'You look pretty good.'

'That's weird. Because I feel fucking awful.'

She seemed to be looking up at him from a deep pit. She couldn't move anything but her eyes. The various cramps and jags of her damage were distant reports from another city, voices in another room.

Vic Gayle said, 'They put you in what they call an induced coma to help your body heal. They brought you out of it a couple of days ago, but only just now let me in to talk. I don't have long, though. If you have any questions you'd best fire them straight at me.'

'Fahad?'

'He's safe. Squared away in an apartment in the UN building. He wanted to go home, but by the time we'd sorted out the little problem of his illegal entry the shuttle had departed.'

'He has a little sister, back on Earth.'

It felt odd, saying that. Earth. You don't need to think about the name of your home until you've left it.

'He talks to her by q-phone every day,' Vic said.

'Is he still drawing?'

'Not that I know of. Playing video games, complaining that we won't let him go out . . . Drury's organisation has fallen apart, there's a little civil war over control of drug corners, but some hothead might decide to try to make a name for himself by taking a pop at the kid.'

'The spaceship . . . ?'

'Was Fahad right about that? Has it arrived? I don't know. No one knows. The storm has locked down everything in Idunn's Valley. A UN team is trying to get through to the site, but communications are down all over. If something has happened out there it will take a while for the news to reach us. But don't you worry, Chloe. It's been taken care of. Everything is fine. All you need to do is rest and get better. Can you do that for me?'

'I'm trying.'

'The nurse is giving me a death stare. I have to go. Take care, Chloe. I'll come back soon.'

And then the nurse was bustling around her and did something to her morphine drip, and everything sank away.

When Chloe woke again the room was lit only by the glow of the monitors and a wedge of light under the door. She listened to the noises of the hospital, and slept. When she woke, dry-mouthed and cottony, the policeman was there again.

'Water,' she said.

Vic called the nurse, who let her sip ice water through a metal straw. It was heavenly. When she had finished, she asked him about Henry Harris's body.

'It should go home. Back to Earth.'

'It's still in Winnetou. But as soon as the dust storm lifts I'll make sure it's sent back.'

'Nevers. Is he still here?'

'In jail. But not for long, I reckon. The British consulate has lodged a complaint, and there's a rumour of some under-the-counter deal. We're having more luck with Cal McBride. He's been charged with the murder of Hanna Babbel. Fahad told us what you told him; at some point we'll need a statement from you. McBride made bail, but he's tagged, and he knows we're watching him. And we're still looking into his involvement in the death of Nevers's partner, and a stack of old cases. One way or another, he's going down.'

'The avatar?'

'No sign of it. Nevers claims he doesn't remember anything. The scientists have been doing all kinds of tests on the memory wire he was carrying, but it seems to have burned out. No trace of activity left in it.'

'The ship?'

'Still no word. Fahad wants to visit, by the way. If I can swing permission for him, will you be up for it?'

'Love to see him.'

'He's been having tests here, as a matter of fact.'

'I think Ugly Chicken has finished with him. But if he starts drawing again . . .'

'That's one of the signs. Right.'

Vic changed the subject and talked about preparations for the arraignment of Cal McBride and predictions about the dust storm's duration until the nurse sent him away.

Chloe had lost twelve centimetres of her colon to Drury's bullet, and it had chipped her pelvis and caused some nerve damage. She'd also contracted pneumonia and suffered congestive pressure to her heart. And there was something else, something growing under the skin of her wrist. When the biochine had bitten her, it had left something behind.

One of the consultants treating her said that she'd seen similar examples of biochine infection amongst prospectors and ruin miners. Fibrous growths of carbon whiskers with complex nano-structures incorporating copper and iron and other elements, with a pathology similar to neurofibromatosis.

'In your case, fortunately, the fibroid is localised and highly organised. As if it has a purpose or function. Although what that is, I'm afraid we do not yet know.'

'Is it still growing?' Chloe said. The idea of a weird alien para-site stealthily invading her flesh was simultaneously unnerving and queasily fascinating.

'The scans show that it appears to have stabilised, although threads resembling afferent nerves have extended up your arm and made connections to your sensory and paranervous systems at the fifth cervical vertebra.' The consultant touched her neck to show what she meant. 'You aren't the only person infected, by the way. Your friend, Fahad Chauhan, has a similar growth.'

'He must have been bitten too. He didn't mention it . . .'

'The other good news is that it appears to have had no effect on your immune system or brain activity,' the consultant said. 'And there is no loss of mobility in your wrist or hand. You'll hardly notice it's there.'

It took a moment for Chloe to realise what she meant. 'You aren't going to remove it?'

'Surgical excision is often unsuccessful – the fibroids grow back. And any attempt to remove the threads embedded in your spinal cord could cause paralysis. We'd like to do some more tests,' the consultant said. 'With your permission, of course.'

'Maybe when I've healed up.'

Chloe had a good idea what the growth was for. A terminal. A connector. She had been prepared. Fahad had been prepared too. And maybe the idea that she'd been prepared was part of that preparation.

She gave Vic Gayle a statement about witnessing Hanna Babbel's murder, and over several days told him about everything else, from the breakout in Dagenham to the final confrontation at Site 326. One day she realised just how ill she had been, and knew then that she was getting better. Soon afterwards, she was able to begin physical therapy. It would be a while before she could walk again, but the cheerful young Romanian physiotherapist who put her through her gruelling routines said that if she continued to exercise regularly she would probably only have a trace of a limp.

Vic told her about progress in the case against McBride. The dust storm was still blowing and communications were still down between the city and Idunn's Valley: there was no news from the excavation site.

'Which almost certainly means there's no sign of a ship yet,' Vic said.

'One is on its way. Fahad was sure of it.'

'Maybe this Ugly Chicken lied to him. Or he misunderstood. I wouldn't blame the kid if he did.'

'This ship, or whatever it is, it may have been asleep for a long time. Thousands of years. Tens of thousands . . . It may need a while to get back up to speed again. Take it from me.'

Fahad visited her, too. He showed her a brief video message from Rana, sent via q-phone. They talked about the confrontation between Ugly Chicken and the Jackaroo avatar, and discovered that they'd seen different things.

'It was inside our heads. Real and not real,' Fahad said. 'We were trying to make sense of something we didn't understand.'

Which as far as Chloe was concerned just about summed up the last month.

Their patches were identical: pale oval blotches sitting just beneath the skin, flexible, very thin. Like Chloe, Fahad was absolutely certain that they had something to do with the spaceship. Some kind of connection.

'We'll find out what they can do when it comes,' he said.

'If the Jackaroo let us keep it. If the UN lets us visit it.'

'I've tried to talk to Mr Gayle about that, but he always changes the subject. I don't think he has the authority to help us. I've decided to stay on,' Fahad added. 'The UN asked me if I wanted to go home on the next shuttle, but I want to be here when the ship arrives. If it ever comes.'

'Maybe it's waiting for the dust storm to blow out,' Chloe said.

*

The storm blew through the rest of Mangala's night-year. Every day, Chloe spent four excruciating hours in physiotherapy. She endured batteries of tests that reminded her of her time in Ada Morange's lab. The doctors were excited by the discovery that pulses of ultrasound at particular frequencies focused on her wrist patch induced a form of parathesia – made her see geometric patterns, taste salt, feel transient pulses of heat or cold travel up her arm. Chloe, only half-joking, said that it made her feel like a broken robot. 'Maybe you can find the code that'll help me walk in a straight line.'

She gave a statement to two UN investigators, who wanted to know more about Nevers and Ada Morange than she could tell them. A lawyer paid a visit and told her that he had been instructed by Ada Morange to provide any legal aid she required. She told him that as far as she knew she wasn't in any trouble and sent him away.

The storm was still blowing when Vic Gayle visited Chloe again, early one morning. He found her in the hospital's physio room, heaving herself back and forth along a set of parallel bars. She was supporting most of her weight with her arms, taking baby steps. It still hurt. It hurt a lot.

'They're here!' he said as he strode towards Chloe. 'They're here!'

The physiotherapist tried to intercept him, telling him off for interrupting the session. Vic sidestepped her. He was grinning hugely.

'This is more important. The damn kid was right! They're here!'

There were two ships, he said, and pulled out his phone and showed Chloe images of a pair of elongated teardrops shaped from a froth of bubbles and pierced at random by gleaming spars. They hung above neighbouring mounds at Site 326 like the ugliest balloons in the universe. They had sunk down through the atmosphere two days ago, Vic said. It had taken that long to get the news back to Petra because comms were still down.

The ships were each about as big as a three-storey house. Close-ups showed that their skin was mottled with subtle shades of grey and blue.

'Both of them opened ports. Right there,' Vic said, zooming in on what looked like a tear or wound at the tapering base of one of the ships. 'And that's all they've done. No coherent electromagnetic activity, although there are random emissions in the ultraviolet spectrum, and a steady pulse at around fifty megahertz. That's what the report said. I don't know what any of that shit means.'

Chloe asked if anyone had been inside; Vic said not yet, although the team on site had sent in camera drones.

There were views of a space webbed with spars of various thicknesses, illuminated by a harsh blue-white glare which came from nowhere in particular. Irregular blisters on the walls which might contain the machinery of the ship's drive and its lifesystem.

'The temperature is about forty degrees Celsius, very humid,' Vic said. 'And the air is thin, about half ordinary atmospheric pressure at sea level on Earth, with just enough oxygen to make it breathable. The light is rich in ultraviolet, too. The Elder Culture that made these things seems to have come from a world with a hotter, bluer sun.'

He told Chloe that a specialist team had been rushed out. 'Engineers, physicists. Also a retired astronaut and a couple of jet-plane pilots. Hopefully they'll figure out how they work. If they can.'

'The UN should take Fahad back there. In fact, he should be the first to go aboard.'

Chloe was stroking the oval patch under the skin of her left wrist. Two ships. Two pilots. A thought amazing and terrifying.

Ada Morange's lawyer visited her the next day. He told her that she would profit immensely by helping Ada Morange pursue her claim to the find.

'If she wants to buy me out, I'm not interested in selling,' Chloe said, and didn't listen to anything else the lawyer had to say before the ward nurse came and ejected him.

The day-year dawned and the storm started to die back. According to the news feed from Earth, the Jackaroo's only reaction to the appearance of the two ships was that it was 'an interesting development'. Adam Nevers was still refusing to answer questions about why they had supported his attempt to stop Fahad and Ugly Chicken calling down the ships.

362

One day, Vic told Chloe that the UN had taken Fahad out to Site 326; a week later Vic was on his way there too. A couple of days later, the UN commissioner held a press conference: one of the ships had gone into orbit, and had returned safely. Ada Morange's lawyer phoned Chloe while the commissioner was still speaking.

'We really do have things to discuss.'

'Tell Dr Morange I'll be happy to talk to her any time she likes,' Chloe said, and hung up.

56· Unlikely Astronaut

Mangala | 13 September

When he returned to Petra, Vic told Chloe that he'd brought back Henry Harris's body and had made arrangements for it to be transported to Earth. And then he told her about his trip into space.

The young woman listened with rapt attention, the shine of a true believer in her gaze. She'd had her hair cut while he'd been away, a boyish bob that made her look younger, vivacious. But although she'd lost the drawn look of the truly ill and had exchanged her hospital gown for a tracksuit, she was still sitting in a wheelchair, and crutches leaned against the wall of her room.

Vic told her that he'd travelled in a small convoy of UN vehicles out along the new road, really just a bulldozed track still mostly unpaved, that linked Winnetou and the ferry crossing to Site 326. Which was a bustling village of tents and prefabs now – labs and workshops, dormitories and mess tents, even a tent that doubled as a church and a mosque. A small frontier town dominated by the two ships that hung like strange fruit above adjacent mounds.

Fahad had made a connection with one of the ships through his patch, and there had been several secret tests, with Fahad taking the ship into the sky to different heights, straight up and straight down like a tethered balloon. But this time he was going to take it on a real flight: out of Mangala's atmosphere and into orbit.

Vic went aboard as Fahad's guest. He and the other passengers – technicians, scientists and a former astronaut – sat in a horse-shoe of padded chairs on a plywood platform suspended in the middle of the ship's vault, watching as the ship recognised Fahad and gave him access to its systems. A weirdly solemn moment, like being in a cathedral or temple at some ceremony of investiture, although everyone was dressed in shorts and T-shirts because of the tropical heat, wearing sunglasses to filter the UV in the blue light that glared on webs of black struts, and now and then taking sips of oxygen from face masks connected to portable tanks.

There was an air of jocular tension, and not just because they were all about to take a huge fucking step into the unknown. There was the possibility that the Jackaroo might intervene; jokes about being shot down by alien starfighters now seemed suddenly real. A photographer was videoing Fahad as he engaged in an internal dialogue with the ship. A surgeon was measuring his vital signs; a neurologist was measuring his brain activity. Technicians studied arrays of readouts on their tablets, exchanged cryptic jargon.

At last the astronaut, a petite French woman with a cap of silvery hair, reached over and lightly gripped Vic's wrist and said, 'The entrance has closed. It begins.'

She was grinning hugely.

It was gentle at first. Like riding a very fast elevator. Vic's weight slowly increased, pressing him into the aerogel padding of his chair. He was too excited to be scared. Everyone was excited, even the scientists and technicians pretending to be monitoring changes on their tablets.

The force of acceleration peaked at 2.2 times Earth's pull. And then it abruptly went away and they were in free fall. One of the technicians switched on cameras stuck to the ship's hull; everyone cheered and applauded as images of Mangala's ochre crescent appeared on the big TV screens hung here and there from spars. Pouches of wine were passed around to toast the historic moment. Fahad refused to make a speech; the kid seemed dazed, but maybe that was because he was still plugged into the ship, one arm engulfed in a mass of jostling black bubbles that hung from a spiny many-jointed limb.

The astronaut shoved off from her chair, turned neatly in mid-air, caught a spar with one hand and held the other out to Vic, as if asking him to dance. He unsnapped his harness, kicked towards her, and shot past, tumbling head over heels. He snatched at a thin spar as it went past; momentum swung him around it and he clung there, dizzy, foolish and exhilarated, as the astronaut swam neatly towards him.

'Don't use too much force,' she said. 'Look at where you want to go and push. Like this.'

She glided across the width of the ship and Vic followed, and soon they were flitting amongst the spars like birds in an aviary, swimming and somersaulting through the air, while the ship swung around the planet and the scientists tried to work out whether various readings meant that the ship was functioning normally. Mostly, they seemed to be arguing about what 'normal' meant. Fahad sat alone in his big chair, arm cased in stiff black foam to the elbow, eyes closed. He seemed happy and calm. Serene. As if he had reached the place where he had always wanted to be.

'And after two orbits he brought the ship back down,' Vic told Chloe, 'and that was that.'

'It's just the beginning,' Chloe said.

'Are you going to go up? Try to fly one of those ships, I mean, not just as a passenger.'

'I don't know. It's a big thing. Enormous. How was Fahad, afterwards?'

'We talked for about ten seconds after he brought us down. He seemed pleased. And then the scientists hustled him away for tests.'

'Maybe I've had enough of tests,' Chloe said, with a quietness that touched Vic. She was a tough young woman, no doubt, but she'd been through the fire and it had definitely left its mark on her. He felt a pang, a tender protectiveness. You save someone's life, you're responsible.

'Well,' she said brightly. 'What about you? When Fahad decides to dive through a wormhole, will you go with him?'

'Oh, I'm an unlikely kind of astronaut, don't you think? Besides, I've already *been* through a wormhole. And I have work here. Making sure that McBride goes down for what he did, to begin with. I was police before I came up and out, and I'm still police. I like to think I'm good at it. Or I try to be. My partner, Skip, now he definitely knew the job. He wanted to do the right thing by his dead, even if it was the hard thing. I'm going to dedicate myself to that, I guess.'

Vic didn't tell Chloe that he had a date with Astrid Pelissier. The French astronaut. He wanted to see how it worked out first. They'd had a moment, on the ship, and afterwards, back on the ground in a corner of one of the tent cafeterias, they'd fallen to talking about themselves. He'd told Astrid about tracking Drury and McBride to Site 326; she'd told him about her tour on the International Space Station, six months orbiting Earth – one of the last tours before the Jackaroo came and that was the end of the space programme. But now, she'd said, who knows?

'We have no idea what the ship can do yet, but it's clear that it is powered by some kind of reactionless drive. Possibly a bias drive that alters the gravitational constant to create a local propulsive gradient, the scientists say. If so, we could go anywhere we wanted to go. I could be the first woman to step on Mars.'

Astrid was a few years older than Vic, scary-smart, capable, cosmopolitan, certain about who she was and what she wanted. He wasn't sure what she saw in him, but believed it might be fun, finding out what they had in common. Maybe one day they would walk the sands of Mars together. Meanwhile, he could most definitely use some certainty in his life.

57. The Gift
Mangala | 15-28 September

Fahad visited Chloe in hospital a couple of days after Vic had told her about the first real flight of the spaceship, and said that he was planning to return to Earth on the next shuttle.

'What about the ships?' Chloe said.

Fahad shrugged. 'They won't be going anywhere for a little while. And I have to see Rana. See that she is safe. Tell her about the gift that her friend gave us.'

'Tell me everything. What was it like, flying that ship? Was it easy, was it scary, what?'

'I was scared that I would fail. But then the ship's systems settled around me and I knew exactly what to do . . . It was wonderful, Chloe. Better than anything. I can't really describe it, but when you go up you'll see exactly what I mean.'

Fahad was dressed in a green denim jacket and green work pants and a red T-shirt. Sort-of-but-not-quite military gear. He'd grown out his hair and it hung loose around his face and there was a gold earring in his left ear. To mark his first voyage, he'd said. He also told her that he'd come to an arrangement with Ada Morange. Her lawyers would fight his legal battle for control of his ship; he would share with her everything he knew.

Chloe said, 'Are you sure that's wise?'

'She helped me find what I needed to find,' Fahad said. 'And she'll help me keep control of it, too. To start with, her people have worked out what Rana's drawings mean.'

It took Chloe a moment to remember what he meant. The starburst of lines radiating out from a central point.

Fahad said that it was a map. 'There are these tiny dense stars, pulsars, which rotate really quickly, and emit beams of electro-magnetic radiation. Like radio signals. You can only detect the pulsar beams when they're pointed at you, so they tick like very precise clocks. Some in milliseconds, some in seconds. Every one is different, so if you know the period of the tick, you can identify the pulsar. Dr Morange's people think that's what Rana's map shows. The marks on each line are a code, giving the period. And the length of the line is the distance from the pulsar to the place the map is aimed at.'

'Do they know where this place is?'

'Not yet. The same kind of maps were put on these robot probes that went out into deep space, beyond the edge of the solar system. In case aliens found them, and wanted to know where they came from. Those had a key, a way of working out the time periods. That's what we need to find first. And when we do, we can find the pulsars, and find the place we're supposed to find.'

'Whatever it is.'

'We'll know it when we find it. You should talk to Dr Morange, Chloe. You're the only other person who can control the ships. You can name your price.'

Fahad had acquired a definite air of glamour. A raffish, pirat-ical confidence. The rock-star chic of a kid from the streets who'd made good on talent, luck and dedication. Chloe saw in him one half of the future struggle between the fearful and jealous conservative heartland of humanity and the bold impa-tient energy of the frontier. And she knew, thanks to her gift, her curse, that she was going to have to decide which side she was on.

'It scares me,' she confessed.

'It's only just begun,' Fahad said. 'There are other ships out there. The first thing we have to do is go and find them.'

'Did the ship tell you that? Or was it Ugly Chicken?'

'There were many Elder Cultures,' Fahad said. 'And even if only one of them possessed ships, this can't be the only system where they stashed them. Maybe that's what the map is about. We'll find out, you'll see.'

His serene self-assurance was marvellous and frightening. It reminded Chloe, just a little, of the messianic gleam of the leader of the New Galactic Navy. Who had also believed that he'd been chosen to fly to the stars.

She said, 'We have to get past the lawyers and politicians first. And maybe that's not such a bad thing. It gives us a chance to think about what we want to do, what we should do, before we fly off into the unknown.'

'When I come back we'll go up together,' Fahad said. 'It'll be the beginning of a great adventure!'

But the lawyers and politicians were still arguing about the disposition of the ships when the shuttle arrived. Chloe had been discharged from hospital by then. She still needed a crutch to walk, and she couldn't walk very far before the grinding pain in her hip became too much, but she had moved into a little apartment in the UN building and liked to sit in the café in the plaza and watch the people of this new world go by. That was where Ada Morange's lawyer found her, and told her that his boss would like to talk to her.

'Any time. Just put her on the phone.'

The lawyer smiled. 'Actually, she would prefer a face-to-face meeting.'

Ada Morange had come up on the shuttle to Mangala, accompanied by a small entourage of scientists and lawyers, and the !Cha, Unlikely Worlds. Chloe met with her in a suite in the Petra Carlton. They sat facing each other in their wheelchairs; Unlikely Worlds's tank squatted next to Ada Morange, its articulated legs folded around it.

'We have been given a chance to change history,' the entrepreneur said, after they had got past the niceties of congratulation on a mission accomplished, and concern about Chloe's recuperation. 'We have been entirely dependent on the Jackaroo's shuttles and their fixed schedules. But now we will be able to travel freely between Mangala and Earth. And between Earth and the other worlds . . .'

'As long as the Jackaroo allow it,' Chloe said.

'Sometimes, I'm told, the Jackaroo make something attractive by forbidding it,' Ada Morange said. 'They push people towards it by pretending to push them away.'

Chloe looked at the !Cha's tank, said, 'Is that true? Or is it another of your stories?'

While she'd been bedridden, she'd had plenty of time to think about the Jackaroo, and the !Cha. About why the avatar that called itself Bob Smith had visited her on that beach in Norfolk; about what the avatar carried by Adam Nevers had said to Vic.

Bob Smith had told her that she had been standing at a place where small actions could have large and unintended consequences: that had definitely turned out to be true. And it had said that there were others here, with their own agenda. Perhaps it had meant people like Adam Nevers. Or perhaps it had meant the !Cha, who collected stories they used to attract the attention of a female mate, back home, wherever their home was. Who reshaped stories that were not pleasing, according to the avatar carried by Nevers; who liked to accelerate change.

Unlikely Worlds said, in its amiable baritone, 'Your species is hardwired to be curious. One of your oldest stories is about a forbidden fruit. Would your female progenitor have tasted it, if it had not been forbidden? Would the serpent have been able to tempt her with it?'

'Are you saying that Ugly Chicken wasn't an Elder Culture eidolon? That the Jackaroo planted it?'

'Perhaps they made it seem important.'

'They tried to stop it calling down the ships,' Chloe said, seeing in her mind's eye the hallucinatory war in the air between the bright shards and the quick dark ghosts. 'Why would they do that if they wanted us to have them?'

'The avatar carried by Adam Nevers was not a true avatar,' Unlikely Worlds said. 'It was a partial. An independent copy. Perhaps it was given to Nevers because he wanted to stop the eidolon. After all, they came here to help.'

'They'd help both sides?'

'Why not? Perhaps, as far as they are concerned, the differences between both sides are trivial.'

'And what about you?' Chloe said. 'What kind of help have you been giving us?'

'You are thinking of claims made by the avatar carried by Adam Nevers.'

'Very much.'

'It was, as I said, only a partial. And perhaps the story it told was a story that Adam Nevers wanted to hear. That he needed to believe, so that he could justify his actions. You are all heroes of your own stories.'

'Then tell me that you haven't been manipulating Dr Morange. That you haven't been manipulating me and everyone else. That you haven't been fucking up our lives so you can go back to some pond and spawn children.'

Chloe heeled away tears, and felt a naked humiliation. She'd meant to confront the !Cha with reasoned argument, but instead she'd lost her temper.

Unlikely Worlds said, in a perfect imitation of kindness, 'Your story has no need of embellishment, Chloe.'

'I wish I could believe it.'

'The Jackaroo are of course a great imponderable,' Ada Morange said, after a short silence. 'But this much we know: they see things differently. And they are not yet, as far as we are concerned, a problem. What I would like to do today, Chloe, why I invited you here, is begin negotiations about revising your status within my company, and to secure your unique skill set.'

'You're offering me a job.'

'You already have a job. I'm offering you a new one.'

She handed Chloe a slim folder, explained that it contained a draft contract, and quoted two six-figure sums. One for what she called the basic salary, the other a bonus to acknowledge Chloe's help, and to provide compensation for her injuries.

'There will be other bonuses, equally generous, based on your performance. Although if you are only half as gifted as Fahad, you will have no difficulty in securing them. I know that this is a life-changing proposition. So I do not expect you to make your decision immediately. Study it. Take your time. And I would advise you to hire a good lawyer to check the contract. We've

372

worked well together, Chloe. I hope that we will continue to work together for many years.'

'You have Fahad,' Chloe said. 'You don't need me.'

'There's no need to make up your mind now. Think about my offer. Take as long as you need.'

'I've already made up my mind. No one should have both of us.'

'You'd rather work for the British government, or the UN? I don't see you as a good fit for sclerotic bureaucratic organisations like that.'

'You're right. I'm at my best when I do my own thing. That's how I found Fahad, after all.'

'While working for me. As you still do, in fact.'

'I was working for Disruption Theory. Which you shut down. And anyway, I quit.'

Ada Morange studied her. Chloe tried her best to meet that deep dark gaze. There was nothing human in it that she could see, no anger, no disappointment, no pity.

'My offer still stands,' the entrepreneur said. 'And meanwhile I will continue to pay your hospital bills, and to pay for your protection also. There have already been threats to your life from fanatical elements, you know, back on Earth. If you really do want to do your own thing, you should bear that in mind.'

That was as close to a threat as she came. Chloe knew there would be years of trouble ahead, trying to stay out of Ada Morange's orbit, but she also knew that she had a singular advantage. Only she and Fahad could control the ships. Sooner or later someone would figure out an interface that anyone could use, but meanwhile people who wanted easy travel to other planets would have to rely on their goodwill. Ada Morange had Fahad. And if she dared to use her gift, Chloe thought, everyone else would have her.

They parted on an amicable note. Ada Morange gave Chloe two gifts, both double-edged.

The first was a return ticket to Earth that Chloe knew she would not need. When she was ready, she could go back on her own terms, in her own ship. The second was a memory stick containing a video message from Neil and his family – they were glad she was safe, and hoped she would be coming home soon – and an up-to-date archive of the Last Minute wiki.

'I know how much it means to you,' Ada Morange said.

As Chloe wheeled around, ready to go, Unlikely Worlds said, 'I enjoyed your story, Chloe. I hope that I will be able to continue to enjoy it.'

And he also said, in a startlingly intimate whisper transmitted through her wrist patch, that he had left a little gift of his own in the archive of the Last Minute wiki.

It wasn't hard to find. *All The King's Horses*: a short video shot from somewhere above Trafalgar Square. The viewpoint yawed and pitched, turning this way and that – Chloe, who knew everything about those last moments, believed that it had been recorded by the balloon that had been adrift high in the sunlight air. And knew, with a deep thrill of absolute conviction, remembering another untethered balloon above Mr Archer's meeting, that it had been no child's balloon.

She also knew that the King's Mews had been demolished to make way for Trafalgar Square. That the site of the National Gallery had once been a stable block.

There would be time later to think about what all this implied, to wonder how long the aliens had been observing humanity, and wonder what else they might have been doing. Now, Chloe watched with narrow and absolute concentration as the balloon's unstable viewpoint crossed the roof of the National Gallery and turned towards the narrow street on the far side, and the entrance at the rear of the National Portrait Gallery. The video froze at that point. After a minute, she dared to zoom in. And saw the woman caught in mid-step as she walked down the long ramp, on her way to meet her friend for lunch, not knowing that this was the last minute of her life, the last minute before everything changed.

Before the aliens came, eager to help.

Acknowledgements

I first developed ideas about the Jackaroo and their double-edged gifts in a number of short stories. My thanks to Lou Anders, Peter Crowther, Gardner Dozois, Simon Ings, William Schafer, Jonathan Strahan and Sheila Williams, the editors of the anthologies and magazines where they first appeared. My agent, Simon Kavanagh, shepherded the novel through every stage of composition, and was its first reader. His critical eye and unstinting encouragement were hugely helpful throughout. Thanks also to my editor, Marcus Gipps, for suggesting many improvements large and small, to my copy-editor Nick Austin for his thorough, microscopic scrutiny, and to Georgina Hawtrey-Woore and the NHS for life support.